Books by Jude Deveraux

The Velvet Promise
Highland Velvet
Velvet Song
Velvet Angel
Sweetbriar
Counterfeit Lady
Lost Lady
River Lady
Twin of Fire
Twin of Ice
The Temptress
The Raider
The Princess
The Awakening
The Maiden
The Taming
The Conquest
A Knight in Shining Armor
Wishes

Mountain Laurel
The Duchess
Eternity
Sweet Liar
The Invitation
Remembrance
The Heiress
Legend
An Angel for Emily
The Blessing
High Tide
Temptation
The Summerhouse
The Mulberry Tree
Forever . . .
Wild Orchids
Forever and Always
Holly
Always

Jude Deveraux

The Taming
The Conquest

POCKET BOOKS
New York   London   Toronto   Sydney

POCKET BOOKS, a division of Simon & Schuster, Inc.
1230 Avenue of the Americas, New York, NY 10020

This book is a work of fiction. Names, characters, places and inci-
dents are products of the author's imagination or are used ficti-
tiously. Any resemblance to actual events or locales or persons,
living or dead, is entirely coincidental.

The Taming copyright © 1989 by Deveraux Inc.
The Conquest copyright © 1991 by Deveraux Inc.

These titles were previously published individually by
Pocket Books.

ISBN-13: 978-1-4165-0744-4
ISBN-10:   1-4165-0744-2

First Pocket Books trade paperback edition January 2005

10 9 8 7 6 5 4

POCKET and colophon are registered trademarks of
Simon & Schuster, Inc.

Manufacured in the United States of America

For information regarding special discounts for bulk
purchases, please contact Simon & Schuster Special Sales
at 1-800-456-6798 or business@simonandschuster.com

"Forget garden-variety ghosts and poltergeists—the devil himself makes an appearance in Deveraux's romantic suspense novel. . . . A superb job."

—*Publishers Weekly*

"Incredible, wonderful, fantastic, superb. . . . An unforgettable read."
—*Romance Reviews Today*

THE MULBERRY TREE

"A twisted, unpredictable story."

—*Romantic Times*

"Mystery, romance, and good cooking converge in [*The Mulberry Tree*]."

—*People*

THE SUMMERHOUSE

"Deveraux . . . blends three love stories into an emotionally stirring novel."

—*The State* (Columbia, NC)

"Deveraux is at the top of her game."

—*Booklist*

TEMPTATION

"[The] lively pace . . . will keep readers turning pages."
—*Publishers Weekly*

HIGH TIDE

A *Romantic Times* Top Pick

"*High Tide* is packed full of warmth, humor, sensual tension, and exciting adventure. What more could you ask of a book?"
—*Romantic Times*

The Taming

CHAPTER ONE

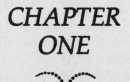

England
1445

*E*ither your daughter goes or I do," Helen Neville said sternly, hands on hips as she looked down at her husband, Gilbert. He was stretched out on a cushioned window seat, the sun streaming in through the old stone window past blue-painted wooden shutters. He was rubbing the ears of his favorite hound while eating tasty little bits of ground meat.

As usual, Gilbert didn't make any response to Helen's demand, and she clenched her fists in anger. He was twelve years older than she and lazy beyond anything she'd ever known. In spite of the fact that he spent most of his time on a horse following a soaring hawk, his belly was large and growing bigger by the day. She had married him for his money, of course, married him for his gold plate, for his thousands of hectares of land, for his eight castles (two of which he'd never seen), for his horses, his army of men, for the beautiful clothes he could give her and her two children. She had read a list of Gilbert Neville's

possessions and said yes to the marriage proposal
without even asking to see the man.

Now, a year after their marriage, Helen asked
herself, If she had met Gilbert and seen his slothful-
ness, would she have wondered who ran his estates?
Did he have a superior steward? She knew he had only
one legitimate child, a pale, shy-looking girl who said
not a word to Helen before the marriage, but perhaps
Gilbert had an illegitimate son who ran his estates.

After they were married and Helen knew she had a
husband who was as lazy in bed as he was out of it, she
found out who ran the Neville lands.

Liana! Helen wished she'd never heard the name.
That sweet-looking, shy-seeming daughter of Gilbert's
was a devil in disguise. Liana, like her mother before
her, ran everything. Liana sat at the steward's table
while the peasants paid their yearly rents. Liana rode
through the countryside and saw to fields and ordered
broken roofs repaired. Liana decided when a castle
had become too dirty and the crops depleted and told
the retainers it was time to move. Three times in the
last year Helen had first heard that they were moving
when she saw a maid packing her bedding.

It had done no good to explain to Gilbert or Liana
that she, Helen, was now the lady of the manor and
that Liana should relinquish her power to her stepmother. Both of them had merely looked at Helen
curiously, as if one of the stone heads of the gutters
had begun to speak, then Liana had gone back to
ruling and Gilbert had returned to doing nothing.

Helen had tried to take charge on her own, and for a
while she thought she was succeeding—until she
found out that each servant was asking Liana for
verification before carrying out her order.

At first, Helen's complaints to Gilbert had been
mild, and usually after she had pleased him in bed.

Gilbert had paid her little mind. "Let Liana do what she likes. You can't stop her. You could no more stop Liana or her mother than you could stop the fall of a boulder. It was and is best to get out of their way." He'd turned over and gone to sleep, but Helen had lain awake all night, her body hot with rage.

By morning she was ready to be a boulder, too. She was older than Liana and, if need be, much more cunning. After her first husband had died and his younger brother had inherited the estates, Helen and her two little girls had been pushed aside by her sister-in-law. Helen had had to stand by and watch as duties that had once been hers were taken over by a younger, much less competent woman. When Gilbert Neville's proposal came, she leaped at the chance to once again have her own household, her own home. But now her place was being usurped by a small, pale girl who should have been married and sent away from her father's house years ago.

Helen had tried to talk to Liana, had tried to tell her of the pleasures of having her own husband, her own children, her own household.

Liana had blinked at her with those big blue eyes of hers, looking as meek as an angel on the chapel ceiling. "But who will take care of my father's estates?" she'd asked simply.

Helen gritted her teeth. "*I* am your father's wife. *I* will do what needs to be done."

Liana's eyes twinkled as she looked at Helen's sumptuous velvet dress with a train in back, at the low V neck in front and in back that exposed a great deal of her beautiful shoulders, at the heavily embroidered, padded headdress, and smiled. "The sun would burn you in that."

Helen found herself defending her words. "I would dress suitably to ride a horse. I'm sure I can ride as well as you can. Liana, it's not proper that you remain in your father's house. You are nearly twenty years old. You should have your own home, your own—"

"Yes, yes," Liana said. "I'm sure you're right, but I must go now. There was a fire in the village last night and I must see to the damage."

Helen had stood there, her face red, her temper black. What good did it do her to be married to one of the richest men in England, to live in one castle after another where the riches were more than she'd ever believed possible? Thick, colorful tapestries hung from every wall, every ceiling was painted with biblical scenes, every bed, table, and chair was covered with an embroidered cloth. Liana kept a roomful of women who did nothing but bend over tapestry frames and ply their needles. The food was divine, as Liana enticed cooks with excellent wages and fur-trimmed gowns for their wives. The latrines, the moat, the stables, the courtyards were always clean, as Liana liked cleanliness.

Liana, Liana, Liana, Helen thought, putting her fists to her temples. With the servants, it was always what Lady Liana wanted, what Lady Liana had ordered, or even what Gilbert's first wife had established. Helen might not have existed for all the power she had in the running of the Neville properties.

It was when Helen's two little girls had begun to quote Liana that Helen's anger came to the boiling point. Young Elizabeth had wanted a pony of her own, and Helen had smiled and said she could have it. Elizabeth had merely blinked at her mother, then said, "I'll ask Liana," and run off.

It was that incident that had caused Helen to now give her husband an ultimatum. "I am less than nothing in this house," she said to Gilbert. She didn't

4

bother to keep her voice down, even though she was well aware of the listening servants around them. They were Liana's servants, well-trained, obedient men and women who knew their young mistress's generosity as well as her wrath and who would, upon request, have laid down their lives for her.

"Either your daughter goes or I do," Helen repeated.

Gilbert looked over the tray of meats that were molded into shapes of the twelve apostles. He chose St. Paul and popped him into his mouth. "And what am I to do with her?" he asked lazily. There wasn't much on earth that could excite Gilbert Neville. Comfort, a good hawk, a good hound, good food, and peace were all he asked in life. He had no idea what his first wife had done to increase the wealth his father had left him and the huge dowry she had brought to the marriage, nor did he know what his daughter did. To his mind, the estates ran themselves. The peasants farmed; the nobility hawked; the king made laws. And it also seemed that women quarreled.

He had seen the beautiful young widow Helen Peverill as she rode across her dead husband's land. Her dark hair had been streaming down her back, her large breasts were nearly coming out of her gown, and the wind plastered her skirts to strong, healthy thighs. Gilbert had experienced a rare moment of lust and had told her brother-in-law he'd like to marry Helen. Gilbert hadn't done much after that until Liana told him it was time for the wedding. After one lusty wedding night, Gilbert was satisfied with Helen and expected her to go off and do whatever women did all day. But she hadn't. Instead, she had begun to nag and nag—about Liana, of all things. Liana was such a sweet, pretty child, always seeing that the musicians

Jude Deveraux

played songs that Gilbert liked, telling the maids to bring him food and, on long winter evenings, telling stories to entertain him. He could not understand why Helen wanted Liana to go away. Liana was so quiet, one hardly knew she was around.

"I guess Liana can have a husband if she wants one," Gilbert said, yawning. He believed in people doing what they wanted to. He thought the men worked in the fields from daylight to dark because they wanted to.

Helen tried to calm herself. "Of course Liana doesn't want a husband. Whyever should she want a man to tell her what to do when she has absolute freedom—and absolute power—here? If I had had such power in my dead husband's home, I would never have left." She threw up her hands in a gesture of helpless anger. "To have power and no man to cater to! Liana has heaven on earth. She will _never_ leave here."

Even though Gilbert didn't understand Helen's complaints, her screeching was beginning to bother him. "I will speak to Liana and see if there is a husband she wants."

"You have to command her to take a husband," Helen said. "You have to choose a man for her and tell her she is to marry him."

Gilbert looked down at his hound and smiled in memory. "I crossed Liana's mother once and only once. I am not about to make the same error again and cross her daughter."

"If you do not get your daughter out of my house, you will regret crossing _me,_" Helen said before turning on her heel and leaving the room.

Gilbert scratched his hound's ears. This new wife was as a kitten to a lion compared to his first wife. He

6

really couldn't understand what Helen was angry about. It had never crossed his mind that a person would actually *want* responsibility. He picked up a molded St. Mark and ate it thoughtfully. Vaguely, he remembered someone warning him against having two women in the same household. Perhaps he would talk to Liana and see what she thought of this idea of getting a husband. If Helen carried out her threat and moved to another estate, he'd miss her in his bed. But if Liana did marry, perhaps she would marry someone with good breeding hawks.

"So," Liana said softly, "my esteemed stepmother wants to throw me out of my own home, out of the home my mother worked to increase and I have managed for three years."

Gilbert thought perhaps his head was beginning to hurt. Helen had ranted at him for hours on end last night. It seems Liana had given some order for new cottages to be built in the walled town at the foot of the castle. Helen was horrified that Liana planned to use Neville money to pay for these cottages rather than let the peasants pay for them themselves. Helen had been so angry and screeched so loudly that all six of Gilbert's hawks had flown from their perches into the rafters. They had been hooded to keep them calm and the blind, panicked flight had caused one bird to break its neck. Gilbert knew that something had to be done; he couldn't bear losing more of his beloved hawks.

His first thought was to fit the two women with armor and let them joust for who remained and who left, but women had weapons harder than steel: They had words.

"I think Helen believes you'll be, well, happier in

7

your own home. With your own husband and a few brats." Gilbert couldn't imagine being happier than on the Neville lands, but who knew about women?

Liana walked to the window and looked out across the inner courtyard, across the thick castle walls and below to the walled town. This was just one of the estates her family owned, only one of the many she managed. Her mother had spent long years training Liana how to treat the people, how to check the steward's records, and how to bring in a profit every year that would be used to buy more land.

Liana had been angry when her father said he was going to marry a pretty young widow. She didn't like the idea of another woman's trying to take her mother's place and she had a premonition of trouble, but Gilbert Neville had his own stubborn streak and sincerely believed he should be allowed to do whatever he wanted whenever he wanted. For the most part, Liana was pleased he wasn't one of those men who thought of nothing but war and weapons. He stayed with his hounds and his hawks and left the more important matters first to his wife, then to his daughter.

Until now. Now he'd married the vain Helen, whose foremost thought was profit so that she could buy more and richer clothes. Helen kept five women working long hours sewing on her gowns. There was one woman who did nothing but sew on seed pearls. Last month alone, Helen had purchased twenty-four pelts of fur, and the month before that she had bought a basketful of ermine pelts, thinking no more of the expense than if she'd purchased a basket of corn. Liana knew that if she turned over the running of the estates to Helen, she'd bleed the peasants dry just so she could have a belt of gold and diamonds.

"Well?" Gilbert asked from behind Liana. Women!

he thought. He was going to miss the day's hunting if he didn't get an answer from his daughter. The way Helen was acting, she might climb on a horse and follow him just so she could continue to berate him.

Liana turned to her father. "Tell my stepmother I will marry if I find a *suitable* man."

Gilbert looked relieved. "That seems fair enough. I'll tell her, and she'll be happy." He started out the door, then paused and put his hand on his daughter's shoulder in a rare display of affection. Gilbert wasn't a man to look at the past, but at this moment he wished he'd never seen Helen, never married her. He hadn't realized how comfortable he'd been with his daughter to look after his simple needs and a maid now and then to care for his baser needs. He shrugged. There was no use regretting what couldn't be changed. "We'll find you a lusty young man who'll give you a dozen brats to fret over." He left the room.

Liana sat down hard on the feather mattress of her bed and waved her maid out of the room. Liana held her hands up and saw how they were shaking. She'd once faced a crowd of peasants armed with sickles and axes alone, with three terrified maids behind her, yet she'd kept her head and turned the rabble away by giving them what food she carried with her and jobs on her land. She'd dealt with drunken soldiers; she had once escaped a rape by an overzealous suitor. She had been able to deflect one disaster after another with calmness, assurance, and peace of mind.

But the idea of marriage terrified her. Not just frightened her, but deep-down, inside-her-soul terrified her. Two years ago she had seen her cousin Margaret married off to a man chosen by the girl's father. Before the marriage the man had written love sonnets to Margaret's beauty. Margaret used to talk about how her forthcoming marriage was a love match and she so looked forward to a life with this beloved man.

After the marriage, the man showed his true self. He sold most of Margaret's immense dowry to pay his huge debts. He left Margaret in an old, decaying, cold castle with but a few retainers, then went to court, where he spent most of the rest of her dowry on jewels for his many high-born whores.

Liana knew how fortunate she was to have the power of running her father's estates. She knew that no woman had any power unless it was granted to her by a man. Men had been asking for her hand in marriage since she was four years old. She had been betrothed once, when she was eight, but the young man had died before she was ten. Her father had never bothered to accept any offers after that and so Liana had quietly been able to escape marriage. When some suitor had pressed his petition, all Liana had had to do was remind Gilbert of what chaos her marriage would cause and Gilbert refused the offer.

But now this greedy Helen was interfering. Liana considered turning all power of running the estates over to her stepmother and retiring to their estate in Wales. Yes, that would be remote enough. She could live there in privacy, and soon both Helen and her father would forget about her.

Liana stood up, her fists clenched at her side, her simple, unornamented velvet gown sweeping the tile floor. Helen would never allow her to live in peace. Helen would pursue her to the ends of the earth to make sure her stepdaughter was as miserable as all women seemed to be in marriage.

Liana picked up her hand mirror from a little table by the window and stared at her reflection. In spite of all the love poems eager young men who wanted to marry her had written, in spite of the songs the traveling singers who were paid by her had sung, she could not see that she was a beauty. She was too pale, too blonde, too . . . too innocent-looking to be a beauty. Helen was beautiful, with her snapping dark eyes that let everyone know she had secrets, with her sultry way of looking at men. Liana sometimes thought the reason she could control the servants so well was because she was sexless. When Helen walked across the courtyard, men stopped what they were doing and looked at her. Men tugged their forelocks in respect to Liana, but they didn't stand gaping or guffaw and punch each other when she passed.

She moved to the window and looked down into the courtyard. A pretty milkmaid was being teased by an assistant farrier, the boy's hands reaching for the girl's round, shapely body.

Liana turned away, for the sight was too painful for her to bear. Never could she hope for some young man to chase her around a well. She could never find out if some young man *wanted* to chase her. Her father's people would always treat her with the respect of her station and address her as "my lady." Her suitors would do anything to win her hand because they wanted her dowry. It wouldn't matter if she were a hunchback with three eyes; she would still receive flowery compliments and glowing praise of her beauty. Once, a man had sent her a poem about the beauty of her feet. As if he'd ever seen them!

"My lady."

Liana looked up to see her maid, Joice, standing in the doorway. Joice was the closest thing to a friend that Liana had. Being only ten years older than Liana, Joice was almost like a sister. Liana's mother had hired Joice to care for Liana when Liana was just a baby and Joice had been little more than a child herself. Liana's mother had taught her daughter to run

11

estates, but when Liana had had a bad dream, it was Joice who'd comforted her. It was Joice who'd stayed up with her through childhood illnesses and Joice who'd taught her about things other than estate management. Joice had explained how babies were made and what the man who'd tried to rape her had wanted.

"My lady," Joice said, always careful to show respect to her young charge. Liana could afford to be friendly, but Joice was always aware of her place, always aware that tomorrow she could be without a roof over her head or food on the table. She did not volunteer advice that might not be wanted. "There is a dispute in the kitchen and—"

"You are fond of your husband, Joice?"

The maid hesitated before answering. The entire castle knew what Lady Helen was demanding, and the people were of the belief that if Liana left, the Neville estates would be dust in six years. "Aye, my lady, I am."

"Did you choose him or was he chosen for you?"

"Your mother chose him, but I believe she wanted to please me, so I was married to a young and healthy man and I have come to love him."

Liana's head came up. "Have you?"

"Oh yes, my lady, that often happens." Joice felt she was on safe ground here. All women were afraid before their marriage. "When one spends long winter nights together, love often follows."

Liana turned away. *If* one could spend time together, she thought. *If* your greedy husband didn't send you away. She looked back at her maid. "Am I pretty, Joice? I mean actually pretty enough so that a man might be interested in me and not in all this?" She moved her arm to indicate the silk-hung bed, the tapestry on the north wall, the silver-gilt ewer, the carved oak furniture.

"Oh yes, my lady," Joice answered glibly. "You are *very* pretty, beautiful actually. There is no man high or low who could resist you. Your hair—"

Liana put up her hand for the woman to stop. "Let's see to the kitchen dispute." She could not keep the heaviness out of her voice.

CHAPTER
TWO

*S*ix months!" Helen screamed at her husband. "For six months that daughter of yours has been finding fault with men! Not one of them is 'suitable.' I tell you, if she is not out of here in another month, I shall take this child of yours that I carry and never return."

Gilbert looked out the window at the rain and cursed God for sending two weeks of foul weather and for creating women. He watched Helen ease herself into a chair with the help of two maids. From the way she complained, it would seem that no woman had ever carried a child before, but what amazed him was how pleased he was at the prospect of another child and a chance to have a son at last. Helen's words and tone grated on him, but he was inclined to do anything she wanted—at least until his son was safely delivered.

"I shall speak to her," Gilbert said heavily, dreading another scene with his daughter. But now he realized that one of the women had to go, and since

14

Helen was able to produce sons, it had to be Liana who left.

A servant found Liana, and Gilbert met her in one of the guest rooms off the solar. He hoped the rain would clear soon and he could go hawking again and not have to deal with this unpleasant business further.

"Yes, Father?" Liana asked from the doorway.

Gilbert looked at her and hesitated for a moment. She was so like her mother, and at all costs he didn't want to offend her. "Many men have come to visit us since your mother—"

"Stepmother," Liana corrected. "Since my step-mother announced to the world that I was ready to be sold, that I was a bitch in heat and needed stud service. Yes, many men have come here to look at our horses, our gold, our land and also, as an afterthought, at the plain-faced Neville daughter."

Gilbert sat down. He prayed that in heaven there would be no women. The only female allowed would be the kestrel hawk. He wouldn't even allow mares or female dogs. "Liana," he said tiredly, "you're as pretty as your mother, and if I have to sit through one more dinner with men telling you, at length, of your beauty, I shall go off food forever. Tomorrow I may have my table set up in the stables. At least the horses will not regale me with how white my daughter's skin is, how radiant her eyes, how golden her hair, how rose-red her lips."

There was no answering smile from Liana. "So I am to choose one of these liars? I am to live like Cousin Margaret while my husband spends my dowry?"

"The man Margaret married was a fool. I could have told her that. He canceled a day's hawking to diddle with some man's wife."

"So I am to marry a man who likes hawking best? Is

15

that the solution? Perhaps we should hold a hawking tournament and the man with the hawk with the biggest kill wins me as a prize. It makes as much sense as anything else."

Gilbert rather liked that idea, but wisely didn't say so. "Now see here, Liana. I've liked some of the men who've been here to visit. What about that William Aye? Good-looking fellow he is."

"Every one of my maids thought so, too. Father, the man is stupid. I tried to talk to him about the bloodlines of the horses in his stables and he had no idea what they were."

Gilbert was taken aback at that. A man should know about his horses. "What about Sir Robert Fitzwaren? He seemed smart enough."

"He told everyone he was smart. He also said he was strong and brave and fearless. According to him, he's won every tournament he's ever entered."

"But I heard he was unseated four times last year at— Oh, I see what you mean. Bragging men can become tiresome."

Gilbert's eyes lit up. "What about Lord Stephen, Whitington's boy? Now there's a man for you. Good looking. Rich. Healthy. Smart, too. And the boy knows how to handle a horse and a hawk." Gilbert smiled. "I'd guess he knows something about women. I even saw him *reading* to you." Reading, in Gilbert's opinion, was an unnecessary burden for a person to carry.

Liana remembered Lord Stephen's dark blond hair, his laughing blue eyes, his skill with a lute, the way he controlled an unruly horse, how he'd read from Plato to her. He was charming to everyone he met, and everyone in the household adored him. He'd not only told Liana she was lovely, but one evening in a dark corridor he'd grabbed her and kissed her until she was breathless, then whispered, "I'd love to take you to bed with me."

Lord Stephen was perfect. Flawless. Yet something . . . Maybe it was the way he glanced at the gold vessels lined up on the mantelpiece in the solar or the way he'd looked so hard at Helen's diamond necklace. There was something about him that she didn't trust, but she couldn't say what. It wasn't wrong, exactly, for him to take note of the Neville wealth, but she wished she saw a bit more lust in his eyes for her person and not her wealth.

"Well?" Gilbert prompted. "Is there anything wrong with young Stephen?"

"Nothing, really," Liana said. "He's—"

"Good, then it's done. I shall tell Helen, and she can start planning the wedding. This should make her happy."

Gilbert left Liana alone, and she sat down on the bed as if her body were made of lead. It was settled. She was to *marry* Lord Stephen Whitington. To spend the rest of her life with a man she didn't know yet who would have absolute power over her. He could beat her, imprison her, impoverish her, and he'd have a perfect, and legal, right.

"My lady," Joice said from the doorway, "the steward asks to see you."

Liana looked up, blinking without seeing for a moment.

"My lady?"

"Have my horse saddled," Liana said, and damn the steward, she thought. She wanted a good long run, with the horse pounding beneath her. Perhaps enough exercise would help her forget what awaited her.

Rogan, the oldest of what was left of the Peregrine family, squatted on his heels and stared at the castle

on the horizon. His dark eyes were full of his thoughts
—and his fears. He would rather face a battle than
what he faced today.

"Putting it off won't make it any easier," his brother
Severn said from behind him. Both men were tall and
broad-shouldered like their father, but Rogan had
inherited a sheen of red to his dark hair from their
father, while Severn, who had a different mother, had
more delicate facial features and hair streaked with
gold. Severn was also quicker to be impatient, and
now he was impatient with his older brother's immo-
bility.

"She won't be like Jeanne," Severn said, and behind
him the twenty knights stopped moving and held their
breath. Even Severn stopped breathing for a moment,
fearing that he'd overstepped himself.

Rogan heard his brother, but he didn't betray the
emotion that went through him at the mention of
Jeanne's name. He did not fear war; he did not fear
charging animals; he did not fear death, but the
thought of marriage made him hesitate.

Below them ran a deep stream, and Rogan could
almost feel the cold water on his body. He stood and
went to his horse. "I will return," he said to his
brother.

"Wait a minute!" Severn said, grabbing the reins.
"Are we to just sit here and wait for you while you
decide whether or not you have courage enough to
visit a slip of a girl?"

Rogan didn't bother to answer but looked at his
brother with hard eyes.

Severn released the reins. Sometimes Severn
thought Rogan could tumble stone walls with those
eyes of his. Even though he'd lived all his life with this
older brother, Severn felt he knew very little about
him; Rogan was not a man to reveal much about

himself. As a boy, when that bitch Jeanne had betrayed him so publicly, Rogan had withdrawn into himself, and in the ten years since, no one had penetrated his outer shell of hardness.

"We will wait," Severn said, stepping out of the way and allowing Rogan to pass.

When Rogan was gone, one of the knights behind Severn grunted. "Sometimes a woman changes a man," he said.

"Not my brother," Severn answered quickly. "No woman anywhere is strong enough to change my brother." There was pride in his voice. The world around them might change from day to day, but Rogan knew what he wanted and how to go about getting it. "A woman alter *my* brother?" he said derisively.

The men smiled at the impossibility of such an idea.

Rogan rode down the hill, then along the stream for a while. He wasn't sure what he wanted to do, just put off the time when he had to go to the Neville heiress. What a man had to do for money disgusted him. When he had heard the heiress was being put up for sale, so to speak, he had told Severn to go and get her and bring her back with her wagonloads of portable wealth and the deeds to some of her father's estates. Or, better yet, return with the gold and papers alone and leave the woman behind. Severn had said that a man as rich as Gilbert Neville would want only the oldest Peregrine, the man who would become duke as soon as the Peregrines wiped the Howards off the face of the earth.

As usual, Rogan's body tightened with hatred when he thought of the Howards. The Howards were the cause of everything bad that had happened to the Peregrines for three generations. They were the reason he was now having to marry some old-maid heiress,

19

the reason he wasn't at home now—in the *real* Peregrine home, the place the Howards had stolen. They had stolen his birthright, his home, and even his wife.

And marrying this heiress, he reminded himself, would bring him one step closer to regaining what was rightfully his.

There was a clearing in the trees and the stream spread out to catch in a beautiful rock-edged pool. On impulse, Rogan dismounted, then began to shed his clothes, undressing down to the loincloth tied about his waist. He stepped into the icy pool and began to swim as hard and as fast as he could. What he needed was a good long hunt to expend the pent-up energy in his body, but swimming might do as well.

He swam for nearly an hour, then stepped out of the pool, his sides heaving with exertion. Stretching out on a patch of sweet green grass in the sun, he was soon sound asleep.

He slept so soundly that he did not hear the quiet gasp of the woman as she came to the pool for water. Nor was he aware that the young woman stepped back into the trees and watched him.

Liana rode hard and fast, outdistancing her father's knight who tried to keep up with her. Her father's men ate rather than trained and she knew the trails of the land better than they did; it was easy to escape them. Once she was alone, she headed for the pool north of the castle. She'd be alone there and she'd be able to think about her forthcoming marriage.

She was still some distance away from the pool when she saw a bit of faded red through the trees. Someone was there. She cursed her luck, then cursed her foolishness at having left her guard behind. She halted her horse, tied him to a tree, then crept quietly toward the pool.

The red was the dress of one of the farmers' wives who lived in town and had three small fields outside the walls. Liana saw that the woman was standing absolutely still and was so absorbed in what she was looking at that she didn't hear Liana approach. Curious, Liana started to move softly forward.

"My lady!" the young woman gasped. "I . . . I came to get some w-water."

Her nervousness increased Liana's curiosity. "What were you looking at?"

"Nothing of any importance. I must go. My children will need me."

"You're leaving the pool with an empty water jug?" Liana pushed past her and looked through the bushes and immediately saw what had held the woman's attention. Lying on the grass in a patch of sunlight was a splendid-looking man: tall, broad-shouldered, slim-hipped, heavily muscled, with a strong-jawed face shadowed with dark whiskers and long, dark hair that glinted red in the sunlight. Liana looked from his feet to the top of his head, wide-eyed with interest as she gazed at the honey-colored skin of his nearly nude body. She'd had no idea a man could be so beautiful.

"Who is he?" she whispered to the farm wife.

"He's a stranger," the woman whispered back.

Near the man was a pile of clothes of coarse wool. With the sumptuary laws, it was often possible to guess a person's income and station in life by his clothes. This man wore no fur of any kind, not even the lowly rabbit allowed the lower classes. He had no musical instrument nearby, so he was no traveling musician.

"Perhaps he is a huntsman," the farm wife whispered. "Sometimes they come to trap game for your father. With your wedding, more game will be needed."

Liana shot the woman a quick look. Did everyone know of her life? Her wedding was what she'd come here to contemplate. She looked back at the man on the grass. He looked like a young Hercules, power and muscle now asleep, merely waiting to be awakened. If only Lord Stephen looked like this man, she wouldn't mind marriage so much. But even asleep, this man radiated more strength than Lord Stephen had when clad in full armor. For a moment she smiled as she pictured telling Helen she'd decided to marry a lowly huntsman, but then her smile left her because she doubted that this man would want her if she weren't endowed with wagonloads of silver and gold. For just one day she'd like to be a peasant girl, to see if she were woman enough to interest a handsome man.

She turned to the farmer's wife. "Take off your dress."

"My lady!"

"Take off your dress and give it to me, then return to the castle. Find my maid, Joice, and tell her no one is to search for me."

The woman paled. "Your maid will never talk to the likes of me."

Liana tugged an emerald ring from her finger and handed it to the woman. "Nearby is a knight, probably searching for me. Give him this and he will take you to Joice."

The woman's expression changed from fearfulness to slyness. "He is a handsome man, isn't he?"

Liana narrowed her eyes at the woman. "If I hear one word of this in the village, you'll regret it. Now, get out of here." She sent the woman away wearing only a coarse linen undergarment, as Liana wasn't about to allow the woman's filthy body to touch the velvet of her gown.

The peasant dress Liana put on was very different from her high-waisted, full-skirted gown. The scratchy wool was one piece that clung to her body from her neck to below her hips, showing the slim curves of her body. The wool was crude and dirty and it stank, but it was revealing. She rolled the sleeves, stiff with years of grease, back to her elbows. The skirt reached only to her ankles and the shortness made her feel free to walk or even run through the ferns.

With this dress on, Liana felt she was ready to face what lay ahead. She peeped through the branches to look at the man again. Every time she'd ever seen the peasants laughing and chasing one another through the fields came back to her. She'd once seen a boy give a flower to a girl. Would this divinely handsome man offer her flowers? Perhaps he'd weave a garland for her hair as one knight had done for her a few months ago—except this time it would be for *real*. This time the man would present her with flowers because of her person and not for her father's wealth.

Her heavy headdress removed and hidden in the bushes, her long pale hair streaming down her back, Liana stepped forward into the clearing and toward the man. He did not awaken even when she stumbled over a pile of rocks.

She moved closer to him, but he didn't stir. He was indeed a beautiful man, made the way God intended a man to look. She could hardly wait for him to see her. She'd been told that her hair was like spun gold. Would he think so?

His clothes were in a heap not too far from him, and she went to them and lifted his shirt, holding it at

23

arm's length, putting her hands out to the wide edges of the broad shoulders. The wool was thickly spun, and she thought what a better job her women did at spinning.

As she looked at the shirt she saw something odd, then leaned forward for a closer look. Lice! The shirt was crawling with lice.

With a little squeal of disgust, she threw the shirt from her.

One moment the man was asleep on the ground and the next he was standing before her in all his nude glory. He was indeed magnificent: tall, powerfully muscled, not an ounce of fat. His thick shoulder-length hair was dark, but it looked almost red in the sunlight, and there was a reddish stubble on his heavy jaw. His eyes were dark green and alive with emotion.

"How do you do?" Liana said, holding out her hand to him, palm downward. Would he sink to one knee before her?

"You threw my shirt in a bog," he said angrily, looking down at the pretty blue-eyed blonde.

Liana withdrew her hand. "It was crawling with lice." What did one say to a huntsman when one was his equal? Lovely day, isn't it? Would you like to fill my water jug for me? There, that seemed ordinary enough.

He gave her an odd look. "You can get my shirt out of the bog and wash it. I have to go somewhere today."

He had a very pleasant voice, but she didn't like what he was saying. "It's good the shirt sank. I told you it was covered with lice. Perhaps you'd like to pick blackberries. I'm sure we could find—" To her consternation, the man grabbed her shoulders and turned her toward the pool, then gave her a shove.

"Get my shirt out of the bog and wash it."

24

How dare he touch her without permission! Liana thought. Wash his shirt, indeed! She'd leave now and go back to her own clothes and her horse and the safety of her father's castle. She turned away, but he caught her forearm.

"Can't you hear well, girl?" he said, spinning her about. "Either you get the shirt out or I throw you in after it."

"Throw me in?" she asked. She was on the verge of telling him who she was and just what she would or would not do when she looked into his eyes. Handsome eyes, yes, but also dangerous eyes. If she told him she was Lady Liana, daughter of one of the richest men in England, would he perhaps hold her for ransom?

"I . . . I have to get back to my husband and . . . and children. Lots of children," she said haltingly. She had liked this man's aura of power when he was asleep, but when he was holding her arm, she didn't like it nearly as much.

"Good," he said, "then, with lots of brats, you'll know how to wash a shirt."

Liana looked toward the oozy black bog where only his shirtsleeve could be seen. She had no idea how to wash a shirt, and the idea of touching the lice-infested thing repulsed her.

"My . . . my sister-in-law does my laundry," she said, and was pleased with herself for having thought of such a good idea. "I'll go back and send her to you. She'll be glad to wash it."

The man didn't say a word but pointed at the bog.

She realized he was not going to allow her to leave. Grimacing, Liana walked toward the bog and leaned forward to reach the edge of the sleeve. She couldn't reach it, so she stretched further—then further.

25

She fell face forward into the rich, thick ooze of mud, her arms sinking to her elbows, her face covered. For a moment she struggled to get out of the bog, but there was nothing to hold on to. Then an arm swooped down and pulled her up to dry land. She stood there sputtering for a moment, then the man pushed her backward into the pond.

Face forward into a bog, then backward into ice-cold water.

She managed to get to her feet and started out of the pond. "I am going home," she muttered, feeling close to tears. "Joice will make me a hot posset and build me a fire, and I'll—"

The man caught her arm. "Where do you think you're going? My shirt is still buried."

She looked up into his cold green eyes and all fear of him left her. Who did he think he was? He had no right to order her about even if he thought she was the lowliest field gleaner. So he thought he was her master, did he?

She was wet through and freezing, but anger was keeping her warm. She smiled what she hoped was an ingratiating smile at him. "Your wish is my command," she murmured, and managed to keep a calm face when he grunted with satisfaction, as if that was the answer she was supposed to give.

She turned her back to him and got a long stick from under a tree, then went back to the bog. She fished the shirt out, held it on the end of the stick for a moment, then with all her might, she sent it flying to hit him cold and hard smack across the face and chest.

While he was peeling the shirt from his body, Liana began to run. She knew the woods better than any stranger ever could, and she went straight to a hollow tree and disappeared inside it.

She heard him crashing through the woods nearby and she smiled to herself at his inability to find her. She'd wait until he was gone, then go to her horse on the other side of the pond and make her way home. If he was a huntsman, tomorrow she'd greet him in her father's house and have the satisfaction of hearing his apology for his conduct today. Perhaps she'd borrow one of Helen's gowns, something covered in furs, with a jeweled headdress. She'd sparkle so brightly he'd have to shield his eyes from the glare.

"You might as well come out," he said from just outside the dead tree.

Liana held her breath.

"You want me to come in after you? Or shall I chop the tree down around your ears?"

Liana couldn't believe he really knew where she was. Surely he was bluffing. She didn't move.

His big arm came into the tree, caught her waist, and pulled her out—and against his hard chest. His face was smeared with black mud, but those eyes of his burned, and for a moment Liana thought he might kiss her. Her heart began to pound in her breast.

"Hungry, are you?" he said, his eyes laughing at her. "Well, I haven't got time. I have another wench waiting for me." He pushed her from him and back toward the pond.

Liana decided that merely appearing before him in a radiant gown would not be enough. "I shall make him crawl," she muttered.

"Will you, now?" he said, overhearing her.

She whirled to face him. "Yes," she said through clenched teeth. "I will make you crawl. I will make you regret treating me like this."

He didn't smile, in fact his face seemed made of marble, but his eyes showed amusement. "You'll have

27

to wait for that day, because now I intend to make you wash my clothes."

"I'd sooner—" She broke off.

"Yes? Name your price, and I'll see if I can manage it."

Liana turned away from him. It was better to just get it over with, to get his clothes washed and get away from him. Today he had the power, but tomorrow she would be the one who held the reins—and the whip and the chains, she thought with a smile.

At the pond's edge she stopped, refusing to obey him with any semblance of acquiescence. Her attitude seemed to amuse him further. He picked up his muddy shirt and slammed it against her chest so that, by instinct, she caught it.

"Might as well do these too," he said, and heaped her arms full of his other lice-infested clothing, then knelt down and washed the mud off his face.

Liana gasped and dropped the load to the ground.

"Get busy," he said. "I need those clothes for courting."

Liana realized that the sooner she got this over with, the sooner she could get away from him. She grabbed a fist full of shirt, dunked it into the water, then slammed it against a rock. "She won't have you," Liana said. "She might like the look of you, but if she has any sense, she'll jump from the town wall before she'll agree to marry you."

He was stretched out on the grass in the sun, his head propped on his hands as he watched her. "Oh, she'll have me, all right. It's a matter of whether I'll want her. I'll marry no shrews. I'll take her only if she's biddable and soft-spoken."

"And stupid," Liana said. She wanted to kill the lice, so she picked up a small rock and began pounding the clothes. Then, as she turned the shirt over, she saw the tiny holes the rock was making. Her eyes widened in horror, then she smiled. She'd clean his clothes for him all right, but they'd look like a fisherman's net when she finished. "Only a stupid woman would have you," she said loudly, hoping to distract him from what she was doing.

"Stupid women are best," he answered. "I want no clever woman. Clever women cause a man trouble. Are you done with those yet?"

"They are filthy and need a lot of work," she said as sweetly as she could manage. Thinking of his appearing at a girl's door in clothes filled with holes pleased her. "And I guess women have given you a great deal of trouble in your life," she said. His vanity was overwhelming.

"Very little trouble." He was watching her.

Liana didn't like the way he was looking at her. In spite of her wet clothes, he was making her feel very warm. He seemed lazy and quiet now, but she'd seen his anger and felt the violence just under his skin.

"How many children did you say you have?" he asked softly.

"Nine," she said loudly. "Nine little boys, all of them big and strong like their father. And their uncles," she added nervously. "My husband has six huge brothers, strong as oxen, and tempers! I never saw such tempers. Only last week—"

"What a liar you are," he said calmly, putting his head back down on the ground and not looking at her. "You've never had a man."

She stopped pounding the clothes. "I've had a hundred men," she said, then stopped. "I mean, I've had my husband hundreds of times and—" She was making a fool of herself. "Here are your clothes. I

29

hope they itch you to death. You *deserve* a body covered with lice."

She stood over him, then dropped the wet clothes on his hard, flat belly. He didn't flinch from the cold but stared up at her with eyes that seemed warm and compelling. She wanted to leave him and she knew she was now free, but somehow she just stood there, her eyes locked with his.

"Such good work must be rewarded. Bend to me, woman."

Liana felt herself sinking to her knees before him while he came up to meet her. He put his big hand behind her head, his fingers entwined in her hair, and pulled her lips to his.

A few men had tried to kiss Liana, but they had never been so expert as this. His lips, so unlike his manner, were soft and warm and she closed her eyes to the sensation.

The kiss was all she'd hoped a kiss could be and her arms moved to encircle his neck as she pressed her body to his, feeling his sun-warmed skin through her cold clothes. He moved his lips on hers, opening his mouth slightly, and she followed his lead. Her hands moved to his hair. It was clean from his swim and so warm she thought she could feel the redness of it.

When he broke the kiss and moved away from her, she kept her eyes closed and leaned toward him, wanting more of him.

"There, that's enough," he said with amusement in his voice. "A virginal kiss for a virgin. Now, go along home to whoever should have been protecting you and don't go chasing after men again."

Liana's eyes flew open. "Chasing after men? I was not—"

He gave her a quick kiss, a twinkle in his eyes, before rising. "Spying on me from the bushes. You ought to learn what lust is before you try to inspire it. Now, off you go before I change my mind and give you what you've asked for. I've got more important business to tend to today than some hungry virgin."

It didn't take Liana long to recover herself. She was on her feet in seconds. "I will freeze in hell before I am hungry for the likes of you."

He paused as he started to put a leg into a pair of wet braies. "I'm tempted to make you eat those words. No," he said and began moving again, "I have other things to do. Perhaps later, after I'm married, you might come to me. I'll see if I have time for you then."

There were no curse words vile enough to describe what Liana was feeling. "You will see me again," she managed to say. "Oh yes, you will, but I do not think you will be so arrogant when we meet again. Pray for your life, peasant." She stormed past him.

"I do every day," he called after her. "And I'm not—"

She didn't hear any more as, once in the trees, she pulled her gown and headdress from their hiding place and ran toward her horse. The animal waited quietly while Liana tore the woolen dress from her body. She flung it to the ground, then stamped on it, grinding it into the dirt.

"Disgusting!" she said. "Filthy, dirty people," she muttered. And she had thought the peasants' lives romantic. They were so *free!* "They have no one to protect them," she said to her horse. "If my guard had been here, he'd have skewered that swine. If Lord Stephen had been here, he'd have made him crawl. I

would have laughed to see that red-haired devil kiss Lord Stephen's shoe. What shall I do with him, Belle?" she asked the horse. "The rack? Drawing and quartering? Disembowelment? Burning at the stake? Yes, I like that. I'll have him burned. I shall serve dinner, and his burning shall be the entertainment."

Dressed in her own clothes once again, she mounted her horse and gave a glance of hatred in the direction of the pond. She tried to imagine the man's violent death, but then she remembered his kiss. She shook her head as if to clear away those thoughts. Again she tried to think of his burning, but she couldn't get past imagining his beautiful form tied to the pole.

"Damn him!" she cursed, and kicked her horse forward.

She had not gone but a short distance when she came to fifty of her father's knights, suited in heavy armor as if going to war. *Now* they decide to look for me near the pond, she thought. Why didn't they come when he was tossing her in the water or making her wash his clothes . . . or when he was kissing her?

"My lady!" the lead knight exclaimed. "We have been searching for you. Have you been harmed?"

"Actually, I have," she said angrily. "In the forest on the east side of the pond is—" She stopped. She didn't know why, but suddenly fifty men against one unarmed peasant seemed very unfair.

"Is what, my lady? We will kill it."

"Is the largest flock of the prettiest butterflies I have ever seen," she said, giving the man her most dazzling smile. "I lost track of time. I am so sorry if I worried anyone. Shall we return?" She turned her horse and rode ahead of the men, greatly puzzled by what she'd

done. It would be better, of course, to wait and tell her father what had happened and how that awful man had treated her. Yes, that was it. She was just being sensible. Her father would know how to deal with him. Perhaps seal him inside a nail-studded barrel. Yes, that sounded like a good idea.

CHAPTER
THREE

Rogan watched the girl go and regretted the fact that he hadn't had time for her. He would have liked to touch that pale skin of hers—and that hair! It was the color of the mane of a horse he'd owned as a boy.

A horse killed in battle by the Howards, he remembered with bitterness, and pulled hard on the knitted, footed stockings.

His big toe came through a hole just below the knee. Without thought, he pulled the hose over his toe then yanked on the braies again. His little toe stuck at the ankle. This time his clothing got his attention. He held the braies up to the sunlight and saw the hundreds of tiny holes. Now the stockings were holding together out of habit, but in a matter of days they'd start unraveling. He grabbed his shirt and saw that it too was full of holes, as was his woolen overtunic.

Damn the presumptuous snippet of a girl, he thought with anger. Here he was to marry the Neville heiress and his clothes were falling off his body. If he ever saw that wench again, he'd—

Rogan stopped his thoughts and looked at the shirt again. She'd not wanted to wash his clothes. What she'd wanted was a good tumble in the grass. When she didn't get it, she'd had her revenge on him, and revenge was something Rogan understood very well.

In spite of his anger, in spite of the fact that he was now going to have to go to the expense of new clothes, he looked at the sunlight shining through the holes in his shirt and he did something he rarely did: He smiled. Saucy wench, she wasn't afraid of him. She had risked a well-deserved beating when she'd pounded holes in his clothes. If he'd caught her, he would have . . . He would probably have given her the tumble she wanted, he thought, still smiling.

He tossed the shirt into the air, caught it, then began to dress. He felt better now about marrying the Neville heiress. Perhaps after his marriage he'd find the blonde beauty and see if he could give her what she wanted. Maybe he'd take her with him and maybe he'd fill her belly with the nine brats she claimed to have.

Once dressed, he mounted his horse and rode up the bank to where his brother and his men waited.

"We've waited long enough," Severn said. "Have you built your courage now? Can you face the girl?"

Rogan's humor left his face. "If you want to keep that tongue of yours, you'll hold it still. Mount and ride. I go to marry a woman."

Severn went to his waiting horse, and as he put his foot in the stirrup, something blue in the grass caught his attention. He picked it up and saw that it was a piece of yarn. He dropped it again and gave it no more thought as he rode after his hardheaded brother.

"My lady," Joice said again, then waited. But Liana made no response. "My lady!" she said louder, but

35

still no response. Joice looked at Liana staring out the window, her mind far away. She had been this way since yesterday, when she'd returned from her ride. Perhaps it was her impending marriage—the messenger had been sent to Lord Stephen this morning—or perhaps it was something else altogether. Whatever it was, Liana was not telling anyone. Joice eased out of the room and closed the heavy oak door.

Liana hadn't slept during the night and she'd given up all attempts at work. She just sat on the window seat in her room and stared at the village below. She watched people scurrying, laughing, cursing.

The door opened with a bang. "Liana!"

There was no possibility of ignoring the angry, hate-filled voice of her stepmother. Liana turned cool eyes to her. "What do you want?" She couldn't look at Helen's beauty without seeing Lord Stephen's smiling face, his eyes shifting to the gold salver on the mantel.

"Your father wants you to come to the Hall. He has guests."

There was a bitterness in Helen's voice that piqued Liana's curiosity. "Guests?"

Helen turned away. "Liana, I don't think you should go down. Your father will forgive you; he forgives you everything. Tell him you have seen this man and do not want him. Tell him you have given your heart to Lord Stephen and want no one else."

Now Liana was indeed interested. "What man?"

Helen turned back to look at her stepdaughter. "It's one of those dreadful Peregrines," she said. "You probably don't know of them, but my former husband's land was near theirs. For all their long line of ancestors, they are poor as a honey-wagon driver—and about as clean."

"So what do these Peregrines have to do with me?"

"Two of them arrived last night and the oldest one says he has come to marry you." Helen threw up her hands. "It's like them. They don't ask for your hand— they announce that one of the filthy beasts is here to marry you."

Liana remembered another filthy man, a man who had kissed her and teased her. "I am pledged to Lord Stephen. The acceptance to his proposal has already been sent."

Helen sat down on the bed and weariness made her shoulders droop. "That's what I've told your father, but he won't listen. These men brought two huge hawks as gifts for him, two big peregrine falcons like their name, and Gilbert has spent all night with them recounting one hawking story after another. He is convinced they are the best of men. He doesn't notice the stench of them, the poverty of them. He ignores the stories of their brutality. Their father wore out four wives."

Liana looked steadily at her stepmother. "Why do you care who I marry? Isn't one man as good as another? What you want is for me to get out of your house, so what difference does it make who I marry?"

Helen put her hand on her growing belly. "You will never understand," she said tiredly. "I merely want to be mistress in my own house."

"While I must leave and go to some man who—"

Helen put up her hand. "It was a mistake for me to try to talk to you. Go to your father, then. Let him marry you off to this man, who will probably beat you, a man who will take every penny you have and leave you without so much as the clothes on your back. Clothes! Clothes are nothing to these men. The oldest one dresses worse than the kitchen boys. When he moves, you can see holes in his filthy garments." She heaved herself off the bed. "Hate me if you must, but I pray that you do not ruin your life merely to do what I say you should not." She left the room.

Liana wasn't much interested in this new man who had announced he planned to marry her. Men like him had been coming night and day for months now. For her part, she couldn't see a great deal of difference in them. Some were old, some were young, some had brains, some did not. What they had in common was a desire for the Neville money. What they wanted was—

"Holes in his clothes?" Liana said aloud, her eyes wide. "Holes in his clothes?"

Joice came into the room, "My lady, your father—"

Liana pushed past her maid and ran down the steep spiral stairs. She had to see this man, had to see him before he saw her. At the bottom of the stairs she ran out the door and through the courtyard, past knights lounging about, past horses waiting for riders, past spitcock boys resting in the sun, and into the kitchen. The enormous open fireplaces made the rabbit warren of rooms feverishly hot, but Liana kept running. She pulled open a little door near the slophole and went up the steep stone stairs to the musicians' gallery. She put her finger to her lips to silence the fiddle player as he started to address her.

The musicians' gallery was a wooden balcony at one end of the Great Hall, with a waist-high wooden rail blocking the musicians from view. Liana stood in one corner of the gallery and looked down into the Hall.

It was *him.*

The man she'd seen yesterday, the man who had kissed her, sat at her father's right hand, an enormous falcon on a perch between them. Sunlight streaming through the windows seemed to make the red in his hair catch fire.

Liana leaned back against the wall, her heart pounding. He wasn't a peasant. He had said he was off to do some courting, and he'd meant her. He had come to *marry* her.

"My lady, are you all right?"

Liana waved the harpist away and looked back at the men below, not sure of what she'd seen. There were two men with her father, but to her eyes, she could see only one of them. The dark man seemed to dominate the hall with his sprawling way of sitting and the intensity with which he spoke and listened. Her father laughed and the blond man laughed, but her man did not.

Her man? Her eyes widened at the thought.

"What is his name?" she whispered to the harpist.

"Who, my lady?"

"The dark man," she said impatiently. "There, that one. Below."

"Lord Rogan," the musician answered. "And his brother is—"

"Rogan," she murmured, not caring about the blond man. "Rogan. It suits him." Her head came up. "Helen," she said, then flung open the door and started running again. Down again through the kitchens, past a dog fight the men were laying odds on, across the cobbled yard to the south tower, then up the stairs, nearly knocking over two maids who had their arms full of laundry, and into the solar. Helen sat before a tapestry frame and barely glanced up when Liana came rushing in.

"Tell me about him," Liana demanded, panting from her run.

Helen was still smarting from Liana's remarks of an

hour before. "I know nothing about any man. I am merely a servant in my own home."

Liana grabbed a stool from against the wall and went to sit before Helen. "Tell me all you know about this Rogan. Is he the one who has asked for me? Reddish hair? Big, dark? Green eyes?"

Every person in the solar came to a standstill. Lady Liana had never shown the least interest in a man before.

Helen looked at her stepdaughter with concern. "Yes, he is a beautiful man, but can you not see more than his beauty?"

"Yes, yes, I know, his clothes are crawling with lice. Or they were until I— Tell me what you know of him," Liana demanded.

Helen did not understand this young woman at all, but she'd never seen her so alive, so flushed, so pretty. A feeling of dread was spreading over her. Sensible, sane, mature Liana could not possibly fall for a man's beauty. There had been hundreds of handsome men here in the last months and not one of them—

"Tell me!"

Helen sighed. "I don't know a lot about them. Their family is old. It's said their ancestors fought with King Arthur, but a few generations ago the eldest Peregrine gave the dukedom, the family seat, and the money to the family of his second wife. He had his eldest children declared illegitimate. After he was dead, the wife married a cousin of hers and the son of Peregrine became a Howard. Now the Howards own the title and the lands that once belonged to the Peregrines. That's all I know. The king declared all the Peregrines bastards and they were left with two decaying old castles, a minor earldom, and nothing else."

Helen leaned toward Liana. "I have seen where they

live. It is hideous. The roof has fallen in places. It's filthy beyond belief, and those Peregrines care nothing for dirt or lice or meat covered with maggots. They live for only one thing and that is to revenge themselves on the Howards. This man Rogan doesn't want a wife. He wants the Neville money so he can wage war on the Howards."

Helen took a breath. "The Peregrines are horrible men. They care only for war and death. When I was a child there were six sons, but four of them have been killed. Maybe only these two are left, or perhaps the men breed sons like rabbits."

On impulse, Helen took Liana's hand. "Please do not consider this man. He would eat you alive for breakfast."

Liana's head was reeling. "I am made of stronger stuff than you think," she whispered.

Helen drew back. "No," she whispered. "Do not think of it. You cannot consider marriage to the man."

Liana looked away from her stepmother. Perhaps there was some other reason Helen wanted to keep her away from Rogan. Perhaps she wanted him for herself. Perhaps they had been lovers when she'd lived near him, while her first husband was alive.

Liana was about to say as much when Joice entered the room.

"My lady," she said to Liana. "Sir Robert Butler has arrived. He asks for your hand in marriage."

"Accept him," Helen said instantly. "Accept him. I know his father. An excellent family."

Liana looked from Joice to Helen and knew she could take no more. She pushed past the two women and hurried down the stairs, Helen and Joice following her as fast as they could.

In the courtyard below stood eleven men, all splendidly dressed, their velvet tunics trimmed in gold, their caps fashionably arranged in the latest extravagance, jewels on their fingers sparkling in the sunlight.

Liana tried to pass them to reach the stables in the outer courtyard. A hard ride might clear her head. But Helen stopped her by grabbing her elbow.

"Sir Robert?" Helen said.

Reluctantly, Liana turned to look at the man. He was young, handsome, with dark brown hair and eyes. He was beautifully dressed and he smiled at her sweetly.

She hated him at first sight.

"This is my stepdaughter, Lady Liana," Helen said. "How is your father?"

Liana stood there stiffly, listening to the two of them exchange pleasantries and wanting desperately to get away. She had to go somewhere and think, for she had the decision of her life to make. Should she marry a man who smirked at her, who made her wash his clothes?

"I'm sure Liana would love to go with you. Wouldn't you, Liana?" Helen asked.

"What?"

"Sir Robert has agreed to accompany you on your ride. He will protect you from any harm as well as your own father would, won't you, Sir Robert?"

Liana hated the way Helen smiled at the man. Was she actually sleeping with men besides her husband? "And who will protect me from him?" Liana said sweetly, looking at Helen. "But then I wear no jewels, so perhaps I'll be safe."

Helen gave Liana a quelling look. "My stepdaughter is indeed amusing." She glared at Liana. "But not *too* amusing, I hope." She pushed Liana forward. "Go with him," she hissed.

Hesitantly, Liana walked through to the outer courtyard, where her horse was stabled.

"I had hoped to win your hand because of your father's lands," Sir Robert said in a pleasant voice, "but now that I have seen you, you are a prize in yourself."

"Oh?" She stopped and turned to face him. "Are my eyes like emeralds or sapphires?"

His eyes widened in surprise. "I would say sapphires."

"My skin is like ivory or the finest satin?"

He gave her a little smile. "I would say the petals of the whitest rose."

Her eyes hardened. "And my hair?"

His smile widened. "Your hair is hidden."

She jerked off her headdress. "Gold?" she asked angrily.

"Sunlight on gold."

She turned away from him angrily and missed seeing Sir Robert's repressed laughter.

"Would you allow me to escort you on a ride?" he asked politely. "I swear on my mother's soul that I will not compliment one part of your lovely form. I will call you a hag if you so wish."

She didn't look back at him as she went toward her horse, which the stableboy was already saddling. She didn't find anything humorous in what he was saying. Of course he'd tell her she was a hag. He'd say anything she wanted him to.

She ignored him as she rode through the outer gate, across the drawbridge, and toward the nearby forest. She didn't think about where she was going, but she headed for the pond. Behind her, she knew Sir Robert was having a difficult time keeping up with her, but she didn't slow down for him.

When she halted near the edge of the pond, she sat still on her horse for a moment, remembering yesterday, when she'd seen Rogan lying there. She smiled in memory of the look on his face when she'd slammed the muddy clothes into his chest.

"My lady is as good a rider as she is beautiful," Sir Robert said as he reined his horse near hers. When Liana started to dismount, he protested that he must help her.

She spent two hours with him at the pond and found him to be an utterly perfect man. He was kind, considerate, pleasant, and learned, and he treated her as if she were a fragile flower that might break at any second. He talked to her about love songs and fashions and assumed she'd be wildly interested in what was going on at King Henry's court. Three times Liana tried to direct the talk to land management and the price of wool, but Sir Robert would hear none of it.

All the time she was with him she kept thinking about the time she'd spent with Lord Rogan. He was a dreadful man, of course. He was dirty, demanding, and arrogant. He'd ordered her about as if she were his slave. Of course she had been dressed as a peasant and he had known he was an earl—or if what Helen had said was true, then perhaps he was actually a duke. But there was something about him, something strong and magnetic that made her able to think of little else except him.

"Perhaps I can teach you the new dance. Lady Liana?"

"Yes, oh certainly." They were walking side by side down a wide wagon path through the forest. Twice he'd offered to take her arm, but she'd refused him. "How does a man want a wife to act?" she asked.

She wasn't aware of how Sir Robert's chest swelled

with pride as her words raised his hopes. "Wives were meant to give a man comfort and support, to make a home for him, to bear his children. Wives are to give a man love."

She raised one eyebrow at him. "And as much land as her father can afford?"

Sir Robert chuckled. "That helps, of course."

Liana was frowning as she remembered Rogan's words: "I'll marry no shrews. I'll take her only if she's biddable and soft-spoken."

"I guess all men like soft, obedient women," she said.

Sir Robert looked at her with lust in his eyes, lust for her beautiful person as well as for the wealth that came with her. For his part she could be a vixen, in fact he rather liked her spitefulness, but he would never tell a woman that. It was better to tell them to be obedient and hope for the best.

They walked in silence, but Liana's head was reeling. Why would she even consider marriage to someone like Lord Rogan? There was nothing to recommend him. He had treated her with every discourtesy, but then he'd thought she was a peasant. He'd probably have kissed her hand and murmured pleasant phrases about the perfume of her skin if he'd known who she was. And would lice crawl up her arm? she wondered.

She looked at Sir Robert and gave him a weak smile. He was clean and pleasant and boring—oh so very, very boring. "Would you kiss me?" she asked on impulse.

Sir Robert didn't have to be asked twice. Gently, he took her in his arms and pressed his lips against hers.

Liana could have fallen asleep. She stepped back and looked at Sir Robert in surprise. So *that* was why she considered marrying Lord Rogan. She desired him. When he kissed her, her toes curled. When he stood before her with almost no clothing on, her own body grew hot. Right now Sir Robert could remove every stitch of his clothing and she knew she'd feel nothing.

"Liana," he whispered, and took a step toward her.

Liana turned away so quickly, his hair ruffled in the breeze she caused. "I have to return. I have to tell my father I agree to the marriage."

Sir Robert was so stunned he stood still for a moment, unable to move. Then he ran after Liana, grabbed her into his arms, and began kissing her neck and throat. "Oh my darling, you have made me the happiest man on earth. You don't know what this means to me. We've been plagued with fires for the last year. I had nearly lost hope of being able to rebuild."

She pulled away from him. "I thought it was my golden hair and my sapphire eyes you desired."

"That, too, of course." He took both her hands in his and began kissing them enthusiastically.

She snatched her hands away and hurried toward her horse. "You'll have to find someone else to rebuild for you. I've decided to marry the oldest Peregrine."

Sir Robert let out a yelp of genuine horror as he ran after her and caught her arm. "You cannot possibly consider any of them. They are—"

She put her hand up to stop him. "It is not for you to decide. Now, I'm going to return to my house and you may remain here or go with me. When you do return, I suggest you take your men and leave the Neville lands and go in search of another heiress to repair your damaged estates. And next time, perhaps you'll take better care of your properties and prevent the fires before they start." She went to her horse and mounted.

Sir Robert looked after her for a moment, his disappointment leaving him. Perhaps he was better off without this termagant. Marriage to a woman like her could be hell. Perhaps he'd rather lose a bit of land than saddle himself with this woman for the rest of his life.

Like hell he would, he thought. Damn those Peregrines! Women seemed to like them in spite of their dirt and their lifelong battle for lands and titles that weren't theirs. If Liana marries one of those Peregrines, within three years she'll be old and worn out from being used harder than a plow horse, he thought with some satisfaction.

He mounted his horse and followed her. It would be better to take his men and leave right away. He couldn't bear to see the betrothal ceremony of the lovely Lady Liana and one of those Peregrines. He shrugged his shoulders. It was no longer any concern of his.

Liana stood before her father and stepmother in the solar and made the announcement that she was going to marry Lord Rogan.

"Wise choice, girl," Gilbert said. "Best falconer in all of England."

Helen's face was slowly turning purple. "Do not do this," she said, gasping. "You are trying to spite me."

"I have done what you wanted and chosen a husband," Liana said coolly. "I would think you'd be pleased with me."

Helen tried to calm herself, then she sank down heavily in her chair and threw her hands up in surrender. "You win. You may stay here. You may run the estates and the servants. You may have it all, for all I care. When I go to meet my God, I will not have it on my head that I forced my husband's daughter to this living death. You win, Liana. Does this give you pleasure? Go now. Go from my sight. At least leave me this one room, where neither you nor your dead mother still rule."

Liana was puzzled by her stepmother's speech and she thought about it as she turned to leave the room. She was nearly to the door when she realized what Helen was saying. She turned back quickly.

"No," she said with some urgency in her voice, "I *want* to marry this man. You see, I met him before. Yesterday. We were alone for a while and . . ." She looked down at her hands, her face red.

"Oh dear God, he has raped her," Helen said. "Gilbert, you must hang him."

"No!" Gilbert and Liana said in unison.

"The hawks—" Gilbert began.

"He didn't—" Liana began.

Helen put up her hands for silence, then clutched her belly. Her child would no doubt be born with cloven feet after the hell her stepdaughter had put her through during her pregnancy. "Liana, what has the beast done to you?"

Made me wash his clothes, she thought. Kissed me. "Nothing," she said. "He has not touched me." She meant to say penance at mass for that lie. "Yesterday while I was riding, I met him and I . . ." She what? Liked him? Loved him? Hated him? Probably all of them. Whatever she felt for him, it was strong. "And I want to accept his offer of marriage," she finished.

"Good choice," Gilbert said. "The boy is a man if ever I saw one."

"You're a fool, Liana," Helen whispered, her face pale. "Rarely does a girl have such a doting father that he will let her choose her own husband, and now I understand why. I would never have guessed you to be

48

so stupid." She sighed. "All right. It's on your head now. When he beats you—if you're still alive—you may return here and have your wounds dressed. Go now. I can't bear the sight of you."

Liana didn't move from where she was. "I do not want to meet him before the ceremony," she said.

"At last, some wisdom," Helen said sarcastically. "Stay away from him as long as you can."

Gilbert was eating grapes. "He hasn't asked to see you. I guess yesterday was enough, eh?" He grinned and winked at his daughter. He didn't know when a woman had pleased him so much. The Peregrine boys might be a little rough around the edges, but that was because they were *men,* not popinjays ruled by women.

"I guess so," Liana said. She was afraid that if he saw her and realized she was the woman who'd tossed the clothes at him, he'd refuse to marry her. He didn't like shrews, and if Rogan wanted a soft-spoken wife, then she was going to *be* a soft-spoken wife.

"Well, it's easy enough to arrange," Gilbert said. "I'll say you have the pox and he can exchange rings with a proxy. We'll set the wedding for . . ." He looked at Helen, but she was stony and silent. "Three months. Is that all right with you, daughter?"

Liana looked at Helen, and instead of hating her stepmother, she remembered the way Helen was ready to allow Liana to remain as a spinster in the Neville household. Perhaps Helen didn't hate her after all. "I will need gowns," Liana said softly. "And I will need household goods. Do you think you could help me choose what I need?"

Helen looked bleak. "I cannot make you change your mind?"

"No," Liana said. "You cannot."

"Then I will help you," Helen said. "If you died, I would help lay out your body for burial, so I will ready you for this."

"Thank you," Liana said, smiling, and left the room feeling wonderfully light and happy. She had a great deal to do in the next three months.

The Peregrine banner of a rampant white falcon on a red background with three horses' skulls in a diagonal band across the falcon's belly flew over the campsite. Some of the men slept in tents or under the baggage wagons, but Rogan and Severn lay on blankets on the ground, their bodies surrounded by weapons.

"I don't understand why she agreed to marry you," Severn said once again. It was something he'd been puzzling on since Gilbert Neville had said his daughter had agreed to the marriage. Rogan had merely shrugged, then started negotiating what was to be included in the dowry. Neither Rogan nor Gilbert seemed to think it was odd that the young woman, after refusing most of England, should take Rogan sight unseen.

"She turned down everyone else," Severn said. "Not that I approve of allowing a girl to choose her own husband, but why would she say no to a man like Stephen Whitington?"

Rogan turned onto his side, away from his brother, and grunted. "The girl has a head on her shoulders. She made the right choice."

It was Severn's turn to grunt. "There's more to it than you're telling me. You didn't seduce the girl in private, did you?"

"I never laid eyes on her. I was too busy trying to seduce Neville out of his gold. Maybe he beat the girl and told her who she was to marry, just as he should have done in the first place."

"Perhaps," Severn said. "But I still think you—"

Angrily, Rogan looked across the night at his brother. "I never met the girl, I told you. I was with Neville from morning till night."

"Except when you went off alone before we went to Neville's castle."

"I didn't—" Rogan began, then stopped and remembered the girl who'd complained about his clothes. He had forgotten about her until this moment. He'd have to remember to look for her when he returned in three months' time for his wedding. "I didn't see the heiress," Rogan said softly. "Her father must have arranged the marriage. He's a fool of a man and I could buy his soul for a dozen or so hawks."

"I doubt if you'd have to pay that much," Severn scoffed, then paused a moment. "Weren't you curious about the woman? I'd want to see a woman I was to marry before I married her. She could be fat and old for all you know."

"What do I care about a wife? It's her lands I want. Now go to sleep, little brother, for tomorrow's Wednesday and Wednesday takes a lot of energy."

Severn smiled in the darkness. Tomorrow he'd see Iolanthe and everything would be the same. But in three months' time Lady Liana Neville would enter their lives and things would still remain the same, for if she was anything like her father, she was a cowardly little thing.

CHAPTER FOUR

No, no, no, my lady, good wives do not screech.
Good wives *obey* their husbands," Joice said. She was
tired and exasperated. Lady Liana had asked her to
teach her how to be a good wife, but Liana had had
too much control for too long and it was almost
impossible to make her understand how a wife was
supposed to behave.

"Even when he is a fool?" Liana asked.

"*Especially* when he is a fool," Joice answered.
"Men like to believe they know everything, that they
are always right, and they want absolute loyalty from
their women. No matter how wrong your husband is,
he will expect you to stand by him."

Liana listened to this carefully. This is not what her
mother thought of marriage, nor did Helen. And
neither of them had been beloved wives, she thought
with a grimace. In the last month she'd come to realize
how different she wanted her marriage to be from the
two she'd seen. She didn't want to live in hatred for
the rest of her life. Her mother hadn't seemed to mind

the fact that she despised her husband, nor did Helen, but Liana wanted her life to be different. She'd seen a love match once of a couple who, after years of marriage, still gave one another long looks and sat for hours talking to each other. Liana wanted *that* kind of marriage.

"And he'd rather have obedience than honesty?" Liana asked. "If he is wrong, I am not to tell him so?"

"Most certainly not. Men like to think their wives believe them to be next to God in everything. Take care of his house, bear him sons, and when he asks your opinion, tell him that he knows much more about such matters than you do, that you are merely a woman."

"Merely a . . ." Liana said, trying to understand this. The only man she'd ever really known was her father, and she hated to think what the Neville lands would be like if her mother had refused to govern them. "But my father—"

"Your father is not like most men," Joice said as tactfully as possible. She had been stunned when Lady Liana had asked for her advice about men, but she thought it was high time. Liana had better learn what men were actually like before she tied herself to someone like those Peregrines. "Lord Rogan will not allow you such freedom as your father has."

"No, I guess not," Liana said softly. "He has said he will marry no shrew."

"No man wants a shrew. He wants a woman who will praise him, who will see to his comfort, and who will be eager in bed."

Liana thought she could handle two of those points easily. "I'm not sure Lord Rogan believes in comfort. His clothes are dirty and I believe he does not bathe often."

"Ah, now there is where a wife can have power. Al¹

men like comfort. They like a certain dish for eating, a certain cup for their favorite drink, and whether your Lord Rogan knows it or not, he likes an orderly, quiet household. His wife should take care of the servants' quarrels, she should see that his table is loaded with delicious food. You can replace his scratchy, dirty clothing with soft new ones. These are ways to a man's heart."

"And if his lands are in a muddle, then I—"

"Then that is his business. It is not a woman's concern," Joice said sharply.

Liana thought it might be easier to run a hundred estates than to please one man. She wasn't sure she could remember all the rules of what a man did and did not like. "You are sure of all this? Staying in the solar and tending merely to household business will win my husband's heart?"

"I am sure of it, my lady. Now, will you try on this new gown?"

For three months Liana tried on new gowns. She ordered furs, Italian brocades, jewels. She set every woman who could hold a needle to embroidering. Not only did she order her own wardrobe, but she had a splendid set of clothing made for Lord Rogan. The only time her father took any notice of the proceedings was to remark that the bridegroom should dress himself. Liana took no notice of him.

When she wasn't with Helen working on her new wardrobe, Liana was supervising the packing of her dowry. All the Neville wealth that was not in land was in portable goods. Gold plates and ewers were packed in straw and put into wagons, as were precious glass vessels. She took tapestries, linens, pieces of carved-oak furniture, candles, feather pillows and mattresses.

There were carts full of rich fabrics, furs, a fat iron-bound chest full of jewels and another of silver groats.

"You will need everything," Helen said. "Those men have not one comfort in their lives."

Liana smiled at that because perhaps the comfort she brought would help her husband love her.

Helen saw Liana's lovesick smile and groaned, but she didn't try to talk to Liana again, as she'd seen how impossible it was to attempt to reason with her. Helen just helped to denude the Neville castle of its riches, and she gave Liana no more advice.

The wedding was to be a small one, as the Nevilles were not favorites among the aristocracy and royalty of the land, for Gilbert's father had purchased his earldom from the king only a few years before he died. There were still many people who could remember when the Nevilles were merely rich, ruthless merchants charging five times what they paid for an item. Liana was glad for the excuse to save the expense of an enormous wedding celebration so she'd have more to take with her to the Peregrine castle.

Liana didn't sleep much the night before her wedding. She kept going over in her mind the things she had learned about pleasing a husband, and she kept trying to visualize her new life. She tried to imagine lying in bed with the handsome Lord Rogan. She thought about his touching her and caressing her and saying tender words to her. She had decided not to be "married in her hair," but to wear a jeweled headdress because she knew her long flaxen hair was her best feature and she wanted to share it with him and him alone on their wedding night. She imagined long walks together, as they laughed and held hands. She imagined sitting before the fire on a cold winter evening and reading aloud to him, or playing a game of draughts. Perhaps they'd play for kisses.

She smiled in the darkness at the thought of what he would say when he discovered he'd married the woman by the pool. Of course *that* woman had been a shrew, but Rogan's wife would be the demure, quiet, loving Lady Liana. She imagined his gratitude when she changed those dirty, rough clothes of his for fine silks and wools. She closed her eyes for a moment and imagined how incredibly handsome he would be dressed in dark velvet, green perhaps, with a jeweled chain extending from one broad shoulder to the other.

She would introduce him to the pleasures of bathing with rose-scented oil in the tub. Perhaps afterward he'd rub oil into her skin, even between her toes, she thought with a sigh of heavenly pleasure. She imagined lying on a clean, soft featherbed and laughing together over their first meeting—how childish they'd been not to have known at first sight that they were the love of each other's lives.

Just before dawn she dozed off, a smile on her lips, only to be awakened moments later by an unearthly clatter in the courtyard below. By the sound of the shouts of men and the clank of steel, they were being attacked. Who had left the drawbridge down?

"Oh Lord, don't let me die before I marry him," Liana prayed as she leaped out of bed and began running.

In the hall, Helen was also running, as was half the household, it seemed.

Liana made her way through the chaos to her stepmother. "What is it? What has happened?" she shouted above the noise.

"Your bridegroom has at last arrived," Helen said angrily. "And he and all his men are drunk. Now someone who doesn't value his life will have to get this Red Falcon of yours off his horse, bathed, dressed, and sober enough to say his vows to you." She paused and gave Liana a look of sympathy. "You vow away your life today, Liana," she said softly. "May God have mercy on your soul." Helen turned and started down the stairs to the solar.

"My lady," Joice said from behind Liana. "You must return to your room. You cannot be seen on your wedding day."

Liana went back to her room and she even allowed Joice to coax her into bed, but she could not sleep. Once again Rogan was under the same roof as she was and soon . . . soon he'd be here in bed with her. Just the two of them. Alone and quiet and intimate. What would they talk about, she wondered. They knew so little about each other. Perhaps they'd talk about first learning to ride a horse or maybe he'd tell her about where he lived. This Peregrine castle would be Liana's new home and she longed to know about it. She had to plan where her mother's tapestries would be hung, where her gold plates would be set to best display them.

She was so happy in her thoughts that she dozed off for a while until Joice came to wake her and four giggling maids began to dress her in red brocade with a cloth-of-gold underskirt. Her double-horned head-dress was red, embroidered with gold wire, and strung with hundreds of tiny pearls. A long transparent silk veil hung down her back.

"Beautiful, my lady," Joice said, tears in her eyes. "No man will be able to take his eyes from you."

Liana hoped so. She hoped she was as physically appealing to her husband as he was to her.

She rode sidesaddle on a white horse to the church

and she was so nervous she barely saw the crowds of people lining the sides of the road and yelling their wishes that she bear many children. Her eyes were straining ahead to see the man standing by the church door. Her palms were wet as she drew nearer to him. Would he take one look at her, see that she was the woman who hit him with a mud-soaked garment, and refuse to marry her?

When she was close enough to see him, she smiled with pride that he looked as good as she'd imagined in the green velvet tunic that she'd had made for him. The tunic barely reached the tops of his thighs and his powerful, muscular legs were tightly encased in dark knitted hose. On his head he wore a short-brimmed fur hat with a large ruby twinkling on the band.

She swelled so in pride at the look of him that her ribs ached against the steel bones in her corset. Then she held her breath as he stepped down from the church steps and started toward her. Was he going to lift her from her horse himself and not wait for her father, who rode ahead of her, to do it?

Her horse moved maddeningly slowly. Perhaps he could see she was the woman from the pond and he was pleased. Perhaps she had haunted his thoughts for the past three months as he had hers.

But Rogan did not come to her horse. In fact, as far as she saw, he did not so much as glance her way. Instead, he went to her father's horse and caught the bridle. The entire procession halted as Liana watched Rogan talk earnestly to her father. Liana watched in puzzlement until Helen moved her horse forward to stand beside her stepdaughter.

"What is that red devil up to now?" Helen spat out. "Those two are wrong if they think we will wait while they talk of hawks."

"Since he is to be my husband, I assume we must wait," Liana said coolly. She'd had enough of Helen's complaints about Rogan.

Helen kicked her horse's ribs and went to stand on the far side of her husband. Liana could not hear what was being said over the noise of the crowd, but she could see Helen's anger. Gilbert remained impassive and even leaned back in the saddle while Helen talked angrily to Rogan, but Rogan merely looked across at her with unseeing eyes.

Liana hoped he would never look at her like that. After a moment Rogan looked about him, as if seeing the crowd for the first time, and as an afterthought he looked at Liana sitting quietly on her horse. Liana held her breath as his cool eyes scanned her from toe to head. She did not see any recognition in his eyes and she was glad, because she didn't want to risk his refusing to marry her. When his eyes rose to meet hers, Liana lowered her lashes, hoping to seem modest and obedient.

After a moment, she looked up to see Rogan returning to the church steps and Helen riding toward her.

"That man you plan to marry," Helen said with a sneer, "was asking for twelve more knights' fees. He was saying he would walk away now and leave you here if he didn't get them."

Liana's eyes widened in alarm. "Did my father agree?"

Helen closed her eyes for a moment. "He agreed. Now, let's get this over with." She kicked her horse forward to ride behind Liana.

Gilbert helped his daughter from her horse, and she walked up the stairs to meet her husband. The ceremony was brief, the vows no different from what they had been for centuries. Liana kept her eyes lowered throughout, but when she vowed to be "meek and obedient in bed and at board," the crowd cheered her. Twice she stole looks at Rogan, but he merely seemed impatient to be away—as she was, she thought with a smile.

When they were pronounced man and wife, again the crowd cheered and the bride and groom, their family and guests went inside to mass, for the wedding was of the state and therefore outside the church, but mass was of God. The priest blessed their marriage and began the mass.

Liana sat quietly beside her new husband and listened to the Latin incantations for what seemed to be hours. Rogan did not look at her, did not touch her. He yawned a few times, scratched a few times, and sprawled his long legs in the aisle. At one point she thought she heard a snore coming from him, but his brother punched him and Rogan sat up straighter on the hard bench.

After mass, the wedding group rode back to the castle while the peasants threw grains at them and shouted, "Plenty! Plenty!" For three days and nights every man, woman, and child would have all the food and drink they could hold.

Once over the drawbridge and into the inner courtyard, Liana sat on her horse and waited for her husband to lift her down. Instead, she watched as Rogan and his brother Severn dismounted and went to the wagons loaded and waiting along the stone wall.

"He cares more for your goods than for you," Helen said as a groom helped Liana from her horse.

"You have had your say," Liana snapped. "You do not know all there is. Perhaps he has reasons for his actions."

"Yes, such as not being human," Helen said.

"There's no use reminding you of what you've done. It's too late now. Shall we go in and eat? It is my experience that men always come home when they're hungry."

But Helen was wrong, because neither Rogan nor his men came in to the feast Liana had spent weeks organizing. Instead, they stayed outside, going through the wagons that were packed with her dowry. She sat alone at her father's right side, the groom's place next to her empty. All around she could feel the tittering of the guests as they looked at her with sympathetic eyes. She kept her chin up and refused to let them see she was hurt. She told herself it was good that her husband was interested in his property. A man who was so concerned about his estates wasn't likely to gamble them away.

After a couple of hours, when most people had finished eating, Rogan and his men came into the Hall. Liana smiled, for now, surely, he'd come to her and apologize and explain what had kept him. Instead, he stopped beside Gilbert's chair, reached between Gilbert and Helen, and picked up a two-pound piece of roasted beef and began to gnaw on it.

"Three wagons are full of feather mattresses and dress goods. I want them filled with gold," Rogan said, his mouth full.

Gilbert had had nothing to do with the packing of the wagons and so could not answer Rogan's complaint. He opened his mouth to speak, but nothing came out.

Helen had no such problem. "The mattresses are for my daughter's comfort. I don't imagine that place of yours has even the barest comforts."

Rogan turned cold, hard eyes on her and Helen almost backed down. "When I want a woman's opinion, I will ask for it." He looked back at Gilbert. "I am having an accounting made now. You will regret it if you have cheated me." He stepped away from the table, the meat eaten, and wiped his greasy hands on the beautiful velvet tunic Liana had had made for him. "You can keep your feathers."

Helen was on her feet instantly as she confronted Rogan. He was much taller than she and overpoweringly large, but she held herself rigid before him. Her anger gave her courage. "Your own wife, the wife you have chosen to ignore, supervised the loading of those wagons and she has not cheated you. As for the household goods, either they go with her or she remains here in her father's house. Choose now, Peregrine, or I'll have the marriage annulled. No daughter of mine goes from my house naked."

The entire room was silent. Only a dog snuffling in a corner could be heard and it, too, soon quietened. Guests, acrobats, singers, musicians, jesters all paused in what they were doing and looked at the tall, handsome man and the elegant woman confronting each other.

For a moment Rogan did not seem to know what to say. "The marriage has been performed."

"And not consummated," Helen flashed back at him. "It will be easy to have it annulled."

The anger in Rogan's eyes increased. "You do not threaten me, woman. The girl's goods are mine and I will take what I want." He took a step backward and grabbed Liana's arm, pulling her out of her chair. "If the girl's virginity is a problem, I'll take it now."

This statement made the half-drunk crowd laugh, and their laughter increased as Rogan pulled Liana up the stairs and out of sight.

"My room . . ." Liana said nervously, not exactly sure of what was going on. She was aware only that at last she was going to be alone with this magnificent man.

Rogan flung open a door to a guest room that was being used by the Earl of Arundel and his wife. The countess's maid was folding clothes. "Out," Rogan commanded the girl, and she scurried to obey him.

"But my room is—" Liana began. This was not the way things were supposed to happen. She was to be undressed by her maids and to be put nude between pure clean sheets and he was to come to her and kiss her and caress her.

"This room is good enough," he said, and pushed her back onto the bed, then grabbed her skirt hem and flung it over her head.

Liana fought her way out from under several heavy layers of cloth, then gasped as Rogan's considerable weight covered her. The next moment she cried out in pain as he entered her. She was unprepared for such pain and she pushed away from him, but he didn't seem to notice as he began to make quick, long strokes. Liana gritted her teeth to keep from crying and she clenched her fists against the pain.

Within minutes he was finished and he collapsed on her, limp and relaxed. It took Liana a moment to recover from the onslaught of pain, but when she opened her eyes she could see Rogan's dark hair, could feel the softness of it against her cheek. His face was turned away from her, but his thick, clean hair covered her cheek and forehead. How heavy yet how light he felt. His broad shoulders covered her small body, yet his hips didn't seem as wide as hers.

She lifted her hand and touched his hair, put her fingers into it, then her nose, and inhaled the fragrance of him.

Slowly, he turned to face her, his lids heavy with fatigue. "I slept for a moment," he said softly.

She smiled at his closed eyes and stroked the hair at his temple. His lashes were thick, his nose finely cut, his skin dark and warm and as finely pored as a baby's. His cheeks were stained dark with unshaven whiskers, but they didn't take away from the relaxed softness of his mouth.

Her finger moved from his temple and down his cheek to his lips. When she touched his lower lip, his eyes sprang open and the greenness of them was startling. Now he will kiss me, she thought, and for a moment she held her breath as he looked at her.

"A blonde," he murmured.

Liana smiled at him since her hair color seemed to please him. She put up her hand to pull off her headdress and all three feet of her hair cascaded out. "I wanted to save it for you," she whispered. "I hoped you would like it."

He picked up a strand of the fine, golden hair and curled it about his fingers. "It's——"

He halted in mid-sentence and all softness left his face. Immediately he got off of her and stood, glaring down at her. "Cover yourself and go to that hellion of a stepmother of yours and tell her the marriage is consummated. Tell her there will be no annulment. And you can ready yourself, for we leave here tonight."

Liana pushed her skirts down over her bare legs and sat up on the bed. "Tonight? But the marriage celebration goes on for two more days. Tomorrow I have planned dancing and——"

Rogan hastily straightened his clothes. "I have no time for dancing, and I have no time for back-talking wives. If this is how you plan to start, then you can stay here with your father and I will take the goods with me. My men and I leave in three hours' time. Be there or not, it doesn't matter to me." He turned and left the room, closing the door loudly behind him.

Liana sat where she was, too stunned to move. He would leave her behind!

There was a soft knock on the door, then Joice entered. "My lady?" she said.

Liana looked up at her maid, all her puzzlement showing in her eyes. "He leaves here in three hours and he says I may go with him or not. He doesn't care one way or the other."

Joice sat down on the bed and took Liana's hand. "He thinks he does not need a wife. All men think that. It is up to you to prove to him that he does need a wife by his side."

Liana pulled away from her maid, and when she moved her legs, she felt pain. "He hurt me."

"It's always like that the first time."

Liana stood and anger began to race through her. "I have *never* been treated like this before. He did not bother to even come to his own wedding feast. I had to sit there and endure the stares and smiles from the people. And this!" She glanced down at her skirt. "I may as well have been raped. I'll let him know who he's dealing with." She had her hand on the door latch when Joice's words stopped her.

"And he will look at you with hatred as he looked at Lady Helen."

Liana turned back.

"You saw how he despised her," Joice continued, and suddenly felt very powerful. Her young charge might be beautiful and rich, but she was listening to and obeying Joice. "Believe me, I know what men like Lord Rogan want. He will hate you just as he does her if you defy him."

Liana rubbed the fingers of her right hand together.

She could still feel his hair against her skin and she remembered that, for a moment, there had been softness in his eyes. She did not want to take that away. "What do I do?" she whispered.

"Obey him," Joice said firmly. "Be ready in three hours. Lady Helen will no doubt protest your leaving, but stand with your husband against her. I have told you how men want loyalty from their wives."

"*Blind* loyalty?" Liana asked. "Even now, when he is wrong?"

"Most especially when he is wrong."

Liana listened to this, but still she didn't understand.

Seeing that her young mistress was still confused, Joice continued. "Swallow your anger. All married women feed on anger that they keep to themselves. You will see. You will learn to swallow so much anger that it will become a way of living to you."

Liana started to say something, but Joice cut her off.

"Go and get ready now or he will leave you."

Feeling very confused, Liana hurried out of the room. She was going to do whatever she could to prove to this man that she could be a good wife, and if it meant repressing her rage, then so be it. She'd show him that she could be the most loyal of wives.

As Lord Rogan went down the stone steps, a frown on his handsome face, the first person he met was Lady Helen. "The deed is done," he said to her. "There will be no annulment. If there is anything to be added to the wagons, then do it, for we leave in three hours' time." He started past her, but Helen put herself in front of him.

"You will take my stepdaughter away from her own wedding feast?"

Rogan didn't understand what these women were making such a fuss about. If it was food they wanted, they could take plenty with them. "I will not starve the girl," he said, making an effort to take the hatred from Helen's eyes. He was not used to women hating him. For the most part they were like that girl he'd married: adoring and soft-eyed.

"You *will* starve her," Helen said, "as your father starved his wives of warmth and companionship." Her voice lowered. "As you starved Jeanne Howard."

Helen stepped back when she saw the look on Rogan's face. His eyes hardened and he looked at her with such rage that she began to tremble.

"Never come near me again, woman," he said coldly, in a low undertone. He then stalked past her, ignored the calls of the guests to come and join them in a drink, and went outside to the courtyard.

Jeanne Howard, he thought. He could wring that woman's neck for mentioning Jeanne to him, but it made him remind himself to be careful with this new wife, not to allow pretty blue eyes and blonde hair to sway him.

"You look ready to run someone through," Severn said jovially. His face was flushed from too much food and drink.

"Are you ready to leave?" Rogan growled at him. "Or have you been too busy bedding the wenches to tend to the business at hand?"

Severn was used to his brother's constant anger and he'd had too much wine to let it bother him now. "I have anticipated you, brother, and filled a wagon full of food. Do we leave the feather pillows or take them?"

"Leave them," Rogan snapped, then hesitated. In his mind he heard Helen Neville saying, "As you

67

starved Jeanne Howard," and felt a knife twisting in his gut. The girl he'd married—what was her name? —seemed simple enough. "Let her have her feather mattresses," he growled to Severn, and went to check on his men.

Severn watched his brother walk away and wondered what his pretty little sister-in-law was like.

CHAPTER
FIVE

Liana hurried to dress herself, to make sure all her new clothes were packed, and to direct her maids to pack her personal articles. Three hours was such a short time to ready herself for her new life.

All the while that she was rushing about, Joice lectured her.

"Do not complain," Joice said. "Men hate women who complain. You are to take whatever he gives you and never say a word in protest. Tell him you are *glad* to be leaving your wedding feast, glad to have three hours to prepare yourself. Men like their women to be smiling and cheerful."

"He hasn't liked me yet," Liana said. "He hasn't taken any notice of me yet except to abolish the risk of an annulment," she said with some bitterness.

"It will take years," Joice said. "Men do not give their hearts easily, but if you persevere, love will come to you."

And that's what she wanted, Liana thought. She

wanted her beautiful husband to love her and to need her. If swallowing a little anger now and then would make him love her, then so be it.

She was ready before the three hours were up, and she went downstairs to say goodbye to her father and stepmother. Gilbert was drunk and talking of hawks with some men and barely had a word of farewell to say to his only child, but Helen hugged her tightly and wished her all the best in the world.

Outside, with the Peregrine knights mounted and waiting to ride, the big white falcon banner before them, Liana felt a momentary terror. She was leaving all that she knew behind and trusting her fate to these strangers. She stood frozen where she was and looked for her husband.

Rogan, atop a big roan stallion, came riding in front of her, so close she put up her arm to shield her face from flying gravel. "Mount and ride, woman," he said, and moved to the head of his men.

Liana hid her clenched fists in the folds of her skirt. Swallow anger, she thought, and tried to calm herself at his rudeness.

Out of the dust came Rogan's brother, Severn, and he smiled at her. "May I help you mount, my lady?" he asked.

Liana relaxed and smiled at this handsome man. He was as ill dressed as Rogan had been and his dark golden hair was too long and ragged at the edges, but at least he was smiling at her. She put her hand on his extended arm. "I would be honored," she said, and walked with him toward her waiting horse.

Liana was just mounted when Rogan rode back to them. He did not look at her, but he scowled at his brother.

"If you are through playing lady's maid, come with me," Rogan demanded.

"Perhaps your wife would like to ride in front with us," Severn said pointedly over Liana's head.

"I want no women," Rogan snapped, still not glancing at Liana.

"I don't think—" Severn began, but Liana cut him off.

Even she knew that she would not please her husband by being the cause of an argument with his brother. "I would rather stay here," she said loudly. "I will feel safer surrounded by the men, and you, sir," she said to Severn, "are needed by . . . by my husband."

Severn frowned for a moment as he looked at her. "As you wish," he said, and with a little bow he rode away from her, to position himself beside his brother at the head of the line.

"Oh excellent, my lady," Joice said as she came to ride beside her mistress. "You have pleased him now. Lord Rogan will like an obedient wife."

As they rode through the courtyard, across the drawbridge, and onto the dusty road, Liana sneezed at the dust. "I have been the obedient wife, but now I must ride behind ten men on horses and half a dozen wagons," she muttered.

"You will win in the end, though," Joice said. "You will see. Once he sees that you are obedient and loyal, he will love you."

Liana coughed at the dust and rubbed her nose. It was difficult to think of love and loyalty when one had a mouthful of dirt.

They rode for hours, Liana remaining where she was in the middle of the procession, none of her husband's men talking to her. The only voice she heard was Joice's, lecturing her on obedience and duty, and when Severn asked her if she was comfortable, Joice answered for her mistress, saying that if

Lord Rogan wanted his wife here, then of course Lady Liana was happy where she was.

Liana gave Severn a weak smile and choked on a cloud of dust.

"That one shows far too much interest in you," Joice said when Severn was gone. "You had better let him know his place right away."

"He is only being kind," Liana said.

"If you accept his kindness, you will cause problems between the brothers. Your husband will wonder where your loyalties lie."

"I am not sure my husband has yet looked at me," Liana mumbled to herself.

Joice smiled through the cloud of dust that surrounded them. With each day she was feeling more and more powerful. As a child, Lady Liana had never listened to her and several times Joice had been punished because Liana had escaped her rule and gotten into some mischief. But at long last here was something she knew which her mistress didn't.

They rode well into the night and Liana knew Joice and her other six maids were drooping with exhaustion, but she did not dare ask her husband to stop. Besides, Liana was too excited to rest. Tonight would be her wedding night. Tonight she would lie all night in her husband's arms. Tonight he would caress her, touch her hair, kiss her. A day spent riding in a little dust was worth such a nightly reward.

By the time they did stop to make camp, her senses were alive with anticipation. One of the knights perfunctorily helped her dismount, and Liana told Joice to see to the other women. Liana looked about for her husband and saw him disappearing into the trees.

Behind her, Liana was vaguely aware of the complaints of her women, who weren't used to riding horses such a distance, but she had no time for them. Taking her time, and trying to act casually, she followed her husband into the woods.

Rogan answered a call of nature in the woods, then walked deep into the still darkness toward the little stream. With every step he took, his muscles tightened harder. It had taken longer to get here than when he traveled without wagonloads of goods, and now the darkness was so complete he had to feel his way along the bank.

It was a while before he found the cairn, the six-foot-high pile of stones that he'd built to mark where his eldest brother, Rowland, had fallen to a Howard blade. He stood for a moment, his eyes adjusting to the faint moonlight on the gray stones, and heard the sounds of battle once again in his head. Rowland and his brothers had been hunting and Rowland, feeling safe since they were two days' ride from the Howards' land—the Peregrine land, in truth —had walked away from the protection of his men and sat by the river to drink a jug of beer alone.

Rogan knew why his older brother wanted to be alone and why he so often drank himself into a stupor each night. He was haunted by the deaths of three brothers and their father—all at the hands of the Howards.

Rogan had watched his beloved brother walk off into the darkness and he hadn't tried to stop him, but he'd signaled a knight to follow and keep watch over his brother, to protect him while he lay in drunken oblivion.

Rogan looked at the stones and remembered, and once again cursed himself for having fallen asleep that night. Some small sound woke him, or maybe it wasn't a sound but a premonition. He jumped from his pallet on the ground, grabbed his sword, and started running. But he was too late. Rowland lay beside the stream, a Howard sword through his throat, pinning him to the ground. The knight who guarded him was also dead, his throat slashed.

Rogan had thrown his head back and given a long, loud, piercing cry of agony.

His men and Severn were beside him instantly and they tore the woods apart looking for the Howard attackers. They found two of the men, distant cousins of Oliver Howard's, and Rogan made sure their deaths were long and slow. He ended one man's life when the man mentioned Jeanne.

The demise of the two Howards did nothing to bring back his brother, nor did it lessen Rogan's sense of responsibility now that he was the eldest of the Peregrines. Now it was his job to protect Severn and young Zared. He had to protect them, provide for them, and most of all, he had to get the Peregrine lands back, the lands the Howards had stolen from his grandfather.

His senses were dulled with memory, but at a snapping branch he whirled and put his sword to the throat of the person behind him. It was a girl, and for a moment he couldn't remember who she was. Yes, the one he'd married that morning. "What do you want?" he snapped. He wanted to be alone with his thoughts and his memories of his brother.

Liana looked down at the sword pointed at her throat and swallowed. "Is that a grave?" she asked hesitantly, remembering every word Helen had said about the violence of these men. He could kill her now that he had her dowry, and all he had to do was say he'd found her with another man and he would escape unpunished.

"No," Rogan said curtly, having no intention of telling her about his brother, or anything else for that matter. "Go back to the camp and stay there."

It was on the tip of Liana's tongue to tell him she'd go where she pleased, but Joice's warning to be obedient echoed in her head. "Yes, of course I'll return," she said meekly. "Will you return with me?"

Rogan wanted to stay where he was, but at the same time he didn't want her walking in the woods alone. For all that he couldn't remember her name, she was a Peregrine now and therefore an enemy of the Howards. They would no doubt love to hold another Peregrine woman captive. "All right," he said reluctantly. "I'll return with you."

Liana felt a little thrill of pleasure run through her body. Joice was right, she thought. She had meekly obeyed her husband and he was walking her back to the camp. She waited for him to offer her his arm, but he didn't. Instead, he turned his back on her and started walking. Liana ran after him for a few steps, but then her gown caught on a fallen log. "Wait!" she called. "I'm caught."

Rogan came back to her and, as always, Liana's heart seemed to beat a little faster when he was near.

"Move your hands," he said.

Liana looked into his eyes, saw the way the moonlight made them sparkle, and was aware of nothing else—until he brought his sword down on the log and hacked away a big piece of her skirt. She gaped at the hole and was utterly speechless. That embroidered silk had cost her quarterly rents from six farms!

"Now, come on," he commanded, and turned his back on her again.

Swallow! she commanded herself. Fight the anger down and do not display it. A woman is always loving and kind. A woman does not point out her husband's faults. Fighting her anger, she began to follow him and wondered if he was looking forward to their wedding night with as much anticipation as she was.

With every step he took, Rogan remembered ever more vividly his brother's death. Two years' time had done very little to dull the memory. Here he and Rowland had talked of buying horses. Here he and Rowland had talked of James and Basil's deaths eight years before. Here Rowland had spoken of protecting Zared. Here—

"Could you tell me something of your castle? I'll need to know where to hang my tapestries."

Rogan had forgotten the girl was with him. William, who had been three years older than Rogan, died as a boy of eighteen. His dying words were to get the Peregrine lands back and that would make sense of his death.

"Is it a large place?" the girl asked.

"No," he answered gruffly. "It is very small. It's the discards of the Howard bitch." He halted at the edge of the forest and gaped at the campsite. Before him was a sea of big feather mattresses on the ground. They might as well set up torches and blow trumpets to announce their whereabouts to the Howards.

Angrily, he strode across the campsite to reach his brother, who was talking and smiling at one of the Neville maids. He punched his brother's shoulder to turn him around.

"What stupidity is this?" he demanded. "Why not invite the Howards down on our heads?"

Severn pushed Rogan's shoulder. "We're well guarded, and there are only a few mattresses for the women."

Rogan punched Severn's chest. "I want them out of

sight. The women can sleep on the ground or they can go back to Neville."

Severn doubled his fist and planted it in Rogan's chest, but his heavier brother didn't waver. "Some of the men want to sleep with the women."

"All the better that they do not sleep too well. If a Howard comes, we'll be ready—as we were not ready the night Rowland was butchered."

Severn nodded at that and went to tell the men to stow the feather cushions.

At the edge of the forest, Liana stood and watched her husband and brother-in-law punch each other as if they were sworn enemies. She held her breath for fear their fight would erupt into bloodshed, but after a few minutes of low, guttural sentences, they separated, and Liana released her breath. She looked about her and saw some of her women staring, but none of the Peregrine knights seemed to take any notice of their masters' rough exchange. Yet Liana knew that any one of those blows would have felled most men.

At that moment, Joice came running to her, her face contorted with emotion. "My lady, they have no tents. We are to sleep *on the ground."* She said the last with horror.

Usually when they traveled, Liana, her father and stepmother, and most of the women, if they were not guests of another landowner, slept in sumptuous tents. Since they moved most of their furniture with them from castle to castle, the beds and even tables were set up inside the tents.

"And there is no hot food," Joice continued. "We have only cold meats that were taken from your wedding feast. Two of the women are in tears."

"Then they'll have to dry their tears," Liana snapped. "You have told me that a good wife does not complain. That goes as well for her maids." Liana was much too excited about the prospect of the coming night to worry about cold meats and tents.

At a noise, both turned to see the Peregrine knights removing the feather pallets from the ground and returning them to inside the wagons.

"No!" Joice gasped, and went toward the men.

For the next hour, all was chaos as Liana settled her maids to sleeping on the ground under the stars. She removed bags full of furs from the wagons and had them put on the ground, skin side down, and this helped mollify the tears. A few of the Peregrine knights put their arms around the women and comforted them.

Liana had furs placed outside the camp, in the deep shade of an oak tree, for herself. Joice helped her remove her mutilated gown and put on a clean linen nightshirt, then Liana lay down and waited. And waited. And waited. But Rogan did not come to her. She had not slept the night before, and that and the long journey made her sleep even though she tried to stay awake to greet him. But she went to sleep with a smile on her lips, knowing how her husband would wake her.

Rogan lay down on the coarse woolen blankets near Severn, where he always slept on their journeys.

Sleepily, Severn turned to him. "I thought you had a wife now."

"The Howards attack and I'm thrusting away at some girl," Rogan said sarcastically.

"She's a pretty little thing," Severn said.

"If you like rabbits. The only way I can tell which one she is is by the color of her dress. Is today Thursday?"

"Yes," Severn answered. "And we'll be home Saturday night."

"Ah, then," Rogan said softly. "I'll not have rabbit for dinner on Saturday."

Severn turned away and went to sleep while Rogan lay awake for another hour. His memories in this spot were too strong to allow him to sleep. His mind was filled with plans of what he'd do with the Neville gold now that he had it. There were war machines to build, knights to hire and equip, food to be purchased for the long siege ahead, for he knew that regaining the Peregrine lands was going to take a long, long time of warfare.

Not once did he think of his new wife, who waited for him on the opposite side of the camp.

The next morning Liana's temper was not the best it had ever been. Joice came to her mistress with a stream of complaints from the maids. The Peregrine knights had been harsh in their lovemaking and two of the maids were bruised and sore.

"Better bruised and sore than well and comfortable," Liana snapped. "Bring me the blue gown and headdress and tell the women to stop complaining or I'll give them something to complain about."

Liana saw her husband through the trees and once again choked her anger down. Were all marriages like this? Did all women suffer one injustice after another and have to bite their tongues? Was this truly the way to love?

She wore a blue satin gown with a gold belt set with diamonds. There were also small diamonds on the tall padded headdress she wore. Perhaps today he'd look at her with desire. Perhaps last night he had been shy about lying with her when his men were about. Yes, perhaps there were reasons for his behavior.

He didn't greet her that morning. In fact, he walked past her once and didn't even look at her. It was as if he didn't recognize her.

Liana mounted her horse with the help of a knight and once again rode in the middle of the men, behind the dust and horse manure.

Toward midday she grew restless. She could see Severn and Rogan at the head of the line talking earnestly and she wanted to know what interested them so much. She reined her horse to the side.

"My lady!" Joice said in alarm. "Where are you going?"

"Since my husband does not come to me, I will go to him."

"You cannot," Joice said, eyes wide. "Men do not like forward women. You *must* wait until he comes to you."

Liana hesitated, but her boredom won out. "I will see," she said, and kicked her horse forward until she rode beside her brother-in-law, Rogan next to him. Severn glanced at her; Rogan did not. But neither man gave her a word of greeting.

"We'll need all the grain we can get," Rogan was saying. "We'll have to store it and ready ourselves."

"And what about the fifty hectares along the north road? The peasants say the fields won't produce and the sheep are dying."

"Dying, ha!" Rogan snorted. "The bastards are no aoubt selling them to passing merchants and keeping the coin. Send some men to burn a few houses and whip a few farmers and we'll see if their sheep keep dying."

Here was a place where Liana felt at home. Discussions of sheep and peasants were what had occupied her life for years. She didn't think of "obeying" or of keeping her counsel to herself. "Terrorizing peasants never did any good," she said loudly, not looking at either man. "First we must find out if what they say is true. It could be many things: The land could be overused, the water could be bad, or a curse could have been put on the sheep. If it's none of these things and the peasants are cheating us, then we banish them. I've found that banishment works as well as torture, and it's so much less . . . unpleasant. Once we get there, I shall look into it." She turned to smile at the men.

Both of them were staring at her with their mouths open.

Liana didn't understand their expressions at all. "It could also be the seeds," she said. "One year a mold destroyed all our seed and—"

"Back!" Rogan said under his breath. "Get back to the women. If I want an opinion from a woman, I will ask," he said in the same tone as he might say that he'd ask his horse about the grain before he asked a woman.

"I was merely—" Liana began.

"I will tie you inside a wagon if you say more," Rogan said, his eyes hard and angry.

Liana swallowed more anger as she turned her horse and went back to the women.

Severn was the first to speak when they were again alone. "The water? What could be wrong with the water? And a curse. Do you think the Howards put a curse on our sheep? How do we get rid of it?"

Rogan was staring straight ahead. Damned woman, he thought. What was she trying to do, interfere in men's work? Once he'd allowed a woman to interfere. Once he'd listened to a woman, and she had repaid him in treachery. "There is no curse. Merely greedy peasants," Rogan said firmly. "I'll show them whose land they farm."

Severn was thoughtful for a moment. He was not possessed of the same hatred of women that his brother was. There were many things that he discussed with Iolanthe, and he often found her answers were wise and useful. Perhaps there was more to this Neville heiress than he'd thought when he first saw her.

He turned in the saddle and looked back at her. She sat rigid on her horse, her back straight, her eyes glittering with anger. Severn turned and grinned at his brother. "You've offended her now," he said jovially. "Her temper won't be so sweet tonight. I've found that a gift will usually put a woman in a better mood. Or perhaps compliments will work. Tell her that her hair is like gold, tell her that her beauty tempts you from your soul."

"The only thing that tempts me is the gold in the wagons, not in her hair. And I think that tonight you'd better take one of the maids to keep you from thinking of women's hair."

Severn kept smiling. "While you lay with your pretty wife and give her a few sons?"

Sons, Rogan thought. Sons to help him fight the Howards. Sons to live on the Peregrine lands once he took them back. Sons to ride beside him. Sons to teach to fight and ride and hunt. "Yes, I'll give her sons," Rogan said at last.

Liana was convinced Joice was right after her confrontation with Rogan. It was going to take a while to teach herself to be obedient and to listen and to keep her ideas to herself.

That night they camped again, and again Liana put furs under a far tree. But again Rogan did not come to her. He did not speak to her or even look at her.

Liana refused to cry. She refused to remember Helen's words of warning. Instead, she remembered the time at the pool of water when he'd kissed her. He seemed to find her desirable then, but not now. She slept fitfully and woke before dawn, before the rest of the camp was awake. She rose, a hand at her stiff back, and made her way into the woods.

Stooping down to take a drink from a little spring, she became aware of eyes on her and whirled to see a man standing in the shadows. She gasped and put her hand to her throat.

"Do not leave the safety of the camp without a guard," came Rogan's low voice.

She was acutely aware that she wore only her thin silk robe over her nudity, her hair hanging loose down her back, and he wore only his braies, the hose covering him from waist to toe, his broad chest bare. She took a step toward him. "I could not sleep," she said softly. She wished he'd reach for her, take her in his arms. "Did you sleep well?"

He frowned at her. Somehow, she was familiar, as if he'd seen her before. She was tempting enough in the early morning light, but he felt no raging desire for her. "Get back to the camp," he said, then turned away from her.

"Of all the—" she said under her breath but caught herself. Was there some reason this man ignored her? Joice said she'd be able to make herself indispensable to him once she was in his home. There she'd be able to make him comfortable and see to his many needs.

And there they'd share a bed, she thought with pleasure.

She hurried forward to catch up with him. "Do we reach the Peregrine castle today?"

"It's the Moray castle," he said tightly. "The Howards occupy the Peregrine lands."

She was having to rush to keep up with him, her long robe causing her to trip over branches and stones.

"I've heard of them. They stole your lands and title, didn't they? You would be a duke now if it weren't for them."

He halted abruptly in front of her and turned angry eyes on her. "Is that what you hope for, girl? That you have married a duke? Is that why you married me and turned down the others?"

"Why no, I didn't," she said, astonished. "I married you because . . ."

"Yes?" he demanded.

Liana couldn't very well say that she lusted after him, that her heart was pounding in her throat even now at being so close to him, and that she greatly wanted to touch the bare skin of his chest.

"There you are," Severn said from behind them, thus saving Liana from answering. "The men are ready to ride. My lady," he said, nodding to Liana.

His eyes studied her so hard that she blushed, then looked up through the curtain of her hair to see if Rogan saw. He did not. He had started toward the camp, leaving Liana where she was. She made her way back to the camp by herself, following along behind the brothers.

"She's prettier than I first thought," Severn said to his brother as they rode.

"She doesn't interest me at all," Rogan said. "No woman who has 'wife' attached to her interests me."

"I would imagine that you'd fight hard enough if someone tried to take her." Severn was jesting with his brother, but the minute the words were out, he regretted them. Ten years ago someone had indeed tried to take a wife of Rogan's and he'd fought so hard to get her back that two of their brothers had been killed.

"No, I would not fight for her," Rogan said softly. "If you want the woman, take her. She means less than nothing to me. The gold she brought me is all I want of her."

Severn frowned at his brother's words, but he said no more.

CHAPTER
SIX

Moray Castle came into sight at midday, and a more depressing sight Liana had never seen. It was the old-style castle, made for protection, and left unchanged for over a hundred and fifty years. The windows were arrow slits, the tower was thick and impenetrable-looking. Men lined the battlements, which were broken in places, looking as if the castle had been attacked and never repaired.

As they drew closer, she could smell the place. Over their own horses and the unwashed bodies of the Peregrine knights came the stench of the castle.

"My lady," Joice whispered.

Liana did not look at her maid, but stared ahead. Helen had told her of the filth of the place, but she was not prepared for this.

They came first to the moat. All the latrines of the castle emptied into this protective body of water and it was thick with excrement as well as kitchen slops of rotting animal carcasses. Liana kept her head high and her eyes forward while, around her, her maids coughed and gagged at the smell.

They rode in single file through a long, low tunnel and overhead Liana saw three openings for heavy, spiked iron gates that could be dropped on intruders. At the end of the tunnel was a single courtyard, half the size of her father's outer bailey, yet there were three times the people here. Her nose already outraged, now it was her ears' turn. Men hammered hot iron on anvils; dogs barked; carpenters hammered; men yelled at each other above the noise.

Liana could hardly believe the noise and the stench of stables and pigsties, which looked as if they'd not been cleaned in years.

To her right a maid squealed and her horse sidestepped into Liana's. Liana looked up to see what had frightened the girl. A urinal from the third story opened into the courtyard and now a heavy waterfall of urine was cascading and splashing down the wall into a deep puddle of filth on the ground below.

After the maid's squeal, neither Liana nor her maids said another word. They were too horrified to be able to speak.

To Liana's right were two stone staircases, one leading to the single tower, the other to the lower two-story slate-roofed building. With this small castle there were no inner and outer courtyards, no separation of lord and retainer, but everyone lived together in this small space.

At the head of the stairs Liana saw two women. They searched the crowd of newcomers until they saw Liana, then one of them pointed at her and they both laughed. Liana could see they were maids, but the filth of the place made it obvious they did no work. She'd soon fix them and teach them not to laugh at their betters.

The girls sauntered down the stairs and as they rounded the short stone wall, Liana saw their figures. They were both short, buxom, small-waisted, big-hipped girls with lots of coarse dirty brown hair hanging in long braids down their backs. Their clothes were tight and revealing and they walked with an insolent, exaggerated sway to their hips. They strutted across the courtyard in a slow way that made their big breasts move under their clothes, and most of the men stopped to watch them.

As a knight helped Liana from her horse, she saw the maids ooze their way toward Rogan. He was yelling at some men about the Neville wagons, but Liana saw him glance down at the girls. One of them turned and gave Liana such a look of triumph that Liana's fingers itched to slap her face.

"Shall we go inside, my lady?" Joice said meekly. "Perhaps inside it's . . ." Her voice trailed off.

It was obvious that her husband was not going to show her her new home and by now Liana didn't expect him to. Assuming that the staircase the insolent maids had used led to the lord of the manor's quarters, she lifted her skirts and went up them, kicking bones and what looked to be a dead bird out of the way as she ascended.

At the top of the stairs was a large room, the doorway partitioned off by what once must have been a beautiful carved wooden screen, but now axe heads were buried in the wood and nails had been driven into it to hold maces and lances. Through the wide wooden doors of the screen, one of which hung by only one hinge, was a room about forty-five feet long by twenty-five feet wide, with a ceiling as high as the room was wide.

Liana and her maids stepped into this room in silence because no words could express what they saw.

Filthy would not describe it. The floor looked as if every bone from every meal that had been eaten in this room for over a hundred years was still on it. Flies swarmed around the maggot-covered bones, and Liana could see things—she refused to consider what things—crawling about under the thick layer of refuse.

Spider webs with fat occupants hung from the ceiling almost to the floor. The double fireplaces at the east end of the hall had three feet of ashes in them. The only furniture in the room were a thick, heavy table made of a slab of blackened oak and eight scarred, broken chairs, all covered with grease from years of meals.

There were several windows in the room, some of them fifteen feet above the floor, but the glass and the shutters were gone, so the smell of the moat, the courtyard, and this room mingled.

When one of the maids behind her swooned and began to faint, Liana wasn't surprised. "Stand up!" she commanded, "or we'll have to lay you on the floor." The girl uprighted herself immediately.

Taking her courage in her hands, as well as her silk skirt, Liana made her way across the room to the stairs in the northwest corner. These too were covered with bones, straw crushed to powder, and what was possibly a dead rat. "Joice, come with me," she said over her shoulder, "and the rest of you remain here."

Up eight stairs was a room, opening to the left, and a toilet, to the right. Liana just looked into the room but did not enter it. It contained a small round table, two chairs, and hundreds of weapons of war.

Liana continued up the circular stairs, a timid Joice behind her, until she reached the second floor of the tower. Before her was a short, low round-topped hallway, and a few feet along it was a door leading off to the right. This was a bedchamber with a filthy straw-filled mattress on the floor, the straw so old, it was merely two pieces of coarse wool on the floor. A latrine led off this room.

Joice stepped forward and put her hand down as if to touch the two blankets heaped at the foot of the mattress.

"Lice," was all Liana said, and moved on down the hallway.

She entered the solar, a large, spacious room filled with light from the many windows. Along the south wall was a wooden staircase that led up to the third floor. A rustle overhead made Liana look up. Along the carved corbels that held the ceiling beams were wooden perches and here sat hawks, all of them hooded and jessed. There were peregrines, kestrels, merlins, goshawks, and sparrow hawks. The walls were coated with bird droppings, which had dripped down to form hard hills on the floor.

Liana lifted her skirt higher and went across the filthy floor to the east side of the room. Here were three arches, the center one creating a little room, one wooden door barely hanging, the other missing. Set in the stone wall was a little piscina, the basin used by the priest for ablutions after mass.

"It is sacrilege," Joice whispered, for this was a private oratory, a holy place for the saying of mass for the family.

"Ah, but here we have an excellent view of the moat," Liana said, looking out the window and trying to bring some humor into this hideous place. But Joice did not laugh or smile.

"My lady, what shall we do?"

"We shall make my husband comfortable," Liana said with assurance. "First we will prepare two bedrooms for tonight, one for my husband and me," she could not prevent the flush that crept over her face, "then one for you and my maids. Tomorrow we shall start on the rest of the place. Now, stop standing and staring. Go and get those women I saw below. A little work should take the insolence out of them."

Joice was afraid to move about the castle alone, but her mistress's manner gave her courage. She was afraid of what lurked in the shadows and corners of the castle. If something attacked, how long would it be before they found her bones among the others?

In the solar, Liana went to the other arched rooms flanking the oratory. The bird droppings were less in evidence here and she could see that under the dirt the walls had once been painted with scenes. Once they were cleaned she could have them repainted, and there on that far west wall she'd hang a tapestry. For a moment she could almost escape the smells of the room, the ominous sound of birds' wings rustling, and the sound of whatever was moving about under the refuse on the floor.

"They won't come, my lady," said a breathless Joice from the doorway.

Liana came back to reality. "Who won't come? My husband?"

Joice was indignant. "The maids! Lord Rogan's maids won't come. When I told them they were to come and clean, they laughed at me."

"Did they?" Liana said. "Let's see what they say to me." She was ready for a good fight. She'd been so obedient and had swallowed so much anger in the past few days that she wanted an outlet for it, and overdeveloped maids who pointed at her and laughed would be an excellent target.

Liana stormed down the steep stairs, across the lord's chamber, down the outside stairs, and into the loud, dirty courtyard. The two maids she'd seen before were lounging near the well, allowing three young knights to draw buckets of water for them while they brushed their big breasts against the men's arms.

"You!" Liana said to the first one. "Come with me."

Liana turned on her heel and started back toward the castle only to realize that no maids were following her. She looked back to see the two maids smiling at her as if they knew something she did not. Liana had never had a maid disobey her before. Always before, she'd been backed by her father's power.

For a moment, Liana didn't know what to do. She could feel the eyes of the other people in the courtyard on her, and she knew that now was the time to establish her power as mistress of the castle. But she couldn't do that unless they knew she had her husband's backing.

Rogan was near the far wall of the courtyard, directing the unloading of a wagon that contained several suits of armor that were part of Liana's dowry. Angrily, she made her way across the courtyard, sidestepping three fighting dogs, overstepping a pile of rotting sheep entrails.

She knew what she wanted to say, the demands she wanted to make, but when Rogan turned to her, annoyed that she was interrupting him, her confidence faded. She so much wanted to please him, wanted to have his eyes change when he looked at her. Now he seemed to be trying to remember who she was.

"The maids will not obey me," she said quietly.

He looked at her in consternation, as if her problem had nothing to do with him.

"I want the maids to start cleaning, but they won't obey me," she further explained.

That seemed to relieve his puzzlement. He turned

back to the wagons. "They clean what's needed. I thought you brought maids."

She moved between him and the wagon. "Three of my maids are *ladies,* and the others . . . well, there's just too much for them to do."

"Dent that armor and I'll dent your head," Rogan shouted to a laborer who was unloading the wagon. He looked down at Liana. "I have no time for maids. The place is clean enough as it is. Now, go away and let me get these wagons unloaded."

He dismissed her as if she didn't exist, and Liana stood there staring at his back and feeling the eyes of every man and, most of all, those two maids on her. So this was what Helen had warned her about. This was what marriage was like. A man courted you until he got you, then you were less than . . . than a piece of steel to him. Of course, with Rogan, she hadn't even received the courting.

Now she knew that at all costs she must keep her dignity. She didn't look right or left but walked straight ahead toward the stone steps and went up them and into the castle. Behind her she could hear the noise of the courtyard resume with tripled force, and she even heard some high-pitched female laughter.

Liana's heart beat quickly with the humiliation she'd received. Helen had said she'd been spoiled by her power at the Neville estates, but Liana had had no real idea of what she meant. She suspected that few people realized how different other people's lives were from their own. She'd expected her married life to be somewhat different, but this feeling of being powerless, of not existing, was something altogether new to her.

This must have been how Helen felt at the Neville

estates when the servants obeyed Liana and not her. "She felt like this, yet she was still good to me," Liana whispered.

"My lady," Joice said softly.

Liana blinked at her maid and saw the fear on the older woman's face. Liana didn't seem so sure of herself now as she had before the wedding. At the moment she was too tired to think what she was going to do in the future. For now the immediate needs were for food and a place to sleep.

"Send Bess to find the kitchens and bring up supper—I do not want to eat in company tonight. Then get some of my bedding sent up to the solar." She put her hand up to stop Joice from speaking. "I don't know how to accomplish that. It seems that I have no power in my husband's home." She tried to keep the self-pity out of her voice, but she didn't succeed. "And find some shovels. Tonight we will empty two rooms of enough filth to be able to sleep. And tomorrow we'll—" She stopped because she didn't like to think of tomorrow. If she had no power, even in directing a maid, she would be a prisoner just as if she were locked in a dungeon.

"Find out what you can about this place," Liana said as an afterthought. "Where is Lord Severn? Perhaps he could . . . help us." There was little strength in Liana's voice.

"Yes, my lady," Joice said meekly and left the room.

Slowly, Liana made her way up the circular staircase to the solar. The hawks moved on their perches at the sound of her, then settled again. If the whole castle were not littered with the remains of people's living, she might have thought the place deserted. It was so unlike her father's house, with people moving in and out of rooms, people laughing and teasing. Here there were only men, hard-faced, unsmiling men with scars on their bodies and weapons in their hands. There were no children, and no women except for the two bitches who'd laughed at her and refused to obey her.

She looked below at the moat and in the fading light saw the head of a cow bob in the black, thick ooze. This place was to be her home. Here she was to bear children and raise them. And what love she was to have was to come from a husband who didn't seem to recognize her from one hour to the next.

How was she to make him love her? Perhaps if she and her maids cleaned the place, perhaps if she made this castle a fit place to live, he would be glad he married her. He would think of her as more than just the person who came attached to the dowry.

And food, she thought. Perhaps if she hired some good cooks and covered his table with delicious, delectable food. Surely the man who ate well, slept between clean sheets, wore clean clothes, would be pleased with the woman who made this possible.

And then there was the bed. Liana had heard her maids say a woman who pleased a man in bed could control him out of it. She'd get one bedroom clean by tonight and he'd seek her out, for now that they had privacy, he'd want his wife. She smiled for the first time since seeing Moray Castle. She just had to be patient and what she wanted would eventually come to her.

Moments later all seven of her maids came to the solar, their arms loaded with food, pillows, and blankets, and chattering all at once.

It took Liana a while to understand what the women were saying. Lord Severn was with someone called the Lady and wasn't likely to be seen for three or four days. Other than the Lady and her maids, there were only eight women in the whole castle.

"They do no work," Bess said, "and no one would tell me what they do."

"And they're named for the days of the week. Sunday, Monday, Tuesday, and so forth, except one is called Waiting. They didn't seem to have any other names," Alice said.

"And the food is awful. The flour is full of weevils and sand. The baker just bakes it into the bread."

Bess leaned forward. "They used to buy bread from a baker in town, but he filed an order of a feud against the Peregrines for nonpayment and . . ."

"And what?" Liana demanded, trying to eat a piece of meat that could have been used for saddle leather.

"The Peregrine men tore the door off the baker's house and . . . and used his flour bins for a toilet."

Liana put her inedible meat down. The women had cleaned off a seat under one window and now sat there together. Below them they could hear the sounds of steel on steel, of men yelling, of food being eaten with open mouths. It seemed that her husband and his men were eating in the room below, but no one had thought to ask the wife of their lord to join them.

"Did you perhaps hear which bedchamber is Lord Rogan's?" she asked, trying to keep her dignity.

The women looked at each other, pity in their eyes.

"No," Joice murmured. "But surely that one there, the large one, is his room."

Liana nodded. She hadn't yet felt strong enough to mount the wooden stairs of the solar and see what rooms were above—or, more likely, what manner of filth was there. If birds were kept in the solar, were pigs kept in the upper bedrooms?

It took two hours of hard work to shovel out two bedrooms. Liana wanted to help, but Joice refused to allow it and Liana understood. At the moment her maids were almost her equals, as they all felt lost and alone in this strange, foul-smelling place, but Joice did not want her mistress to lose her power over these women. So Liana sat on the window seat in the solar and held a clove-studded orange to her nose to block out the smell of the moat.

When at last her room was ready—not clean, but at least she could walk in it without tripping over bones—a maid persuaded a farrier to bring up two mattresses, and Liana, with Joice's help, undressed and went to bed. She lay awake for a while, waiting for her husband to come to her. But he didn't.

In the morning she awoke to loud noises and hideous smells. What she had thought was a bad dream was reality.

In the morning Rogan walked into the Lord's Chamber to see Severn sitting at the table, his head resting tiredly on his hand, and eating bread and cheese. "I didn't expect to see you for a while. Want to go hunting with me?"

"Yes," Severn answered. "I need the rest after last night with Io. You look well rested. Your wife didn't bother you too much last night?"

"Last night was Saturday," Rogan gave for an answer.

"And you didn't spend it with your wife?"

"Not on Saturday."

Severn scratched his arm. "You'll never get any sons like that."

"Are you ready to go or not? I'll get around to her. Maybe next . . . I don't know when. She's not something to stir a man's blood."

"Where is she now?"

Rogan shrugged. "Upstairs, maybe. Who knows?"

Severn washed the rest of the bread down with sour wine and spit sand onto the floor. What his brother did was none of his business.

For three days Liana and her maids worked at cleaning the solar. And for three days she was afraid to go belowstairs. She couldn't bear to show her face to the people of Moray Castle. They all knew that she had been rejected by her husband, that he not only refused to sleep with her but that he refused to give her power over his servants.

So Liana stayed alone, never seeing her husband, never having any contact with the people of the castle. So far, she thought, not only wasn't she winning her husband's love with her meekness, but he wasn't even noticing her, meek or otherwise.

It was on the afternoon of the fourth day that she dared to venture up the wooden stairs. The upper floor was as dirty as the solar had been, except there were no signs that anyone had been here for years. She wondered where the people of the castle slept and instantly pictured them altogether in a heap.

She walked along the hall and looked into one empty bedroom after another, scaring rats as she went along, creating little dust storms behind her. When she was about to leave to go downstairs again, she thought she heard a spinning wheel. Lifting her skirts, she ran to the far bedroom and pushed open the heavy door.

Sitting in a stream of sunlight was a very pretty older woman with dark hair and brows, working at a flax wheel. The room was clean, there was cushioned furniture here, and the windows had glass in them. This had to be the Lady who Lord Severn visited. Perhaps she was an aunt or some other relative.

"Come in, dear, and close the door before we both choke on the dust."

Liana did as she was bid and smiled. "I didn't know anyone was here. What with the state of everything, that is." She felt very comfortable with this lovely woman, and when she nodded at a chair, Liana took it.

"It is awful, isn't it?" the lady said. "Rogan wouldn't notice the dirt even if it were so deep he had to swim through it."

Liana quit smiling. "He wouldn't notice me if I were drowning in it," she said under her breath to herself, not meaning for the lady to hear.

But she did hear. "Of course he wouldn't notice you. Men never notice the good women who see that their clothes are clean, that their food is well cooked, and who bear their children in silence."

Liana's head came up at this. "What women *do* they notice?"

"Women like Iolanthe." She smiled at Liana. "You haven't met her. She's Severn's greensleeves. Well, not an actual greensleeves. Actually, Io is the wife of a very wealthy, very old, very stupid man. Io spends his money and lives here with Severn, who is neither old nor wealthy and not at all stupid."

"She lives *here?* She chooses to live in this . . . this . . ."

"She has her own apartments over the kitchen, quite the best apartments in the castle. Io would demand the best."

"I demanded help from the servants," Liana said bitterly, "but got nothing."

"There are demands and there are demands," the lady said, spinning her flax into a fine, smooth strand. "Do you love Rogan very much?"

Liana looked away and didn't even question her intimacy with this woman. She was so tired of having only maids to talk to. "I think I could have loved him once. I agreed to marry him because he was the only man who was honest with me. He didn't praise my beauty then look at my father's gold."

"Rogan is always honest. He never pretends to be what he is not, to care about what does not matter to him."

"True, and he does not care about me," Liana said sadly.

"But then you do lie, don't you, dear? The Liana who hides from the laughter of maids is not the Liana who ran her father's estates, the Liana who once faced a mob of angry peasants."

Liana didn't ask how the woman knew these things about her, but she felt tears welling in her eyes. "I don't think a man could love that Liana. Joice says men like—"

"And who is Joice?"

"My maid. Actually, she is somewhat like a mother to me. She says—"

"And she knows all about men, does she? Raised by one, married to one, mother to many?"

"Well, no, actually, she grew up with me. She was an orphan before that and lived in the women's quarters. She is married, though, no children, but then she only sees her husband three times a year so . . . Oh, I see what you mean. Joice has not had a great deal of experience with men."

"No, I thought not. Remember, dear, it isn't the woman who cleans a man's house who has battles fought for her, it is the woman who sometimes wields a whip."

That made Liana laugh. "I can't imagine taking a whip to Lord Rogan."

"Only a muddy shirt," the woman said, eyes smiling, then her head came up. "Someone comes up the stairs. Go, please. I don't want to be disturbed."

"Yes, of course," Liana said and left the room, closing the door behind her. She almost went back into the room to ask how she'd known about the muddy shirt, but Joice came to the head of the stairs and said Liana was needed.

The rest of that day Liana spent in isolation in the solar, only her maids for company, and Liana kept hearing the woman's words. She was so confused about what to do. She thought of going to Rogan and demanding that he make the servants obey her, but the idea was ridiculous to her. He'd merely turn away. She couldn't imagine he would listen to her merely because she shouted at him. Of course she could always draw a sword on him. That idea almost made her giggle. So all she could do was wait. Perhaps someday he'd come to the solar, perhaps to get one of his hawks, and he'd see how clean the place was and he'd want to remain, then he'd turn to her with love in his eyes and—

"My lady?" Joice said. "The hour grows late."

"Yes," Liana said heavily. She'd go to her empty, cold bed once again.

It was hours later that she awoke to an odd sound and a light. "Rogan!" she gasped, and turned over to see not her husband but a tall boy, a very pretty boy, with dirty shoulder-length dark hair and a ragged velvet tunic over baggy knit hose. He was standing by the wall, one leg on a stool, elbow on knee, eating an apple and staring at her in the light of a fat, bright candle.

Liana sat up. "Who are you and what are you doing in my room?"

"Come to have a look at you," he said.

He must be younger than his height indicated because his voice hadn't changed yet, she thought. "You've seen me, now get out of here." She did not have to put up with insolence in the room she'd chosen for her own.

He loudly munched on his apple and made no move to leave. "I guess you've been waiting for my brother for a while now."

"Your brother?" Liana remembered Helen's saying she didn't know how many Peregrine sons were left.

"I'm Zared," the boy said, putting his foot on the floor and throwing the apple core out the window. "I've seen you now. You're just like they said, and Rogan won't be coming tonight." He started out the door.

"Wait just a minute!" Liana said in a voice that made the boy halt and turn back. "What do you mean I'm like they said, and where is my husband that he won't be here tonight?" Liana hoped the boy would say Rogan was on some secret mission for the king, or perhaps had taken a temporary vow of chastity.

"Today's Wednesday," Zared said.

"What has the day of the week to do with my husband?"

"I heard you met them. There're eight of them. One for each day of the week and one for when one of the Days has female trouble. Sometimes two of them at a time have female trouble, then Rogan is hell to live with. Maybe he'll come to you then."

Liana wasn't sure, but she thought she was beginning to understand. "Those maids," she said softly. "Do you mean that my husband sleeps with a different one each night? That they are a . . . a *calendar?*"

"He tried one for each day of the month once, but he said it made for too many women around the place. He's made do with eight. Severn is altogether different. He says Iolanthe is enough for him. Of course, Io is—"

"Where is he?" Anger was beginning to surge through Liana. Anger swallowed from the first time she met Rogan was pumping through her veins. She was regurgitating it, like something as vile as the moat below. "Where *is* he?"

"Rogan? He sleeps somewhere different every night. He goes to the Days' rooms. He says they get jealous if they come to his room. Tonight, this being Wednesday, he'd be on the top floor of the kitchen apartments, first door on the left."

Liana stood. Her entire body was filled with rage. Every muscle was taut.

"You aren't going there, are you? Rogan doesn't like to be bothered at night, and I can tell you, his temper isn't pleasant. One time he—"

"He hasn't seen *my* temper yet," Liana said through clenched teeth. *"No one treats me like this and lives to tell about it. No one!"* She pushed past Zared and went out into the hall, where she grabbed a flaming torch from the wall. She wore her robe and her feet were bare but she didn't notice the bones she stepped on, and when a snarling dog got in her way, she used the torch as a sword and the dog skulked away.

"I heard you were a rabbit," Zared said from behind her, following her in wonder. But this wife didn't look like a rabbit now as she marched down the stairs and through the Lord's Chamber. What was Rogan's wife going to do? Whatever was going to happen, Zared knew Severn must be fetched.

CHAPTER
SEVEN

*L*iana wasn't sure where the kitchen apartments were, but she seemed to find them by instinct. Instinct was the only thing she had to direct her feet because her brain was taken over by memories of the humiliations she had suffered since her wedding. He hadn't asked to see her before their marriage. He had demanded more money at the church door. He *raped* her after their wedding—and merely to consummate the marriage, not because he'd had any desire for her. For days he had ignored her, dumped her in this cesspit of a castle, and not so much as introduced her to the castle staff as his wife.

She went down the stairs to the courtyard and then up narrow stone stairs to what she guessed was the kitchen, then up a steep spiral stone staircase. Something slimy squished under her foot, but she took no notice. Nor did she notice the people who were beginning to rise from their beds and follow her, looking with interest at this meek and mild rabbit of a woman who their lord had brought home.

Liana went up and up the stairs, kicking once at an overzealous rat that tried to make a meal of one of her toes, until she reached the top floor. She quietly opened the first door on the left and stepped inside the room. There, sprawled on his stomach, his beautiful body bare—the body she had once lusted for—was her husband. And his right arm was thrown across the plump, nude body of one of the maids who'd refused to obey Liana.

Liana didn't think about what she was doing but put the torch to the corner of the mattress—one of the mattresses she had brought with her—then set another corner on fire.

Rogan awoke almost immediately, and he reacted instantly by grabbing the sleeping maid from the fiery bed, then leaping up. The girl awoke and began screaming and kept screaming when Rogan dropped her on the far side of the room. He grabbed the smoldering blanket from the bed and began to beat at the spreading flames. The door burst open and Severn came in and helped his brother put out the fire before it reached the rafters of the wooden ceiling. When the flames were at last out, the two brothers shoved the charred remains of the mattress out the window, where they fell below into the moat.

The maid's screams had stopped, but now she stood huddled into a corner of the room, her eyes alive with terror. She made little whimpering sounds.

"Stop that!" Rogan commanded. "It was just a little fire," he said, then followed the girl's eyes to where Liana stood, still holding the torch. It took Rogan a moment to understand what had happened, and then he didn't believe what he thought to be true. "You set the bed on fire. You tried to kill me," he stated, then turned to Severn. "She's with the Howards. Take her and burn her in the morning."

Before Severn could answer, before any of the many people, including Zared, who were crowding at the doorway could reply, Liana's rage erupted.

"Yes, I tried to kill you," she said, and advanced on him with the flame of the torch toward him, "and I wish I had succeeded. You have humiliated me, dishonored me, ridiculed me—"

"I?" Rogan said, utterly astonished. He could have easily taken the torch away from her, but she looked rather good with all that fair hair and thin robe in the firelight. And her face! Was she the girl he'd thought plain? "I have paid you every respect. I have hardly been near you."

"True!" she hissed at him, taking another step toward him. "You left me alone at my own wedding feast. You left me alone on my wedding night."

Rogan wore the look of a man unjustly accused. "You are no longer a virgin. I saw to that."

"You *raped* me!" she half yelled at him.

Now Rogan was beginning to get angry. In his view, he had never raped a woman in his life. Not because he was morally opposed to it but because with his face and form, he'd never found the act necessary. "I did not," he said under his breath, watching the way her breasts moved under her robe.

"I can see we aren't needed," Severn said loudly, but Rogan and Liana were so intent on each other they didn't hear him. Severn pushed the others out of the room and shut the door behind him.

"But she must be punished," Zared said. "She nearly killed Rogan."

"Interesting wench, that one," Severn said thoughtfully.

"She has my room!" Wednesday wailed, a charred blanket wrapped around her nudity.

Severn smiled. "She may have taken more than

your room. Go sleep with Sunday. And you," he said to Zared, "go to bed."

Inside the room, Liana and Rogan faced each other. Rogan knew he should punish her—after all, she might have killed him—but now that he knew her action was merely a woman's jealous fit, he knew it was nothing to be concerned about. "I should have you flogged."

"You lay a hand on me, and the next time I'll set your *hair* on fire."

"Now, see here—" he said. She was going too far. He was willing to put up with women's little tempers —after all, they were women—but this was too much.

Liana jabbed the torch at him. He seemed utterly unaware that he was wearing not a stitch of clothing. "No, it is *your* turn to listen to me. I have stood by silently and watched as you have ignored me, belittled me. You allow those . . . those Days of yours to laugh at me. Me! The lady of the castle. I am your wife, and I am going to be treated as I deserve. So help me God, you will treat me with courtesy and respect—I do not demand love—or you had better never sleep when I am by, for you will never wake up again."

Rogan was speechless. It was one thing to be threatened by an enemy, but this woman was his *wife!* "No woman threatens me," he said quietly.

Liana jabbed the torch at him and in one swift gesture he took it from her, then caught her waist. He meant to haul her from the room, to take her below and lock her in the cellar, but when her face was close to his, his anger turned to desire. Never had he desired a woman as much as he desired this one. He would die if he could not have her.

He put his hand to her shoulder and started to tear the robe from her.

"No!" she said, pulling back from him.

He was blinded with passion, his brain given over to the wanting of her. He wrapped his hand in her hair and pulled her toward him.

"No," she whispered, her lips against his. "You do not rape me again. You may make love to me all night, but you do not rape me."

Rogan was taken aback by her. Women gave themselves to him, women had seduced him, but he'd never had a woman make demands of him. And suddenly, he wanted to please her. It had never occurred to him before whether he was pleasing a woman or not, but this one he wanted to please.

His hands on her shoulders loosened their grip until his fingers were softly holding her skin. Gently, he pulled her toward him. He didn't usually trouble himself much with kissing the women he bedded because they were always ready and eager for him and it was a waste of time to kiss them. But he wanted to kiss this woman.

Liana leaned her head back and gave herself to his kiss, feeling the softness of his lips, her hands reaching up to touch his hair. His lips moved over hers, enveloping hers, then his tongue tip touched hers and Liana moaned and leaned her body into his.

Rogan could wait no longer for her. His arms tightened about her, then one hand bit into her thigh as he lifted her right leg to wrap it about his waist. Then his other hand lifted her left leg.

Liana, having had so little experience with sex, had no idea what was going on, but she loved the kissing and the feeling of her bare bottom against his skin. She was unprepared for when he slammed her back against the stone wall and entered her with all the force of a man using a battering ram to attack a locked door. She cried out in pain and protest, but her face was buried in the muscle of his chest and she could not be heard.

It seemed that he kept up his deep, hard thrusts for hours, and at first Liana hated the act, the man, everything that was being done to her, but after a while, her eyes opened wider, for she felt a deep inner pleasure that was beginning to spread through her body.

She cried out in surprise, then clutched Rogan's hair in her hands, pulling it hard while she brought her mouth down on his.

Her sudden passion was enough to finish Rogan and with a final thrust, he went limp against her, pushing her back hard against the stones as he leaned against her, his heart pounding.

Liana wanted more. She wasn't sure exactly what she wanted, but what she'd received wasn't enough. Her nails bit into his shoulders.

Rogan drew his head away from her shoulder and looked at her, startled. He could see that he had not pleased her. Instantly, he dropped her legs and stepped away from her and began searching for his braies in the debris on the floor. "You may go now," he murmured, feeling anger rising in himself.

Liana was energized by the too-brief lovemaking. "I have a bedroom off the solar prepared for us."

"Then you can go there and sleep," he said with anger, but when he turned to look at her, his anger vanished. Her eyes were bright and alive and her hair was wild and free about her head. He almost reached for her again, but he forced his hands to remain at his side. Women who were new to him were always exciting, he told himself.

Liana didn't try to repress the anger she felt. The vision of him in bed with another woman was too fresh and too painful. "So that you can go to another woman?" she hissed at him.

"Why, no," he said, surprised. "So that I can sleep. There is no bed in here."

This statement, delivered so solemnly, made Liana smile. "Come with me," she said softly, holding out her hand to him. "I have a clean, fragrant bed ready for us."

Rogan didn't want to take her hand and he knew he shouldn't sleep with her, because he'd learned from experience that when you slept the whole night with women, they began to think they owned you. He'd been "owned" by a woman once and— In spite of his sensible thoughts, he took her hand, and her smile at him deepened.

"Come," she whispered, and he followed her like a little dog on a leash as she led him down the stairs to the kitchen, then out into the courtyard. It was quiet now and she paused to look up at the stars. "They're beautiful, aren't they?"

At first Rogan didn't know what she meant. Stars were to guide you when traveling at night. "I guess they are," he said softly. The moonlight on her hair made it silver.

She stepped back against him, her back against his chest. This was what she'd imagined marriage to be, her husband holding her in the moonlight. But Rogan made no move to put his arms around her, so Liana put her hands about his wrists and guided his arms about her shoulders.

Rogan was startled for a moment. It was such a waste of time to be standing outside in the middle of the night, holding a bit of a girl and looking up at the stars. Tomorrow he had so much to do. But then he put his nose in her hair, smelled the clean, spicy fragrance of it, and he couldn't remember what he had to do tomorrow. "What's your name?" he whispered against her hair. He had trouble with women's names and had years ago assigned them a date as opposed to a name.

Liana didn't let her little lump of anger rise to the surface. "I am Lady Liana, your wife," she said, then turned in his arms and put her face up to be kissed. When he didn't kiss her, she kissed him, her hands caressing the back of his neck as she did so. Then she put her head against his shoulder and snuggled her body close to his.

Rogan found himself holding her, just standing there and holding her close to him. He'd never done this before. Women were for sex, for fetching what a man needed, for doing whatever a man wanted. They were not for standing in the middle of a courtyard and just holding. There was no purpose behind such an action, yet he was powerless to move.

Liana heard the movement behind her, someone who couldn't sleep, perhaps. She was not used to being married and so immediately felt wrong for touching a man so intimately. "Come, let's go before they find us."

Again, Rogan followed her as she led him up the stairs, past the Lord's Chamber and up to the hall that led to the solar. Here was the bedroom that had once belonged to his father and his wives. He hadn't been in it for years. This girl, this Liana, had hung a tapestry on one wall. There were fat, fragrant candles burning. There was a bed against one wall, a holy cross above it.

Rogan took a step backward, but the girl tugged on his hand.

"Come, I have wine, good wine from Italy, and I will pour you a glass."

Rogan wasn't sure how she did it but moments later

he was nude and in her soft, clean bed, a silver goblet of wine in his hand and her pressed to his shoulder, his arm holding her to him, his fingers playing with her hair.

Liana snuggled her body against his as if she were trying to become part of his skin. There were so many questions she wanted to ask him about the castle, about the people. Who was the Lady she'd seen spinning? She wanted to know more about Severn's Iolanthe. And why wasn't Zared fostered to another knight and in training?

But she'd poured out too much emotion tonight and was now too tired to talk. She put her hand on the hair of his chest, felt his big, strong body next to hers and, contentedly, she drifted into sleep.

Rogan heard her soft breathing of sleep and thought that he should go. He should leave her now and go find somewhere else to sleep. He remembered the way she'd set the bed on fire. If he hadn't wakened, he could have burned to death. By rights she should be in the dungeon now and at dawn he should tie her to a stake and burn her—just as she tried to burn him. But he made no movement. Instead, he lifted her hand from his chest and looked at it with curiosity. It was such a small, weak, useless hand, he thought just before he fell asleep, still holding her in his arms.

When he awoke, it was full morning and he could hear the noise of the courtyard below. With the daylight, his senses returned. He was wrapped about the girl as if they were the entwined roots of a tree. He shoved her from him and rolled out of the bed, then started toward the garderobe. There was a urinal in the little hall before the room with the seat and he paused to relieve himself.

Liana awoke and stretched luxuriously in the bed. She had never felt so good in her life. This was what

marriage was supposed to be: standing in the courtyard in the night in your husband's arms and looking
at the stars, sleeping in his arms, waking to know that
he's near you, hearing a man in the garderobe. He
walked out of the latrine, scratching his bare chest and
yawning.

"Good morning," she said, moving her legs about
under the blankets.

Rogan's mind was on the day's work. Now that he
had the Neville gold, he could begin hiring knights to
help him fight the Howards. Of course he'd have to
train them properly. Most men were lazy louts with
the strength of children. And speaking of lazy, he'd
better get Severn out of that witch-woman's bed or
there'd be no strength left in his brother. He left the
room without once looking at, or remembering, his
wife.

Liana sat up in the bed in shock when he walked out
without acknowledging her. She had half a mind to
run after him and— What? she wondered. She lay
back against the pillows and smiled. She had been
quiet and meek and obedient and he had ignored her.
She had tried to burn him to death and he'd spent the
night with her. The lady who'd been spinning had said
men never fought battles for women who were meek
and mild. Would Rogan perhaps fight a battle for a
wife who tried to set him on fire?

"My lady!" Joice said excitedly as she burst into the
room and began chattering.

Liana's thoughts were so occupied with her husband that she did not at first hear Joice's words.
"What? Fire Lady? What are you talking about?"
When Liana began to understand the story, she
laughed. It seemed the story of Liana's lighting
Rogan's bed had traveled all over the village as well as
the castle, and she had been dubbed the Fire Lady.

"Two of the Days have already gone back to their parents in the village," Joice said, "and the others are afraid of you."

There was pride in Joice's voice, and Liana thought it was ironic coming from this woman who had counseled meekness. If she'd continued to follow Joice's advice, last night would never have happened.

"Good!" Liana said firmly, flinging the covers back and getting out of bed. "We shall use the fear while we have it. Perhaps you and the other women should mention poison and . . . snakes—yes, that's good. If a maid doesn't do her work, I might have snakes put in her bed."

"My lady, I don't think—"

Liana whirled on her maid. "You don't think what, Joice? That I should use my own judgment? Do you think that I should continue to rely on your advice?"

Joice knew she'd lost her power over her mistress. "No, my lady," she whispered. "I meant . . ." She couldn't finish.

"Fetch me the green silk, then come and do my hair," Liana said. "Today I begin to clean my house."

The people of Moray Castle found that the Pale Rabbit had indeed turned into the Fire Lady. They were used to working for the Peregrine brothers, who demanded five things at once of each person, but this little woman, in her brilliant green dress, her fat blonde braids down her back, demanded ten times the work of the masters. She took every man and knight from his usual task and set him to hauling trash. Fireplaces were shoveled out. Bucket after bucket was filled with bones and filth and dumped into the now-empty Neville wagons and hauled away. Liana got Zared to find three other boys and the four of them set about killing rats. She sent men to the village to hire women to scour the walls and floors and furniture. She also hired men to use weighted nets to start dragging the moat and when the nets would not sink into the filth but floated on top, she ordered the men to dig a trench and drain the filth away—if it will move, she thought. The men balked at that, fearing Lord Rogan's sword more than they feared her fire.

"My husband will give permission," she said to the two men before her, both of them afraid for their lives.

"But, my lady," one man said, "the moat is for defense and—"

"Defense!" Liana gasped. "An enemy could *walk* across it as it is now." But no matter what she said, the men would not start digging. She gritted her teeth. "Where is my husband, then? I will go to him and we will settle this between us."

"He is beating farmers, my lady."

It took Liana a moment to understand. "What?" she whispered.

"Someone is stealing, and Lord Rogan beats men until someone tells him who the thieves are."

Liana raised her skirts and ran inside the castle walls. While her horse was being saddled, she got directions to where Rogan and his brother were and minutes later she was riding furiously across the countryside, six armed knights close behind her.

The sight that greeted her was one of horror. One man was tied to a tree, his back bloody from whip lashes. Another three men stood together, shaking with terror as a man held his bloody whip aloft. Four women and six children stood by crying, two of the women on their knees and begging Rogan for mercy. Six Peregrine knights stood to one side of Rogan and Severn, who were deep in conversation, seemingly oblivious to what was going on around them.

"Stop!" Liana screamed, and came off her horse while it was still running. She hurled herself before the cringing farmers. "Do not kill them," she said, looking into Rogan's hard green eyes.

Rogan and his men were so shocked, the knight lowered his whip for a second. "Severn, take her," Rogan commanded.

"*I* will find who is stealing from you," she shouted, twisting away before Severn could grab her. "I will deliver the thieves to you and you may punish them, but not these random people."

Her actions and her words effectively silenced everyone, from Rogan down to the children whose father was tied to the tree.

"You?" Rogan said, as much surprised as anything.

"Give me two weeks' time," Liana said breathlessly, "and I will find your thief. Terrorized peasants do not produce good crops."

"Terrorized . . ." Rogan began, then his bewilderment left. "Get her the hell out of here," he commanded his brother.

Severn's big arm caught Liana's waist and pulled her from in front of the three condemned men. Liana thought fast. "I'll lay you odds I can find your thieves in two weeks," she shouted. "I have a chestful of jewels that you have not seen. Emeralds, rubies, diamonds. I'll give them to you if I do not produce the thieves in two short weeks."

Once again, Rogan and the people quietened and stared at her. They were all wondering what manner of woman she was, Rogan wondering most of all.

Severn's grip on her waist loosened, and Liana went to her husband and looked up at him as she put her hand on his chest. "I have found that terror breeds terror. I have dealt with thieves before. Let me do this now. If I am not right, in two weeks' time you may kill all of them and you will have the jewels."

Rogan could only gape at her. She had nearly

burned him to death last night and now she was making a wager with him like a man and interfering in his business. He had half a mind to yet send her to the dungeon.

"I could take the jewels," he heard himself saying as he looked at her and remembered how alive she'd been last night. A sudden wave of desire overtook him, and he turned away before he touched her in front of his men.

"They are well hidden," she said softly and put her hand on his arm. The same desire was also flooding her veins.

Rogan shook her hand away. "Take the thieving bastards," he said gruffly, just wanting to get away from her. "In two weeks I will have the jewels and I will have taught a woman a lesson," he said, trying to make light of the matter and not unman himself before his men. But a glance at his brother and his men showed they were not close to laughing. They were looking at Liana with deep interest.

Rogan cursed under his breath. "We ride," he growled, moving toward his horse.

"Wait," Liana said, running after him. Her heart was pounding in her throat, for she knew that what she was about to say was greatly daring. "What do I get if I win the wager?"

"What?" Rogan said, glaring down at her. "You get the damned thieves. What else do you want?"

"You," she said, hands on hips, smiling at him. "If I win the wager, I want you as my slave for one whole day."

Rogan gaped at her. He was going to have to remove some of this woman's hide and teach her how a wife should act. He didn't say a word but put his foot in the wooden stirrup.

"Wait a minute, brother," Severn said, grinning. He

was recovering from his shock faster than the others. No one, including him, had seen but a few men and even fewer women challenge Rogan. "I think you should take the lady's wager. After all, you can't possibly lose. She'll never find the thieves. We've been looking for months. What do you have to lose?"

Rogan, iron-jawed, cold-eyed, glanced at his knights and then at the peasants. He would win the stupid wager and he'd send her away before she interfered again. "Done," he said, and without another look at Liana, he mounted his horse and started riding hard. His thoughts were black with anger. Damned bitch, she'd made a fool of him before his men!

His anger hadn't subsided when he reached the castle. And once inside the gate, he sat on his horse to stare in disbelief at his men, his laborers, his women, all shoveling manure, sweeping, and scouring.

"I'll be damned," Severn muttered from beside Rogan as he stared at one old knight while he stuck a pitchfork into a four-foot-high pile of manure.

Rogan felt as if his own men were betraying him. He threw back his head and gave a loud, long, hideous war cry—and the people in the courtyard came to a halt. "To work!" he bellowed at his men. "You are not women! Work!"

He didn't wait to see if he was obeyed, but dismounted and strode angrily up the stairs to the Lord's Chamber, then to the private room to one side of it. This room was his and his alone. He slammed the door shut and sat down on the old oak chair that had belonged to the head of the Peregrines for three generations.

He sat, then stood abruptly and glared at the chair. There was a puddle of cold water in the seat, where someone had been scrubbing it. So angry he could barely see, he looked about the room and saw that it was clean. The foot-deep debris was gone from the floor, the spider webs that connected the weapons on the wall were gone, the rats were gone, the grease was gone from the table and chairs.

"I'll kill her," he said from between his teeth. "I'll have her drawn and quartered. I'll teach her who owns the Peregrine lands, who rules the Peregrine men."

But as he put his hand on the door, he noticed a little table against the wall. He remembered seeing Zared's mother use that table, but he hadn't seen it for years. He wondered if it had been in this room all that time and he just hadn't seen it. On top of the table, neatly placed, was a stack of precious, clean, expensive paper, beside it were a silver inkwell and half a dozen quill pens, the points sharp and ready for use. The paper and pens drew Rogan like a moth to a flame. For months he'd had an idea for a trebuchet, a wooden war machine that could throw large stones with great force. He'd been thinking that if it were built with two cranks instead of one, he could make the throwing arm much higher and get more power behind the stones. Several times he'd tried drawing his ideas in the dirt, but he hadn't been able to make a line fine enough.

"The wench can wait," he muttered, and went to the table and slowly and clumsily began to draw his ideas. He wasn't as familiar with a pen as he was with a sword. The sun set, he struck a flint and lit a candle, and kept on laboriously drawing his design for the trebuchet.

CHAPTER
EIGHT

After Rogan left the peasants, it took a while for Liana's heart to calm. She was certainly doing a poor job of pleasing her husband, wasn't she? She could see his dark form, still wearing his wedding clothes, which were becoming greasier by the day, riding toward the castle and she wanted to run after him and apologize. It had hurt her to see the rage in his eyes. Perhaps it was better when he ignored her. Perhaps it was better—

"My lady, thank you."

Liana looked down to see a thin, tired-looking peasant woman, her head bowed beneath her ragged hood as she took the hem of Liana's gown and kissed it.

"Thank you," the woman repeated.

The other peasants came to her and bowed down before her, and their groveling made Liana feel sick. She hated to see people as downtrodden as these. The peasants on her father's land were fat and healthy, while these were gray with fatigue and ill health and fear.

"Get up, all of you," she commanded, then waited while they slowly obeyed her, the fear increasing in their eyes. "I want you to listen to me. You heard my husband: He wants the thieves, and *you* are going to deliver them to him." She saw the way their eyes hardened at her words. There was pride left in these people, a pride that made them protect the thieves from a hard master.

Her voice softened. "But first you are going to eat. You"—she pointed to a man who, if she had not intervened, would have a bloody back now—"go and slaughter the fattest cow on all the Peregrine lands and two sheep, then bring them here and roast them. You shall eat, because you have a great deal of work to do in the coming weeks."

None of the peasants made a move.

"The hour grows late. Go!"

One man went to his knees, his face showing his agony. "My lady, Lord Rogan punishes any person who touches what is his. We cannot kill his animals or eat his grain. He keeps all of it and sells it."

"That was the way it was before I came," Liana said patiently. "Lord Rogan has not as much need for money as he once did. Go and kill the animals. I will take the lord's wrath on my head." She swallowed at that, but she couldn't allow the peasants to see her fear. "Now, where is the baker's shop? The one who has the feud against my husband?"

It took Liana hours to set in motion what she meant to do. Two weeks was so little time. The six knights with her, at first silently standing by and watching with that special expression of amusement that men affect when a woman does something that they can not, she put to work.

She ordered a wheat field cut, the grain given to the baker, the sheaves to be used to thatch the decayed roofs of the peasants' houses. She ordered a knight to supervise a mass cleaning of the streets, which ran with human and animal excrement. Another knight supervised a washing of the peasants, who were as dirty as the streets. At first she was appalled at the refusal of the merchants to take her word that they would be paid, but remembering the story of what her husband's men had done to the baker, she forgave the merchants and gave them silver coins from the bag she carried on her horse.

It was sundown when she returned to Moray Castle, and she smiled as she saw two knights nodding sleepily in their saddles. Her plan was to make the peasants comfortable enough so that their loyalty would be to the master and not to a few thieves who were probably sharing their booty with the hungry farmers. It was not going to be easy to clean up a village within two weeks, but she was going to try.

The stench of the moat greeted her nostrils as she neared the castle, and she knew she'd have to get Rogan's permission to drain the thing before the men would proceed. But inside the walls, she could see the difference. There was less filth on the ground, less piled up in the stables and around the shallow buildings built along the walls. When she rode up, the workers looked up at her and some men tugged at their forelocks in respect of her. Liana smiled to herself. They were beginning to notice her now.

She mounted the stairs to the Lord's Chamber. Here the women had concentrated their efforts. It wasn't clean yet, not by Liana's standards—the walls would have to be whitewashed anew—but she could walk across the tile floor without tripping over bones.

Inside the room, at the clean table and chairs, sat

Severn and Zared, their heads down on the table. Stretched along the length of the table was a long, three-deep pile of the fattest dead rats Liana had ever seen. They looked as if they were meant to be trophies of war.

"What is this?" she asked sharply, startling Severn and Zared awake.

Zared smiled at her and Liana thought again what a pretty, beardless boy he was.

"We killed them all," Zared announced proudly. "You wouldn't by chance know how to count, would you? Rogan does, but not as high as this many."

Liana didn't want to get near the rats, but Zared was so proud she felt she had to. She pointed and began counting. Each one she counted, Zared threw out the window into the moat below. Liana meant to protest, but a few rats weren't going to make the moat worse than it already was. One of the rats was still alive and Liana jumped back while Zared brought a fist down on the rodent's head. Severn grinned proudly.

Liana counted fifty-eight rats, and when they were gone from the table, she tiredly sat down next to Severn and looked about the room.

"Fifty-eight!" Zared was saying. "Wait until I tell Rogan."

"Someone forgot to throw those bones out," Liana said wearily, looking at the wall over the double fireplace. There were six horses' skulls hanging there. She hadn't noticed them before since they were probably covered with cobwebs, she thought.

She became aware of Severn and Zared gaping at her, looking as if she'd suddenly grown horns. She glanced down at the front of her gown, which was dirty but not hideously so. "Is something wrong?" she asked.

"Those are the Peregrine horses," Zared said in a strained whisper.

Liana had no idea what the boy meant, so she looked to Severn. His handsome face was changing in expression from astonishment to a kind of cold, deep rage that, until now, Liana had thought only Rogan capable of.

Severn's voice was quiet when he spoke. "The Howards laid siege to Bevan Castle and starved our family. My father, Zared's mother, and my brother William died there. My father went to the walls and asked the Howards to allow the woman freedom, but they would not." Severn lowered his voice. "Before they died, they ate the horses." He turned to the skulls hanging on the walls. *"Those* horses." He looked back at her, his eyes burning. "We do not forget, and the skulls will not be removed."

Liana looked at the skulls with horror. To be so hungry that one was reduced to eating horses. It was on the tip of her tongue to say that the Peregrine peasants were condemned to a lifelong siege and would probably be glad of horses to eat, but she refrained.

"Where is my husband?" she asked after a while.

"In his brooding room," Zared said cheerfully, while Severn cast the youngster a warning look.

Liana didn't pursue Zared's words because she understood more than she had at first. Perhaps there were reasons for her husband's anger, for his obsession with money. She stood. "If you will excuse me, I must bathe. Tell my husband I—"

"Bathe?" Zared said, sounding as if Liana had said she planned to jump from the parapets.

"It's a pleasant occupation. You should try it," Liana said, especially since Severn and Zared were now the dirtiest objects in the room.

Zared leaned back in the chair. "I think I'll pass. Did you really tell the Days to go home at night?"

Liana smiled. "Yes, I did. Good night, Severn, Zared." She started up the stairs, then paused when she heard their voices.

"The woman has courage," she heard Zared say.

"Or else she's an utter fool," Severn answered.

Liana continued up the stairs, and an hour later she was in her bedroom, soaking in a wooden tub full of scented hot water and watching the play of flames on the logs.

To her right the door was thrown open with a crash, and Rogan entered like a sudden storm on a peaceful day. "You have gone too far, woman," he bellowed at her. "You have not my permission to dismiss my women."

Liana turned her head to look at him. He wore only his big white shirt, which hung to the top of his thighs, a wide leather belt about his waist, and his braies. His sleeves were rolled up to his elbows, exposing thickly muscled, scarred forearms.

Liana could feel perspiration breaking out on her forehead. He was still yelling at her, but she didn't know what he was saying. She stood in the tub, her slim, firm, full-breasted body rosy and warm from the hot water. "Would you please hand me that drying cloth?" she asked softly in the silence, for Rogan had ceased speaking.

Rogan could only gape at her. For all the many women he'd had, he'd never had the leisure to look, really *look*, at a woman, and now he didn't think he'd ever seen anything as beautiful as this rosy-skinned beauty with the curtain of blonde hair hanging almost to her knees.

I won't let her use her body to make me forget what she has done today, he thought, but his feet took a step

125

toward her and one hand reached out to touch the curve of her breast.

Liana told herself to not lose her head. She wanted this man, oh yes, she so much wanted him, but she wanted more than a few minutes of rutting. She put her hand out and untied the strings of his shirt at his throat, then touched his skin with her fingertips. "The water is still hot," she said softly. "Perhaps you'd allow me to wash you."

A bath was a great waste of time to Rogan's mind, but the idea of being washed by a nude woman . . .

He was out of his clothes in seconds, and when he stood nude before her—*all* of him standing upright— he made a grab for her. But Liana, laughing, side-stepped him.

"Your bath, sir," she said, and Rogan found himself stepping into the tub.

The hot water felt good to his dirty skin and the herbs floating on the water smelled good, but best of all was the woman, his wife, this beautiful . . . "Leah?" he asked, looking at her as she knelt over the foot of the tub, her breasts, pink-tipped and luscious, just grazing the wooden rim.

"Liana," she answered, and smiled at him.

She began to wash him, running soapy hands over his arms, his chest, his back, his face. He leaned against the tub and closed his eyes. "Liana," he said softly. Vaguely, he seemed to remember that this woman had done something unpleasant today, but he couldn't at the moment remember what it was. She was so small and angelic, so pink and white, that he couldn't imagine her doing anything he disapproved of.

He lifted his legs so she could wash them, then obeyed her when she told him to stand and her small, warm soapy hands washed between his legs. The pleasure he felt at her action was so overpowering that he spilled his seed on those small hands. His eyes flew open in alarm and, to hide his embarrassment, he roughly shoved her shoulder and sent her flying hard against the wall.

"You have hurt me," she cried out.

Rogan had killed many people and never felt a thing, but this girl's cry struck some chord in him. He had not meant to hurt her; he had only been unmanned in front of her. To his consternation, he found himself stepping from the tub and kneeling down to her. "Let me see," he said, and bent her forward. Where she had hit the stones, her skin was bruised but not cut.

"It's nothing," he said. "Your skin is too fragile, is all." He ran his big, scarred, callused hand down her small, slim back. "It's skin like the underbelly of a newborn colt," he said.

Liana rolled her eyes at him and almost giggled, but she didn't. Instead, she turned in his arms and put her head on his shoulder. "You enjoyed your bath, didn't you?"

Rogan could feel the blood rushing to his face in embarrassed memory, then as he looked at her, her eyes twinkling, he realized she was *teasing* him. He had seen his brothers laugh with women, but Rogan had found very little that was humorous about women. But this woman made him feel different. "I enjoyed the bath too much," he heard himself say, and was astonished.

Liana giggled against his shoulder. "Can it be enjoyed again?" she asked slyly. "Or is that your last 'enjoyment'?"

For a moment Rogan considered beating her for her

insolence, but then his hand slid down her bare rump. "I believe I can manage a bit more." He then did something he'd never done before: He lifted her in his arms and carried her to the bed and gently laid her on it.

As he stood over her and looked down at her, he didn't want to jump on her, thrust inside her, then go to sleep as he usually did. Perhaps it was because of his earlier "enjoyment," as she called it, or perhaps he wanted to touch her as she had touched him, but he lay on the bed beside her, propped on one elbow, and reached out his hand to feel the skin of her belly.

Liana had no idea how new all this was to Rogan, but this was what she had imagined being in bed with a man to be like. He explored her body with his hand as if he'd never seen a woman before. Liana closed her eyes as his hand caressed her legs, running between her thighs, his fingers curling over the smooth, firm roundness of them, then his fingertips entwined in her short woman's hair. His hand moved up to her belly, his thumb running along the side of her navel, then slowly, ever so very, very slowly, his hand moved up to the underside of her breast. He cupped first one then the other, his thumb just grazing the sensitive, hard little point.

She opened her eyes to look at him and saw the softness in his eyes and suddenly she knew why she had agreed to marry him. She had sensed that under his toughness, under his hard outer shell, was a softness he had never let anyone see. A shudder passed through her body as she thought of the pain this man must have experienced in his life to make him into the cold, unfeeling man he showed to the world. But somehow she sensed that the Rogan the world saw was not the inner man.

I love him, she thought. I love him with all my soul

and all my being, and so help me God, I am going to make him love me too.

She put her hand to his jaw, felt the whiskers there, soft now from days without shaving as he seemed to shave only once a week. I'm going to make you need me, she said to herself. And I'm going to make you feel safe enough that I can see the softness in your eyes even when I have clothes on.

The last made her smile and she rolled her body toward his. He held her to him and she could feel his rising passion as his hands stroked her back, then his mouth took hers and he kissed her deeply. His lips ran down her throat and at last to her breast. Liana arched backward and let out a little cry of pleasure.

Rogan was aware of her reactions, and because of the episode in the tub, he was able to control his own need for her. The women he'd had had either been frightened virgins or very willing, experienced women, and always they had wanted to please him. Of course none of them had offered to bathe him, nor had any of them left paper and pens in his room. Perhaps it was merely a wish to repay a debt, but he was enjoying feeling this woman squirm beneath his searching hands. Her pleasure was giving him pleasure.

His lips followed his hands down her body and he found the smell of her and the taste of her sweet and fresh, so unlike the Days, who sometimes smelled so bad he kicked them out of bed. This girl smelled like wood smoke and herbs.

When his head came back up to her lips, he was amazed at how much he wanted her. Her hands clutched at his shoulders and when he entered her, she rose to meet him with a force and power to match his.

Never had he spent such a time in bed with a woman! She was lusty beyond all belief, at one point pushing him to his back and climbing on top of him, her hair wrapping around the two of them like a soft yet strong prison.

Rogan had never considered the woman's pleasure before, but this woman, with her moans and groans, her movements here, her movements there, sent his own pleasure into a fevered pitch until he thought he might die. When he finished at long last, it was an earth-shattering experience to him, affecting him from his toes to the top of his head.

He collapsed on the girl and instead of pushing her away, as he usually did to the women he bedded, he clutched her to him as if he were drowning and she were a buoyant log.

Liana snuggled against him. He seemed to pour over her body as if he were sauce over a pudding. She had never felt so good in her life. "That was wonderful," she whispered. "That was the best thing that has ever happened to me. I knew marriage to you would be like this."

Rogan released his hold on her and moved to the far side of the bed, but Liana moved with him, her head on his shoulder, her arm across his chest, her thigh across his. She was happier than she'd ever been, happier than she'd thought possible.

She had no idea of the turmoil that was coursing through Rogan. He wanted to get away from her, yet he couldn't move.

"What did your brother William look like? Did he have red hair like yours?" she asked.

"I don't have red hair," Rogan said indignantly.

"In the sunlight your head looks as if it's on fire," Liana retorted. "Was William like you?"

"Our father had red hair, but I inherited my mother's black hair."

"So both of you had red hair, then."

"I don't—" Rogan said, then stopped and he almost smiled. "On fire, eh?" Every other woman he'd had had told him he had black hair without a trace of his father's red. That was what he'd wanted them to say and therefore they had.

"What about your other brothers? Were they redheads too?"

He thought of his now-dead brothers, remembering the youth of them, the strength of them. How well they could fight! He never thought he'd someday be the oldest Peregrine and have the responsibility of it all. "Rowland, Basil, and James had a dark mother, so they all had black hair."

"And what of Severn and Zared?"

"Severn's mother was a blonde like . . ." He trailed off. She had taken his hand in hers and now lay there looking at his fingers, entwining hers with his. It was such an odd thing to do, he thought. He should push her out of bed and get some sleep rather than talk to her about painful memories. But remembering his brothers as alive was not painful.

"Like me," Liana said, smiling. "And she was Zared's mother also? But Zared is such a dark young man."

Liana did not see Rogan smile in the dim light. "Yes, indeed. Zared is dark because of a dark mother. Severn's mother died giving birth to him."

"So your father had four wives and seven sons?"

Rogan hesitated before answering. "Yes."

"It must have been good to have brothers. I often wished for another child to be born to my mother. Did you often play together, or were you fostered out to other people?" She felt him stiffen beneath her and wondered what she'd said wrong.

"There was no play in our lives, nor did we foster." His voice was cold. "We trained for war from the time

131

we could stand. The Howards killed William when he was eighteen, James and Basil at twenty and twenty-one, and they killed Rowland two years ago, before he was thirty. Now I must protect Severn and Zared." He took her shoulders and lifted her to look into her eyes. *"I* killed James and Basil. I killed them over a woman, and I'll die before I let it happen again. Get away from me, and stay away from me."

He shoved her back into the feather mattress, then got out of bed and began tugging on his clothes.

"Rogan, I didn't mean—" Liana began, but he was already gone. "Damn, damn, damn," she said, slamming her fist into the pillow, then she turned onto her back and stared at the white-painted ceiling. What had he meant that *he* killed his brothers? And over a woman? *"What* woman?" she said aloud. "I'll have her for breakfast."

The thought comforted her and the thought of there being tomorrow night also calmed her. But most of all, she thought of winning her wager. If the peasants turned over the thieves to her, Rogan would be her slave for an entire day. What would she do with him? Have him make love to her all day? Perhaps just to have him stay with her for a day would be enough. Stay with her and answer her questions, maybe. She drifted off to sleep.

The next morning Liana rose early, meaning to find her husband, but the sight belowstairs made her temporarily forget Rogan. No one was in the Lord's Chamber, so she went down the stairs and outside and took the stairs leading to the retainers' hall. She had not been in this area before, but she was not surprised to find it as filthy as the other part of the castle had been. In the enormous hall, twice as big as the Lord's Chamber, sat about two hundred men at greasy tables on slimy benches eating sand-filled bread and drinking sour wine. No one paid any attention to her when she entered, but they continued scratching, shouting, swilling, belching, and breaking wind.

Liana's good mood and sense of accomplishment left her. Quietly, she left the hall and went outside into the sunlight.

Severn was standing near the south wall stroking the breast of a big peregrine falcon.

"Where is my husband?" she asked.

"Rode out for Bevan this morning," Severn answered, not looking up.

"Bevan? Where your family was starved?"

Severn gave her a quick glance and put the bird on its perch. "That's the one."

"When will he return?"

Severn shrugged and walked away.

Liana followed him, lifting her skirts so she could hurry. "He just rode out? No word to anyone? He didn't tell anyone when he planned to return? I want you to give the men permission to drain the moat."

Severn stopped, turned, and looked down at her. "Drain the moat? Are you crazy, woman? The Howards could—"

"Walk across the thing as it is now," Liana said, glaring up at him. "When will my husband return?"

The stern expression left Severn's face and his eyes began to twinkle. "My brother rode out of here before dawn, saying only that he was going to Bevan Castle. If you asked him to order the moat drained, I imagine that had something to do with his leaving."

Liana didn't say a word.

"Scared to, eh?" Severn said, beginning to smile.

Liana couldn't stop the blood from creeping into her face, as he had guessed correctly.

"I'm not about to give permission and have Rogan come back and see the moat empty," Severn said, and turned away again.

Liana stood staring after him. It upset her that Rogan was gone, but she thought she could perhaps more easily put the castle and the village in order if he weren't there. Severn was a much softer man than Rogan was, she could see that, and she thought perhaps there was a way to persuade Severn, a way she had used to persuade her father to do anything she wanted: food.

Liana sent Joice to fetch her precious recipe book, then Liana straightened her headdress and went up the stairs to the kitchen rooms.

It was late that night when Liana climbed alone into her bed. She was exhausted but happy too, for she now had permission to have a ditch dug to drain the filthy moat.

It had taken all day, but she'd managed to get the kitchens and the retainers' hall somewhat clean and she'd laid before Severn and the Peregrine knights a banquet fit for a king. She'd served roasted beef, pink and juicy, capon in orange sauce, rabbit cooked with onions and raisins, spinach and cheese tarts, eggs in mustard sauce, spiced pears, mince pies, and apple mousse.

By the time Severn and his men stopped gorging themselves, Liana knew she could have anything she wanted from them. Patting his swollen belly, Severn not only agreed to her request, he offered to help dig. She'd smiled and said that wouldn't be necessary, then handed him a plate heaped high with sweet jellied milk cubes.

If only my husband were so easy to win, Liana thought as she sank wearily onto the feather mattress.

She tried not to wonder what her husband was doing at Bevan Castle. Was he in the arms of another woman?

Rogan sat before the fireplace in Bevan Castle, as unaware of the filth and disrepair around him as he was at Moray Castle. He had eyes only for the pretty young peasant girl before him.

When he'd left Moray early that morning, he wasn't sure why he was leaving. He knew only that he'd awakened from sleep and his first thought was of that blonde-haired she-devil he'd married. He'd scratched at the fleas that had so willingly left the old mattress he'd slept on and jumped on his skin, and knew he wanted to put some distance and time between him and the girl.

He'd ordered some men to ready themselves and had ridden out, stopping in the village to pick up Thursday to take her with him. But Thursday had cringed and cried and begged him not to force her to go with him as the Fire Lady would kill her. Rogan had left the girl in disgust. He heard the same from Sunday and Tuesday, so he'd ridden with no woman to Bevan.

Bevan Castle was isolated atop a tall, steep hill, and before he began the climb, he stopped in the village below and took the first pretty, healthy-looking girl he saw and pulled her across his saddle. Now, the girl stood trembling before him.

"Stop shaking," he commanded her, scowling. She was younger than he'd first imagined. He saw her shaking increase and his scowl deepened. "Come here and give me a kiss," he ordered.

Tears began to run down the girl's face, but she stepped toward him and gave him a quick kiss on the cheek. Rogan grabbed her greasy hair and pulled her

135

Jude Deveraux

mouth down to his and kissed her angrily. He felt the girl whimper under him. He released her, pushing her so she fell to the floor.

"Do not hurt me, please, my lord," the girl begged. "I will do as you say, but please do not hurt me."

Rogan's desire left him. He remembered too well a woman who was eager for him, a woman who didn't smell of grease and pig manure. "Get out of here," he said under his breath. "Go before I change my mind!" he yelled when the girl was too frightened to move. He turned away as she scurried from the room.

Rogan went to one of the barrels along the wall and tapped a stream of dark, bitter beer into a dirty wooden mug. One of his knights lay sleeping nearby. Rogan kicked him in the ribs. "Get up," he commanded. "And get some dice. I will need something to help me sleep tonight."

CHAPTER
NINE

*L*iana put her hand to her aching back. Two long weeks Rogan had been gone, and in those two weeks she'd wrought miracles in the castle and the village. At first the peasants had been afraid to obey her, afraid of Lord Rogan's wrath, but when a few obeyed Liana and were not punished, the others began to believe in her.

Village houses were repaired, new clothes purchased, and animals slaughtered to feed the hungry people. By the end of the first two weeks, the peasants were looking at Liana as if she were an angel.

The cleaning of the village and castle gave Liana great satisfaction, except for one aspect: the number of red-haired children running about. At first she'd thought it was a coincidence that Rogan should have the same distinctive dark red hair as some of the villagers. It was when a little boy, about eight years old, looked up at her with the same hard eyes of her husband that Liana demanded to know who was the father of the boy.

The peasants around her stopped their tasks and stared at the ground in silence. Liana repeated her question, then waited. At last a young woman stepped forward. Liana recognized her as one of the Days, one of the women who used to sleep with Rogan.

"Lord Rogan is the father," the woman said defiantly.

Liana felt the peasants around her cringe as if in anticipation of a blow. "How many of my husband's children are there?"

"A dozen or so." The girl's chin came up a little higher. "And the one I'm carrying."

Liana stood for a moment, unable to move or speak. She didn't know if she was angrier at her husband for having so many bastards or for leaving his own children to exist in poverty. She knew the peasants were watching her, waiting to see what she would do. She took a deep breath. "Gather the children and send them to me at the castle. I will see to their needs."

"With their mothers?" the Day said, her voice and attitude showing she felt herself to be triumphant.

Liana glared at the girl. "You may choose to put your weaned child in my care or you may keep the responsibility of raising it. But no, I do not take on the mothers of the children."

"Yes, my lady," the girl said dutifully, bowing her head.

Near her, Liana heard a few women snicker in approval.

It was late when she left the village, and she wished she could crawl into bed beside Rogan. As usual, she began to daydream about what she would ask of him when he was her slave for a day. Perhaps she'd plan a meal served beside a stream, for just the two of them. Perhaps she'd make him *talk* to her. Just to have him spend a day with her, an *hour* with her, when they both had their clothes on would be an accomplishment. He seemed to put her in the same category as the Days—that she was to sleep with and nothing else.

The loudness of her horse's hooves on the wooden bridge over the now-empty moat brought her back to reality. Behind her rode the ever-present, silent Peregrine knights.

The castle grounds were almost clean now and Liana was able to walk up the stairs to the Lord's Chamber without tripping on refuse.

Once upstairs, she avoided Joice, who had a list of questions and complaints, and climbed upward to the bedchambers above. Several times in the last weeks Liana had sought out the Lady, the woman she'd met that first week, the woman who'd reminded her that men never fought battles over quiet, meek women, but each time the door to her room had been locked.

The upstairs rooms were clean now and a few of them were occupied by her maids, but for the most part they remained empty, waiting for the appearance of guests. At the end of the corridor was the locked door, only this time the door was standing open. Liana paused for a moment to watch the woman, the sunlight on her braided hair as she bent over on a tapestry frame.

"Good evening, my dear," the woman said, turning and smiling pleasantly. "Please come in and shut the door. It makes a draft."

Liana did as she was bid. "I have come to see you before, but you weren't here. Rogan has gone to Bevan Castle." Once again, there was the feeling of having known this woman forever.

The woman separated strands of scarlet silk. "Yes, and you have a wager with him. He's to be your slave for a day?"

Liana smiled and walked toward the woman, looking over her shoulder at the fabric stretched on the frame. It was a tapestry-worked, almost-complete picture of a slim blonde lady with her hand on the head of a unicorn.

"She could be you," the Lady replied, smiling. "What do you have planned for your day with Rogan?"

Liana smiled dreamily. "A long walk in the woods, perhaps. A day spent alone. No brothers, no castle duties, no knights, just the two of us. I want him to . . . to give me his full attention." When the Lady didn't reply, Liana looked at her and saw the smile was gone. "You don't approve."

"It's not for me to say," she said softly. "But then I believe he and Jeanne used to take walks together."

"Jeanne?"

"Jeanne Howard."

"Howard!" Liana said, gasping. "The same Howards who are the sworn enemies of the Peregrines? I have heard little else since I was married—about how the Howards stole the Peregrine lands, killed the Peregrines, starved the Peregrines. Are you saying that Rogan once *courted* a Howard?"

"Rogan was once married to Jeanne before she was a Howard."

Liana sat down on a window seat, the sun warm on her back. "Tell me all," she whispered.

"Rogan was married to Jeanne Randel when he was only sixteen and she was fifteen. His parents and his brother William had been starved at Bevan the year before and the three oldest Peregrine sons were busy waging war on the Howards and so were too busy to marry themselves. They decided Rogan should marry, get a girl's dowry, and give them a few sons to grow to help them fight. Rogan fought against the marriage, but his brothers persuaded him."

The Lady turned to look at Liana. "Rogan has known only hardship and pain in his life. Not all the scars on his body are from battles. His brothers and father put their share on him, too."

"So they 'persuaded' Rogan to marry?" Liana said softly.

"Yes, but he wasn't reluctant after he saw her. She was a pretty little thing, so quiet and soft-spoken. Her mother had died when she was quite young and as a ward of the king she was raised by nuns in a convent. Perhaps going from a convent to marrying a Peregrine was not the easiest thing a child ever did."

The Lady looked at Liana, but Liana did not respond. This morning she'd discovered a dozen illegitimate children of her husband's and this evening she'd discovered he'd had another wife.

The Lady continued. "I think Rogan began to fall in love with her. He'd never had any softness in his life and I think Jeanne's gentleness fascinated him. I remember once they came back from a walk and they both had flowers in their hair."

Liana looked away, not wanting the hurt on her face to be seen. He gave his first wife flowers and he couldn't remember the name of his second wife.

"They were married for about four months when the Howards took Jeanne. She and Rogan were alone in the woods. Rowland had told Rogan not to go out alone, but Rogan thought he was immortal, that when he was with Jeanne, nothing could harm him. I believe they'd been swimming and . . ."—the Lady looked at Liana's stricken face—". . . and napping when Oliver Howard's men set upon them and took her. Rogan couldn't get to his sword, but he managed to pull two

Howards off their horses. He strangled one of them before the others could pull him away. I'm afraid that one of the Peregrines had just killed Oliver's younger brother and Oliver was in a vile mood. He had his men hold Rogan while he shot three arrows into him, not to kill him but to show Oliver's power. Then Oliver and his men rode away with Jeanne."

Liana stared at the woman, imagining the awful scene. "And what did Rogan do?" she whispered.

"Walked back to the castle," the Lady said. "Four miles, with three dripping wounds, he walked back to his brothers. He went with them the next day when they attacked the Howards. He rode with them and fought with them, until, on the third day, he fell off his horse, burning with fever. When he was sensible again, it was nearly two weeks later and his brothers Basil and James were dead."

"He said he killed his brothers," Liana said softly.

"Rogan has always taken his responsibilities very seriously. He and Rowland and young Severn fought the Howards for over a year. The Peregrines did not have the strength or the money to properly attack the Howard castle and it is a vast, strong place, so they fought however they could, stealing Howard supplies, burning the peasants' houses, poisoning what water they could reach. It was a bloody year. And then . . ." the Lady trailed off.

"And then what?" Liana encouraged.

"And then Jeanne returned to Rogan."

Liana waited, but the Lady said no more. Her needle flew lightning-fast in and out of the tapestry silk. "What happened when Jeanne returned?"

"She was six months' pregnant with Oliver Howard's child and very much in love with him. She came to Rogan to beg him to give her an annulment so she could marry Oliver."

"That poor boy," Liana said at last. "How could she do that to him? Or did Oliver Howard force her to come to him?"

"No one had forced Jeanne. She loved Oliver, and he, her. In fact, Oliver had forbidden her to go to Rogan. Oliver planned to kill the husband of the woman he loved. I think Jeanne must have felt something for Rogan because I think her visit saved his life. Rogan came home after he saw Jeanne, and while Rogan petitioned for the annulment, the Peregrines and the Howards did not war with each other."

Liana stood and walked to the far side of the room. She was silent for quite some time. At last she turned back to look at the Lady. "So Rogan and Jeanne used to walk in the woods together, did they? Then I shall plan a celebration. We will dance. I will have singers and acrobats and—"

"As you did at your wedding?"

Liana stopped talking and remembered her wedding day, when Rogan had ignored her. "I want him to spend time with me," she said. "He doesn't notice me except in bed. I want to be more to him than . . . than a day of the week. I want him . . ."

"You want what from him?"

"I want what that slut Jeanne Howard had and threw away!" Liana said violently. "I want Rogan to love me."

"And you are going to accomplish this with walks in the woods?" The Lady seemed amused.

Liana suddenly felt very tired. Her dream of a husband who walked with her and held her hand was not the man who, after being shot with three arrows, continued to fight for days. She remembered Zared's saying Rogan was in his brooding room. Well, no wonder he brooded; no wonder he never smiled; no wonder he wanted nothing to do with another wife.

143

"What do I do?" she whispered aloud. "How do I show him I'm no Jeanne Howard? How do I make a man like Rogan love me?" She looked to the Lady and waited.

But the Lady shook her head. "I have no answer for you. Perhaps it is an impossible task. Most women would be content with a husband who did not beat them and who used other women's bodies for their needs. Rogan will give you children, and children can be a great comfort to a woman."

Liana's mouth tightened. "Children who can grow up to fight and die for the Howards? Am I to stand by and watch while my husband points to the horses' skulls and teaches my children to hate? Rogan drains all income from me, from the peasants, from wherever he can get it, in order to make war machines. His hatred is more to him than any life on earth. He breeds sons on the peasant girls, then leaves the boys to starve. If for one day he could forget the Howards, forget that now he is the oldest Peregrine. If he could just *see* how his hatred is causing the slow death of his people, then he might—" She stopped, her eyes wide.

"He might what?"

Liana's voice was low. "Weeks ago the peasants asked my permission to celebrate St. Eustace's day. Of course I gave permission. If Rogan could see these people, talk to them . . . If perhaps he could see his own children . . ."

The Lady was smiling now. "He has rarely been away from his family, and I doubt if he will agree to spending the day alone with you. Once, when he was alone, his wife was taken and that eventually led to the death of his two brothers. No, he will not readily agree to whatever you request of him."

The Lady looked at the door and listened. "I believe

I hear your maid searching for you. You must go
now."

"Yes," Liana said, distracted, her thoughts on what
they'd talked about. She moved to the door then
turned and looked back. "May I see you again? Your
door is often locked."

The Lady smiled. "Whenever you need me, I will be
here."

Liana smiled in return and left the room. She heard
the lock turn in the door as soon as it closed. She
wanted to knock on the door. There were questions
she'd meant to ask the Lady, but she never seemed to
remember them when she was in that room.

She changed her mind and didn't knock but went
down the hall, then down the stairs. Joice was indeed
looking for her. Lord Rogan had returned, and close
behind had come nearly the entire village of peasants,
a handcart in their midst. On the cart lay two dead
men, a father and son.

"They're your thieves," Joice said, eyes wide. "Just
like you said. The peasants hanged them. Some of the
knights said it was so Lord Rogan wouldn't torture the
men. They say the thieves were Robin Hoods, who
shared all they stole, and the peasants loved them. But
they hanged them for you, my lady."

Liana grimaced at this dubious honor, then
smoothed her skirts and went down the stairs to meet
her husband. Her heart was pounding in her throat.

Rogan was still on his horse, the fading rays of
sunlight flashing on his hair, the big roan stallion
between his powerful legs prancing dangerously as it
felt its master's anger. Rogan was looking at the castle
grounds, frowning at the cleanliness of the place,
frowning at the clean peasants who'd lost their lean,
gaunt look.

Liana sensed there was to be trouble. She could see it in Rogan's handsome face. "I have won the wager," she said as loudly as she could, trying to draw his attention to her and away from the peasants. Since she was in an advantageous position at the top of the stone stairs, her voice carried to the people below.

She watched, breath held, as Rogan reined his horse around to look at her. He remembers me, she thought with pleasure. And more, he desires me. Her heart began to hammer harder.

But then her breath stilled as she looked into his eyes. He seemed to be angry with her—not just angry, but enraged. No doubt this was how he looked at the Howards. I am not your first wife, she thought as she kept her chin upright and tried to still the trembling in her body. She wanted to run up the stairs to her bedroom and hide under the covers. She wanted to get away from this man's fierce gaze.

"I have won," she forced herself to say. "Come and be my slave." She turned away, no longer able to stand Rogan's glare, and went upstairs to the solar. Perhaps a few minutes alone in the chapel would calm her.

Rogan watched the woman go upstairs, then dismounted, handing the reins to a red-haired stableboy. He watched the boy walk away and he was somehow familiar.

"A woman's slave for a day?" Severn said from beside his brother, laughter in his voice.

Rogan turned his glare on Severn. "Did you give permission to drain the moat? And this?" He waved his arm to include the very different courtyard and the dead men in the cart. "Is all this your idea? When my back is turned—"

"Your wife deserves the credit, not me," Severn said, not losing his good humor. "She has done more in these few weeks than you and I—" He stopped as Rogan pushed past him and went up the stairs.

"Will the killings stop now?" one of the peasants dared to ask.

Severn had his own temper and he strode up the stairs two at a time. Zared was the only person in the Lord's Chamber. "Where is he?" Severn snapped.

"There." Zared pointed to the room they called the brooding room. It traditionally belonged to the head of the Peregrine family—their father, then Rowland, now Rogan. Its privacy was sacred. When a man was inside it, he was to be disturbed for nothing less than imminent attack.

Severn strode up the few steps to the door, then shoved it open without hesitation.

"Get the hell out of here," Rogan bellowed, his voice showing his shock.

"And listen to the men call my brother a coward? To hear them say he won't honor a wager?"

"A *woman's* wager," Rogan sneered.

"But a wager made in public, made in front of me, your men, even the peasants." Severn calmed himself. "Why not give the woman what she wants? She'll probably have you sing a duet with her or carry flowers for her. How bad can it be to be a woman's slave for a day? Especially this woman. All she seems to care about is a clean house and . . . and you. The Lord only knows why. She asked Zared and me hundreds of questions about you."

"And you no doubt told her everything. You seem to like talking to women. You and that married duchess of yours—"

"Don't say anything you'll regret," Severn said in warning. "Yes, I talk to Iolanthe. She has a head on her shoulders, and this wife of yours seems to have one, too. She was right when she said she'd get the peasants to present the thieves. For two years we've flogged people and beat them and they still steal us blind. Yet all she did was feed them and make them take a bath and they're groveling at her feet."

"They'll get so used to eating our cows they'll stop working and expect us to provide them with everything. What will they want next? Silk gowns? Furs to keep out the winter's chill? Peacocks' tongues for dinner?"

"I don't know," Severn answered honestly, "but the woman did win her wager with you."

"She's like the peasants. If I give her what she wants today, what will she demand tomorrow? Will she want to run the whole estate? Shall I let her judge the courts as well? Perhaps I should let her train the men."

Severn looked at his brother for a long moment. "Why are you afraid of her?"

"*Afraid* of her!" Rogan yelled. "I could break her in half with my bare hands. I could order her locked away. I could send her and her uppity maids to Bevan and never see her again. I could . . ." He stopped and sat down heavily in a chair.

Severn looked at his brother in amazement. Here was his big, strong, invincible brother, the man who never flinched before a battle, looking like a frightened child. He did not like to see it. Rogan was always sure of himself, always knew what to do. He never hesitated when a decision was to be made and never wavered once he'd decided what to do. No, Severn amended, Rogan didn't make decisions, he *knew* what to do.

Severn stepped toward the door. "I will make some excuse to the men. Of course no Peregrine will be a slave to a woman. The very idea is absurd."

"No, wait," Rogan said. He didn't look up. "I was a fool to have agreed to her wager. I had no idea she would produce the thieves. Go to her and ask her what she wants of me. Perhaps she wants a new gown or two. I don't want to spare the money, but I will."

When Severn didn't answer, Rogan looked up. "Well? You have something else to do? Go to her."

Severn felt warmth rising at his neck. "She might want something . . . ah, personal from you. If Io won me as a slave for a day, she'd probably tie me to a bed or—" He broke off at the look of interest in Rogan's eyes. "Who knows what your wife wants from you? Maybe she wants you to wear a donkey's tail and scrub the floors. Who knows? This woman listens more than she talks. I guess she knows more about us than we do about her."

"Like a good spy," Rogan said heavily.

Severn threw up his hands. "Spy or not, I like the smell of this place better. Go see what the woman wants. She seems simple enough." He left the room, closing the door behind him.

Moments later, Rogan left his brooding room and mounted the stairs to the solar. He had been in here in the last few years only to fetch a hawk. But the hawks were gone now and the walls looked almost damp with fresh whitewash. Three big tapestries hung on the walls, and his first thought was that he could sell them for gold. There were chairs, tables, stools, and women's sewing frames scattered about the room.

The women in the room stopped their chattering when they saw him and stared at him as if he were a demon from hell. Across the room, sitting on a window seat, was his wife. He remembered that calm stare of hers, but most of all he remembered the feel of her body.

149

"Out," was all he said, then stood there and waited while the scared women scurried past him.

When the two of them were alone, he didn't move any closer to her. The thirty or so feet separating him from his wife was fine, in his opinion. "What do you want of me?" he asked, his dark brows drawn together in a scowl. "I will not make a fool of myself before my men. I'll scrub no floors or wear any donkey's tail."

Liana blinked at him in astonishment, then smiled. "I have never received any pleasure from making another look like a fool." Very slowly, she reached up and removed her headdress, letting her long blonde hair cascade about her shoulders and down her back. She gave her head a little shake. "You must be tired after your journey. Come and sit by me. I have wine and sweetmeats here."

He stood where he was, glaring at her. "Do you try to entice me?"

Liana gave him a look of exasperation. "Yes, I do. And what is so wrong with that? You're my husband and I haven't seen you in weeks. Come, tell me what you did while you were away and I will tell you of what was found in the moat." She took a silver goblet from a table and poured it full of wine, then carried it to him. "Try it, it's from Spain."

Rogan took the wine and drank, his eyes never leaving hers, then he looked into the cup in surprise. The wine was delicious.

Liana laughed. "I brought some recipes with me and I persuaded your cooks to try them." She put her hand on his arm and gently began pulling him toward the window seat. "Oh, Rogan, I could have used your help. Your people are so stubborn, it was like talking to rocks. Here, try this. It's a pickled peach, and you might like this bread, there's no sand in it."

Before Rogan knew what he was doing, he was half sprawled on the softness of a window-seat cushion, eating one delicious food after another and wasting the day listening to a lot of frivolous nonsense about cleaning. He should, of course, be out training with his men, but he didn't move. "How many gold coins?" he found himself asking.

"We found six gold coins, twelve silver, and over a hundred copper pennies in the moat. There were also eight bodies, which we buried." She crossed herself. "Here, you look uncomfortable. Stretch out and put your head on my lap."

Rogan knew he should leave and he hadn't asked her yet about the wager, but he was tired and the wine was relaxing him. He stretched his legs on the long seat and put his head in her soft lap. The silk of her skirt felt good against his cheek and she caressed his temples and his hair with soft, smooth fingertips. When she began to hum, he closed his eyes.

Liana looked down at the beautiful man sleeping in her lap and she never wanted this moment to end. He looked so much younger when he was asleep, no scowl marring his handsomeness, the weight of responsibility not as heavy on his broad shoulders.

He slept peacefully for nearly an hour until Severn came clanging into the room wearing fifty pounds of armor.

War-trained Rogan sat up with a jolt. "What has happened?" he demanded, all softness leaving him.

Severn looked from his brother to his sister-in-law. He had never seen Rogan even look at a woman before sundown, much less put his head in her lap. It was startling to see such softness in his hard older brother. He found himself frowning.

Severn had been on his sister-in-law's side, but then

Rogan's hardheadedness often made Severn take an opposite side when arguing with his older brother. But he did not like this. He didn't like this woman making Rogan forget where he was supposed to be. Just hours ago Rogan had been dreading seeing his wife again after weeks away from her. Severn had been a bit amused at his brother's temerity, but perhaps Rogan had cause to fear the power of this woman. Could she make him forget his duties? His honor? She was peace-loving with the peasants, but did her nonviolent ways extend to making Rogan forget the Peregrines' war with the Howards?

Severn did not want to see his older brother change. He did not want Rogan's edges softened. It was one thing to play childish games with a woman and quite another to neglect duties to lay about with her in the afternoon.

"I had no idea today was a holy day and meant to be spent in pleasure," Severn said sarcastically. "I beg your pardon. I will leave the men to train alone, without me, and I will go to judge the peasants' disputes since you are too . . . busy."

"Go and train the men," Rogan snapped. "I will judge the courts, and if you do not want to find yourself eating that tongue of yours, keep it still."

Severn turned away in time to hide a smile. This was his brother, the man who scowled and growled, the man who treated him as if he were still a boy. It was all right for the woman to change the castle, but Severn didn't like her trying to change Rogan. As if she could! he thought with a grin. Nothing and no one could change Rogan.

Liana felt like throwing something at Severn. She saw what he was doing, saw the disbelief in his eyes when he'd seen Rogan asleep on a woman's lap. It seemed that everyone conspired to keep all softness from Rogan's life. She reached up to put her hand on his shoulder. "Perhaps I could help in the judgments. I often helped my father," she said. Actually, since her mother's death she had had sole responsibility for judging the peasants' disputes because her father couldn't be bothered.

Rogan was on his feet at once, scowling down at her. "You go too far, woman. *I* will make the judgments. *I* will give justice to my own peasants."

She was on her feet also. "And you have done a fine job of it until now, haven't you?" she said angrily. "Is starving them your idea of justice? Is letting the roofs of their houses fall on their heads what you think they need? If two men come to you with a dispute, what do you do, hang both of them? Justice! You have no idea what the word means. You only know how to punish."

As Liana looked at the rage on his face, she was sure he was going to add her to the long list of people he'd killed. In the heat of that rage, she almost backed away from him, but some great force of willpower made her stay where she was.

Suddenly, his eyes changed. "And what would you do to a man who stole another man's cow? Have them bathe together? Perhaps have them clean their fingernails twice a day as their punishment?"

"Why, no, I'd—" Liana began, then realized he was *teasing* her. Her eyes twinkled. "I'd have them live with your foul temper for a day. That and the stench of you after weeks without washing should be enough."

"Oh?" he said softly, and stepped toward her. "You do not seem to mind my stench."

He pulled her to him with one arm, and Liana

melted against him. No, she did not seem to mind his stench or his temper or his glares or his disappearances. He kissed her gently at first, then deeper and deeper, until he had to fully support her weight against his strong body.

He pulled his mouth from hers, still holding her. "And what do you want of me as your slave? Shall we spend all day in bed? Shall you stand over me wearing just my helmet and make demands of me?"

Liana opened her eyes. What an interesting idea, she thought, and almost said yes to his suggestion. But she controlled her lust. "I want you to wear peasants' clothes and attend a fair with me."

Rogan blinked a few times, then released her so abruptly she fell back against the window seat. "Not in my lifetime," he said, anger in his face again. "You ask me to go to my death. You *are* a spy. The Howards—"

"Damn the Howards!" Liana yelled. "I care nothing for them. I merely want you to spend a day with me. Alone. With no guard watching us, with no brother taunting you for daring to spend an hour with your wife. I want a whole day with you—*with* my clothes on. It cannot happen here, they would not leave you alone. So I ask you to stop, for one whole day, being Lord Rogan and share with me an ordinary day at a peasants' festival." She slowed down, put her hands on his forearms. "Please," she said. "They are such simple people, and their pleasures are so simple. It will be a day of dancing, of drinking, of eating. I believe they plan to put on a play. Can you not spare one day for me?"

Rogan's face did not betray how much her words appealed to him. A day spent in merriment . . . "I cannot go unarmed among the peasants," he said. "They—"

"Wouldn't recognize you. Half the men of the village are the offspring of your father—or you." She said the last with some disgust.

Rogan was shocked at the insolence of her words. He should have locked her away moments after he married her. "And you think they will not recognize you, either?"

"I will wear a patch over one eye. I do not know how I will disguise myself. The peasants will never believe their lord and mistress to be among them. One day, Rogan, please?" She leaned toward him and he could smell lavender from her clothes.

He heard himself say, "Yes," and didn't believe his own voice.

Liana flung her arms about his neck and kissed all the skin she could reach. She couldn't see the look of shock on Rogan's face that slowly softened. For just a moment, a quick, brief moment, he hugged her in return, not a sexual caressing, but just a little squeeze of pleasure.

He released her immediately. "I must go," he murmured, stepping away from her. "And you stay here and don't interfere in my court judgments."

She tried to look hurt, but she was too happy to succeed. "Of course I wouldn't. I'm a good and dutiful wife and I obey my husband in all things. I am merely trying to make your life more pleasant."

Rogan wasn't sure if she was making sport of him or not. He really did need to stop her insolence. "I must go," he repeated, then when she held her hand out to him and he found himself hesitating, he almost ran from the room. He'd go with her to the fair, he thought as he ran down the stairs, and afterward he'd send her to Bevan to stay. And he'd have his Days returned. Yes, he'd do that. This wife was getting entirely out of hand and interfering in his life.

But even as he was thinking of sending her away, he was also thinking of taking his helmet to their bedchamber that night.

CHAPTER
TEN

*L*iana looked at her husband's sleeping profile in the early morning light and smiled. She shouldn't be smiling at him, but she was. Last night she'd waited in bed for him for hours, but he hadn't come to her. At last, with her jaw set, a torch in her hand, she went downstairs to look for him.

She didn't have to go far. He was in the Lord's Chamber just below, alone with Severn, the two of them drunk almost to the point of oblivion.

Severn lifted his head from the table and looked at Liana. "We used to get drunk," he said, his words thick and slurred. "My brother and I used to be together all the time, but now he has a wife."

"And you *still* get drunk together," she said pointedly. "Here," she said to her husband. "Put your arm about my shoulders and let's go upstairs."

"Wives change things," Severn mumbled from behind her.

Liana had all she could do to help Rogan up the

157

stairs. "Your brother needs a wife," she said to Rogan. "Perhaps he'll leave us alone if he has his own wife."

"She has to have lots of money," Rogan said as he leaned heavily on her and concentrated on the steep, narrow spiral stairs. "Lots of money and lots of hair."

Liana smiled at his words as she pushed open the bedroom door. Rogan staggered to the bed and was asleep instantly. So much for a night of lovemaking, Liana thought, then snuggled against his dirty body. He was right. She didn't seem to mind his stench at all.

Now in the early morning, smiling down at him, she felt exhilarated and happy because today was the day he was to spend with her. For one whole day he was hers.

"My lady?" Joice's voice came through the door.

"Yes," Liana called, and Joice entered, careful the door didn't squeak.

Joice took one look at the sleeping Rogan and frowned. "You aren't ready? The others will be up soon and they will see you." Her voice was full of disapproval of her mistress's plan.

"Rogan," Liana said, leaning over her husband, whispering softly in his ear. "Rogan, my love, you must wake up. Today is the fair."

He put his hand up and touched her cheek. "Ah, Thursday," he murmured. "You get on top today."

"Thursday!" Liana gasped, then punched him in the ribs. "Wake up, you drunken dung heap! I'm your *wife,* not one of your women."

Rogan put his hand over his ear, then turned, blinking, to look at her. "What are you yelling about? Is something wrong?"

"You just called me by another woman's name." When he looked blank, having no idea why that should bother her, she sighed. "You have to get up. Today's the fair."

"What fair?"

"Men!" Liana said through her teeth. "The fair you promised to take me to. The wager, remember? I have peasants' clothes for us and we're to leave the castle the moment the gates are open. My maid is going to lock herself in this room all day, and I have put it about that what I want from you is a day in bed. No one will know we're gone."

Rogan sat up. "You have taken a lot on yourself," he said, frowning. "My men should know where I am at all times."

"If they do, they will hover about you and all the peasants will know who you are. Are you going back on your word?"

Rogan thought that women who talked of honor and keeping one's vows should be put in the same category with flying pigs. They shouldn't exist, and if they did, they were a damned nuisance since they wouldn't stay in their pens.

Liana leaned toward him, her beautiful hair spilling over his arms. "A day in pleasure," she said softly, "nothing but eating, drinking, dancing. No men to worry over. Nothing at all to worry about." She smiled as she had an inspiration. "And you might be able to hear whether the peasants know anything about the Howards' doings."

Rogan considered that. "Where are the clothes?"

Once he'd made up his mind, Liana was able to get him to move quickly. When they were dressed, she was sure no one would recognize them—as long as Rogan remembered to drop his shoulders and keep his head slightly bowed. Peasants didn't walk the way the lord of the manor did.

They left the bedroom and got to the gate just as Rogan's men were lifting the portcullis. No one looked at them. Once across the drawbridge, over the empty moat, Rogan stopped. "Where are the horses?"

"Peasants don't ride horses. They walk."

Rogan balked. Just stood there unmoving.

Her first thought was to remind him that he used to walk with Jeanne Howard, but she restrained herself. "Come on," she coaxed. "We'll miss the play if we don't hurry. Or maybe I can purchase that old donkey over there. For a few coins I imagine he'll—"

"There's no need to spend money. I can walk as well as the next man."

They walked the four miles to the village together, and around them swarmed many people, strangers arriving to sell goods, travelers, relatives from other villages. As they neared the village, Liana could feel Rogan begin to relax. His eyes were still wary, for he was a soldier and he watched the people suspiciously, but when they all seemed to be laughing and looking forward to the day, some of his suspicion left him.

"Look there," Liana called, pointing at the pennants flying from the tops of the tents set up by the visiting merchants. "What shall we have for breakfast?"

"We should have eaten before we left," Rogan said solemnly.

Liana grimaced and hoped he wasn't going to starve them all day in order to save a few pennies. The fair had been set up on a barren field outside the walls of the village.

"This field will never grow grain again," Rogan grumbled. "Not after all these feet have trampled it."

Liana gritted her teeth and wondered if taking Rogan to the fair had been such a good idea after all. If he spent all day looking at what the peasants did wrong, he'd have a lot to punish them for later.

"The play!" Liana said, pointing toward a big wooden stage that had been set up at one end of the field. "Some of the players have come from London, and the whole village has been working on it for the last week. Come on or we won't get a seat." She took Rogan's hand and began pulling him forward, leading him to a place on one of the benches in the middle of the audience. Near her was a woman with a basket of rotten vegetables that she could sling at the performers if she didn't like what they did.

Liana nudged Rogan to look at the vegetables. "We should have brought some too."

"A waste of food," Rogan growled, and Liana wondered again if this had been such a good idea.

There was a patched and dirty curtain across the stage and now a man dressed in harlequin clothes, one leg red, one black, opposite arm red, the other black, with a black and red tunic, came out to announce that the name of the play was *The Taming of Lord Buzzard.*

For some reason, this announcement made the people around them howl with laughter.

"I guess it's a comedy," Liana said, then added, looking at Rogan's dour face, "I *hope* it's a comedy."

The curtain was pulled aside to reveal a bleak scene: Bare trees in pots stood at the back, and in the foreground was an ugly old man squatting down over a heap of straw that was dyed red to look like a fire. He held a stick out that had three rats on it.

"Come on, daughter, dinner is almost ready," the man called.

From behind the curtain to the right came a woman —or what looked to be a woman. She turned toward the audience and she was actually a very ugly man.

The audience howled. In her arms was a fat straw doll, and when she bent to put the "baby" down then stood, the audience saw that she had an enormous bosom, so enormous its weight tipped her forward. She looked at the rats. "They look delicious, Father," she said in a high voice as she squatted down across from him.

Liana smiled up at Rogan and saw that he was barely watching the play. He was looking at the people around them as if he were trying to find enemies.

From the left side of the stage came another actor, a tall man, his shoulders thrown back, his head held high. On his head was a red wool wig and on his nose was a paper beak like a hawk's.

"What is going on here?" the tall actor demanded. "I am Lord Buzzard and you are eating my livestock."

"But, my lord," the father whined, "they are only rats."

"But they are *my* rats," Lord Buzzard said arrogantly.

Liana began to feel a little nervous. This play couldn't possibly be a parody of Rogan, could it?

On the stage, Lord Buzzard grabbed the old man by the scruff of the neck and pushed him face down into the straw fire.

"No, my lord," cried the ugly daughter as she stood up, her tattered cloak falling away from her vast bosom.

"Ah-ha!" Lord Buzzard said, leering. "Come here, my beauty."

The reference to the woman-dressed man as a beauty made the audience laugh.

The daughter took a step backward as Lord Buzzard came toward her. He kicked the straw baby with his foot, sending it flying across the stage.

It was then that Lord Buzzard opened his long cloak. Affixed around his waist, strapped to his legs, was an enormous set of genitals. It was padded straw, eighteen inches long, eight inches around, and below it hung two big round gourds.

Liana's heart dropped to her feet. "Let's go," she said to Rogan, said really loudly, because the audience was screaming with laughter.

Rogan's eyes were now fixed on the stage. He clamped a hand down on Liana's shoulder and held her in place. She had no choice but to watch.

Onstage, Lord Buzzard, with his coat held open, went across the stage after the ugly woman until they were out of sight. Instantly, one of Rogan's red-haired sons came onto the stage and took a bow. He was obviously the product of Lord Buzzard's union with the woman.

From stage left came an old woman carrying a dark bundle, which she put in the middle of the stage, not far from where the father still lay in the straw fire.

"Now, daughter, we will at last be warm," she said, and from the right came another very ugly man dressed as a woman. Only this man stuck out behind instead of in front. He had padded buttocks that could have been used as a shelf and an absolutely flat chest.

While the audience was watching this, another of Rogan's red-haired sons ran across the stage, sending the audience into new gales.

Liana didn't dare look at Rogan. Tomorrow he'd probably order the whole village drawn and quartered.

Onstage, as the mother and her jut-butted daughter were warming their hands over the pile of black, Lord Buzzard strutted onstage, his paper hawk beak looking even larger.

"You are stealing my fuel," Lord Buzzard shouted.

"But it is only cow dung," the old woman wailed. "We were freezing to death."

"You want fire, I will give you fire," Lord Buzzard said. "Take her and burn her."

From the left came two men, big, fierce-looking brutes with scars painted on their faces so that they looked like monsters more than men. They took the old woman's arms, as she wailed and screamed, and pulled her to the back of the stage, where they tied her to one of the barren trees and placed red-dyed straw bundles about her feet.

Meanwhile, Lord Buzzard looked at the daughter. "Ah, come to me, my beauty," he said.

The ugly man playing the daughter turned to the audience and made a face so ugly—he pushed his lower lip up over the tip of his nose—that even Liana gave a bit of a laugh. Once again Lord Buzzard pulled his cloak back to reveal the grotesque genitals and chased the "girl" off the stage, while behind them the mother screamed. Two red-haired boys came running from opposite sides of the stage and crashed into each other.

"There's more where we came from," one boy announced gleefully to the audience.

Liana was about to insist to Rogan that they leave when she got an even greater shock. From the left came a young girl, very pretty, wearing a long white gown and a blonde wool wig that reached all the way to her feet. Liana knew this actress was supposed to be her. And how would these cruel people portray her?

From the right came Lord Buzzard and a man dressed as a priest; the priest began to read a marriage ceremony. Lord Buzzard, obviously bored, didn't look at the pretty girl in white. Instead, he played to the audience, making kissing faces at the girls, winking, flipping his cloak open now and then to show what he had. The girl in white kept her head down, her hands clasped.

When the priest pronounced them married, Lord Buzzard grabbed the girl's shoulders then picked her up and began shaking her. Coins fell out of her clothes, and Lord Buzzard's men ran onto the stage and scurried to pick them up. When there was no more money falling from the lady in white, he set her down, turned his back on her, and strutted offstage, still flirting with the audience and flipping his cloak. The lady walked to the back of the stage, her head bowed.

Immediately, onstage came a man leading a cow. Lord Buzzard met him center stage.

"What is this?" Lord Buzzard demanded.

"My lord," the man said, "this cow ate your vegetables."

Lord Buzzard patted the cow's head. "Cows need to eat." He started to walk away, but then turned back to glare at the man. "Did *you* eat any of my vegetables?"

"I had one bite of turnip that fell from the cow's mouth," the man said.

"Hang him!" Lord Buzzard ordered, and his scarred knights hurried onstage.

The man fell to his knees. "But, my lord, I have six children to feed. Please have mercy."

Lord Buzzard looked at his men. "Hang the whole family. There'll be fewer to feed."

The knights dragged the man to the back of the stage and put a rope around his neck. He stood beside the man in the fire, the old woman at the stake, and the lady in white.

The lady looked at these people and shook her head sadly.

Onstage sauntered two pretty, plump young women

who Liana recognized as two of the Days. The audience, especially the men, cheered and whistled and the Days stretched and bent over and did what they could to show off their voluptuous bodies. Liana stole a look at Rogan. He was sitting as immobile as a statue, his eyes and attention totally on the stage.

On instinct, she reached across him and took his hand in hers, and to her surprise, he clung to her hand.

She looked back at the stage. Lord Buzzard came back onstage, halted at the sight of the Days, then leaped at them, his cloak flying open. The three of them went tumbling to the floorboards.

It was at this sight that the lady in white came alive. She hadn't minded when her husband had ignored her at their wedding or shaken coins from her or when he'd hanged a man for eating a bit of turnip a cow had spit out—but she minded about the other women.

She ripped off her white dress to reveal a red one underneath. From behind a pot containing a bare tree, she took a red headdress with tall paper flames attached to it and jammed it on her head over the blonde wig.

"The Fire Lady!" the audience yelled in delight.

The red-dressed Fire Lady took bundles of red-painted straw from the feet of the old woman tied to the tree and began throwing them at the three people tumbling about in the center of the stage. The Days jumped up, screaming and acting as if they were putting out fires from their clothes and hair, and ran offstage.

The Fire Lady looked down at Lord Buzzard and from her pocket she withdrew a big collar such as used to tie up a mean dog. She fastened it onto Lord Buzzard's neck, took a leash, and led him offstage.

The audience yelled and cheered and jumped on the benches and danced, while onstage all the dead people came to life again. Six of Rogan's sons came out and threw flower-covered nets over the dead trees so that it looked as if even the trees were coming back to life. The people onstage began to sing and all the actors came onstage, the Fire Lady leading Lord Buzzard on all fours. He tried to flip his cloak aside to show the audience, but the Fire Lady smacked him across the head and he was quiet again.

At long last, the curtain was pulled closed, and when the audience stopped cheering and laughing, they began to file out of the benches.

Rogan and Liana sat still, neither of them moving, hands clasped in Rogan's lap.

"I don't guess the peasants are so simple, after all," Liana managed to say at last.

Rogan turned to look at her, his eyes telling her what an understatement her words were.

CHAPTER ELEVEN

The audience filed out of the benches, laughing, slapping one another's backs, and recalling one scene of the play after another. "Did you see—?" "I liked the part where—"

Liana and Rogan sat where they were, hands clasped, until the last person had left the audience.

Gradually, as her shock left her, Liana felt her body filling with anger. In the last weeks she had dared her husband's rage for these people. She had exhausted herself seeing that they were fed and clothed, and they repaid her with this . . . this ridiculing farce.

She clutched Rogan's hand. "We'll go back and get your men," she said, anger pounding in her temples. "We shall see if these people will be so ungrateful after your men get through with them. They think they have seen the Peregrine wrath, but they have seen nothing."

Rogan didn't say anything, but when she looked at him, he didn't appear to be angry as much as thoughtful.

"Well?" she said. "You didn't want to come, and you were right. We'll return and—"

"Who played Lord Buzzard?" Rogan asked, interrupting her.

"He looked like one of your father's by-blows," Liana snapped. "Shall I return alone?" She stood and started to move past him, but he still held her hand and wouldn't let her pass.

"I'm hungry," he said. "Do you think they sell food here?"

Liana gaped at him. A moment ago he'd refused to part with the few pennies needed to buy them food. "The play didn't make you angry?"

He shrugged as if he didn't care, but there was something deeper in his eyes—something that Liana meant to discover. "I never killed anybody for eating my rats," he said somewhat defiantly. "They can have all the rats they want."

"What about using your cow dung for fuel?" she asked softly. She was standing between his big legs and he was still holding her hand. Somehow, this hand-holding was more intimate than their few couplings. He said the play didn't bother him, but the way he was holding on to her told another story.

"I have never *killed* anyone for that," he said, looking off into the distance, "but the dung does fertilize the fields."

"I see," Liana said. "Flogging?"

Rogan didn't answer, but his dark skin seemed to flush. She felt very motherly toward him at that moment. He wasn't a vicious man, a man who enjoyed killing or got pleasure from seeing others suffer. He had been trying to protect his family and provide for them the best way he could.

"I am starving," she said, smiling at him, "and I

saw a stall heaped with cream cakes. Perhaps a few cakes and some buttermilk will cheer both of us."

He allowed her to lead him away, and she wanted very much to know what he was thinking. When he reached inside his coarse woolen peasant garb and withdrew a little leather bag and gave the cream-cakes vendor some pennies, she felt elated. She couldn't be sure, of course, but she doubted if he'd ever spent money on a woman before.

He bought them a mug of buttermilk and they shared the mug while the vendor waited for the return of the wooden cup.

With food in her belly, Liana began to be able to think of the play with less anger. In fact, looking back on it, it was almost humorous. She would never have guessed that the peasants could be so daring—or so honest.

She looked into the mug and tried to keep from smiling. "They may have been wrong about the rats, but they were right about certain physical attributes of the lord," she said.

Rogan heard her, but at first he didn't understand her meaning. Then, remembering the outrageously exaggerated straw genitals of Lord Buzzard, he began to feel the blood creep to his face. "You have a sharp tongue on you," he said, meaning to chastise the wench.

"If I remember correctly, you liked my tongue."

"Women shouldn't talk of such things," he said sternly, but his eyes betrayed him.

Liana knew by the way he was looking at her that she had sparked his interest. "Did you *really* bed ugly women? Ugly but sticking out in front or back?"

He looked as if he were about to reprimand her again, but instead his eyes softened. "Your father should have beat some manners into you. Here," he said, taking the empty mug away from her. "If you are through eating me into poverty, let's go see the games over there."

Her teasing had pleased him and pleasing him made her feel joyous. As they walked, she slipped her hand into his and he did not push her away.

"Will it change back?" he asked, looking ahead as they walked.

She had no idea what he was talking about.

"Your hair," he said.

Liana squeezed his hand and laughed in delight. Joice had dyed her blonde hair and eyebrows black so that the peasants wouldn't recognize Liana's distinctive hair. There wasn't much of it visible beneath the coarse linen covering pinned over her braided hair. "It will wash out," she said, then looked up at him. "Perhaps you'll help me wash it."

He looked down at her, desire in his eyes. "Perhaps."

They walked on together, saying nothing, holding hands, and Liana felt jubilant.

Rogan paused on the outskirts of a crowd of people. He could see over their heads, but Liana couldn't. She stood on tiptoe, then squatted down, but she couldn't see through the people. She tugged on Rogan's sleeve. "I can't see," she said when he looked at her. She had a romantic vision of his lifting her to his shoulders and holding her, but instead, acting as if he owned the place—which he did—he pushed his way through the crowd to the front. "Don't call attention to us," she hissed, but he paid no attention to her. She gave weak smiles of apology to the people around them as she was pulled along by Rogan.

The people were looking with curiosity at Rogan, especially at his hair curling along his neck beneath his woolen hood. Liana began to stiffen in fear. If these people, hating the Peregrines as they did, should find out the master was alone and unprotected among them, they would no doubt murder him.

"Another of the old lord's bastards," she heard a man near them whisper. "Never seen this one before."

She began to relax and for once thanked God for the fertility of the Peregrines. Still clutching Rogan's hand, she looked at what he did. On a flat grassy place, in the middle of a large circle, were two men, both naked from the waist up, fighting each other with long wooden poles held in both hands. One man, short, muscular, with short arms, looked to be a forester or a woodcutter. He was very ordinary-looking.

Liana's eyes went to the other man—as did the eyes of every other woman in the crowd outside the circle. This was the man who'd played Lord Buzzard. He'd looked good onstage, but now, half-nude, skin glistening with sweat, he was magnificent.

Not as magnificent as Rogan, Liana reminded herself and stepped closer to her husband.

Rogan was intent on the fight, interested in the way this half-brother of his handled himself. He was crude and untrained, of course, but there was speed in his movements. The little woodcutter was no match for him.

Rogan's attention was taken from the fight when his wife stepped closer to him. He glanced down at her. She was watching his half-brother with wide-eyed interest, and Rogan began to frown. It was almost as if she found this half-Peregrine desirable.

Rogan had never felt jealousy before. He'd shared the Days or any of his women with his brothers, with his men. As long as he wasn't inconvenienced, he didn't care what the women did. But right now he didn't like the way his wife was looking at his scrawny, weak, bumbling, incompetent, red-haired—

172

"Think you could beat 'im?" said a toothless old man standing next to Rogan.

Rogan looked down his nose at the old man.

The man cackled, his bad breath filling the air. "Just like them Peregrines," he said loudly. "The old master bred arrogance in his sons."

The Peregrine half-brother in the ring glanced at the old man, then at Rogan, and in his surprise, he looked away from his opponent. The woodcutter clipped the young man on the side of the head. The man stepped back, put his hand to his temple, and looked at the blood on his fingertips. Then, with a look of disgust on his face, he sent the woodcutter sprawling in three hard blows.

Immediately, he went to stand before Rogan on the sidelines.

Liana saw that the two men were about the same age, but Rogan was heavier and, to her eyes, much, much more handsome. Beside her, a young woman gave a sigh of lust. Liana clutched Rogan's hand hard with her own and plastered herself to the side of him.

"So, I have another brother," the young man said.

His eyes were as piercing as Rogan's, Liana thought, and something in them made her sure that he knew who Rogan was. "Don't—" Liana began.

"Shall we give the people a fight or not?" the man challenged. "Or are you ruled by a woman?" He lowered his voice. "As Lord Rogan is?"

Liana felt her heart sink, for she knew Rogan would never resist the challenge. The two of them had politely ignored the last scene of the play, when the Fire Lady had collared Lord Buzzard, but she knew Rogan was aware of it. He wouldn't allow himself to be insulted twice in one day.

Rogan released her hand and stepped into the

circle. Liana knew she could do or say nothing without putting both their lives in jeopardy. Her breath held, she watched the two men walk together into the ring, facing each other. They were so much alike: same hair, same eyes, same square, determined jaw.

Rogan looked down at the pole on the ground, then to Liana's horror, he removed his concealing hood, then pulled his shirt off over his head. There was a moment's pleasure as he tossed his garments to her and she caught them, but then Liana's fear returned. Surely someone would recognize him now. She didn't like to think *who* would recognize him, since it could be one or all of the women he'd bedded. "Half the village," she muttered to herself.

She scanned the crowd and saw two of the Days standing on the opposite side of the circle. Now their faces showed puzzlement, but Liana had no doubt that soon the women would realize who Rogan was.

Swiftly, she began to make her way toward the women.

"You say one word and you will regret it," she said when she reached the women. One of the Days cowered, her face showing her fear, but the other woman was bolder and smarter. She saw the danger Liana and Rogan were in.

"I want my son to be raised as a knight," the woman said.

Liana opened her mouth to refuse this outrageous and bold request, but she closed it. "You will see that no one else knows," she countered.

The woman looked Liana in the eyes. "I will tell people he comes from a village to the south and that I have met him before. My son?"

Liana couldn't help admiring this woman who risked so much for her child. "Your sons will be educated and trained. Send them to me tomorrow."

She moved away from the women and made her way back to where she had been.

Rogan and his half-brother were circling each other, long poles held horizontally in their hands. They were imposing men, both young and strong, broad-shouldered, slim-hipped, muscles well defined.

But it didn't take half a brain to see who was the better fighter. Rogan was obviously testing his half-brother, toying with him to see what he could do, while the half-brother, anger in his eyes, was fighting with all his might. The brother attacked and Rogan easily sidestepped, then quickly brought his pole to the back of his brother's knees.

"Are you used to fighting only women?" Rogan taunted.

Anger was getting the best of his brother, causing him to make stupid mistakes.

"No one has ever beaten Baudoin before," the toothless old man next to Liana said. "He'll not like being bested."

"Baudoin," Liana said aloud, frowning. She didn't think it was a good idea for Rogan to make an enemy of this brother as he was doing. Rogan had spent most of his life training with sticks and swords, while this young man no doubt spent most of his time behind a plow.

After a while, it was obvious to everyone watching that Rogan was growing tired of this game that gave no challenge. He stood in front of his brother, put his pole in one hand, standing it on end and . . . stretched.

It was an insulting move, and Liana's sympathies went to Baudoin at being so humiliated.

Baudoin's eyes turned dark with rage, and he lunged at Rogan, murder in his face. The crowd gasped.

Barely looking at his brother, Rogan sidestepped and brought his stick crashing down on the back of Baudoin's head. The young man went sprawling, face down, unconscious, in the mud and grass.

Without a look of concern for his brother, Rogan stepped over his inert body and walked toward Liana, took his clothes from her, and slipped them over his head. He pushed his way through the crowd, his shoulders and head back, not looking at Liana but obviously expecting her to follow him. He ignored the peasants about him, who clapped him on the shoulder in congratulations and asked him to have a drink with them.

Rogan was feeling very proud of himself. He'd bested the man who'd made his wife look at him with desire. He'd shown her who was the best man. And he was proud of how he'd done it. There would be no doubt in her mind as to who was the better man. He could have beat that overconfident half-brother with one hand tied behind his back.

Very aware that Liana was following him, he led her toward the woods. When she showed how pleased she was with him, he wanted to be alone with her. Once, after he'd won a tournament, two young ladies had come to his tent to congratulate him. That had been a night to remember!

But now all he wanted was his wife's praise. Perhaps she'd kiss him the way she had when he'd said he'd go to the fair with her. He didn't stop walking until he was deep in the woods, then he turned and looked at her.

She didn't throw her arms about his neck, nor did she give him one of her smiles that he'd come to know: a smile that was beginning to make him think of pleasure and softness and laughter.

"I won," he said, his eyes alive.

"Yes, you won," she said flatly.

He didn't understand her tone. It was almost as if she were angry with him. "I beat the man rather easily."

"Oh yes, it was very easy for you. Easy to humiliate him, to make the people laugh at him."

Rogan didn't understand her and he didn't try. She had gone too far this time. He drew back his hand to strike her.

"Will you beat me now? Will you beat someone else who is weaker than you? Will you beat *all* your relatives? Me, your wife, your brothers. Why not get your children and tie them to the trees and flog them?"

Rogan knew the woman was crazy; she made no sense. He lowered his hand and turned away from her to walk back to the village.

Liana planted herself in front of him. "What were you thinking of to beat the boy so badly? You made him look like a fool."

Rogan's own temper came to the surface. He grabbed her shoulders and yelled into her face. "Did you hate seeing him made a fool of? Would you rather it was *me* on the ground? Would you have comforted *him* with his head in your lap?" He dropped his hands from her shoulders. He had revealed too much of himself. He walked past her.

Liana stood alone for a moment, staring at the ground as she thought about his words. His meaning came slowly to her and she had to run to catch him. She stood before him. "You were jealous," she said, wonder in her voice as she looked up at him.

He didn't answer but walked around her.

She stepped in front of him again and put her hands on his chest. "Did you really beat that boy so badly just to impress me?"

Rogan looked into the distance over her head. "I wanted to test his strength and quickness, and when I'd done that, I was finished with him." He glanced at her, then away. "He is not a boy. He is my age or perhaps older."

Liana began to smile. She didn't like what he'd done to his half-brother, but oh how good it felt to think her husband was jealous of the way she'd looked at another man. "He may be as old as you, but he's not as strong as you or as skilled nor as handsome." She took his arm and tried to lead him into the forest, but he stood where he was.

"I have been too long away from my men. We should return to the castle." His body was rigid.

"But the wager was for you to be my slave for a whole day," Liana said, unable to keep from whining slightly. "Come, we'll sit here in the woods. We won't have to return to the fair."

Rogan found himself following the woman. Somehow she was able to make him forget duty and responsibility. He had neglected his work more since he'd married her than he had ever done before.

"Come, sit here beside me," she said, indicating a grassy, flower-strewn patch beside a little stream.

She could see by his face that he was still angry and she started to smile at him when a movement in the trees behind him caught her eye. "Look out!" she managed to shout.

Rogan instinctively sidestepped and so missed the knife that came at his back.

Liana stood where she was and watched, horror on her face, as Baudoin attacked Rogan with a knife. She saw blood on Rogan's arm, but in the frenzy of activity, she couldn't tell how bad the wound was.

This time Rogan did not have such an easy time of

subduing his half-brother. Baudoin was enraged, and he meant to kill.

Liana could do little more than watch as the men wrestled with each other, tumbling, rolling over and over on the grass, the knife flashing between them now and then. Rage added strength to Baudoin, and Liana could see that Rogan was fighting for his life.

Glancing about her, she saw a short, stout tree branch. She picked it up, weighing it in her hands, then moved closer to the two powerful men. She had to jump back as they rolled near her, then step forward when they rolled away. The two heads, their faces buried in each other's bodies, were so alike she was afraid she'd hit the wrong man.

Then there was a chance. Baudoin wrenched his right arm free and held the knife above Rogan's throat.

The next moment he collapsed helplessly as Liana brought the club down on his head.

For a moment Rogan didn't move. He lay there, his limp half-brother sprawled on top of him. He didn't like to admit to himself that he might have been killed if it hadn't been for a . . . a woman.

He pushed Baudoin off him and stood, unable to look at his wife. "We'll go back and send the men for him," he murmured.

"And what will your men do to him?" Liana asked as she examined the wound on Rogan's arm. The skin was barely broken.

"Execute him."

"Your own *brother?*" Liana asked.

Rogan frowned. "It will be quick. No burning or torturing."

Liana was thoughtful for a moment. "You go and get the men. I will join you in a while."

Rogan looked at her and his pulse pounded in his temple. "You mean to stay here with him?"

Her eyes met his. "I mean to help him escape your injustice."

"My—?" Rogan said, aghast. "He just tried to *kill* me. If that means nothing to you, it means a great deal to me."

She went to him and put her hands on his arms. "You have lost so many brothers, and most of them were half-brothers. How can you bear to lose another? Take this man and train him. Train him to be one of your knights."

He stepped away from her, gaping at her. "Do you tell me how to run my men? Do you ask me to live with a man who tried to kill me? Do you hope to rid yourself of me so you can have this man?"

Liana threw her hands in the air in a gesture of helplessness. "What a fool you are! I chose *you*. Do you have any idea how many suitors I had? They desperately wanted my father's money, and they courted me in every possible way. They wrote poetry to me, sang songs to my loveliness. But *you!* You shoved me in a bog and told me to wash your clothes and, fool that I am, I agreed to marry you. And what have I received in return for my stupidity? Other women in your bed while you ignore me. The stench of you. And now you dare to accuse me of liking other men. I have cleaned that cesspit you call a home. I have given you better food, I have been an enthusiastic bed partner, and you dare to accuse me of adultery? Go on, kill the man. What do I care? I will return to my father and you can have all the gold and no troublesome wife."

Her anger was leaving her and she felt tired and deflated, and near to tears. She had failed with him. Just as Helen had warned, she had failed.

"What bog?" was all Rogan said after a moment.

Liana was swallowing her tears. "By the pond," she said tiredly. "You made me wash your clothes. Shall we go now? He will waken soon."

Rogan stepped toward her, put his fingertips under her chin, and lifted her head to look at him. "I had forgotten that. So you're the hellion who beat the holes in my clothes?"

She jerked away from him. "I replaced your clothes. Shall we go now? Or perhaps I should leave and you can stay behind and kill your brother. Perhaps he has sisters and you can abduct them and get yourself a new set of Days."

Rogan caught her arm and turned her to face him. Yes, she was that girl at the pool. He remembered lying there, aware that he was being watched and pleased to find it was a pretty woman. She'd shown fire then and even more fire the night she'd put a torch to his bed.

He gave her something he hadn't given a woman in years: He smiled at her.

Liana felt her knees grow weak at his smile. His handsome face was transformed into boyish good looks. Was this the man his first wife had seen? If so, how could she have ever left him?

"So," he said, "you agreed to marry me because I tossed you in a bog?"

No matter how good he looked, she wasn't going to answer him—not when he used that tone of voice. He made her sound like a brainless, lustful peasant girl, no more than one of his Days. She turned away, her back straight, head held high, and started back toward the village.

He caught her and, to her disbelief, lifted her in his arms like a baby, then tossed her high. "What do you have planned for me now? Another bed burning? Or maybe you'll set the whole castle on fire this time?" He tossed her up again. "For someone so little you have a mighty way of getting what you want."

Her arms went about his neck to keep from falling.

"That's better," he said, and kissed her neck.

Liana's anger melted and Rogan knew it because she could feel his silent laughter against her neck. "You!" she said, and smacked his shoulder. "Put me down. Are you going to kill your brother?"

He looked at her and shook his head. "You don't let go of something, do you?"

She put her hand up and caressed his cheek. "No," she said softly. "When I decide I want something, I never let it go."

His eyes turned serious as he looked at her as if he were puzzled about something, and he started to reply to her, but a groan from Baudoin on the ground behind them caught his attention. Rogan put Liana down so quickly she stumbled against a tree.

When she recovered her balance, she saw Rogan standing over his half-brother, the knife in his hands.

Liana began to pray. She prayed fervently, with all her heart, for her husband to show mercy to this young man.

"And how will you kill me?"

She opened her eyes to see Baudoin standing straight and proud before Rogan, showing no fear.

"Fire?" Baudoin asked. "Or will your torturers work on me? Are your men hidden in the woods and spying on us? Will they burn the village because of what was in the play?"

Liana looked at the two men, Rogan with his back to her, and held her breath. She knew her husband could kill Baudoin easily if he wanted, but she prayed he would not. Rogan tossed the knife from one hand to the other and remained silent.

"What do you do to earn your keep?" Rogan asked at last.

The question seemed to startle Baudoin. "I buy and sell wool."

"Are you an honest man?"

Baudoin's face showed his anger. "More honest than the man who fathered us. More honest than my illustrious brothers. *I* do not leave my children to starve."

Liana could not see Rogan's face, but she feared Baudoin's taunts were signing his own death warrant.

When Rogan spoke, it was softly and somewhat hesitantly. "I have lost several brothers in the past few years. I cannot lose more. If I were to bring you into my household, would you swear an oath of fidelity to me? Would you honor it?"

Baudoin was stunned—so stunned he could not speak. He had hated his half-brothers in their castle on the hill all his life. He had lived in poverty while they had had everything.

Liana could see Baudoin's hesitation and she could guess its meaning. She could also guess that Rogan's generosity would soon turn to anger if it weren't readily accepted. Quickly, she stepped between the two men.

"You have children?" she said to Baudoin. "How many? What are their ages? When you come to live with us, I'll see that they're educated. They can go to school with Rogan's sons."

"What sons?" Rogan said, glowering down at her. This wool merchant was refusing to pay homage to him! He should have killed him an hour ago, but he hadn't because of his interfering wife. He stepped toward her.

Liana took Baudoin's arm in such a way that she was protecting him and herself. "All your little red-haired sons, of course," she said brightly. "Can your wife sew?" she asked Baudoin. "I need some women who can sew. Or spin. Or weave. When you're out training with Rogan, she can stay with me. Rogan, why don't you tell your *brother"*—she emphasized the word—"how hard you'll work him. Perhaps he'd rather continue buying and selling wool."

"I am to try to *persuade* him?" Rogan said in disbelief. "Shall I tell him of the comfort of the bed? Or tantalize him with offers of meat every day?"

Baudoin was recovering from his shock. He had inherited their father's intelligence and no one had ever accused him of being a fool. "Forgive my hesitancy, my lord," he said loudly, taking Rogan's attention from his wife. "I am most grateful for your offer and I . . ." He paused and his eyes hardened. "I will defend the Peregrine name with my life."

Rogan looked at the man for a long moment, and Liana could see that he was wrestling with something inside himself. Please, she prayed to herself, please believe him.

"Come to me tomorrow," Rogan said at last. "Now, go."

When Baudoin was gone, tears of relief came to Liana's eyes. She went to Rogan and put her arms about his neck and kissed him. "Thank you," she said. "Thank you so much."

"Will you be so thankful when I am returned with that man's sword in my heart?"

"I do not think . . ." she began, but she didn't *know* that Rogan wasn't correct. "Perhaps I have made an error. Perhaps you should make him a clerk or send him to your other castle or—"

"Are you turning coward on me?"

"When it comes to your safety, I will risk nothing."

"Women have said such to me before," he said, "and it turned out they were not to be trusted."

She put her lips next to his. "Who said this to you? Jeanne Howard?"

One moment she was in his arms and the next she was on the ground, looking up into the face that had made grown men tremble.

CHAPTER TWELVE

*H*e turned on his heel and started walking quickly through the forest, away from her and away from the village.

Liana began to run after him. She was glad for the short peasant skirt as she leaped over logs and around trees. But she couldn't catch Rogan. He was out of sight within minutes.

"Damn him and his temper," she said aloud, stamping her foot in anger.

She hadn't realized she was so close to the edge of the stream or that the land fell away so sharply. The bank gave way under her and she went sliding downward, on her back, for about twenty feet, screaming as she went.

When she hit bottom, Rogan was there, a short sword drawn from someplace under his tunic, standing over her.

"Who did this?" he demanded.

Liana had no time to bless her good luck at having

brought him back. "I fell," she explained. "I was chasing you and I fell."

"Oh," he said, uninterested, as he put his sword back under his rough garment.

He stood there looking as if he had no idea of what to do next. "Carry me to the water, slave," Liana commanded, holding out her hand in an arrogant way. When he didn't move, she said, "Please."

Bending, he picked her up in his arms and walked her to the stream. She put her arms around his neck and nuzzled against him. "Was Jeanne pretty?" she asked.

He dropped her into the ice-cold water.

Sputtering, Liana came up for air. Rogan was already walking away again. "You're the worst slave there ever was!" she called after him. "You're going to forfeit the wager."

As she stood up in the water, he came back to her and by the look on his face Liana almost wished he hadn't.

"I'll forfeit no wager to you, woman," he said in a low growl. "There are some things in my life that are no one else's business and . . . and . . ."

"Jeanne Howard," she said. Her teeth were beginning to chatter.

"Yes, that woman has caused the deaths of—"

"Basil and James," she supplied.

He stopped and glared at her. "Do you make light of me?" he whispered.

Her eyes were pleading with him. "Rogan, I've never meant to make light of something as awful as death. I was merely asking my husband about his first wife. Every woman is curious about the other women in her husband's life. I've just heard so much about Jeanne and—"

"Who told you?"

"The Lady." When Rogan obviously didn't know who she meant, she said, "I believe she's Severn's lady, although she's somewhat older than he is."

Rogan's face lost its hard look. "I wouldn't dare remind Iolanthe that she's older than Severn if I were you." He paused. "Io told you about . . ."

He didn't seem able to say his first wife's name, and this bothered Liana. Was he still so much in love with her? "I've never met Iolanthe, but the Lady mentioned her. Rogan, I'm freezing. Couldn't we talk over there? In the sun?"

Twice he'd walked away from her when she'd mentioned that woman's name and both times he'd returned, and now he was considering remaining with her to "talk." He grabbed Liana's hand and pulled her from the stream.

When they were in the sun, he folded his arms across his chest and set his jaw. He was never, ever again in his life going to agree to spend a day with a woman—especially not this one. She had a talent for picking at his sorest spots. "What is it you want to know?" he asked.

"Was she pretty? Were you very much in love with her? Is she the reason the castle was so dirty? Did you vow to never love another woman because she hurt you so? Why would she want Oliver Howard instead of you? What's he like? Did she make you laugh? Is it because of Jeanne that you never smile? Do you think I can ever replace her in your heart?"

When the questions at last stopped, Rogan just stood there looking at Liana. His arms were at his sides and his mouth was open a bit in astonishment.

"Well?" Liana said, encouraging him. "Is she? Was she? Tell me!"

Rogan wasn't sure what he'd expected from her

when he'd asked her what she wanted to know, but these frivolous, unimportant, lovesick questions were not it. His eyes began to twinkle. "Beautiful?" he said. "The moon was afraid to come up over Moray Castle because it couldn't compete with the beauty of . . . of . . ."

"Jeanne," Liana said thoughtfully. "Then, she was much prettier than me?"

He couldn't believe she was taking this seriously. Truthfully, he didn't remember what his former wife looked like. It had been so many years since he'd seen her. "Much," he said in mock seriousness. "She was so beautiful that . . ." He searched for a comparison. ". . . that charging war horses would halt before her and eat from her hand."

"Oh," Liana said, and sat down on a rock, her wet clothes making squishing noises. "Oh."

Rogan gave the top of her bowed head a look of disgust. "She could never wear pretty clothes because if she did, she hurt men's eyes. She had to wear peasants' clothes all the time just to keep from blinding people. If she rode into the village, she had to wear a mask or otherwise men would throw themselves under her horse's hooves. Diamonds looked dull next to—"

Liana's head came up. "You're teasing me." There was hope in her voice. "What did she *really* look like?"

"I don't remember. She was young. Brown hair, I think."

Liana realized that this last was the truth, that he didn't remember much about Jeanne's looks. "How can you forget someone you loved so much?"

He sat down on the grass, his back to her, and looked at the stream. "I was just a boy, and my brothers ordered me to marry her. She . . . she beıayed me, all of us. James and Basil died trying to get ıer back."

She went to him and sat beside him, her cold wet ,ide next to the warm dryness of him. "She's what has made you sad?"

"Sad?" he said. "The death of my brothers has ınade me sad. Seeing them die one by one, knowing that the Howards have taken everything I ever wanted in life."

"Even your wife," she whispered.

He turned and looked at her. He hadn't thought of his first wife in a personal way in years. He couldn't remember her face, her body, anything at all about her. But as he looked at Liana he thought that if she left, he would remember a great deal about her—and it wouldn't just be her body either, he thought with astonishment. He'd remember some of the things she'd *said*.

He put his hand out and touched her damp cheek. "Are you as simple as you seem?" he asked softly. "Is whether someone loves you or thinks you're beautiful the most important thing in your life?"

Liana didn't like to sound so frivolous. "I can watch the accounts of the estates. I can produce thieves. I can judge court cases. I can—"

"Judge?" Rogan asked, leaning away to look at her. "How can a woman make a decent judgment? The judgments are not about love and who has the cleanest floor—they're about issues of importance."

"Give me an example," Liana said evenly.

Rogan thought it better not to burden a woman's mind with too many serious matters, but he also wanted to teach her a lesson. "Yesterday a man and three witnesses came to me with a document signed with a seal. The document said the man was the owner of a farm, but the farm's previous owner would not leave. That man had put his seal to the paper as collateral for a debt. Now the debt went unpaid, but the first owner remained on the farm. How would you have settled the matter?" he asked smugly.

"I would make no judgment until I'd heard the first owner's testimony. The king's courts have ruled that a seal is too easy to forge. If the man was educated enough to have a seal, perhaps he could also write his own name. He would have put his seal *and* his mark on the paper. I would also question whether the witnesses were friends of the first man or not. All in all, the case does not sound straightforward to me."

Rogan gaped at her. The document had indeed proved to be a false one, made by a man who was angry at having seen his young wife talking to the owner's son.

"Well?" Liana said. "I hope you did not send men to throw the poor farmer off his land."

"I did not," he snapped. "Nor did I burn anyone for eating rats."

"Or impregnate a daughter?" she said teasingly.

"No, but the farmer's wife was a beauty. Big—" He held his hands in front of him.

"You!" Liana said, and lunged at him.

He caught her, pretended that her weight had knocked him down, then held her closely to him. He kissed her.

"I did well in the judgment, didn't I? The document was false, wasn't it?" She was lying on top of him, feeling his strong, hard body under hers.

"Your clothes are wet," he said. "Maybe you should take them off and let them dry."

"You're not going to distract me. Was the document false or not?"

He lifted his head to kiss her again, but she turned her face away.

"Was it?" she asked.

"Yes, it was false," he said, exasperated.

Liana laughed and began kissing his neck.

Rogan closed his eyes. He'd had so few women in his life who weren't afraid of him. The high-born women of the courts usually turned up their noses at him, so Rogan told himself he preferred the servant girls. They were usually fearful of his scowls and frowns. But this woman laughed at him, yelled at him—and refused to obey him.

". . . and I can help," she was saying.

"Help in what?" he murmured.

"The judgments." She was running her tongue along his collarbone.

"Over my dead body," he said cheerfully.

She wiggled on top of him. "I'm over your body, but it doesn't feel very dead to me."

"You're an impudent wench," he said, kissing her.

"How shall you punish me?"

He put his hand behind her head and rolled her over, throwing his big leg over hers. "I will wear you out."

"Impossible!" she said before his mouth came down on hers.

From the trees came a sound of people walking, which, at first, the lovers did not hear.

"Gaby, I tell you this is a bad idea," came a man's voice.

"Nothing ventured, nothing gained, I always say," answered a woman.

Liana felt Rogan's body stiffen, then quickly he took his short sword from under his tunic and knelt over her in a gesture of complete protection.

Through the trees came Baudoin and a small, plump woman, a little girl in her arms, a basket on her arm, and a boy between them.

Liana and Rogan just stared, not understanding the meaning of this intrusion.

"There you are," the plump woman said, coming forward. "Baudoin has told me everything. You must forgive his temper. I'm his wife, Gabriel, but everyone calls me Gaby, and these are our children, Sarah and Joseph. I told Baudoin that if we're going to live with you, we ought to get to know you. My father was a knight, nothing as high as an earl, mind you, but a man of respect. I knew Baudoin was the son of a lord, so I pleaded with my father to let me marry him." She gave the tall, handsome young man a look of adoration. "And I've never regretted a minute of it. Aren't you cold, my lady, in those wet clothes? The dye's coming out of your hair and it's all over your face. Here, let me help you get clean."

Rogan and Liana, in their astonishment, hadn't moved. He still knelt over her, knife drawn, protecting Liana beneath him. When the woman Gaby held out her hand, Liana didn't move.

Baudoin broke the silence. "Go on," he said. "Everyone does what she says." The words were mean, but there was a tone of love in his voice. The couple didn't look as if they belonged together. Baudoin was tall, lean, exceedingly handsome, and angry-looking. Gaby was short, plump, pretty, but far from beautiful, and she looked as if she'd been born with a smile on her face.

Liana took the woman's offered hand and followed her to the stream. Liana was used to women of Gaby's class being fearful of her, but ever since she'd come to the Peregrine land, nothing had been as she'd once known it.

"Now, sit there and behave yourself," Gaby said as she set her daughter on the ground. She looked back at Liana. "I heard what happened this morning. Brothers shouldn't fight. I always told Baudoin that someday his brothers in the castle would see the light, and I was right. He's a good man, is my Baudoin, and he'll do whatever is needed. Look at them. Two peas in a pod."

Liana looked at the two men standing near one another, not looking at each other, not speaking, the little boy between them just as silent.

"Lean over here and let me wash your hair," Gaby directed.

Liana did as she was bid.

"Does yours talk as little as mine?" Gaby asked.

Liana was unsure of what to do—whether to be friends with this woman or not. It was odd how clothes affected one's mind. If she were wearing her best blue silk she would have expected this woman to bow before her but, somehow, while wearing peasant's wool, she felt almost as if she were . . . well, equal to this woman. "If I chain him in one place he will talk. but not much," Liana finally said.

"Don't give up the fight. He'll pull into himself completely if you allow it. And make him laugh. Tickle him."

"Tickle him?" Black-dyed water was streaming past Liana's face.

"Mmm," Gaby said. "Ribs. They're good men, though. They're not fickle in their affections. If he loves you today, he'll love you forever. He won't be like some men and love you today, somebody else tomorrow, and somebody else the next day. There, that should do it. Your hair is blonde again."

Liana sat up, slinging her wet hair back. "And now we can't return to the fair. Someone might recognize me."

"No," Gaby said seriously. "You don't want to go

back there. There was talk this morning of who the mysterious man was who beat Baudoin. You shouldn't return." Her face brightened. "But I have brought food and we can stay here in this pretty spot."

Gabriel didn't tell Liana that she'd spent a year's savings on the feast she'd brought with her. Under Gaby's happy exterior was a very ambitious woman —but she was not ambitious for herself. She was ambitious for the man she loved more than life itself.

She had been twelve when she'd first seen the handsome, cold-eyed Baudoin and she had decided then that she'd have him no matter what it took to get him. Her father had wanted her to make a good marriage, not to marry some bastard son with no prospects. But Gaby had wheedled and whined and pleaded and nagged until her father at last made an offer to Baudoin's stepfather.

Baudoin had married her for her dowry, and the first years together had been hard. He'd had many other women, but Gaby's love was stronger than his lust. Gradually he began to notice her, to come to her for love and comfort, and when the children were born, he found he enjoyed them, too.

In the six years of their marriage, Baudoin had gone from being a hellion who jumped from one bed to another to being a successful merchant who most of all enjoyed his wife and children.

This morning, when he'd seen Lord Rogan in the crowd, he'd recognized his half-brother immediately. For the first time in years his old rage had come to the surface. Hours later he'd found Gaby and, after much word-pulling from her, had told her what had happened in the forest. He was ashamed of having attacked a man from behind and he told Gaby about the offer he'd accepted, but said that they must leave the area and start over again elsewhere, that he could not bear to face Lord Rogan again.

Gaby gave a quick prayer of thanks to God for at last giving them this opportunity, and then she proceeded to work on Baudoin. She used every technique she could think of to break Baudoin's reserve. Once this was accomplished she knew she had to work on the lord and his kind, forgiving wife. And she knew that today, while the lord and his lady were dressed in peasants' garb, was her opportunity. Tomorrow, when they were in silk and she was in wool, the gulf between them would be too great.

So she'd taken the money from its hiding place, purchased beef, pork, chicken, bread, oranges, cheese, dates, figs, and beer, and put them into a basket and gone in search of Baudoin's illustrious relatives. She didn't let herself think of Rogan's reputation, which had been so well portrayed in the play (and she refused to think about Lord Rogan's having seen Baudoin playing him), but concentrated on being amusing and *equal*.

Liana didn't have to say much when she was near Gaby, but then no one did, for Gaby talked enough for an army. At first Liana was reserved with the woman. She didn't like her presumption, didn't like the way the woman had forced herself into what was to have been her time alone with Rogan.

But after a while, Liana began to thaw. It was so good to hear *talk*. With Rogan she had to force every word from him and there were no guests at Moray Castle, no one to talk with except her maids and the Lady—who too often stayed behind a locked door.

And, too, Liana liked the way Gaby adored Baudoin. Her eyes roamed over him in a possessive way that was part wife, part mother, part she-monster who meant to suck the life from him. I wonder if I look at Rogan like that, she thought.

The men looked at one another warily, not knowing what to say or how to react to each other, until Gaby suggested Rogan teach Baudoin how to fight with long poles.

The women sat on the ground eating cheese and bread and watched the men train. Rogan was a good teacher, if a harsh one. He knocked Baudoin into the cold stream three times. But Baudoin wasn't his father's son for nothing. The fourth time Rogan meant to send his half-brother into the water, Baudoin pivoted and Rogan went splashing face down into the icy water.

Liana was on her feet instantly and running to her husband. He looked so startled as he sat there in the water that Liana began to laugh, as did Gaby. Even Baudoin smiled. It took Rogan a moment, but he smiled also.

Liana put her hand out to help him up but, still smiling, he pulled her down into the water with him. "Not fair," she cried. "I was nearly dry."

He stood, then lifted her out of the water and carried her to the grassy place in the sun and sat down beside her. He removed his shirt, and when Liana shivered, he pulled her into his arms so that she leaned back against him. Liana knew she'd never been so happy in her life.

"What's to eat?" Rogan asked. "I'm starved."

Gaby pulled luscious food from the basket, and the four adults and two children began to eat. For the most part it was Gaby who talked, telling amusing little stories of village life. She was remarkably tactful when it came to avoiding all reference to the Peregrine family's terrorizing of the village.

Liana could feel Rogan beginning to relax. He asked Baudoin some questions about being a wool merchant, even asked him if he had any ideas how to improve the Peregrine wool production.

The little girl, Sarah, only a toddler, just able to walk, picked up a date and on her chubby legs made her way, with her father's help, to Rogan. She stood and stared at him for a while until Rogan turned to look at her. He'd never paid much attention to children, but he noted that she was a pretty child with intense dark eyes that studied him.

The child handed him the date, and when Rogan took it, she seemed to think this was an invitation. She turned and plopped into his lap, snuggling her back against his chest.

Rogan looked down at the soft curly hair in horror.

"Never met a stranger," Gaby said. "That's my Sarah."

"Take her," Rogan said under his breath to Liana. "Get her off me."

Liana suddenly became deaf. "Here, Sarah, give these figs to your Uncle Rogan."

Solemnly, the child took a fig and held it to Rogan's mouth. When he tried to take it from her, she gave a squeal of protest. Looking as if it were the most unpleasant thing he'd ever done, he opened his mouth and allowed her to put the fig inside.

Liana kept up a running stream of conversation with Gaby and pretended she was taking no notice of Rogan and the child, but she kept the little girl supplied with dates and figs. When the child tired of feeding her uncle, she settled back against Rogan and went to sleep.

All too soon, the sun dropped low in the sky and Liana knew it was time to go home. She didn't want this pleasant time to end, didn't want to return to gloomy Moray Castle and, perhaps, a husband who ignored her. She slipped her hand in Rogan's and put her head on his shoulder. For a long while they sat there, entwined, the sleeping baby on his lap.

"This has been the best day of my life," Liana whispered. "I wish it would never end."

Rogan tightened his arm around her. It had been such a wasteful day and he planned never again to be so frivolous, but he agreed that it had been . . . well, pleasant.

It was Sarah's waking and crying that made them realize they had to return to their respective homes.

"You'll come tomorrow?" Liana asked Gaby, and saw tears of gratitude in the woman's eyes. Already, Liana had plans of making Gaby her mistress of the household. Gaby would make sure the maids kept the place clean, and Liana would have more time to spend with her husband.

A few minutes later, in the growing darkness, Rogan and Liana began to slowly walk back to Moray Castle. Hands clasped, they were quiet for a while.

"I wish we didn't have to go back," Liana said. "I wish we could be like Gaby and Baudoin and live in a simple hut somewhere and—"

Rogan snorted. "They were ready enough to give up their simple hut. That meal must have cost them a year's wages."

"Half a year," Liana said in the tone of someone who spends a great deal of time with account books. "But they're in *love,*" she said dreamily. "I could see it in Gaby's eyes." She looked up at Rogan. "It must be how I look at you."

Rogan was looking ahead at the walls of Moray Castle. It had been too easy for them to leave this morning. What if the Howards were to dress as vegetable sellers and beg entry? He'd have to tighten vigilance.

"Did you hear what I said?" Liana asked.

Perhaps he should require a badge to be worn by the peasants who were allowed to enter. Of course a badge could be stolen, but—

"Rogan!" Liana had stopped walking and, clutching his hand, she made him halt too.

"What is it?"

"Were you listening to me?" she asked.

"Heard every word you said," he answered. Perhaps something besides a badge. Maybe a—

"What did I say?"

Rogan looked at her blankly. "Say about what?"

She tightened her lips. "I was telling you that I love you."

Perhaps a password, changed daily. Or maybe the safest thing would be just to designate certain peasants to enter, with no new faces allowed in, ever.

To Rogan's consternation, his wife dropped his hand and marched ahead of him, and from the way she walked, she looked to be angry. "Now what?" he muttered. He'd done everything she wanted of him today and yet she still wasn't pleased.

He caught up with her. "Something wrong?"

"Oh, so you noticed me," she said haughtily. "I hope I wasn't disturbing you by telling you that I love you."

"No," he said honestly. "I was just thinking about something else."

"Don't let my declarations of love interrupt," she said nastily. "I'm sure a hundred women have sworn they love you. All of the Days. But then you even had Months once. And of course Jeanne Howard probably told you every day."

Rogan was beginning to see through her cloud of illogic. This was another one of those woman things and not serious at all. "She wasn't a Howard when she was married to me."

"I see. But you don't deny that she told you repeatedly that she loved you. You've probably heard it so many times it means nothing coming from *me.*"

Rogan thought for a moment. "I don't remember any woman telling me she loved me."

"Oh," Liana said, and slipped her hand back into his. They walked in silence for a few minutes. "Do you love me?" she asked softly.

He squeezed her hand. "I have a few times. And tonight I'll—"

"Not *that* kind of love. I mean, inside of you. Like how you loved your mother."

"My mother died when I was born."

She frowned. "Severn's mother, then."

"She died when Severn was born, when I was two. I don't remember her."

"Zared's mother?" Liana asked softly.

"I don't think I felt much of anything for her. She was scared of us all. Used to cry a lot."

"Didn't anyone try to comfort her?"

"Rowland told her to stop crying so we could get some sleep."

Liana thought about that poor woman, alone with a dirty castle full of men whose chief concern was that her crying disturbed their sleep. And she was the wife who was starved to death at Bevan Castle. If Rogan had not loved the women in his life, he must have loved his brothers. "When your oldest brother died—"

"Rowland did not die, he was killed by the Howards."

"All right then," she said impatiently. "Killed.

Murdered. Slaughtered unfairly without provocation. Did you miss him after his death?"

Rogan took a while to answer as images of his strong, powerful brother floated through his head. "I miss him every day," he answered at last.

Liana's voice lowered. "Would you miss me if I died? Say, if the plague took me?"

He looked down at her. If she died, his life would return to the way it had been. His clothes would be crawling with lice. The bread would be filled with sand. The Days would return. She wouldn't be around to curse him, ridicule him, publicly embarrass him, or make him waste his time. He frowned. Yes, he'd miss her.

And he bloody well didn't like the idea of missing her.

"I wouldn't have to go to any more fairs," he said, and walked away from her.

Liana stood rooted where she was. She didn't like to think how much his words hurt. They had been together such a short time and he meant so much to her, yet she was less than nothing to him.

She vowed to herself that she'd never let him see how he'd hurt her, that she'd keep her pain to herself. She thought her face was impassive, with no expression showing to give herself away, but when Rogan turned back, he saw his pretty little wife with her lower lip extended and her eyes big with unshed tears. He searched his mind to figure out what was wrong with her. Did she dread returning to the castle?

He went to her and put his fingers under her chin, but she jerked away.

"You care nothing for me," she said. "If I were to die, you could get another rich wife and keep her dowry."

Rogan gave a bit of a shudder. "Marriages are too

much trouble," he said. "My father had the stamina of a thousand men. He went through four marriages."

In spite of her intentions, tears began to roll down Liana's face. "If I died, you'd no doubt toss my body in the moat. Good riddance!"

Rogan's confusion showed. "If you died I'd . . ."

"Yes?" she asked, looking up at him through lashes heavy with tears.

"I would . . . know that you were gone."

Liana knew this was the best she was going to get from him. She flung her arms about his neck and began to kiss him. "I knew you cared," she said.

To the consternation of both of them, people around them began to applaud. They had been so involved in their own dispute that they hadn't been aware of the people around them who had been gleefully watching and listening.

Rogan was more embarrassed than Liana. He grabbed her hand and started running. They stopped not far from the castle walls and suddenly he, too, was reluctant for the day to end.

There was a vendor nearby with a wooden tray fastened to a belt around his shoulders. In the tray were painted wooden toys of men that danced at the end of a stick. The vendor, seeing Rogan's glance, hurried forward and demonstrated the funny little doll. When Liana laughed at the doll's antics, Rogan found himself parting with two precious pennies for the thing.

Liana clutched the doll eagerly. If Rogan had given her emeralds, she wouldn't like them as much as the doll. She looked up at Rogan with love.

Rogan turned away from her look. Such a frivolous day, such a waste of time and money spent on a bit of a girl who asked stupid questions. And yet . . .

He put his arm about her shoulders and watched as

she fooled with the toy. He felt good as he watched her. He felt at peace, something he thought he'd never felt before. He leaned down and kissed the top of her head. Never before had he kissed a woman for any reason other than lust.

Liana snuggled her body closer to his and Rogan knew he'd pleased her. It was absurd, of course, but somehow, pleasing her pleased him.

With a sigh of regret, he led them to the castle.

CHAPTER
THIRTEEN

Severn sat at the now-clean table in the lord's chamber, eating cheese that had no mold and perfectly cooked beef, and chuckled.

Zared looked up. "Care to share your humor?"

"A whole day in bed with a woman," he said. "Not even I believed Rogan could do it, but once again I underestimated my brother." His eyes showed his pride. "The woman won't be able to walk. She'll probably spend today in bed, too—resting."

"Maybe Rogan will be the one wanting to rest."

"Ha!" Severn snorted. "You know nothing about men. Especially not about men like our brother. He'll put that woman in her place. You'll see. No more trying to run this place after yesterday. Rogan won't neglect the training field to lay about in her lap." There was bitterness in his voice. "She'll stay in her room from now on and not try to interfere in our lives. No more of this constant cleaning and—"

"Cooking," Zared interjected. "I rather like the place better. I sure like the food better."

Severn pointed his eating knife at Zared. "Luxury

can be the downfall of a man, and no one knows that better than our brother. Rogan—"

"Lost the bet."

Severn squinted his eyes. "Yes, he may have lost the bet, but he got what *he* wanted for payment."

"Perhaps," Zared said, slathering sweet, freshly churned butter onto a thick slice of bread. "But then it was her decision about what she wanted to do, wasn't it? And she did win the wager, didn't she? She produced the thieves when you and Rogan couldn't. And she—"

"Luck," Severn said, jaw set. "Blind, stupid luck. No doubt the peasants were ready to turn the thieves over and she happened to arrive at the right time."

"Uh-huh," Zared said. "Sure."

"I don't like your tone," Severn snapped.

"And I don't like your stupidity. The woman has done a lot of work in a short time and she deserves credit. And what's more, I think Rogan's falling in love with her."

"Love!" Severn gasped. "Love! Rogan would never be so weak. He's had a hundred women, a thousand, and he's never fallen in love. He wouldn't. He's too sensible."

"He wasn't so sensible about Jeanne Howard."

Severn's face began to turn an unbecoming shade of purple. "What do you know of that woman? You were a kid when she was here. Her treachery *killed* Basil and James." He calmed himself a bit. "Anyway, Rogan knows what women are like, especially what *wives* are like." He looked at Zared and grinned. "And besides, Rogan never has any use for a woman once he's bedded her. After yesterday, he'll be so sick of this woman he'll probably send her to Bevan to stay and then things will return to normal around here."

"Normal meaning rats on the stairs and dead

bodies lost in the moat? You know what's wrong with you, Severn? You're jealous. You don't want your brother giving his attention to anyone except you. You don't—"

"Jealous! I'll tell you what's wrong with me: I fear Rogan's attention turning from the treachery of the Howards. If this woman softens him, he'll forget to watch his back and an arrow will pierce it. A man can't be a Peregrine and wear skirts as well. *You* should know that."

"I do," Zared said softly. "But what if Rogan does . . . care for her?"

"He won't. Trust me. I know my brother better than he knows himself. He can't even remember the woman's name, so there's no danger of his loving her."

Zared started to speak, but a noise on the stairs made them both turn.

Rogan and Liana entered the room, both of them resplendent in silk brocade, Rogan's hair damp, as if he'd just washed it. Liana had her arm entwined with his and he had his hand over hers.

More unusual than the clothes and the posture was the look on Rogan's face. If he wasn't quite smiling, he was close to it and his eyes were alive as he looked down into the adoring face of his wife.

"Perhaps," Rogan was saying.

"Are you afraid I will contradict you before the peasants?" Liana asked.

"You contradict *me?*" he asked. "Such a thing might make the peasants believe you'd . . ."—he hesitated—" . . . tamed me."

Liana laughed, touching her forehead to his arm. As they walked to the table, they didn't seem to notice the open-mouthed astonishment on the faces of Severn and Zared.

"Good morning," Liana said cheerfully, then seated herself at Rogan's right hand. "Tell me if any food isn't to your liking and I'll speak to the cook—after the court session."

"I see," Rogan said in mock seriousness. "And if you do not participate in the courts, what will we have for dinner?"

Liana smiled sweetly at him. "What you have always eaten: sandy bread and maggoty meat, with moat water to drink."

Rogan turned twinkling eyes to Severn. "This woman blackmails me. If I do not allow her to help judge the court cases, she will starve me."

Severn had been too stunned by this new behavior of his brother's to be able to speak, and now he did not trust himself. He came out of his chair so quickly it fell to the floor. He turned on his heel and stomped from the room.

Rogan, having lived with brothers who were moody and angry most of the time, paid no attention to Severn.

Not so Liana. She turned to Zared. "What is wrong with him?"

Zared shrugged. "He doesn't like being wrong. He'll get over it. Rogan, you look like you enjoyed yourself yesterday."

Rogan started to say something about the fair, but he thought it best that only a few people know where he'd been yesterday. "Yes," he said softly. "I did."

Zared saw Rogan look at Liana with wonder on his face. Rogan would remember the woman's name now, Zared thought, and again wondered if he was falling in love. What would a Rogan in love be like? Would he turn his brooding room into a chamber for writing poetry?

Zared sat quietly at the table and watched the two

THE TAMING

of them and saw a brother who didn't act like a Peregrine. Perhaps Severn was right. *This* brother would never be able to lead an attack on the Howards.

When Rogan finished eating, he gave Liana a lusty look and said, "Come with me, my beauty," at which Liana convulsed with laughter.

Zared, at that point, began to agree with Severn. This was not the brother Zared had always known, the Rogan who scowled and frowned and hated.

Quietly, thoughtfully, Zared left the table, but Rogan and Liana didn't notice.

Severn's anger stayed with him throughout the day. In the afternoon he was on the training field with the men, but Rogan wasn't. "Probably back in bed with the woman," he muttered.

"My lord?" asked the knight Severn was training with.

Severn took his anger out on the knight, attacking him in the mock battle with a ferocity he usually used only on the battlefield.

"Enough!" Rogan bellowed from behind Severn. "Are you trying to kill the man?"

Severn halted, sword in hand, and turned to his brother. Beside Rogan was a man who looked very much like him. "What's one of our father's bastards doing here?" Severn snarled.

"He is to train with us. I put him in your charge." Rogan started to turn away, but Severn caught Rogan's shoulder and pulled him around.

"Like hell I'll train the bastard. If you want him here, you train him. Or should we let your wife train him, since she seems to run the Peregrines now? Was he her idea?"

Severn had hit too close to the truth, and Rogan grabbed an iron pike from the hands of a knight standing nearby. "You will eat those words," Rogan said, and went for his brother.

Severn took a pike too. The men fought long and hard while their knights watched in silence, for they sensed that this was not like the usual petty fights of the brothers but something deeper and more serious.

Rogan was not fueled by rage as his brother was. In fact, he felt less angry than he had in years, so he merely defended himself against his brother's attacks.

Both men were surprised when Rogan's foot caught behind him and he fell. Rogan started to get up, but Severn held the pointed end of the iron pike to his brother's throat.

"*This* is what that woman is doing to you," Severn said. "She might as well castrate you; she already has a chain about your neck."

It was too close to what the peasants had implied in the play. Rogan's rage came to the surface. He pushed the pike aside and leaped up, going for Severn with his bare hands.

Six knights jumped on Rogan and four on to Severn to hold the men apart.

"You always were a fool about women," Severn shouted. "The last wife of yours cost the lives of two brothers, but I guess we mean nothing to you when you have a wife."

Rogan went dead still. "Release me," he said to his men, and the men stepped back. They should not have interfered. Rogan was the lord and he had every right to do what needed to be done to his brother.

Rogan stepped close to his brother. Severn's blue eyes were still hot with anger; he was held back by the knights. "I have given you another brother to train," he said quietly. "I expect you to do it." He turned and walked back to the castle.

* * *

It was hours later that a sweat-dripping Severn mounted the stone stairs over the kitchen and entered Iolanthe's apartments. Here the richness of this large, sunny room was stunning. Gold glowed, silk embroideries shone, jewels on the ladies' gowns sparkled. But by far the most beautiful thing in the room was Iolanthe. Her beauty, her figure, her voice, her movements, were all without flaw, of such exquisite loveliness that often people could not speak when they saw her.

When Io saw the anger on Severn's face, she lifted her hand and dismissed her three women to their own chambers. She poured delicious wine into a golden goblet, handed it to Severn, and when he downed it in one gulp, she refilled it.

"Tell me," she said softly.

"It's that damned woman," Severn said.

Io knew who he meant because Severn had been complaining about Rogan's new wife for some time now.

"She is a Delilah," he said. "She is taking his very soul from him. She rules him, the men, the servants, the peasants, and even me. She ordered *my* room to be whitewashed! There is no place sacred from her touch. She invades Rogan's brooding room and he doesn't so much as reprimand her."

Io was watching him thoughtfully. "And what has she done today?"

"Somehow she persuaded Rogan to bring one of our father's bastards into the castle, and *I* am to train him. He's a *wool merchant.*" Severn said the last with horror.

"How did you get the lump on your forehead?"

Severn looked away. "So the man had a bit of luck with the poles. He'll never be a knight, no matter how much that woman wants it. And today I heard that she

211

sat beside Rogan at court. What next? Will he ask her permission to piss?"

Iolanthe watched Severn, saw his jealousy, and she wondered what this wife of Rogan's was like. Io had stayed in her pretty apartments, leaving only for walks on the battlements, and watched what was happening below. At first she would have wagered that no woman could effect a change on that hardheaded, insensitive, hate-obsessed Rogan, but the weeks had proved her wrong. She and her ladies had watched with amazement as the castle had been cleaned (Iolanthe and her ladies refused even to walk down the stairs through the filth) and she'd listened for hours to the kitchen maids tell stories of what the Fire Lady was doing. Io especially liked the story of Lady Liana's setting Rogan and one of his whores on fire. "Should have been done a long time ago," she'd said.

Io looked back at Severn. "He cares for her, then?"

"I don't know. It's as if she's put a spell on him. She's draining him of his strength. Today in training *I* knocked *him* down."

"It could have nothing to do with your being angry while he was not?"

"Before she came, Rogan was *always* angry. Now he . . . he *smiles!*"

Io could not hide a smile of her own. She did her best to stay out of the Peregrine-Howard feud. The only thing she cared about was Severn. Of course she did not tell him of her love. She had long ago guessed that at the mention of the word *love,* he would flee. And now she knew she was right. He was raging because his brother cared for his wife.

Io wondered how this Liana had made Rogan notice her. It wasn't beauty, because she'd seen divine-looking women make fools of themselves over

Rogan yet he'd not glanced at them, and she'd heard this little wife of his was pretty but certainly no beauty. No, it wasn't beauty that attracted the Peregrine men or Severn would be in love with Iolanthe.

As Io looked at Severn, his handsome face colored by his anger, she thought she'd sell her soul to the devil if he'd love her. He made love to her, true, he spent time with her, even asked her advice on problems, but she never deluded herself that he loved her. So she took what he gave her and never let him know she wanted more.

"What is this woman like?" Io asked.

"Meddlesome," Severn snapped. "Into everyone's business. She wants to run everyone—the knights, the peasants, Rogan, everyone. And she is simpleminded. She believes if she cleans something, it will cure the problem. No doubt she believes that if we bathed with the Howards, we could forgive each other."

"What does she look like?"

"Ordinary. Plain. I cannot see what Rogan sees in her."

Neither could Io, but she wanted to find out. "I am coming to supper in the Lord's Chamber tomorrow night," she announced.

For a moment Severn looked astonished. He knew Io didn't like Rogan, and the castle outside her apartment disgusted her. "Good," he said at last. "Perhaps you can teach the woman to behave like a woman should. Invite her to spend time with you. Keep her out of the courts and away from the peasants —and away from my brother. Maybe if you can get the woman to mind her own business, things can return to the way they should be."

Or perhaps she can teach me how a woman should behave, Io thought, but said nothing to Severn.

*   *   *

Liana looked out the window for the thousandth time. Yesterday Rogan had returned from the training field and his good mood was broken. Since they returned from the fair, he'd been so sweet, so much like the man she sensed he could be, but in the evening he'd been sullen and angry. He locked himself in his brooding room, as Zared called it, and wouldn't let her in.

It was late that night when he came to bed beside her, and sleepily she rolled next to him. For a moment she thought he was going to push her away, but then he clutched her to him and without a word made violent love to her. Liana almost complained about his fierceness but some instinct told her to be quiet, that he needed her.

Afterward, he'd held her tightly.

"Tell me what happened," she whispered.

For a moment she thought he might talk to her but he rolled away, his back to her, and went to sleep. In the morning he got out of bed and left without a word.

So now she was waiting for him to return from the training field for supper. At dinner he'd eaten with his men, leaving Liana alone with her ladies and Zared. It had been a lonely meal.

Liana dressed carefully to go downstairs. It never hurt to look your best when you were with a man.

When she entered the Lord's Chamber, the air was heavy with silence. Zared, Severn, and Rogan were already seated and eating, none of them speaking. Liana had already guessed that Rogan's anger had something to do with his brother, but she had no idea what had caused it. She could have asked Zared, but she wanted Rogan to tell her what had happened.

She seated herself to Rogan's left and began to eat after she was served. She searched for some topic of conversation. "Did Baudoin arrive today?" she asked.

It didn't seem possible, but the silence increased. When the two older men said nothing, she looked at Zared.

"Not a bad fighter," Zared said. "But then our father always bred good men."

"He's not our brother," Severn snapped.

Zared's eyes flashed. "He's as much my brother as you are."

"I'll teach you who's a Peregrine and who isn't," Severn said.

All three of them were on their feet at once, Severn going for Zared's throat, Rogan going for Severn.

This scene was halted in mid-action by the arrival of a woman. Liana looked under the arch that was formed by Severn's hands around Zared's throat, and her eyes opened wide in astonishment. Standing in the doorway was the most beautiful woman she'd ever seen. No, not just beautiful: perfect, flawless, a standard of beauty for all time. She was swathed in cloth of gold so that she was radiant, like a pillar of sunshine on a dark night.

"I see that nothing has changed," said the woman. Her voice was cool and arresting and at once made everyone feel calmer. She walked forward, as gracefully as an angel, floating, yards of fur-trimmed cloth trailing behind her. "Severn," she said, and looked at him as a mother might look at a disobedient child.

Severn immediately dropped his hands and looked a bit sheepish. Then, obediently, he pulled out a chair for her. When she was seated, she looked up at the three Peregrines who were still standing. "You may sit," she said, as a queen might give an order.

Liana couldn't take her eyes off the woman. She was what every woman hoped to look like. She was so lovely, so elegant, so graceful—and best of all, she had men jumping to do her bidding.

215

"Io, you have honored us," Rogan said. "Why?"

There was no mistaking the hostility in Rogan's voice, and when Liana looked at him, she saw what was almost a sneer on his lips. That sneer pleased her very much.

"I came to meet your wife," the woman said.

Liana almost asked, Me? but she caught herself. Then she drew her breath in sharply. If Rogan forgot her name again in front of this beautiful woman, she just might fall dead on the spot.

"Liane, Iolanthe," Rogan said, and went back to eating.

Close enough, Liana thought and wondered if the blacksmith could make a brand of her name and sear it on Rogan's forearm, where he could see it when he forgot.

"Hello," Liana said. What was she to say to this woman? "Did you buy your dress fabric in London?"

"France. My husband is French."

"Oh." She gave the woman a weak smile.

The meal went downhill after that. Rogan didn't speak; Severn didn't speak. Zared seemed as intimidated by the woman as Liana felt. Only Iolanthe seemed comfortable. Three of her own women stood behind her and served her food on gold plates. She didn't say anything but watched the others with curiosity—especially Liana, who grew so nervous she couldn't eat her soup.

At long last, Iolanthe rose to leave and Liana felt her shoulders relax in relief. "She is very beautiful," she said to Severn.

Severn, nose in his soup bowl, merely grunted.

"Isn't her husband a little concerned about her living here with you?"

Severn turned eyes of hatred on her. "You may interfere in other people's business, but not in mine. Io is *my* business, not yours."

Liana was stunned by his animosity. She looked at Rogan, half expecting him to leap at his brother. But Rogan didn't seem to have heard.

"I meant no insult to you," Liana said, "nor do I mean to interfere. I just thought—"

"Didn't mean to interfere!" Severn mocked. "That's all you've done since you arrived. You've changed everything: the castle, the grounds, the men, the peasants, my brother. Let me tell you, woman, you keep your nose out of my business and you leave Iolanthe alone. I don't want her corrupted."

Liana leaned back in her chair, astounded at this attack. Again she looked at Rogan. Why wasn't he defending her? He was looking at her with interest and she suddenly realized that she was being tested by him. She may be only a Peregrine by marriage, but she had to prove herself to be a Peregrine.

"All right," she said calmly to Severn. "You may have everything you had before I came." She stood and went to the fireplace, where there were cold ashes from that morning, picked up the big scoop nearby, and filled it with ashes. She walked across the room to Severn, with all eyes on her, then dumped the ashes on his food and clothes. "There," she said. "Now you are filthy and so is your food. From now on I will see that you have what you've always had."

Severn, soot on his chin and clothes, stood up, enraged. His hands made claws as he went for her throat.

Liana paled and stepped backward.

Severn never reached her because Rogan, while never looking up from gnawing on a beef joint, stuck his foot out and tripped his brother, sending Severn sprawling.

When Severn caught his breath, he bellowed, "You better do something about that woman."

Rogan ran his sleeve across his mouth. "She looks like she can take care of herself."

Liana had never felt so proud of herself in her life. She'd passed!

"But I wouldn't like it if you laid a hand on her," Rogan continued.

Severn stood, slapping soot from his clothes, which had been clean a few minutes before (Liana had directed the maids to wash his garments). He glared at Liana again. "Stay away from Io," he muttered, then left the room.

Liana felt jubilant. These Peregrines had their own rules of conduct, but she was beginning to understand them. Best of all, Rogan *had* defended her. Not from hateful words, but when his brother might have physically harmed her, he had stepped in.

Smiling—not only visibly, but also deep inside herself—she sat back down at the table. "More peas, Zared?" she asked.

"*Clean* peas?" Zared asked in mock fright. "The way *I* like my peas? Clean, the way I like my clothes and room and the peasants and the men *and* my brother?"

Liana laughed and looked at her husband, and the dear lovely man *winked* at her.

Later that night, Rogan held her in his arms and kissed her and made sweet love to her. Whatever had been bothering him seemed to have solved itself.

Afterward, he didn't turn away but held her close to him and Liana heard his soft, slow breathing as he fell asleep.

"Iolanthe isn't the Lady," she said sleepily.

"What lady?" he murmured.

"The Lady who lives above the solar, who told me about Jeanne Howard. She's not Iolanthe, so who is she?"

"No one lives above the solar, not until you came."

"But—" Liana said.

"Stop talking and go to sleep or I'll let Severn have you."

"Oh?" she replied, faking interest. "He's awfully good-looking. Maybe—"

"I'll tell Iolanthe you said that."

"I'm asleep," Liana answered quickly. She'd rather face Severn than the frightening Iolanthe.

As she drifted into sleep, she wondered again who the Lady was.

CHAPTER
FOURTEEN

The next morning, Gaby and her children arrived at the castle and at last Liana had someone to talk to. And best of all, Gaby told Liana of the disagreement Rogan and Severn had had over Baudoin.

"But my husband defended me?" Liana said softly.

"Oh yes, my lady. He told Lord Severn to keep his mouth shut, and Lord Severn has done everything he can to make my Baudoin quit and return to the village. But my Baudoin will *never* quit."

"No," Liana said with resignation. "Peregrines don't ever seem to quit or back down or even relent."

"That's not so, my lady," Gaby said. "Lord Rogan has changed since you arrived. Yesterday you walked across the bridge and Lord Rogan stopped yelling at one of his knights and watched you."

"Did he?" Those were sweet words to Liana. "And he does defend me to his brother?"

"Oh yes, my lady."

Liana couldn't seem to get enough from Gaby. At

times it seemed she'd had no influence on Rogan, that he was the same man who couldn't remember her name. But he remembered it now. Just this morning he had held her in his arms and kissed her and whispered her name in her ear.

Three weeks after Baudoin and Gaby's arrival, Rogan and Severn were still at such odds that they were barely speaking. Liana tried to get Rogan to talk to her about his anger, but he would not. Yet in bed he clung to her. Sometimes she felt as if he wanted her to make up for all the softness he'd lacked as a child.

In the evenings after supper, sometimes he came to the solar with her and sat sprawled on a cushioned chair and listened to one of her ladies play a lute and sing. She'd started to teach him to play chess, and when he realized it was a game of strategy, rather like war, he quickly became quite good. Zared began to join them, and Liana was pleased to see the young man sitting cross-legged on the floor holding a skein of yarn for one of the women to wind. One evening Rogan had been lounging on the window seat, Zared seated on the floor nearby, and Liana had seen Rogan reach out his hand and caress Zared's head. The boy had smiled up at Rogan with a look of such love and trust and adoration that Liana felt her knees weaken.

With each day Liana felt her love for her husband grow deeper and stronger. She had sensed from the beginning that there was more to him than what people saw, that there was a softer side.

Not that the softer side was easy to see. They'd had a couple of arguments that nearly brought the roof down on their heads. Rogan refused to believe Liana was good for anything but bed pleasure and providing him with food and drink. And no matter how many times she showed him otherwise, he never even remembered, much less learned anything from what she'd done.

Even though she'd passed his test and he even joked with her about it, in the end she had to fight him to allow her to help judge the local disputes. She pointed out how she had delivered the thieves to him, but it made no difference. He had decided she couldn't judge the cases, and no amount of reason or logic was going to dissuade him.

She finally broke down in tears. Rogan was not a man who fell apart at the sight of a woman's tears, but what he hated was her lack of smiles. He seemed to think it was her duty to always be happy and cheerful. After a day and a half of Liana's misery, he relented and said she could sit beside him in the court cases. She had thrown her arms about his neck and kissed him—and then she'd tickled his ribs.

Severn had walked into the Lord's Chamber and seen the two of them rolling about on the floor, Liana's headdress knocked off, her hair cascading about her as she tickled his big brother into helpless laughter. Severn's rage had sobered them immediately.

Severn, Liana thought. She was still amazed that her brother-in-law could cause her so much unhappiness. When she'd first arrived, he'd seemed to be on her side, but as Rogan had changed, so had Severn. Now, it was almost as if he hated her, and he did everything he could to turn Rogan against her. Not that Rogan even mentioned what was going on to Liana. No, she had to rely on Gaby for that information. On the training field Severn taunted his brother, ridiculed him for being led by a woman.

The more Liana heard about what Severn was doing, the more comfort she tried to provide Rogan.

In the evenings she sometimes saw how torn he was, as if he warred inside himself whether he should give in to the pleasures of her solar or stay alone in his brooding chamber.

His brooding chamber caused their second big fight. After he'd spent two nights alone in there, Liana went inside. She didn't knock or ask permission for entry, she just walked in, her heart pounding in her ears. He'd yelled at her. He'd blustered and fumed, but there was something in his eyes that told her he didn't actually mind her invasion.

"What are those?" she'd asked, pointing to the stack of papers on the table.

He'd argued some more, but at last he'd shown her his sketches. Liana didn't know much about war machines, but she knew something about farm machinery and this wasn't all that different. She'd made a few suggestions and they had been good ones.

It had been a lovely evening, just the two of them together in that little room, bent over the papers. Several times Rogan had said, "Like this?" or, "Is this better?" or, "Yes, I think that might work."

As he often did, Severn had ruined the evening. He'd pushed open the half-open door, then stood gaping at the two of them. "I heard she was in here," he'd said softly, "but I didn't believe it. This room was sacred to our brother Rowland and to our father. But now *you* let a woman in here. And for what?" He nodded toward the sketches on the table. "To tell you how to build war machines? Is there nothing of the man left in you?"

Liana was pleased to see that when Severn stomped away, he was scratching his arm furiously. She knew that once again lice were infesting his clothes and she hoped they ate him alive. She turned to her husband. "Rogan . . ." she began.

But he was already on his feet. He left her alone in the room and as far as she knew, he had not visited the room since.

Her heart went out to Rogan as she saw him fight within himself. Part of him wanted the softness and tenderness she offered, but part of him wanted to please his angry brother. He trained and worked many hours during the day, trying to be the leader of the Peregrines, to prove to his men and especially to his brother that he was still worthy of his position as their master. And in the evening he never fully relaxed during the pleasures Liana offered.

She tried her best to keep her rage at Severn under control, but it was difficult. She wrote a letter to her stepmother, asking Helen if she knew of any young heiresses Severn might marry. If she could find a wife for Severn, perhaps he'd leave Rogan to her.

It was the third fight that turned the tables and made Rogan side with Severn against her.

Liana was boiling with rage when she stormed down the stairs into the Lord's Chamber. Severn and Rogan were sitting at the table, calmly eating breakfast but not speaking to each other.

Liana was so angry she could hardly speak. "Your . . . your brother was in bed with three women this morning," she spat at Rogan.

Rogan looked at Severn in wonder. "Three? The most I've ever had was four. I was worn out the next day."

"When was that?" Severn asked, as if Liana weren't there.

"A year ago at the tournament at—"

"Not *him!*" Liana shouted. "Zared! Your little brother, that *child,* spent the night with *three* women."

The two men just stared at her stupidly. She

doubted if they had any idea what was wrong with Zared's being in bed with three women. "I won't have it," she said. "Rogan, you have to stop this."

To further increase her fury, Rogan's eyes began to twinkle. "Yes, I will have to do something."

She advanced on him. "Don't patronize me. That boy looks up to you. He idolizes you. He thinks the sun rises and sets on you and I'm sure he's merely imitating you."

Severn grinned and slapped Rogan's shoulder. "Just imitating his big brother," he said, laughing.

Liana turned on Severn, her anger at him coming to the surface. "At least Rogan is making an effort. But you! You, with a married mistress living in the same house as that innocent child."

Severn was on his feet and glowering down at her. "My life is none of your business," he shouted at her. "And Zared is—"

Rogan stood, cutting his brother off. "We will take care of Zared."

"As you take care of everything else—including your wife?" Severn sneered, then slammed from the room.

Rogan watched his brother go, then sat down heavily in his chair. Severn's words had upset him.

"That man needs a wife," Liana said.

"A wife?" Rogan said. "Iolanthe would tear the woman's eyes out."

He looked so dejected sitting there that she wanted to say something to amuse him. "We'll have to find a woman strong enough to handle Severn and Iolanthe."

"There is no such woman."

She caressed his forehead. "No? I have handled you, and you are stronger than twenty Severns and

Iolanthes." She meant her words as a jest, but Rogan didn't seem to take them as such. He looked up at her with eyes glittering with anger.

"No woman controls me," he said under his breath.

"I didn't mean—" she began, but he stood, his expression still angry.

"No woman controls me or my family. Go back to your sewing, woman, where you belong." He left her alone in the room.

He left her alone all that day, that evening, and that night. She was frantic with worry and she was sure he'd gone to another woman. "I will kill her so slowly she will pray for death," Liana seethed as she paced their chamber.

At midnight she went to Gaby, woke her from Baudoin's arms, and had Gaby find out where Rogan was. It didn't take Gaby long to return and tell Liana that Rogan was getting drunk in the Great Hall with half a dozen of his men.

Somehow the news made Liana feel very good. He was as upset about their argument as she was. No more was he the man who ignored her, who couldn't pick her out from a group of women.

When at last she went to bed, if she didn't sleep soundly, she did sleep.

She was awakened before dawn by the unmistakable sound of steel on steel. "Rogan," she said, her heart tight with fear. She threw a robe over her nakedness and began to run.

The Howards had tried to sneak into the Peregrine castle before dawn. They tossed great hooks over the parapets and started climbing up the ropes.

It had been so many months since the Howards had attacked, and the Peregrines had been so involved in their own internal squabbles, that there had been a feeling of safety. Watchfulness had lulled; senses were no longer as alert.

Twelve of the twenty Howard attackers were over the wall before the sleepy guards on the parapets heard them. Two Peregrine knights died without ever waking up.

Rogan, in the Great Hall, lying on the floor in a drunken stupor, had difficulty rousing himself. Severn was there before he was fully aware of what was happening.

"You sicken me," Severn said, then tossed his brother a sword and ran out of the room.

Rogan made up for lost time. If his head did not clear instantly, his body remembered its long training. He kicked his men awake and within seconds he was in the courtyard fighting beside Severn and Baudoin.

It didn't take long to kill the Howard attackers, and as Severn meant to slay the last one, Rogan stopped him.

"Why?" he demanded of the man. "What does Oliver Howard want?"

"The woman," the Howard man said. "We were to take her and hold her." The man knew he was going to die. He gave Rogan an insolent look. "He said his younger brother needs a wife and the Peregrine brides make excellent Howard wives."

Rogan killed the man. He thrust his knife into the man's heart and twisted and kept twisting until Severn pulled him away.

"He's dead," Severn said. "They're all dead. As well as four of our men."

Fear was coursing through Rogan's body. If Severn had not been here . . . if he'd been a little drunker . . . if his men hadn't heard . . . They could have had Liana by now. "I want this place searched," he said. "I want every granary, every garderobe, every chest searched. I want to make sure no Howards are here. Go!" he shouted at the men standing near him.

"At last you care about the Howards," Severn said. "But only because of *her*. You have placed all our lives in danger—me, Zared, yourself. You risk what little property we have left because of her. Is it nothing to you that tonight four of your men were killed and a dozen others wounded while you were in a drunken stupor? And why? Because of a quarrel with that woman? You have killed two brothers over a wife. Will it take the deaths of the rest of the Peregrines to satisfy you?"

At that moment Liana came flying down the stairs, long blonde hair streaming behind her, her robe opening to show slim bare legs. She threw herself at Rogan, her arms about his neck. "You're safe," she cried, tears wetting his shoulder. "I was terrified for you."

For a moment Rogan forgot the bloodstained men around him, as well as his scowling brother, and hugged her trembling body to his. It was only luck that she was still here and not taken by Howard's men. He stroked her hair and soothed her. "I'm unhurt," he whispered.

He looked up to see the face of one of his men, one of his father's men, a man who'd followed Rowland into battle, and he saw disgust on the man's face. Disgust that a Peregrine would be standing here in the early dawn, two dead men at his feet, and cooing to a woman.

Over the past few weeks, Rogan knew that his men had sided with him over Severn because Rogan had never slacked in his training. And they hadn't seen the way Rogan sat in the solar with his wife in the evening and listened to women singing. Nor had they seen

Rogan allowing his wife to help him design machines of war.

But now, as Rogan looked into the eyes of his men, he knew their loyalty had just changed. How could they follow a man who, because of a quarrel with his wife, was too drunk to hear an attack? How could he control them? In the village play, the peasants had portrayed him as being "tamed," as a man whose wife had put a collar on him and led him away. At the time, the idea had seemed too absurd to consider, but now he saw some truth in the play.

He had to establish his control before his men or lose their respect forever.

He abruptly pulled Liana from him, then shoved her away. "Get back to the house, woman, where you belong."

Liana had some idea of Rogan's embarrassment. She straightened her shoulders. "I will help. How many wounded are there?" She turned to the man who'd been watching Rogan with so little respect. "Take these men to the kitchen, it'll be warmer there. And fetch—"

Rogan had to stop her. "Obey me!" he bellowed.

"But there are wounded men here."

His men, wounded and well, were watching him intently and Rogan knew that it was now or never. "I married you for your money," he said evenly and loudly enough for all his men to hear, "and not for your advice or your beauty."

Liana felt as if she'd been kicked in the stomach. She wanted to reply, but her throat closed and she couldn't speak. Around her she could feel the men's smirks. Here was a woman who had been put in her place. Slowly, she turned and started back into the castle.

For just a moment Rogan almost went after her, but he didn't. "Get these men up," he said. He'd make it up to her tonight. Maybe a gift. She had liked that little doll from the fair so much, maybe—

"Take them where?" Severn asked.

Rogan saw respect once again in his brother's eyes. "The Great Hall," he said. "And get a leech to sew them up. Then bring me the men who were on guard duty."

"Yes, brother," Severn said, and for a moment put his hand on Rogan's shoulder.

To Rogan, the hand felt heavy with responsibility.

"He did it," Severn said proudly to Iolanthe. "I knew that when we needed him, he'd be there. You should have seen him yesterday morning. 'I married you for your money, not for your advice or your beauty.' That's what he told her. Now maybe she'll stop interfering in Peregrine business."

Io looked at him over her tapestry frame. She'd heard all about what had happened yesterday. "Where did your wise brother sleep last night?"

"I don't know." Severn hesitated. "With his men, maybe. He should have broken the bedroom door down. That woman needs to be taught a lesson."

Io watched Severn scratching. It had been so good when, for a while, he was clean. "You have nearly got the castle back to the way it was. Your brother is sleeping with his men, and I imagine he is as unhappy as he ever was. I don't guess he's smiling now, is he?"

Severn stood and walked toward the window. Zared had said Severn was jealous, and part of him was beginning to wonder if that was correct. Yesterday Severn had won. He'd forced Rogan into publicly denying his wife, into making her retreat from him. And what had he won? The last twenty-four hours had been miserable. He hadn't realized how much Rogan had changed since he'd married that woman.

The old Rogan had returned in full force. On the training field he was a vicious taskmaster. He had broken the arm of one knight who wasn't quick enough. He had gashed the cheek of another. And when Severn had protested, one blow from Rogan had sent him sprawling.

Severn turned back to Io. "Rogan is as angry as he ever was."

Iolanthe could read his thoughts. There wasn't a malicious bone in Severn's body—which is one reason why she loved him. But he was like most men in that he didn't like change. He had loved, worshiped, his older brothers and one by one he'd seen them die until only Rogan was left. And now he was afraid of losing him, too.

"So what are you going to do to get them back together?" Io asked as she couched gold thread onto the needlepoint background.

"Together?" Severn gasped. "Have Rogan lounging about in the solar all afternoon? The place will fall apart. The Howards will kill us in our sleep. They'll—"

"Rogan is going to kill you with work if you do not rectify your interference."

He opened his mouth to contradict her but shut it and sat back down in the chair.

"I guess she's not so bad," he said after a moment. "And maybe the place did need a bit of cleaning." He looked at Io. "All right, a lot of cleaning, but she didn't have to—" He stopped, not knowing what else to say. "She didn't have to take him away so completely," he said at last.

"She loves him," Io said. "That's a fatal thing to happen to a woman." She looked at Severn with love, but he didn't notice. Iolanthe admired this pale, plain Liana, who'd been able to do what Io could not. "Send Liana an invitation to supper, make it from Rogan, then send Rogan an invitation from Liana."

Severn scratched furiously at his shoulder. "Do you think she'll have my clothes washed?"

"If you give her back Rogan, I'm sure she will."

"I will think about it," Severn said softly. "If Rogan gets worse, I'll consider it."

"Does he think he can win me back so easily?" Liana asked Gaby. They were alone in the solar, Liana having sent her other women away. "Does he think that a single invitation from him will make me come crawling back to him? After the way he humiliated me?"

"But, my lady," Gaby said pleadingly, "sometimes men say things they don't mean, and it's been a whole week now. Baudoin said Lord Rogan is worse than he ever was, that he never sleeps or lets the men rest. He doubled the guards on the parapets, and any guard who so much as blinks is flogged."

"Of what concern is that of mine? He has my money; he has what he wants." The deep, deep hurt she'd felt at his words had not abated in the past week. She had been lying to herself in thinking that he cared anything about her. He had married her for her money and money was all he wanted from her. Well he had that now and he no longer had to put up with her. She wouldn't try to come between him and the peasants. She wouldn't nag him to allow her to judge the court cases. In fact, perhaps she'd just take her ladies and go to that other castle he owned, or maybe she'd retire to one of the estates of her dowry—if he could spare the revenue.

"You mean to refuse his invitation?" Gaby asked.

"I will pack a bag full of gold plates and put them on the chair in my place. That should satisfy him. Then he wouldn't have to look at my ugliness."

"But, my lady, I'm sure he didn't—"

Gaby kept talking, but Liana didn't listen. The thought of the gold and her lack of beauty had given her an idea. "Fetch the blacksmith to me."

"My lady?"

"Send the blacksmith to me. I have a job for him to do."

"If you will tell me what it is, I'll—"

"No, this is my secret."

Gaby stood where she was. "Do you mean to accept the invitation?"

"Oh yes," Liana said. "I will accept my husband's invitation and he will get my gold and he will not have to look upon my plain face."

Gaby still didn't move. "Sometimes it is better to forgive and forget than to keep on with the fight. Marriage is—"

"*My* marriage is based on gold and nothing else. Now, go!"

"Yes, my lady," Gaby said meekly, and left the solar.

Three hours later, Liana was dressing to attend the supper her husband had invited her to. Joice was helping her, as Liana didn't want Gaby's disapproval —and disapproval she knew it would be.

Nor did she want the Lady's disapproval. As Liana mounted the solar stairs, she'd seen that the Lady's door was unlocked and standing ajar. "I will always be here when you need me," the Lady had said, and it was true. Whenever she'd come to a crisis with Rogan, the door had been open.

But tonight Liana did not want to talk to the Lady, because Liana did not want to be dissuaded from what she was about to do. Her hurt was too deep and too raw to do anything else. Was she to say she forgave him? If she did, what would he do to her next time? He could humiliate her daily and expect her to forgive him anything.

So Liana ignored the invitation that the Lady's open door signaled and instead dressed with Joice's aid.

"Get out of here!" Rogan bellowed to Severn. They were in one of the rooms over the kitchen, a room that had once been occupied by a Day. It was already dirty, since no cleaning had been done in a week, and a big rat gnawed on a bone in a dark corner.

"I thought you might like to wear something that stank a little less, that's all. And maybe shave."

"Why?" Rogan asked belligerently. "To eat with a woman? You were right. It was better before she interfered. I think I'll send her to Bevan."

"And how many men must leave here to protect her? The Howards will—"

"The Howards can have her, for all I care." Even as Rogan said it, he winced. Damn the bitch to hell, anyway! He'd tried to see her after what he'd said, but she'd locked the door against him. His first impulse had been to beat the door down and show her who was master in his home, but then he'd felt like a fool for caring. Let her stay behind the locked door if she wanted, it didn't matter to him. He'd told the truth when he'd said he'd married her for her money.

But during the past week he'd . . . well, he'd remembered things. He'd remembered her laughing, remembered the way she threw her arms about his neck when he'd pleased her, remembered her opinions and suggestions, remembered her warm, willing body at night. He remembered the things she caused to happen: music, good food, a courtyard that he could walk across without stepping in a pile of horse manure, the day at the fair. He remembered holding her hand. He remembered watching Gaby wash her hair.

He glared at Severn. "Since when have you cared whether I dressed for my wife or not?"

"Since there was sand in my bread two days ago and since Io started being less than warm to me."

"Send her back to her husband, and I'll send . . ."—he could hardly say her name—". . . I'll send Liana," he said softly, "away."

"Probably be better for both of us," Severn said. "A lot quieter, certainly. And we could get some work done. And we wouldn't have to worry about the Howards attacking us to get at our women. But on the other hand, the men have been complaining about the bread. Perhaps . . ." He trailed off.

Rogan looked at the dark green velvet tunic Severn still held. Perhaps, since she had sent him an invitation, it meant she was ready to apologize for locking him out of their room and for allowing sand in the bread and rats in the rooms. And if she was ready to apologize, perhaps he was ready to forgive her.

Liana waited until all of Rogan's men were seated in the Great Hall and Rogan and Severn and Zared sat at the high table. Joice lowered the veil over her mistress's face.

"You are sure, my lady?" Joice asked grimly, her disapproval showing in her tight mouth.

"More than sure," Liana said, and put her shoulders back.

235

Every man and the few women in the Hall were quiet as Liana entered, Joice holding her long, fur-trimmed train. Liana's face was covered by a veil that reached to her waist.

Solemnly, slowly, she walked toward the high table and stood there waiting until Severn nudged Rogan, and Rogan stood and pulled her chair out for her. As Liana sat down, still the room was silent, every eye on the master and mistress.

Rogan seemed to have no idea what to do to break the silence. "Would you like some wine?" he asked at last, his voice ringing in the high-ceilinged stone room.

Very slowly, Liana put her arms under her veil and raised it. There was an audible gasp through the room as they saw her. About Liana's face, suspended from strings attached to her headdress, were coins: gold coins, silver coins, copper coins. In each one a hole had been punched, a string attached, and then fastened to her headdress.

As the astonished crowd watched, Liana took a pair of scissors and cut a silver coin from in front of her face. "Will this be enough to pay for the wine, my lord?" She cut off a gold coin. "Will this cover the cost of the beef?"

Rogan gaped at her, looking at the coins she cut away.

"Do not look so fearful, my lord," she said loudly. "I will not eat so much that you will be exposed to my ugliness. I am sure the sight of the money pleases you more than my plain face."

Rogan's face turned cold. He did not say a word to her, but rose and left the Hall.

Zared turned to Severn, who looked as if he might be ill. "Eat up, Severn. Tomorrow we'll probably get

236

rocks in our bread and Rogan is going to work all of you into the grave on the training field," Zared said cheerfully. "You were smart to try to keep Liana from interfering."

Liana, with all the grace and dignity she could muster, left the Hall.

CHAPTER
FIFTEEN

N o!" Liana snapped at Gaby and Joice. "Don't put
that there. Nor over there. And certainly not there!"

Joice backed out of the room as soon as possible,
but Gaby stayed in the solar, looked at the back of
Liana's head, and bit her tongue. Not that she'd kept
her mouth shut in the two weeks since that awful
supper when Lady Liana had appeared wearing the
coins, but she'd learned it did no good. "He has what
he wanted," was all Lady Liana would say to Gaby's
pleadings that she and Rogan talk to each other.

And Lord Rogan was worse than his wife. Gaby had
wheedled Baudoin into broaching the subject to the
lord, but Rogan had nearly put a pike through
Baudoin's belly.

So, because of the anger between the master and
mistress, the whole castle, as well as the village, was
suffering. The bakers refused to deliver fresh bread
because Rogan refused to pay them, and Liana refused
to have anything to do with the household. So there
was, once again, sand in the bread. The courtyard was

full of manure because no one ordered the men to clean it. The peasants were hungry. The moat, with only a foot of water in it, already contained half a dozen rotting cow carcasses. Whereas this had been the normal way of life before, now everyone complained. The men complained about the lice and the fleas in their clothes and the manure under their feet. They complained about Rogan's temper. They complained about Lady Liana not doing her job properly. (No one seemed to remember the way they'd fought her when she first arrived.)

All in all, after two weeks there wasn't a person within a ten-mile radius who wasn't affected by this argument between the lord and his lady.

"My lady—" Gaby began.

"I have nothing to say to you," Liana snapped. Two weeks had done nothing to calm her temper. She had made every effort to please her husband, to be a wife to him, and he had ignored her and humiliated her in public. He, a man of great beauty, might think that the plainer people of the world had no feelings about their lack of looks, but he was wrong. If he thought she was so ugly, then she'd spare him having to look at her.

"It's not me," Gaby said. "The lady Iolanthe asks to see you."

Liana's head came up. "Severn has had his way. He has won and he has his brother the way he was. I see no reason to see Severn's mistress."

Gaby gave a bit of a smile. "The gossip is that Lord Severn and his . . . the Lady Iolanthe are quarreling also. Perhaps she'd like to commiserate with you."

Liana wanted to talk to someone. Gaby constantly preached forgiving Rogan for everything. She thought Liana should go to him and apologize, but Liana was sure he'd reject her. How could a woman as plain-faced as she was have any influence on a man like

Rogan? And how could someone as dazzling as Iolanthe understand Liana's problem? "Tell her I cannot accept," Liana said.

"But, my lady, she has invited you to her apartments. It's said that she's never invited anyone inside there before."

"Oh?" Liana said. *"I* am to go to her? I, the lady of the manor, am to visit my brother-in-law's married mistress? Tell her no."

Gaby left the room, and Liana looked back at her tapestry frame. She was seething over the presumption of the woman, but part of her was also curious. What did the beautiful Iolanthe have to say to her?

The invitation was reissued daily for three days, and each time Liana refused it. But on the fourth day she looked out the window and into the courtyard and saw one of the Days, her generous bosom pushing against the coarse wool of her greasy dress.

Liana turned to Joice. "Fetch my red brocade gown, the one with the cloth-of-gold underskirt. I am going visiting."

An hour later Liana was dressed so that she knew she looked her best. She had to go outside and cross the courtyard to reach the stairs to Iolanthe's apartments, and she could feel every eye on her. But she looked straight ahead and ignored all of them.

When she at last reached the apartment and a maid opened the door, it took Liana a moment to recover her composure—and close her gaping mouth. Never had she seen a room of such wealth. There were gold and silver-gilt dishes everywhere. There were *rugs* on the floor, deep-piled, intricately patterned carpets. The walls were hung with silk tapestries of delicate scenes and so intricately woven, a flower no bigger than a thumbnail had a dozen colors in it. The beamed ceilings were painted with pastoral scenes.

The windows had leaded panes with colored-glass inserts that shone like jewels.

And in the room were carved chairs with cushioned seats, carved sewing frames, beautiful chests inlaid with ivory. There was nowhere she could look that was not of exquisite beauty.

"Welcome," Iolanthe said, and in her silver gown she was the most beautiful object in the room.

"I . . ." Liana took a breath to recover herself. "You had something to say to me?" Earlier, Liana had thought of telling this woman how immoral she was and how she would spend eternity in hell for being married to one man and living in sin with another, but in Iolanthe's presence, no such words came to Liana.

"Won't you have a seat? I have had something prepared for us to eat."

Liana took the seat offered and sipped watered wine from a ruby-studded gold chalice.

"You'll have to go to him," Iolanthe said. "He's too stubborn to give in to you, and besides that, I doubt if he knows how."

Liana set the chalice down with a thunk and stood. "I'll not listen to this. He has insulted me repeatedly, and this is the final straw." She started for the door.

"Wait!" Iolanthe called. "Please return. That was rude of me."

Liana turned back.

Io smiled at her. "Forgive me. It has been difficult lately. Severn has been in the worst temper. Of course I've told him this is entirely his fault, that if he hadn't been so jealous of his brother, Rogan would never have said he'd married you for your money and you would never have had to resort to the veil of coins."

Liana sat back down. "True," she said, and picked up her wine goblet again. "He said, in front of his men, that he couldn't bear my ugliness."

241

Iolanthe stared at the blonde woman. So, she thought, it wasn't the money. It was that Rogan had insulted his wife's looks. Rogan and Severn were such divine-looking men that it was easy to see how a woman could feel intimidated by them. Every morning Io studied her own reflection in the mirror and, at her age, she was teaching herself to smile without crinkling her eyes. She lived in terror of the day when Severn no longer believed her to be beautiful. She couldn't imagine how she'd feel if Severn said that he wanted her husband's money and not her person.

"I see," Io said at last.

"Yes," Liana said. "And *I* see, too. I thought I could make him love me. I thought I could make myself indispensable to him, but he never wanted me. Nor did anyone else want me here. It's ironic. My stepmother tried to tell me this, but I wouldn't listen. I thought I knew more than a woman who'd had two husbands. She was right. Even my maid Joice was right. Joice said men didn't want wives. In my case not only my husband didn't want me, but his brother didn't, his mistresses, his men—no one wanted me except the Lady, and now even her door is locked against me."

Iolanthe listened to this speech of self-pity and understood it very well. As long as a woman felt desirable, she could feel confident. She could set his bed, with him and his mistress in it, on fire; she could dare to make a wager that he would lose; she could tempt his wrath by countermanding his orders for the castle staff. But when a woman felt undesirable, much of her strength left her.

Io had no idea what to do. Never in all of time could she hope to get Rogan to go to Liana. Rogan was a stubborn man who had no idea what was good for him. He wouldn't like thinking any woman had ever had any influence on him. "Who is the Lady?" Io asked, stalling for time while she thought about this problem.

At first Io barely listened to Liana's explanation, but something in her words caught her attention. "She lives above the solar?"

"In a single room that is almost always locked. But she seems to sense when I'm troubled, for then the door is open. She has been my greatest friend since I arrived. She told me about Jeanne Howard. She told me that men do not fight battles over timid women— or over ugly women," Liana added.

"Is she an older woman, quite pretty, with soft brown hair?"

"Yes. Who is she? I've meant to ask her, but every time I see her—" She broke off as she watched Iolanthe ring a little silver bell. A maid appeared, Io whispered something to her, and the maid disappeared.

Iolanthe stood. "Would you mind if we went to this room and met your Lady?"

"The room is locked. It has been since I . . . since I went to supper with my husband."

"I have sent my maid to fetch the key. Shall we go?"

Liana's lone appearance earlier had slowed movement in the courtyard, but when Io and Liana appeared together, everyone came to a halt and stood gaping at the two women. Iolanthe was a rare enough sight, but her with another woman was impossible to believe.

Liana ignored the staring people both inside and outside the castle and led Iolanthe to the locked door above the solar. "When she doesn't want to be disturbed, she keeps the door locked. I think we should respect her privacy."

Io didn't say anything, but when her maid reappeared, a big key in hand, she inserted it into the lock.

"I don't think—" Liana began, but broke off. The room, which had been the one clean place in the castle when she arrived, was bare. No, not bare, for she could see, under years of cobwebs and rodent droppings, the Lady's furniture. There was the cushioned bench Liana had sat on. There was the Lady's tapestry frame. The windows that had had sunlight streaming through them were broken, and a dead bird lay on the floor.

"I don't understand," Liana whispered. "Where is she?"

"Dead. Many years ago."

Liana crossed herself even as she denied this. "Are you saying she's a ghost? That's not possible. I talked to her. She's as real as you or I. She told me things, things other people didn't know." Her eyes widened.

"I've heard she does. I've never seen her, nor has Severn, and I don't know if Rogan has or not, but several other people have. She seems to love helping people in need. Years ago a maid who was pregnant was about to throw herself into the moat when she heard the Lady, as you call her, singing and spinning. The Lady talked her out of suicide. Didn't you wonder why no one lived in these rooms? Half the men refused even to go into the solar to fetch the birds, and *no* one would come up here."

Liana was trying to take this in. "No one told me. No one so much as hinted."

"I guess they thought your cleaning would do away with her. She never harms anyone. As ghosts go, she is benign."

Liana walked through the thick dust on the floor to the tapestry frame. On it was an old, unfinished piece of work of a lady and a unicorn—what the Lady had been sewing when Liana had visited. Liana suddenly felt as if she'd lost a very dear friend. "Who is she? And why does she haunt the Peregrines?"

"She is Severn's grandmother, Rogan and Zared's too. She was Jane, the first wife of old Giles Peregrine. Their son was John, Severn's father. After Jane died, Giles married Bess Howard and it was her family who said Jane had never been legally married to Giles and therefore her son and his children were bastards. This castle and Bevan belonged to Jane's family; she grew up here."

"And so she comes back here to haunt."

"Years after her death, she was in this room when her son John arrived home after the king declared him illegitimate. He locked the door on her and never unlocked it again. Only she unlocks it now. Some people say John was a fool, that his mother came to tell him something and he wouldn't listen."

"She probably wanted to tell him to stay away from the village girls," Liana said bitterly.

"No," Io said. "Everyone believed she wanted to tell him where the parish registers were."

"What registers?"

"John could never prove that his parents had been married. All the witnesses to the marriage either died or mysteriously disappeared and no one could find the registers that recorded the marriage. Most people believed the Howards had destroyed them, but some people said old Giles had hidden them from his grasping second wife." Io smiled. "If you see your Lady again, you might ask her where the registers are. If there were proof the marriage did take place, perhaps the king would restore the Peregrine estates to Rogan and Severn and this feud with the Howards would stop."

Liana wondered if Rogan would love her if she

245

found the registers. No, probably not. She'd still be plain-faced even if she were the richest woman in the world. "We should leave," she said, "and lock the door. She should have her privacy."

They left the room. Io locked the door and handed the key to her maid, who had been quietly waiting outside.

"Will you go to him?" Io asked.

Liana knew who she meant. "I cannot. He does not want me; he wants gold. Now that he has it, he should be content."

"Gold makes a cold bed partner."

A lump formed in Liana's throat. "He has his Days. Now, will you excuse me? I have a bit of embroidery that needs finishing."

They walked down the stairs to the solar, and Iolanthe bid Liana farewell.

That evening Severn came to Iolanthe's apartments. He was limping and there was a blood-dripping gash on the side of his head. Io motioned to her maid and soon Io was bathing his head with a linen cloth.

"I am going to kill my brother," Severn said through his teeth. "That is the only way to stop him. Did you talk any sense into that wife of his?"

"I had as much success talking to her as you have had with your brother."

"Watch that!" Severn said, wincing. "I don't want new wounds. At least I can understand Rogan. He's been very tolerant of that woman, allowing her to sit by him while he judged the courts, letting her do what she could in the village, even giving her a full day in bed."

"He has been *most* generous," Io said sarcastically.

"He has, actually. I never thought he'd be so generous with a wife."

"What did you think? That your sweet-tempered brother would drop her in this filthy castle with servants who ridiculed her, that he'd ignore her, that he wouldn't remember what she looked like until she set him on fire?"

"Women!" Severn muttered. "You are such illogical creatures."

"My logic is fine, it's your brother who—"

Severn pulled her into his lap and kissed her neck. "Let's forget my brother."

She pushed away from him and stood. "How many weeks has it been since you had a bath?"

"You never used to care whether I bathed or not."

"I thought horse manure was your natural scent," she shot back at him.

Severn stood up. "This is all that woman's fault. If she—"

"If *you* hadn't interfered, things would be fine now. What are you going to do to make up for what you've done?"

"We've been through this, remember? I was willing to admit that I'd been . . . well, a little overzealous with Rogan, so at *your* suggestion I sent them invitations to supper. And you saw where that went, didn't you? That stupid bitch showed up wearing coins. Rogan should have accepted her offer of payment. What he should have done was—"

"He *should* have told her she's beautiful," Io interrupted. "She thinks your oversexed brother doesn't desire her. I can't imagine why. He'll bed anything that's even three-quarters female."

Severn smiled proudly. "Great cocksman, isn't he?"

"Let's not go into my opinions of your brother. You

247

have to get Rogan to tell Liana he thinks she's beautiful and he desires her above all other women."

"Sure. And I'll move a few oceans, too. You want London moved while I'm at it? You've never tried to get Rogan to do something he doesn't want to do."

"Is he back sleeping with his Days now?"

Severn grimaced. "No, and I think that's half his problem. This is the longest he's gone without a female since . . ." He thought a moment. ". . . since the Howards took his first wife. Don't give me that look," he said to Io. "My brother can handle women whether he's married to them or not. Maybe he just doesn't want a woman right now. I can understand that, what with the way his wife has behaved. Wearing those coins was the last straw."

"It's up to you," Io said sweetly. "Why don't you get Rogan to send Liana back to her father, get rid of her completely. Then you could bring in a wagonload of beautiful, nubile young girls so your brother could have a dozen per night."

"And which one will see that we have pies to eat?" Severn muttered. "Damn you, Io! And damn that Liana. Damn *all* women! Why can't you leave a man alone? Rogan only married her to get money. Why did he have to . . . to . . ."

"To what?" Io asked innocently. "Fall in love with her? Begin to need her?"

"That isn't what I meant at all. Damn both of them! Somebody ought to lock them in a room together and throw away the key. Both of them make me sick." His head came up.

"What is it?"

"Nothing. Just a thought."

"Tell me," Io urged.

It was a while before Severn began talking.

* * *

That same evening Severn sent a peace offering to Liana. She sat alone in her solar with her ladies, as she did every evening. Usually, she was undisturbed by anyone from the castle—as if she didn't exist, or as if they wished she didn't exist—so she was very surprised when a scarred old knight brought up a jug of wine and said it was from Lord Severn to his beautiful sister-in-law.

"Do you think it's poisoned?" Liana asked Gaby.

"Perhaps with a love potion," Gaby answered. She'd never give up trying to reason with Liana.

The wine was spicy and warm and Liana drank more than she meant to. "I suddenly feel very tired," she said. She was so tired that her head felt too heavy to hold up.

It was at that moment that Severn entered the solar. All of Liana's women perked up at the sight of the handsome blond giant, but Severn had eyes only for Liana.

Gaby was looking at her mistress in alarm as Liana's eyes closed and her head lolled against the back of her chair. "I'm afraid something's wrong."

"She'll sleep it off," Severn said, elbowed Gaby out of his way, then picked Liana up.

"My lord!" Gaby gasped. "You cannot—"

"I *am,*" Severn answered as he carried the sleeping Liana from the room and started up the spiral stairs. He went up past the bedrooms above the solar, up another flight until he came to a heavy iron-clad oak door. He shifted Liana, tossing her over his shoulder while he took a key hanging at the end of a chain suspended from his belt and opened the door.

It was a small room with a garderobe off to one side and another heavy, barred door leading out to the walk along the top of the parapets. The room was usually used for housing guards, but today the guards were gone. Sometimes the room was used as a prison and that's what Severn wanted it for.

Severn pushed the door open and stood for a moment while his eyes adjusted to the dim light. Lying on the bed, sound asleep, was Rogan and for a moment Severn reconsidered his plan. But then a couple of fleas began scurrying about on his back and he knew that what he was doing was right. He dumped his sister-in-law on the bed beside his brother and gouged at the fleas.

"There," he said as he looked down at the two of them. "You can stay in here until we have some peace."

CHAPTER
SIXTEEN

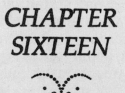

*I*t took Liana a while to wake up in the morning. It was as if she couldn't open her eyes. She stretched her arms, then her legs, as she luxuriated in the soft warmth of the mattress.

"If you want something to eat, you better get up and get it."

Her eyes flew open to see Rogan sitting at a small table devouring chicken, cheese, and bread.

"What are you doing here?" she demanded. "Why have you brought me here? The wine! You drugged it."

"My brother did. My brother, whose days on this earth are limited, drugged the wine."

"And he brought me here?"

"He brought both of us here while we were sleeping."

Liana sat up and looked about the spare little room: a bed, a table and two chairs, and a candle stand. "He has betrayed us to the Howards," she said softly. "Does he mean to turn the castle over to them?"

Rogan looked at her as if she were the village idiot. "My brother may be stupid at times as well as stubborn, but he is not a traitor."

"Then why has he done this?"

Rogan looked back at the food.

Liana got out of bed. "Why has he drugged us and put us in here?"

"Who knows? Now, eat."

Liana felt her temper rising. She went to the doors and pulled on them, then beat her fists against them and shouted to be released, but no one came. She went to each of the two narrow arrow slits and shouted down from them, but no one answered. She turned back to Rogan. "How can you eat? How long are we to be prisoners? How do we get out of here?"

"My father made this room to keep prisoners. We cannot get out."

"Until your stupid, overbearing brother lets us out, that is. Why did I ever marry into a family like this? Do any of you men have any sense?"

Rogan just looked at her with hard eyes, and Liana immediately regretted her words. "I . . ." she began.

He put his hand up. "You may return to your father as soon as we are released from here."

He pushed away from the table and went to stand by the narrow window. She walked beside him. "Rogan, I . . ."

He walked away from her.

The day was spent in silence and anger. Liana looked at Rogan and remembered his telling her that her money meant everything to him. So be it, she thought. She would return to her father or retire to one of her dower estates and live without the Peregrine family, with their horses' skulls hanging over the mantel.

Food was lowered to them in a cloth bundle that would fit through the arrow slit. Rogan took the food and yelled up at Severn about what he planned to do to him when he was released. Rogan took his food to the other side of the room and refused to sit at the table with Liana.

Night came and they still were not speaking. Liana lay down on the bed and wondered where Rogan planned to sleep. She started to protest when he lay down beside her, his back to her, but she didn't. She just made sure she wasn't touching him.

But as the early morning sun touched the arrow slit, Liana woke to find herself held tightly in her husband's arms. She forgot about feuds and arguments and kissed his sleep-softened mouth.

Rogan woke instantly and kissed her with all the hunger he felt. After the kiss, they were both lost and there was a frenzy of clothes being discarded as they frantically sought each other's skin. They came together fast and furiously, with a passion that had built up over the past two weeks.

Afterward, they lay in each other's arms, plastered together by sweaty skin, clinging to one another. Liana's first impulse was to ask if Rogan really thought she was ugly and if he actually meant to send her away, but she refrained.

"I saw the ghost," she said at last.

"In the chamber below us?"

"She's the Lady I thought was Iolanthe. Remember I told you she was older than Severn? She told me about Jeanne Howard."

He didn't answer her, and Liana turned in his arms to look at him. "You've seen her, too, haven't you?" she asked after a moment.

"Of course not. There is no ghost. It's just a—"

253

"A what? When did you see her? Was she sewing or spinning?"

He took a while to answer. "Sewing. The tapestry with the unicorn."

"Did you ever tell anyone?"

"Not until now."

His words made Liana feel triumphant. "When did you see her? What did she say to you?"

His voice was soft. "It was after Oliver Howard took . . . her."

"Jeanne."

"Yes, that one," Rogan answered. "The woman came to me and told me she wanted Howard, that she carried his brat. She asked me to stop the feud. I should have killed the bitch with my own hands."

"But you couldn't."

"I didn't, anyway. I returned here to get supplies— we'd been fighting the Howards for a year—and early one morning I shot an arrow to test a bow and the wind caught the arrow and carried it into a window over the solar. At least, that's what I thought at the time. I also thought I heard a woman scream. I went to the solar, then to the rooms above. No one had lived in them for years because of the stories of the ghost. My father used to curse her because when he had guests, she always appeared and frightened them."

"Were you frightened when you went to get your arrow?"

"I was too angry then at the Howards to care about a ghost. I'd lost my two brothers, and every arrow was needed."

"Was she there?"

She saw Rogan smile slightly. "I thought a ghost would be . . . foggy, I guess. She was so real-looking. She had my arrow and she gave me a scolding, said I'd nearly hit her. At the time I never thought about the fact that I had been shooting away from the castle walls."

"What did you talk about?"

"It was odd, but I talked to her as I've never talked to anyone else."

"Me, too. She knew so much about me. Did you talk about Jeanne?"

"Yes. She told me my wife was not the one."

She looked at him. "The one for what?"

"I don't know. It made sense when I was with her, but none whatever when I left. I guess it had something to do with the poem."

Liana's eyes widened. "What poem?"

"I haven't thought of it in years. Actually, it seems to be more of a riddle. Let's see . . .

"When the red and white make black
When the black and gold become one
When the one and the red unite
Then shall you know."

Liana lay quietly in Rogan's arms and thought about the riddle. "What does it mean?"

"I have no idea. Sometimes I used to lay in bed and think about it, but I never came up with anything."

"What does Severn think? Or Zared?"

"I never asked either of them."

She pushed away to look at him. "Never asked? But it could have something to do with the parish registers. The Lady is your grandmother, and if anyone knows where the registers are, she does."

He frowned. "The woman is a ghost. She's been dead a long time. Maybe I didn't see her and I dreamed the riddle."

"I didn't dream the story about you and Jeanne Howard. The Lady told me how beautiful Jeanne was and how much you loved her."

"I hardly knew the Howard bitch, and I don't remember her as being especially good to look at. Certainly nothing like Iolanthe."

Liana pulled the sheet over her bare breasts and sat up. "Oh, so now it's Iolanthe you want. You could get money *and* beauty."

Rogan's confusion showed on his handsome face. "Iolanthe is a bitch. I'm sure she's the one who planned this." He motioned to the locked door.

"Why? In an attempt to get me to forgive you for telling me before your men that I was hideously ugly?"

Rogan sat up, his mouth dropping open. "I never said any such thing."

"You did! You said you married me for my money, not for my advice or my beauty."

Rogan's confusion deepened. "I only spoke the truth. I didn't even see you before the wedding, except when I didn't know who you were, so how could I have married you for anything besides money?"

Liana could feel tears of frustration coming to her eyes. "I married you because I thought you . . . that you desired me. You kissed me when you didn't know I had any money."

Rogan had never made an effort to understand the female mind and now he knew why. "I also kissed you when I knew you were rich." His voice was rising as he got out of bed and leaned over her. "I kissed you after you interfered between me and the peasants. I kissed you after you wheedled me into seeing a play that made me look like a fool. I kissed you—"

"Because I'm your wife and for no other reason," she said. "You told everyone you thought I was ugly.

Maybe I'm not as beautiful as Iolanthe or as pretty as your first wife, but there are some men who've said I was quite pleasing to look at."

Rogan threw up his hands in exasperation. "You're not bad when you're not sniveling."

Liana started to cry in earnest at that. She lay down in bed, her knees drawn up, and cried so hard her shoulders shook.

As Rogan looked down at her, at first he felt nothing but anger. She was accusing him of something, but he wasn't sure what. She was making it seem that he was in the wrong for what he'd said. He had merely told the truth and he had said it to keep her from stepping between him and his men. What in the world did his words have to do with her looks? And *desire?* Hadn't he just proved this morning that he desired her? And damnation, he hadn't touched another woman in two whole weeks. Two long, long weeks!

He knew he had every right to be angry with her. *He* should be the one being comforted, but as he watched her cry, he felt something inside himself soften. When he was a boy he'd cried just as she was doing now and his big brothers had kicked him and laughed at him.

He sat on the bed by her head. "Tell me . . . what's wrong," he said hesitantly, feeling awkward and embarrassed.

She didn't answer but just cried harder.

After a moment he lifted her and pulled her onto his lap and held her close. Her tears wet his shoulder as he stroked her hair away from her face. "What's wrong?" he asked again.

"You think I'm ugly. I'm not beautiful like you or Severn or Zared or Iolanthe, but the jongleurs have written poems to my beauty."

Rogan started to say that for money anyone would do anything, but he wisely caught himself. "Not as beautiful as me, eh? Or Severn? I might agree with you about me, but we own pigs better-looking than Severn."

"Better-looking than me, too, no doubt," she cried anew.

"I think you're prettier now than when I first saw you."

Liana sniffed and lifted her head to look at him. "What does that mean?"

"I don't know." He smoothed her hair back. "When I saw you at the church, I thought you were a pale little rabbit and I couldn't tell you from the other women. But now . . ." He looked in her eyes. "Now I find you quite pleasant to look at. I have . . . thought about you these past weeks."

"I have thought about you every minute of every day." She clutched him to her. "Oh, Rogan, tell me anything about me, tell me I'm stupid, tell me that I'm a great nuisance and a bother, but please don't tell me I'm ugly."

He held her close. "You should never tell your secrets to a person. They'll use them against you."

"But I trust you."

Rogan couldn't help but feel that her trust was a burden and a responsibility. He held her away from him. "I will tell you that you are the most beautiful of women if you will not unman me before my men."

It was Liana's turn to be shocked. "Me? Never would I do such a thing. *Never!*"

"You countermanded my orders for the peasants."

"Yes, but you were flogging innocent people."

"You tried to burn me in my bed."

"But you were in bed with another woman," she said indignantly.

"You seduce me away from my work with sweetmeats and music and pretty smiles."

She smiled at him as his words convinced her of how right she was to have married him.

"And you disobeyed my orders before my men."

"When?"

"The morning the Howards attacked."

"I was merely—"

"Interfering," he said sternly. "It wasn't any of your business. If I hadn't been drunk, you might have—" He stopped. He didn't want to tell her that while he lay in a drunken stupor, the Howards might have taken her prisoner.

"I might have what?"

His face changed, and Liana could see he was hiding something. "What might I have done?"

Rogan moved away from her and got out of bed. "If that damned brother of mine doesn't send us food, I'll hang him after burning him."

"If you hadn't been drunk, I might have what?" She wrapped a sheet around herself and followed his nude form into the garderobe. Even as he began to use the urinal, she didn't hesitate. "Might have what?"

Rogan grimaced. "If I ever capture a Howard spy and want information, I'll send you to him."

"Might have what?" she asked again.

"Been taken," he snapped, turning back to the room.

"The Howards wanted me?" Liana whispered.

Rogan was angrily pulling on his braies. "The Howards seem to always want what the Peregrines have: our land, our castles, our women."

"We could make them a gift of the Days." Rogan did not find humor in her words. She went to him and put her arms about his neck. "You were so angry that morning because the Howards threatened to take me? Rogan, you *do* love me."

"I don't have time for love. Get dressed. Severn may come in."

She let the sheet fall off her body so that her bare breasts were against his chest. "Rogan, I love you."

"Humph! You haven't spoken to me in weeks. You've made everyone's life miserable. Even Zared's room has rats in it. And I'm so light from lack of decent food, my horse doesn't know me. My life was better when no woman said she loved me." What he said did not agree with how tightly he held her.

"Severn has taught me something," she said. "I swear to you that never again will I leave you alone. If you hurt me—and I've no doubt you will do so often—I promise I will tell you why I am angry. Never again will I shut myself away from you."

"It's not me who matters, but the men need decent food and—"

She stood on tiptoe to kiss him. "It is you who matters to me. Rogan, I will never betray you as Jeanne once did. Even if the Howards were to take me, I would still love you."

"The Howards will never take another Peregrine," he said fiercely.

"And I am now a Peregrine?" she asked, smiling.

"An odd one, but a Peregrine more or less," he said reluctantly.

She hugged him and didn't see the way Rogan smiled into her hair, the way he closed his eyes as he held her. He didn't like to think how much he'd missed her in the past few days or how much her frivolous chatter had come to mean to him. He had lived his life without her and done very well, but she had entered his life meekly, then literally set him on fire. Nothing had been the same since. Pleasure, leisure, softness, had never been part of his life. But this snippet of a girl had introduced them all into his life and it was amazing how quickly he'd adapted.

He pulled away from her, her face held in his big hands. "I think my stupid brother locked us in here to get you to clean his room and to talk to the bakers."

"Oh? And who is to persuade me to do what he wants?"

"Perhaps I can," Rogan said suggestively, and swung her into his arms. "You told everyone we once spent a whole day in bed. Now you shall make your lie true."

They made love to each other long and slowly, their first needy passion already spent. They explored each other's bodies with their hands and tongues, and when they at last came together, it was leisurely, slowly, caressingly. Liana had no idea how Rogan watched her, how he wanted to give pleasure to her, how he wanted her to enjoy their lovemaking.

Afterward, they lay in each other's arms and held one another.

"Do we hang your brother or kiss his feet?" Liana whispered.

"Hang him," Rogan said firmly. "If there was an attack—"

Liana rubbed her thigh over his. "If there were an attack, you'd be too weak to fight, so it wouldn't matter."

"You are a disrespectful wench. You ought to be beaten."

"By whom?" she asked insolently. "Surely not the worn-out oldest Peregrine."

"I'll show you who is worn out," he said, rolling over on her, making Liana giggle.

But a thud on the floor near them caught Rogan's attention. Immediately, he covered Liana's body with his as he looked about for the cause of the noise. "At last, my damned-to-hell brother has sent us food." He scurried off Liana, out of bed, and went to the package that Severn had managed to swing through the narrow arrow slit and then release so it dropped on the floor.

"You're more interested in food than in me?" she asked.

"At the moment, yes." He brought the food to the bed and they ate there. When bread crumbs dropped on Liana's bare breasts, Rogan licked them off.

They stayed in bed together all day. Liana got Rogan to tell her about his life, about when he was a boy, about the things he'd dreamed about and thought about as a child. She couldn't be sure, but she didn't think he'd ever really talked to anyone before in his life.

At sundown Liana mentioned using some of her dowry wealth to add on to Moray Castle. Rogan was speechless with horror at the idea. "This is not Peregrine land," he said. "The Howards took—"

"Yes, yes, I know. But you have now lived here two generations. Our children will make the third. What if it takes another five generations to get the Peregrine lands back? Will all of them have to live in a place where the roof leaks? Or live in a place this small? We could add a wing to the south—a proper wing, with paneled walls. We could add a chapel and—"

"No, no, no," Rogan said, standing up and glaring down at her in bed. "I'll not put money in this puny place. I'll wait until I have the lands the Howards stole."

"And until then you'll spend every penny that I brought you for making war?" Liana's eyes blazed. "You married me so you can wage war?"

Rogan started to yell that yes, that's why he'd married her, but his eyes changed. "I married you because of your beauty that surpasses all other women's," he said softly. "Including my first wife."

Liana looked up at him, her mouth open in astonishment, then she leaped from the bed and threw herself at him, her legs about his waist, her arms about his neck. "My beautiful husband, I love you so much," she cried.

Rogan hugged her tightly. "I will spend the money how I see fit."

"Yes, of course, and as an obedient wife I would never contradict you, but just let me tell you of my ideas for enlargement."

Rogan groaned. "First you part me from my women, then you burden me with a bunch of red-haired brats, and now you propose to tell me how to spend the money I have worked so hard for."

"Worked so hard for!" she said. "You didn't even attend the wedding feast I had planned so carefully. And you insulted my stepmother."

"She needed insulting. She needs a hand applied to her backside."

"And you'd like to do it?" Liana asked archly.

"I wouldn't want to touch her," he said softly, looking at Liana in the fading light. "Now, come to the table because my bound-for-hell brother has sent down supper."

They spent the night in each other's arms, and as they fell asleep, Rogan murmured that he'd "think about" enlarging Moray Castle and Liana felt as if she'd won a great battle.

When she awoke in the morning, she looked up to see Rogan staring stonily straight ahead. She propped herself up on one elbow to follow his line of vision and saw the door to their room standing open. Liana didn't know when any sight had depressed her so much.

Jude Deveraux

"We could close it again," Liana whispered.

"No," Rogan said. "I must face the ridicule of my men."

Liana had not thought how his men would look at their master, who, because of a spat with his wife, had been locked away in a tower chamber.

They were allowed no time to speculate because Gaby came bustling into the room, talking as fast as her teeth and tongue could move. It seemed that Severn had spread the rumor that Rogan had ordered his wife to be locked into the room with him in order to chastise her. Rogan's reputation was intact.

"And what of mine?" Liana asked.

"They believe you to be a proper wife," Gaby said primly.

"A proper wife?" Liana gasped.

"Don't call her that," Rogan said, "or we'll never have any peace. I want no more fiery beds."

Gaby kept her mouth shut on her opinions about Liana's behavior as a wife. Gaby had won her husband through years of self-denying love and she expected every other woman to do the same thing.

Reluctantly, Liana left the chamber with her husband. She had learned something while in this room. She had learned that what was important to a woman was not necessarily important to a man. Rogan had not called her ugly, and better yet, he didn't think she was plain.

Somehow, she felt that they had come to a bridge and had crossed it safely. Liana could see no obstacles in their future path.

CHAPTER
SEVENTEEN

*F*or six long, glorious weeks, Liana was the happiest
person on earth. She and Rogan had feared his men's
ridicule, but what they had not foreseen was that the
men were so grateful to once again have good food on
their table and the rats out of their rooms that they
didn't really care what had brought about the change.

And Moray Castle did indeed change. The men,
rather than ignore her or fight her, now tugged their
forelocks in respect as Liana walked past. Severn
couldn't be nice enough to her, and Iolanthe began to
join them for dinner.

But best of all was Rogan. His eyes followed Liana
wherever she went. He only went into his brooding
chamber to fetch something and instead spent each
evening in the solar with Liana and her ladies. Severn,
instead of fighting his brother, began to join them, as
did Zared and Io.

It was the morning after such a lovely evening that
Liana realized she was going to have a baby. She had
always assumed she'd be ill as she'd seen other women

be in their first months, but she wasn't ill. She hadn't been tired, hadn't felt in any way unusual, except that now she could barely get into her clothes. She put her hands on her hard, expanded belly and dreamed of a little red-haired child.

"My lady?" Gaby said from behind her. "Are you well?"

"Fine. Lovely. I have never felt better. What are you doing?"

Gaby had a basket full of herbs over her arm. "Lord Rogan and Baudoin were wrestling and they rolled into stinging nettles. I shall prepare an infusion of these to help relieve the pain."

Liana winced. Stinging nettles could be very painful. Near her father's house grew an herb that helped stop the pain much more than what Gaby carried. When Liana first arrived at Moray Castle, she remembered seeing the herb along the road. How far away was that? Ten, twelve miles? With a good horse she could be there and back by sundown. And tonight, as she rubbed the herb on her husband's fiery skin, she'd tell him about their child.

She dismissed Gaby. It wouldn't be easy to escape Moray Castle. Rogan had given her strict orders never to leave the grounds without an escort. And since the Howard attack, he'd told her she could not leave the castle even if all the Peregrine knights accompanied her.

Liana looked down at her brocade dress and smiled. Of course if she left the castle as someone else and not as Lady Liana, then she had nothing to fear. She dug into a trunk at the foot of the bed and found the peasants' clothes she'd worn to the fair. All she had to do was cover her hair, keep her face down, and steal a horse.

An hour later she was galloping eastward, away from Moray Castle, away from the village, and toward the herbs that would give her husband relief. The wind on her face and the muscles of the horse between her legs felt wonderful. She laughed aloud to think of the child she was carrying and of the happiness that was hers.

She was so engrossed in her thoughts that she neither saw nor heard the riders come from the trees. They surrounded her before she saw them.

"Look at this," one of the five men said. "A peasant girl on an animal like that."

Liana didn't need to be told who these men were. They were richly dressed, and there was an arrogance about them that could come only from their being retainees to a powerful man. These men were Howards. Her only hope was that they didn't find out who she was.

"I have stolen the horse," she said in a whining voice. "Oh please do not tell my mistress."

"And what will you give us for not telling?" one handsome young man taunted.

"Anything, sir, oh anything," Liana said, tears in her voice.

Another man rode up behind them. He was older, with gray hair at his temples, a thick, muscular body, and what looked to be a permanent frown on what might have once been a handsome face. "Throw the girl off and take the horse," the man commanded. "It's a Peregrine horse, so I'll take it."

In spite of herself, Liana gave the man a sharp look. Could this be Oliver Howard, the man who'd stolen Rogan's first wife? Liana put her head down and started to dismount, but two men had their hands on her, clutching at her body, searching for her breasts

267

and hips. She twisted away from them—and her hood fell off. Her long blonde hair went cascading down her back.

"Look at this," one man exclaimed, touching her hair. "I think I'd like some of this little horse thief."

"Bring her here!" the older man ordered.

With her arms pinned behind her, Liana was taken to stand beside the man's horse. She kept her eyes lowered.

"Look at me," he commanded. "Look at me or I'll make you wish you had."

Defiantly, not wanting him to see her fear, Liana looked up at him. As he studied her, years of anger lines seemed to melt from his face, until at last he threw back his head and gave a roar of mirthless laughter.

"Well, Lady Liana, let me introduce myself. I am Oliver Howard," he said at last. "And you, dear lady, have given me what I have spent my life wanting. You have given me the Peregrines."

"Never," she said. "Rogan will never surrender to you."

"Not even for your return?"

"He didn't surrender for Jeanne and he won't for me," she said, and hoped her voice was as strong as her words. Inside, she was trembling. What would Rogan think when they took her? Would he believe she would betray him as Jeanne had so many years ago?

"Take her," Oliver Howard said to one of his men. "Put her on your horse in front of you. It will be your life if she escapes."

Liana felt too bleak to fight off the man's hands on her body. What was happening was her own fault; she had no one to blame but herself.

The man who held her on his horse whispered into her ear. "The Howards have a charm for Peregrine women. Will you wed one of them? Will you divorce Peregrine and become a Howard as the first one did?"

She didn't bother to answer, which seemed to amuse the man.

"It won't matter what you do," the man said, laughing. "Lord Oliver will make your husband believe you have become a Howard. We will win in the end."

Liana told herself that Rogan would never believe she'd betrayed him, but inside her, she was afraid.

They rode for two days. When they stopped at night, Liana was tied, sitting, to a tree and the men took turns staying awake to guard her.

"Perhaps you should assign two men to me," Liana sneered at Oliver Howard. "I am so strong and mighty that were I to escape the ropes, I might beat them."

Oliver did not smile. "You are a Peregrine and they are treacherous people. You might have the devil help you escape." He turned his back on her and went inside one of the three small tents hidden in the trees.

During the night it began to rain. The men guarding her took turns, no man staying in the rain for longer than an hour. There was no mention of untying Liana and putting her inside the dry warmth of a tent.

In the morning she was cold, wet, and exhausted. The man who held her on his horse didn't grope her as he had before. Instead, he was quiet and Liana felt her weary muscles beginning to relax. She fell asleep against him and didn't wake until sundown, when they reached what Rogan called the Peregrine estates.

They could see the towers from a mile off, and as they approached, Liana's lethargy left her. Never had she seen anything like the buildings looming before her. There were no words to describe the size of the estate: *vast, huge, enormous*—all seemed inadequate. There was a series of six "small" towers guarding the tunnel and outer wall that led to the gate in the inner wall of the castle. Each of these towers was larger than the single tower of Moray Castle.

Behind the inner walls were towers of such magnitude that Liana could only stare at them. She could see another wall inside and slate-roofed buildings.

They came first to a wooden bridge over a moat that was as wide as a river. In time of war, the bridge could easily be chopped away. They rode over a stone bridge, another wooden one, and then they were inside the tunnel. Above her were murder holes that in time of war were used for pouring hot oil on the enemy.

In the fading light again, they crossed another wooden bridge over another moat and at last they reached the inner gate, which was flanked by two tall, massive stone towers. Again, murder holes were above them, as well as the spikes of an iron portcullis.

They entered a grassy area with many half-timbered houses built against the walls. The place was clean and prosperous-looking.

They kept riding to go through another tunnel, this one flanked by two towers that were larger than those of any castle her father owned. Inside, they came to acres of a beautiful courtyard. Here were stone buildings with leaded-glass windows: a chapel, a solar, a Great Hall, storerooms where people bustled in and out with food and barrels of drink.

Liana sat on the horse and stared. She had never, in her wildest thoughts, imagined a place of this size or this wealth. So this is what the Peregrines are fighting for, she thought. This is what has caused the deaths of three generations of Peregrines. This is what makes the Peregrines hate the Howards.

Looking at the wealth around her, she began to understand Rogan better. No wonder he looked on small, decaying Moray Castle with contempt. That castle, including walls, could be placed three times inside the inner ward of this castle.

This is where Rogan belongs, she thought. This is where the size of him, the look of him, the power of him, would fit.

"Take her to the top of the northeast tower," Oliver Howard said, and Liana was pulled from the horse and half-dragged across the long courtyard to the thick, massive tall tower in the northeast corner. The men led her up stone spiral stairs, past rooms she barely glimpsed. But all looked clean and cared for.

There was an iron-barred door at the top of the tower, and one of the men unlocked it and shoved Liana inside, locking it behind her. It was a small room with a mattress on a wooden frame in one corner, a little table and chair in another, and a door to a garderobe to the west. There was one window looking north, and out of it she could see the hundreds of yards of outer wall that surrounded the vast grounds. Men walked on the parapets and kept watch.

"Against the Peregrines' puny force," Liana said bitterly.

She put her hand to her head, feeling dizzy and tired. She'd spent last night tied to a tree in the rain, and that, together with the emotion she'd spent, was exhausting her. She went to the bed, lay down, and pulled the blanket of fulled wool over her and went to sleep.

When she awoke, it was late the next morning. As she struggled from bed to go to the garderobe, she swayed on her feet and when she put her hand to her forehead, her skin felt hot. Someone had been in the room and there was water, bread, and cheese on the little table. She gulped the water, but the food held no appeal for her.

She went to the door and banged on it. "I must speak to Oliver Howard," she shouted, but if anyone heard, he didn't answer. She slid down the door to sit on the cold stone floor. She had to be awake when someone entered her room. She had to talk to Oliver Howard and somehow persuade him to release her. If Rogan and Severn tried to take her from this place, they would be killed.

She fell asleep, and when she awoke, she was in bed, uncovered, and drenched in her own sweat. Again, someone had been in her room, but even opening the door and carrying her to the bed hadn't awakened her. She staggered from the bed and poured a cup of water, her hands so weak she could barely lift the pitcher. She collapsed crosswise on the bed.

When she woke again, it was to someone roughly shaking her. Wearily, she opened her eyes to see Oliver Howard looming over her. The dark room, the candlelight coming from behind him, made him look blurry and indistinct.

"Your husband shows no interest in having you returned," he said fiercely. "He has ignored all ransom requests."

"Why do you want what little he has?" she asked through dry, cracked lips. When he didn't answer, she continued. "Our marriage was arranged. My husband is no doubt glad to be rid of me. If you ask at our village, you will hear of the horrors I have done to him."

"I have heard it all. I have even heard how he went

unarmed into the village to attend a fair. I would have been there, had I heard of it sooner, and I would have taken him. I would have killed this Peregrine as he's killed my brothers."

"As you have killed *his* brothers." Liana's words lost most of their force since she was too weak to lift her head. But even as weak as she was, she wanted to save Rogan. "Release me or kill me, it won't matter to him," she said. "But do it soon. He will want a new heiress for a wife." If it is soon, she thought, then Rogan will not have time to attack.

"I will see how much he doesn't care," Oliver said, and motioned to one of his men.

Liana saw the scissors flash in the candlelight. "No!" she gasped and tried to twist away, but the men's hands were too strong. Hot, feverish tears rolled down her cheeks as the man cut her hair away, leaving it no more than shoulder length. "It was my only beauty," she whispered.

Neither Oliver nor his two men took notice as they slammed from the room. Liana's shorn hair was in Oliver's hand.

Liana cried for a long time, never once touching her shortened hair. "He will never love me now," she kept repeating. Near dawn she fell into a fitful sleep, and when she awoke, she was too weak to get out of bed to get to the water. She went back to sleep.

When she awoke again, there was a cool cloth pressed to her forehead.

"Be quiet now," whispered a soft voice.

Liana opened her eyes to see a woman with gray-flecked brown hair and eyes as gentle and kind as a doe's. "Who are you?"

The woman kept dampening the cloth and wiping away the sweat from Liana's face.

"Here, take this." She held a spoon to Liana's lips, then held her head so she could drink. "I am Jeanne Howard."

"You!" Liana said, choking on the herbal medicine. "Get away from me. You are a traitor, a liar, a demon from hell."

The woman gave a bit of a smile. "And you are a Peregrine. Could you eat some broth?"

"Not from you, I can't."

Jeanne contemplated Liana. "I imagine you are a good match for Rogan. Did you *really* set his bed on fire? Did you wear coins to his table? Were you actually locked in a room with him?"

"How do you know of these things?"

With a sigh, Jeanne rose and went to a table where a small iron pot sat. "Don't you know of the depth of the hatred between the Howards and the Peregrines? They know all there is to know about one another."

Liana, in spite of her fever and her weakness, was studying Jeanne. This was the woman who'd caused so much anger. She was an ordinary-looking woman, of medium height, with plain brown hair—

Hair! Liana thought, and put her hand on her own hair. In spite of herself, she began to cry.

Jeanne turned back to her, cup in hand, and looked in pity as Liana held the ends of her shorn hair. Then Jeanne's face changed and she sat down on the chair by the bed. "Here, eat this. You need the food. Your hair will grow back, and there are worse things."

Liana couldn't stop crying. "My hair was my only beautiful feature. Rogan will never love me now."

"*Love* you," Jeanne said in disgust. "Oliver will probably kill him, so what does it matter whether Rogan loves a woman or not?"

Liana managed enough strength to knock the cup

from Jeanne's hand and send it flying. "Get out of here! You have caused all of this. If you hadn't betrayed Rogan, he wouldn't be as he is now."

Tiredly, Jeanne retrieved the cup, put it on the table, then went to sit by Liana. "If I leave, no one else will come. Oliver has ordered that no one tend you. They dare not deny me entrance, though."

"Because Oliver will kill whoever thwarts the woman he loves?" Liana said nastily. "The woman who betrayed my husband?"

Jeanne stood and went to the window. When she looked back at Liana, her face looked many years older. "Yes, I betrayed him. And my only excuse is that I was a stupid, naïve girl. I was given to Rogan to marry when I was just a child. I had such dreams of my married life. I had been orphaned when I was a baby and I was a ward of the king, so I grew up with nuns, unloved, unwanted, unnoticed. I thought marriage was going to give me someone to love, that at last I'd have a real home."

She paused and slowed down. "You did not meet the older brothers. After Rogan and I were married, they made my life hell. To them, I was money— money for their war with the Howards—and nothing more. If I spoke, no one listened; if I ordered a servant, no one obeyed. Daily I lived in more filth than I had ever imagined."

Liana's anger was leaving her. There was too much truth in Jeanne's words.

"Rogan sometimes came to me in the night, other times he had other women." Jeanne stared at the wall beside Liana. "It was awful," she whispered. "I was less than an orphan to those odious, beautiful men; I was nothing. To them, I didn't exist. They talked to each other over my head. If I was standing where one of them wanted to be, he pushed me aside. And the violence!" She shivered in memory. "To get one another's attention, they threw axes at each other's heads. I never understood how any of them made it to manhood."

Jeanne looked down at Liana. "When I heard that you set his bed on fire, I knew you were right to do so. It was something Rogan would understand. No doubt you reminded him of his brothers when you did that."

Liana didn't know what to say. She knew that every word Jeanne said was true. She'd known how it felt not to exist. And, yes, she'd done the right thing with Rogan, but would it have been enough if she'd had his older brothers to contend with? She caught herself. She was *not* going to side with this traitorous woman. "And was all this"—she motioned toward the window and the vast estate—"worth your betrayal? Two brothers died trying to get you back. Were you glad to hear of their deaths?"

Jeanne's face turned angry. "Those men didn't die trying to get *me* back. They couldn't have picked me out of a crowd. They died fighting the Howards. All I ever heard when I was with the Peregrines was how vile the Howards were, and now all I hear is of the evilness of the Peregrines. When will this hideous feud stop?"

"You did not help with your betrayal," Liana said, and knew her energy was leaving her.

Jeanne calmed. "No, I did not, but Oliver was so kind to me, and this household . . ." She trailed off as she remembered. "There was music and laughter here, and bathtubs full of scented water, and servants who curtsied to me. And Oliver was so very attentive and—"

"So attentive you had his baby," Liana said.

"After Rogan's rough handling, Oliver was a joy to

bed," Jeanne shot back, then stood. "I'll leave you now and let you sleep. I'll return in the morning."

"Don't," Liana said. "I can do well enough on my own."

"As you wish," Jeanne said, then left the room. As Liana heard the bolt lowered, she fell asleep.

For three days Liana was left alone in the room. Her fever grew worse in the cold, unheated room. She neither ate nor drank, but lay in bed, half-asleep, half-awake, sometimes burning hot, sometimes freezing so that her teeth chattered.

On the third day, Jeanne returned and Liana looked up at her in a daze.

"I feared they were lying to me," Jeanne said. "I was told you were well and comfortable." She turned away, then went to bang on the door for the guard to open it. "Pick her up and carry her and follow me," Jeanne told the guard.

"Lord Oliver gave me orders that she was to remain here," the guard said.

"And I am countermanding his orders," Jeanne said. "Now, unless you want to be thrown into the road, pick her up."

Liana was vaguely aware of strong arms picking her up. "Rogan," she whispered. She slept while she was carried down the stairs, woke only a bit as the soft hands of Jeanne's ladies undressed her, bathed the sweat from her body, and placed her on a soft feather mattress.

For three days Liana saw only Jeanne Howard as Jeanne fed her broth, helped her to the chamber pot, bathed the sweat from her body, and sat beside her. Not once did Liana speak to Jeanne in that time. She was too aware that the woman had betrayed her husband.

But by the fourth day, Liana's resolve began to

crumble. Her fever was gone and now she was merely weak. "Is my baby all right?" she whispered, breaking her silence to Jeanne.

"Healthy and growing every day. It takes more than a little fever to harm a Peregrine."

"It takes a traitorous wife," Liana said.

Jeanne put down her needle, rose from her chair, and started for the door.

"Wait!" Liana called. "I apologize. You have been very kind to me."

Jeanne turned back, poured a liquid into a mug, and handed it to Liana. "Drink it. It tastes vile, but you need it."

Obediently, Liana gulped the awful-tasting herbal concoction. When she handed the mug back to Jeanne, she spoke. "What has happened since I was taken? Has Rogan attacked?"

Jeanne took her time in answering. "Rogan sent word that . . . that you were no wife of his, that Oliver could have you."

Liana could only gape.

"I'm afraid Oliver allowed his temper to get the best of him. He ordered your hair cut and sent it to Rogan."

Liana turned away from Jeanne's pitying stare. "I see. But even when they took my . . . hair"—she could barely bring herself to say the words—"it made no difference to him." She looked back at Jeanne. "What will your husband do now, send me back piecemeal to the Peregrines? A hand today? A foot tomorrow?"

"Of course not," Jeanne snapped. In truth, Oliver had threatened just what Liana mentioned, but Jeanne had known they were only words. She was furious with her husband for having taken Lady Liana, but now that she was here and Rogan refused to take the bait, Oliver wasn't sure what to do with her.

"What will you do with me?" Liana whispered, using her weak arms to push herself up. Jeanne handed her a velvet robe to put over her bare body.

Jeanne decided to be honest. "I don't know. Oliver talks of petitioning the king to annul your marriage and then marrying you to his younger brother."

Liana refused to cry. "It's good that Rogan hasn't risked his life and the life of his brothers to come for me."

"Since he has only one brother left, I can see his reluctance," Jeanne said, her tone sarcastic.

"If there were an attack, he'd no doubt have young Zared fight alongside the men."

Jeanne gave her a sharp look. "I doubt that. Even the Peregrines have some standards." She paused. "Did no one tell you Zared is a girl? Are they still dressing her as a boy?"

Liana blinked a few times. "Girl? Zared is a *girl?*" She remembered Zared smashing the head of the rat with his—her—fist. And Zared in her room in the middle of the night. Liana's eyes widened. Then she remembered being so angry because Zared had been in bed with three women. How Severn and Rogan had laughed when she'd raged at them!

"No," Liana said, her jaw clenched tight. "No one bothered to tell me Zared was a girl."

"She was only about five when I was there, and I think the brothers were embarrassed that their father had produced a female. They blamed it on the mewling, cowardly, but rich fourth wife of his. I tried to mother Zared. It was a mistake; she's as fierce as her brothers."

"And I am an even bigger fool, for I never guessed," Liana said. And they never bothered to enlighten me, she thought. They had kept her out of their lives. She had never been a Peregrine, and now they didn't want her back.

She looked at Jeanne. "There has been no response from the Peregrines since they received my . . . my hair?"

Jeanne frowned. "Rogan and Severn have been seen hawking and . . . and drinking together."

"Celebrating, you mean. I thought . . ." She didn't want to say what she thought. She thought that they had come to, if not love her, then need her. She thought Severn had locked her and Rogan in the room because Severn missed the things she had done for the entire castle.

Jeanne took Liana's hand and squeezed it. "They are Peregrines. They are like no other people. They care only for their own. To them, women are a means to get money and nothing else. I don't mean to be cruel, but you should hear this: The Peregrines have your money now, so why do they need you? I heard how you tried to clean their castle and give them better food, but those men won't appreciate such things. The rains last week have half-filled their moat and I hear that already three dead horses are floating in it."

Liana knew that what Jeanne said was true. How could she ever have believed that she meant anything to Rogan? No more would he have to put up with her interfering in his life. "And the Days?" Liana whispered.

"Already they are back," Jeanne answered.

Liana took a deep breath. "So what do you do with me now? My husband does not want me, nor do I think my stepmother would like having me back. I am afraid the joke is on your husband."

"Oliver has not decided yet."

"Rogan and Severn must be laughing heartily. They have gotten rid of me, kept my dowry, and saddled their enemy with a plain-looking, meddlesome shrew."

That seemed to be the gist of it, Jeanne thought, but said nothing. Her heart went out to Liana because she knew how she felt. Those first weeks, so many years ago, after Jeanne had been taken by Oliver Howard, she had been in agony. She had felt no love for her young husband or for his overbearing brothers, but she had suffered as she heard of the deaths that had occurred because of her. For a while it looked as if Rogan was going to die from Oliver's arrows, and when he recovered, he found out his brothers were dead.

Through all Jeanne's misery, there had been Oliver. He had never planned to love the young wife of his enemy, but Oliver's wife of a childless marriage had died over a year earlier and he was lonely, as was Jeanne, and they were drawn to each other. At first Jeanne had been defiant, standing up for a husband who had said very few kind words to her and never held her except during the sexual act. But in a very short time Oliver's quiet kindness made her soften. While outside the walls war raged and men died, inside Jeanne lay in Oliver's arms.

When Oliver knew Jeanne was carrying his child, he became furiously jealous. His hatred of the Peregrines increased because the woman he loved, the mother of his child, was someone else's wife. Jeanne begged him to allow her to go to Rogan and ask for an annulment, but Oliver became enraged at the idea. He was terrified that Jeanne would return to the Peregrines—or even that, upon seeing Jeanne and hearing the news, Rogan would murder her.

But, defying Oliver and endangering her life, she

went to Rogan. It had been an ordeal getting out of a
castle that was under siege. On a black, moonless
night, her ladies had helped her down the wall, a
well-bribed man had rowed her across the inner moat,
then she'd run, crouched, to the outer moat, where
another boat awaited her. It had cost her much gold to
bribe the guards on the parapets to look the other way,
but she'd managed it.

Wearing a roughly woven cloak over her gown,
she'd easily walked through Rogan's camp without
one person recognizing her. If she had not been sure
before, after seeing no recognition on the faces of
people she'd lived with for months, she was sure. She
walked past Severn and young Zared, and they didn't
so much as glance at her. When she faced Rogan, there
was no gladness at seeing her again, no joy that at last
he could stop the siege. She asked him to walk away
into the woods with her, and he had. As quickly as
possible, she told him she had grown to love Oliver
and now carried his child.

For a moment she thought he was going to kill her.
Instead, he had taken her arm and told her she was a
Peregrine and was staying with him, that he'd never
release her to a Howard. She had forgotten what the
Peregrines were like by half. At the thought of never
seeing Oliver again and having to spend the rest of her
life in filthy Moray Castle, she'd begun to cry. She
didn't remember what she'd said, but she believed she
remembered saying she'd kill herself if she had to live
with Rogan.

Whatever she'd said, he'd released her arm and
pushed her hard against a tree. "Go," he'd said. "Get
out of my sight."

Jeanne had started running and hadn't stopped
until she was safe inside a peasant's hut. That day the
Peregrines had stopped the siege, and a month later

Jeanne heard that Rogan had petitioned the king for an annulment.

Jeanne was able to keep Oliver from learning of her visit to Rogan and so saved herself many jealous accusations. But in the years since, over their heads hung the fact that Jeanne had once been married to a Peregrine. For years Oliver looked at their oldest son askance, and once Jeanne saw him inspecting the boy's hair. "There is no red in it," she said, and moved past him. Oliver had been taught to hate the Peregrines from childhood, but now he hated them more. It seemed to him that the Peregrines had first claim to everything he owned: his castle and his wife.

So now, so many years later, Oliver had tried to get back at the Peregrines by yet again taking a wife of theirs. But this time Rogan wasn't going to fight. He wasn't going to risk losing another brother for a woman he'd never wanted in the first place.

Jeanne looked at Liana. "I do not know what happens now," she said honestly.

"Nor do I," Liana answered bleakly.

CHAPTER
EIGHTEEN

*L*iana finished the last stitch on the embroidered dragon on her frame and snipped the thread. She had completed the entire pillow cover in just a few weeks. She'd forced herself to keep her hands busy because if her hands were busy, she thought less.

For five long weeks she had been a prisoner of the Howards. After she was well enough to move about, she had been given a pleasant, sunny guest room and all the sewing supplies she needed. Jeanne had shared two gowns with her.

Other than Jeanne, Liana saw no one but the servants who came to clean, and they were forbidden to speak to her. The first few days she had paced the room until her legs had grown tired, but then she began to sew, using the intricate stitching to take her mind off the news Jeanne brought her each evening.

The Howards kept close watch on the Peregrines, and they reported to Oliver. Rogan was seen every day. He trained with his men, rode with his brother, chased the peasant girls like a satyr.

Oliver renewed his threats to Rogan, saying Liana was in love with Oliver's brother. Rogan's reply had been to inquire if he was invited to the wedding.

Liana jabbed the needle into the tapestry and hit her thumb. Quick tears came to her eyes. Filthy beast, she thought. Daily she went over in her mind all the many terrible things Rogan had done to her. If she ever got away from the Howards, she hoped never to see a Peregrine again. She hoped all of them, including that boy-girl Zared, sank in their own mire and drowned.

At the beginning of the sixth week, Jeanne came to her with a frown on her face.

"What is it?" Liana asked.

"I don't know. Oliver is angry, more angry than I've ever seen him. He wants to force Rogan into a fight." Jeanne sat down heavily. "I can find out nothing, but I think Oliver may have issued a personal challenge to Rogan, a trial by combat."

"That will settle the feud once and for all. The winner will own this place."

Jeanne put her face in her hands. "You can afford to say that. Rogan is years younger than Oliver, and larger and stronger. Your husband will win and mine will die."

In the last weeks Jeanne had become very familiar to Liana, familiar almost to the point of friendship. Liana put a hand on her shoulder. "I know how you must feel. I once believed I loved my husband."

To the right was a clatter.

"What was that?" Jeanne asked, her head coming up.

"The man cleaning the toilet."

"I didn't know anyone was here."

"I forget them myself. They come and go so quietly," Liana said. "At home . . . I mean, at my hus-

285

band's castle, the servants were inept, lazy, and had no idea how to clean anything."

Again came the clatter.

Liana went to the doorway of the garderobe. "Leave us," she ordered to the bent old man who'd been clumsily cleaning her room for the last three days.

"But I haven't finished, my lady," he whined.

"Go!" Liana ordered, and stood there while the old man hobbled out, one leg dragging behind him.

When they were alone, she turned back to Jeanne. "What did Rogan say to the challenge?"

"I don't believe it's been issued. Oliver could not think he could beat Rogan. Oh, Liana, this has to stop."

"Then release me," Liana said. "Help me get away. Once I am gone, Oliver's anger will cool."

"Will you go back to Rogan?"

Liana turned away. "I don't know. I have some property in my own right. Perhaps I'll go there. Surely I can find someplace where I belong, someplace where I'm not a burden."

Jeanne stood. "My first loyalty is to my husband. I cannot help you escape. He is not pleased that I see you every day as it is. No," she said firmly, "it would humiliate him if I betrayed him."

Betrayal, Liana thought. The history of the Howards and the Peregrines was rife with betrayal.

Abruptly, Jeanne left the room, as if she were afraid she'd change her mind if she remained with Liana.

The next day Liana was nervous, jumping at every sound. The door was unlocked and she looked up, hoping to see Jeanne and hear the news, but it was only the old cleaning man. Disappointed, she looked back down at the new piece of linen stretched on her embroidery frame. "Take the food tray away and get out," she said crossly.

"And where should I go?" said a voice that was so familiar to her that chills went up her spine. Very slowly, she looked up. Standing before the heavy door was Rogan, an eyepatch pushed up to his forehead, a padded hump on his back, a leg bandaged so that it looked as if it were crooked.

He was grinning at her in an infuriating way that Liana knew signaled he expected her to leap on him in joy.

Instead, she grabbed a goblet from her empty breakfast tray and threw it at his head. He ducked, and it went slamming against the door. "You bastard!" she said. "You randy satyr. You lying, cheating blackguard. I never want to see you again." One by one she threw items from the tray at him and then began on whatever she could grab in the room. "You left me here to rot. They cut my hair, but you didn't care. You didn't want me. You *never* wanted me. You never even told me Zared was a girl. You said Oliver Howard could have me for all you cared. You laughed while I was held prisoner. You went hawking with Severn while I was locked in this room. You—"

"It was Baudoin," Rogan said.

Having run out of ornaments to throw at him, Liana began to tear the blankets from the bed and threw them. They fluttered through the air, landing at his feet. There was now a large pile of ornaments, pillows, and dishes around him. "You deserve everything the Howards do to you," she yelled. "Your whole family is rotten to the core. I nearly died of a fever while you were enjoying yourself. I'm sure you won't care, but they tied me to a tree all night *in the rain.* I could have lost our baby. As if you'd care. You never—"

"It was Baudoin hawking. I was here," Rogan said.

"That's just like a Peregrine: blame someone else.

That poor, innocent family man. *He* would care if someone cut off his wife's hair. He would—" She paused. There was nothing else left in the room to throw at him. "Here? You were here?" There was suspicion in her voice.

"I have been here searching for you for nearly three weeks. The location of your room has been a well-guarded secret."

Liana wasn't sure she believed him. "How could you be here and not be noticed? The Howards know you by sight."

"Not as well as they think. Their spies have seen Baudoin hawking and chasing the Days, not me. I have been here under disguise. I have cleaned things. I have whitewashed walls, swept floors—and listened."

Liana was beginning to hear him. Perhaps the news she had heard of his denials had been untrue. "*You* clean something?" she said. "I am to believe that? You wouldn't know which end of a broom to use."

"If I had one now, I'd know which end to use on your backside."

It was true. Oh God in heaven, it was true. He *had* been searching for her. Liana's knees weakened on her and she collapsed, sitting, on the bare feather mattress, put her face in her hands, and began to cry as if her heart would break.

Rogan didn't dare touch her. He stood where he was in the midst of the debris and stared at her. He hadn't thought ever to see her again.

The day she'd been taken, he'd rolled in stinging nettles and his skin was on fire. He'd imagined how his wife would have a tub of hot water prepared for him and she would ease his pain. But he'd bounded up the stairs to find a solar full of crying women. He couldn't get anything out of Liana's maids, but Gaby, between sobs, was able to tell him Liana had been taken by the Howards. Oliver Howard had sent a message that, for her return, he wanted the surrender of Moray Castle.

Rogan, without a word, had gone into their bedroom. He had meant to spend some time alone to plan his strategy, but the next thing he knew, Severn and Baudoin were on him, pinning him to the floor. The room was destroyed. In a rage so blind he still remembered none of it, he had taken an axe to the room and chopped up every piece of wood, iron, cloth. Candle wax mixed with cut sheets. Oak chair legs were crushed with a bent iron candle stand. Liana's fine crucifix was in splinters. Pieces of her clothing were everywhere. Red silk, blue brocade, cloth of gold, cloth of silver. Four of her headdresses lay broken, the padding spilling out of them.

The door had been chopped down by Severn and Baudoin as they went in to get their brother and keep him from injuring himself.

When Rogan came to his senses, he was calm— very, very calm. He was so calm that Severn's anger rose.

"We will attack," Severn said. "We have the money now. We'll hire mercenaries. We'll at long last rout the Howards from the Peregrine home."

Rogan looked at Severn and imagined his brother washed and laid out in a coffin—the way he'd seen Basil and James when they had fought to return Rogan's first wife. Rogan knew he must not do anything rash, that he must think clearly and calmly. He could not attack a place as vast as the Peregrine lands without a great deal of planning.

For days he worked long and hard, driving his men to exhaustion as he readied them for war. At night he stopped only when he could move no longer, then he fell into a heavy, dreamless sleep.

But even with all his work, he still missed her. She was the only person in his life who'd ever made him laugh. Neither his father nor his older brothers had ever laughed when they were alive. But then he'd married this girl for her money and nothing had been the same since. She was the only woman who dared to criticize him. Other women were too afraid of him to complain of his treatment. Other women didn't tell him what he did wrong. Other women had no courage, he thought. They didn't set beds on fire, didn't wear coins to dinner, didn't dare ask him about his first wife.

He was supervising the packing of war machines on to wagons when a Peregrine knight came with a package from the Howards. The little oak chest had been catapulted over the wall with a message that it be given to Rogan.

He wrenched the lock off with a steel pick and took out the cloth-wrapped bundle to see Liana's hair inside. Somehow, he managed to remain calm. With her hair, her beautiful, silky hair, clutched in his hand, he started toward the tower.

Severn caught up with him. "Where are you going?" he demanded.

"This is between Oliver Howard and me," Rogan said quietly. "I go to kill him."

Severn swung Rogan around. "Do you think Howard will fight you one on one? That he will fight you fairly? He's an old man."

Rogan felt the hair in his hand. "He has harmed her; I will kill him for it."

"Think what you're doing," Severn pleaded. "If you so much as ride up to Howard's gate, he'll have that thick hide of yours filled with arrows. Then where will your wife be? Come, help us prepare for war. We'll attack Howard properly."

"Properly!" Rogan said, half sneering. "As we did in 'thirty-five? There were five Peregrine brothers then and still the Howards beat us. How can we, as poor as we are, hope to battle the Howards? We will take our tiny force and lay siege and Howard will laugh at us from atop his walls."

"Yet you think that you, one mere man, can do what all our men cannot?"

Rogan had no answer for him. Instead, he went to his brooding chamber, locked the door, and did not come out for twenty-four hours. By then he knew what he was going to do. When he and Liana had gone to the fair, he had seen how easily the peasants walked in and out of Moray Castle. He had always seen them, of course, with their baskets of squawking chickens, their three-wheeled handcarts loaded with crude goods, men with tools strapped to their bodies as they came to do repair work, but he'd never noticed them. Only when he was wearing peasants' clothing did he see the freedom of access these people had, the way they went through the gates without a question asked. Yet if a man in armor on horseback had come within ten miles of Moray Castle, he would have been greeted by armed men.

Rogan called his two brothers into his brooding chamber, for the first time including Baudoin as family. Liana did that, he thought. She had given him that most precious of gifts: another brother. Rogan told his two brothers he planned to dress as a peasant and go alone into the Howard fortress.

Severn's shout of protest made the pigeons fly off the roof. He yelled, he raged, he threatened, but he couldn't sway Rogan.

Baudoin, who had been quiet through Severn's storming, finally spoke. "You will need a good disguise. You're too tall, too easily recognized. Gaby will make you a disguise that not even Lady Liana will see through."

That day Rogan and Gaby and Baudoin had worked on turning him into a one-eyed, humpbacked, crippled old man. Severn had been so angry he'd refused to participate, but Rogan had gone to him and asked for his help. Rogan knew that Howard spies watched them, and he wanted Severn to make them think Rogan was still at Moray Castle. Severn and Baudoin were to make the Howards think that Baudoin was Rogan.

Alone, Rogan had gone to the Howard fortress. As he and Severn had parted in the forest, Severn had clasped his brother to him, a rare gesture between Peregrine men that would not have happened before Liana came and softened them.

"Bring her back to us," Severn said softly. "And . . . I don't want to lose more brothers."

"I will find her." He gave Severn one last look. "Take care of Zared."

Severn nodded, then Rogan was gone.

Rogan found that his stooped, leg-dragging stance made his back ache, and the Howard men who ordered him about often punctuated their orders with kicks and shoves. He made note of their faces and hoped someday to see them on a battlefield.

He skulked about the castle, hauling swill, doing whatever he could to be near people who were talking. The castle was abuzz with gossip about the treachery of the Peregrines, how they were trying to steal what rightfully belonged to the Howards. The people speculated on Liana and said she wasn't good enough for Oliver's young brother. Rogan snapped a broom handle in half at that, which caused a cook to beat him with a leg of mutton.

He ate what he could steal, and since the Howards,

on the Peregrine family's estates, were so wealthy, they never missed the food. He slept in a corner of the stables or in the mews with the birds.

He worked and he listened, keeping his uncovered eye open for anyone who looked as if he might know something.

It was in the third week, when he was about to give up hope, that a man kicked him in the small of his back and sent Rogan sprawling in the dirt. "Come with me, old man," he said.

Rogan picked himself up and followed the man, planning his death as they climbed the stairs. The man handed Rogan a broom. "Go in and clean," he'd said, and unbolted a thick, iron-clad door.

Inside the room, Rogan stood for a moment blinking, for there was Liana, her lovely face bent over a tapestry frame, her hair covered with a cap of white linen. He couldn't move, but just stood there and stared at her.

She looked up. "Well, go on," she said. "You have better things to do than gawk at the Howard prisoner."

He'd opened his mouth to tell her who he was, but then the door was opened behind him. Rogan had scurried into the garderobe, staying by the doorway to listen. He'd breathed a sigh of relief when he heard a woman's voice, but as he continued to listen, he heard Liana call the woman Jeanne. Was this the Jeanne he'd once been married to?

He left the garderobe and began moving about the chamber. Neither woman paid him the least mind. He looked at the woman Jeanne and he thought she was his first wife, but he wasn't sure. Their marriage had been brief and over with a long time ago, and besides, she hadn't been very memorable as a wife.

He listened to the two women and heard stories of

his own indifference, how he was drinking and hawking and couldn't care less about his wife being held prisoner. He smiled when he heard mention of the baby Liana was carrying. But he lost his smile when he saw that Liana believed every word Jeanne was saying. Did women have no loyalty? What had he ever done to deserve his wife's distrust? He had given her a roof over her head, food in her belly—as well as a brat—and he had even given up his women for her. And he had come to save her from the Howards.

He was so disgusted by her disloyal behavior that while he made arrangements, bribing guards and retainers with money that was needed elsewhere, and went to her room every day, he didn't reveal himself to her.

So now he was here, and after all he'd gone through to find her, she wasn't even grateful.

"What were you doing outside the castle walls?" he asked, frowning. "I gave you orders not to leave the grounds." The little cap over her head was so fine it was nearly transparent and he could see how little was left of her hair. If he ever got his hands on Oliver Howard, the man's death would be long and painful.

"I was going to get herbs to soothe the nettles. Gaby said you rolled in them." She was sniffing loudly.

"Nettles!" he said under his breath. "You caused all of this because you went to get herbs for nettles?"

Liana was beginning to realize that he *had* come for her, that all the reports she'd heard of his indifference were false. She leaped off the bed in a flurry of silk and flung her arms about his neck and accurately planted her mouth on his.

He held her so tightly her ribs nearly broke. "Liana," he whispered against her neck.

She stroked his hair, and more tears came to her eyes. "You did not forget me," she whispered.

"Never again," he said, then his voice changed. "I can't stay longer. Tonight there is no moon. I'll come for you and we'll leave here."

"How?" She pulled away to look at him. It seemed that she forgot from one moment to the next how splendidly handsome he was. Even under weeks' worth of ashes and dirt, his face was—

"Are you listening to me?"

"Intimately," she answered, snuggling her hips against his.

"Behave, and listen to me. Do not trust Jeanne Howard."

"But she has helped me. She may have saved my life. I was burning up with fever and—"

"Swear to me," Rogan said fiercely. "Swear to me you won't trust her. Don't confide in her, don't tell her I've been here. She's betrayed my family once, and if she betrayed me again, I would not live. I could not fight off Howard men alone as I am now. Swear to me."

"Yes," Liana whispered. "I swear."

He had his hands on her shoulders, and he gave her one last long look. "I must go now, but tonight I will come to you. Wait for me, and for once, give your loyalty to me." He smiled just a bit. "And clean up this room. I've learned to like cleanliness."

He kissed her once, hard and fiercely, and then he was gone.

For a long while Liana leaned against the door. He had come for her. He hadn't been drinking and hawking while she was held prisoner. Instead, he had risked his life by entering the Howards' domain alone. He hadn't said that he didn't want her.

Dreamily, she began to pick up all the things she'd thrown at him. She didn't want Jeanne to see the mess and ask questions.

Tonight, she thought, he was coming for her tonight. As she began to think less romantically about his coming for her and more realistically, she began to be afraid. What if he were caught? Oliver Howard would kill Rogan. She sat down on the bed, her hands clasped tightly, and the fear beginning to course through her body made her rigid.

As the sun began to set, Liana's fear settled into her bones until she felt as if she were seeing herself from a distance. Slowly, she rose, removed the silk gown Jeanne had loaned her, and put on the peasants' clothes she had been wearing when she had been taken. She put the silk gown back on over the peasants' garb, then sat down to wait.

Every muscle in her body was tense as she sat still and stared at the closed door. She heard the castle grounds quieten as the workers went off to their beds. A servant brought her supper on a tray and lit a candle, but Liana didn't touch the food. Instead, she waited for the night to bring Rogan.

At about midnight, very slowly, the door opened and Liana stood up, her eyes wide.

Jeanne stepped into the room, her eyes on the bed, then, startled, she saw Liana. "I thought you'd be asleep."

"What's wrong?" Liana whispered.

"I don't know. Oliver is very angry and he's been drinking. I overheard . . ." She looked at Liana. She didn't want to say what she'd overheard. In all areas except one her husband was a sensible man, but when it came to the Peregrines, he lost all sense of proportion, of honesty, of sensibility. Today she'd overheard Oliver saying he meant to kill Liana and deliver her body to Rogan. "You must come with me," Jeanne said. "I have to hide you."

"I cannot," Liana said. "I must wait here for—"

"Wait for what?" Jeanne asked. "Or do you wait for someone?"

"No one," Liana said quickly. "No one knows I'm here, do they? How could I be waiting for someone? I was just sitting here, that's all." She closed her mouth. She couldn't tell Jeanne that Rogan was coming for her. Jeanne could tell Oliver. But if she moved, how would Rogan find her? "This room is so nice," Liana said. "I'd rather stay here than move to another. I don't think I could bear a cold room."

"Now is no time to think of luxury. I am concerned for your life. If you wish yourself and your child to live, come with me now."

Liana knew she had no choice. With a heavy heart she followed Jeanne down the torch-lit stairs. She followed her out of the tower, across the dark inner ward, and at last down steep stone steps into the cellar of one of the gate towers. Here were huge bags of grain, in places piled almost to the ceiling. It was a dank, dark, moldy-smelling place, the only window an arrow slit high above her head.

"You cannot mean for me to stay here," Liana whispered.

"It's the only place I could find where no one will look. This grain won't be needed until spring, so no one will come in here. I have put wool blankets there, and there's a chamber pot in the corner."

"Who will empty it?" Liana asked. "The old man who comes to my room seems stupid enough to be safe."

"Not this time. I will come tomorrow night. I trust no one but myself." She feared that when Oliver found Liana gone, he'd offer a reward for her, and if he did, anyone was likely to turn her in. "I am sorry. This is a hideous place, but it's the only safe place. Try to sleep. I will come tomorrow."

When Jeanne left and bolted the door behind her, the sound echoed in the round stone room with its vaulted ceiling. It was absolutely dark and cold as only stone that had never been heated could be. Liana struggled forward, stumbling over bags of grain to find the blankets Jeanne had left. When she found them, she tried to make a bed on the lumpy bags, but there was no way to make them comfortable.

At last, settled with the hard, dusty bags under her and two inadequate blankets over her, she began to cry. Somewhere outside, her beloved Rogan was risking his life to find her. She prayed that he would not do something foolish when he found she was gone. But even if he kept silent, he would never find her in this cellar, for no guards or servants knew where she was now. Only Jeanne Howard knew where Liana was.

Jeanne did not come the next day. Liana had no food, no water, no light, no warmth. And as the day grew into night, she had no hope. Rogan had been right about Jeanne: She could not be trusted. Liana began to remember that it was Jeanne who had told her of Rogan's not caring that she was held prisoner. It was Jeanne who had made her believe in Rogan's treachery.

Jeanne came on the night of the second day. Quietly, she opened the door and stepped into the cold, dark cellar. "Liana," she called.

Liana was too weary and full of anger to answer.

Stumbling over grain bags, Jeanne began to feel her way about the room, gasping when she touched Liana. "I have brought you food and water and another blanket." She lifted her skirt and began untying bundles. She held a gourd of water to Liana's lips, and she drank greedily, then Jeanne handed Liana cold beef, bread, and cheese.

"I could not come yesterday. Oliver suspects that I

have had something to do with your escape. He has set everyone to spying on everyone else. I'm afraid of even my own ladies. I had to plead illness and have my food brought to me in my room in order to get you something to eat."

"I am to believe you gave up your own meal for me?" Liana asked, her mouth full.

It was dark and she couldn't see Jeanne's face, but there was a pause before she spoke. "Something has happened," Jeanne said. "What is it?"

"I have no idea what you mean. I have been here alone in this freezing place. No one has come or gone for two days."

"And it has no doubt saved your life," Jeanne snapped. "You are the wife of my husband's enemy, and I have risked much to keep you healthy and safe."

"What risk? Your lies?" Liana wished she hadn't spoken.

"What lies? Liana, what has happened? What have you heard? *How* have you heard anything?"

"Nothing," Liana said. "I have been held in close confinement. I could not have heard anything."

Jeanne walked away from her. Her eyes were beginning to adjust to the blackness and she could see shadows of the grain bags and the darker outline of Liana. She took a deep breath and looked at Liana. "I have decided to tell you the truth, all of the truth. My husband means to kill you. That's what I overheard when I took you from the tower room. He has no use for you. He never meant to take you, you just appeared, so to speak, and he took you on impulse. He hoped to force Rogan to surrender Moray Castle to him. What he actually wants is to take every blade of grass the Peregrines own." There was bitterness in her voice.

Jeanne continued. "I don't know what to do with

you now. I can trust no one. Oliver has issued a death threat to anyone seen helping you. He knows you're still in the castle, because since he took you, he has had the guards look at the face of every peasant who enters or leaves the walls. His men are even now combing the woods outside the walls."

Jeanne paused. "Damn that Rogan! Why hasn't he tried for your return? I never thought he'd be content to let one of his own rot."

"He hasn't!" Liana said, then bit her tongue.

"You *do* know something." Jeanne grabbed Liana's shoulders. "Help me save your life. It's only a matter of time before Oliver's men search this cellar. I cannot save you if you're found."

Liana refused to speak. Rogan had made her swear not to trust Jeanne, and she was going to keep her word.

"All right," Jeanne said tiredly. "Have it your way. I'll do the best I can to get you out of here as soon as possible. Can you swim?"

"No," Liana answered.

Jeanne sighed. "I will do my best," she whispered, then slipped out the door.

Liana spent a restless night on the bags of grain. She could *not* tell Jeanne that Rogan was within the grounds and that he would help her escape. If she told Jeanne of Rogan's disguise, Jeanne could tell Oliver.

On the other hand, what if Jeanne were telling the truth? It was indeed only a matter of time until she was found. And if they took her, would Rogan stand aside in his beggar's dress and silently watch her be put to death? No, Rogan would not remain silent and Oliver Howard would take both of them.

In the morning, Liana heard noise coming through the arrow slit high in the wall. It took her a long while, but she managed to drag the one-hundred-pound bags of grain around until she formed a pyramid that she could climb on. Climbing up, she was able to see out the bottom of the long slit.

The castle grounds were alive with activity, men and women running and shouting, doors being thrown open, horses taken out of the stables, carts filled with goods being unloaded. She knew they were searching for her.

As she strained up on her toes to see out, far across the grounds she saw an old, crippled beggar man, a hump on his back, one leg dragging behind him. "Rogan," Liana whispered, and stared at the man with all her might, urging him to come to her. As if he sensed her message, he came slowly toward her.

Her heart was pounding in her throat as he drew near. The window wasn't far above the outside ground level, and if he came close enough, she'd be able to call out to him. As he came nearer, she held her breath. She opened her mouth to call to him.

"Here! You!" a Howard knight shouted at Rogan. "You have two good arms. Drive this wagon out of here."

Tears came to Liana's eyes as she saw Rogan awkwardly pull himself up to the wagon seat and drive the horses away. She sat down on the grain sacks and began to cry. What Jeanne had told her was true. Oliver Howard was tearing the place apart to search for her, and if not today, tomorrow he would find her.

A voice inside her head said she had to trust Jeanne, that her only chance for living was to tell Jeanne that Rogan was near and that he had a plan for escape. If she did not trust Jeanne, she was sure to die. If she did trust her, there was a possibility both she and Rogan might live.

By the time Jeanne came that night, Liana's head was pounding from her agony of indecision.

"I have arranged something," Jeanne said. "It is the best I could do, but I do not know if it will work. I have not dared trust any of my husband's men. I fear that one of my ladies is telling my husband everything. Come with me now. There is no time to lose."

"Rogan is here," Liana blurted.

"Here? In this room?" Jeanne's voice was full of fear.

"No. He is in the ward. He came to me in the tower room. He said he had a plan and meant to take me away the night you brought me here."

"Where is he? Quick! People are waiting to help you, and we desperately need your husband's help."

Liana dug her fingers into Jeanne's arm. "If you betray us, I swear before God that I will haunt all the days of your life."

Jeanne crossed herself. "If you are caught, it will be because you have used valuable time threatening me. Where is he?"

Liana described how Rogan was disguised.

"I have seen him. He must care for you to risk coming here alone. Wait, I will return for you."

Liana sat down with a thud on a pile of grain bags. Now was when she'd know if she'd made the right decision. If her decision was wrong, she was as good as dead.

CHAPTER
NINETEEN

J eanne barged into the Great Hall, two silk-clad ladies behind her, in a fury of temper. The floors were covered with straw pallets where men and dogs were sleeping. Other people tossed dice in a corner; one man fondled a maid in another.

"The drains in my garderobe are clogged," she announced. "I want someone to clean them. Now."

Those who were awake snapped to attention at the sight of her ladyship, but no one volunteered for the smelly task.

"I will send someone—" one knight began.

Jeanne saw Rogan in his filthy clothes sitting against a wall. She could feel his eyes on her. "That one will do. Come with me." She turned, hoping he would follow her. He did, and she waited until they were in the deep shadow of a building. She signaled her two ladies to leave her, then turned to Rogan.

Before he could step back, she reached out and flipped up his eyepatch. "It is you," she whispered. "I did not believe what Liana told me could be true. I didn't believe a Peregrine could care whether a woman lived or not."

Rogan's hand caught her wrist, crushing it painfully. "Where is she, bitch? If she's harmed, I'll do to you what I should have done years ago."

"Release me or you'll never see her again."

Rogan had no choice but to obey her. "What did you do to her to make her tell you of me? I'll take pleasure in killing you if—"

"You can give me your sweet words later," Jeanne snapped. "She is hidden now and I mean to get her out, but I need help. She can't swim, so she has to take a boat across both moats. You must row her. Go now to the wall this side of the northeast tower. There is a rope hanging down. Go across the outer ward to the northwest. There will be another rope down that wall, and a boat will be waiting below. Wait for her in the boat. I will help her to the outer wall, then it's up to you to get her across the bank and the outer moat."

"Am I to believe you? Howard's men will no doubt be waiting for me."

"My women are going to divert the guards atop the walls. You *have* to believe me. There is no one else."

"If you betray me again, I will—"

"Go!" Jeanne commanded. "You are losing precious moments."

Rogan left her, rushing, but dragging his leg in case anyone watched. He had never felt so naked in his life. His life and Liana's were in the hands of a lying traitor. Part of him was sure that he was going to reach the northeast tower and find twenty men waiting to murder him. But another part of him knew this was his only chance. He'd been searching in vain for Liana for days and had had no more luck than Howard's men had.

There were no men waiting at the tower. Instead, in

the darkness, a rope hung down from the top of the wall. He threw off his eyepatch, pulled the stuffing that formed a hump from his back, and untied his leg. He took a knife from inside his dirty shirt, put it in his mouth, and began to climb.

He expected men to be waiting for him at the top of the rope, but none were. Silently, he lowered himself down a rope on the other side of the wall.

Once he was on land again, he ran, crouching, across the middle ward. He melted his body into the dark stone of the outer wall as he heard laughter. Two guards walked by, never noticing Rogan a few feet from them or the rope hanging in the shadows down the wall to their right.

Rogan had one more wall to climb before he reached the moat. It took him precious minutes of searching to find the rope and then to start climbing. At the top, he had to pause because he heard a man's voice followed by a woman's giggle. Rogan waited until they were gone, then he heaved himself onto the wide, flat parapets.

The next rope was farther down the wall and Rogan climbed down it swiftly. In the shadows, hidden in tall reeds, was a tiny boat with two oars. He got in it, crouched down, and waited. He kept his eyes on the wall above him, watching so hard that he rarely blinked.

It was a long while before he saw the dark shadows of the heads near the top of the wall where the rope hung. He had begun to give up hope. The Howard bitch had indeed left the ropes and the boat, but would she bring Liana?

Rogan held his breath as he watched the two heads. They seemed to be *talking*. Women! he thought. They must put everything into words. Words were everything to them. They talked when a man tried to bed them. They talked when a man gave them a gift—they wanted him to *explain* why he gave them a gift. But worst of all, they talked when they were on top of a wall surrounded by armed men.

Then everything happened at once. One of the women's hands went into the air as if she meant to strike the other one. Rogan was on his feet and running toward the wall. There was a woman's cry above his head, then the sound of men running along the wall. Rogan had his hands on the rope, ready to climb up, when Jeanne shouted down at him.

"No!" she called to Rogan. "Save yourself. Liana is dead. You cannot save her."

Rogan started up the rope and was six feet off the ground when it fell away and he hit the earth. Someone above had chopped the rope off.

"Go, you fool," he heard Jeanne scream, then her voice was muffled as if someone had put a hand over her mouth.

Rogan didn't give himself time to think, for arrows were beginning to rain down on him. He ran for the boat, but two arrows had hit it and it was sinking. He plunged into the cold water of the moat and began to swim, arrows whizzing past his head.

He reached the bank, then ran, crouching, across the northern bank, just outside the walls of the western bailey. Sleepy guards, hearing the commotion across the moat, were coming awake and looking down the walls at the steep bit of land between the inner and outer moats. When they saw movement, they shot arrows.

Rogan reached the outer moat just as an arrow scraped across his back, searing his skin. He jumped and began to swim northward, away from the walls but into the north lake, which fed the two moats. He was a strong swimmer, but he was losing blood. When he reached the shore, he had to pull himself onto the land, where he lay in the reeds for a moment, coughing water from his lungs, his sides heaving with exertion, blood covering his back.

When at last he could walk, he made for the forest, hearing the hooves of Howard's men on horses not far behind him. He and Howard's men played cat-and-mouse the rest of the night and most of the next day as Rogan hid from them, then they circled back and he hid again.

At dusk he jumped on a Howard knight, slit his throat, and stole his horse. The men chased him, but Rogan whipped the horse until it bled and he outran them. At dawn the horse stopped, refusing to go further. He dismounted and began to walk.

The sun was high in the sky when he saw the outline of Moray Castle. He kept walking, stumbling over rocks, his muscles at last giving out after weeks of abuse.

One of the men on the parapets saw him, and within minutes, Severn was riding furiously toward him. Severn leaped off his horse before it stopped and clasped Rogan to him just as Rogan collapsed.

Severn was sure his brother was dying when he saw blood on his hands from Rogan's back. He started to pull Rogan toward the horse.

"No," Rogan said, pulling away. "Leave me."

"Leave you? By all that's holy, you have put us through hell. We heard Howard had killed you last night."

"He *did* kill me," Rogan whispered, turning away.

Severn saw the wound on his brother's back. It was still bloody and deep, but it was not enough to kill a man. "Where is she?"

"Liana?" Rogan asked. "Liana is dead."

Severn frowned. He had just been beginning to like

that woman. She was a great deal of trouble, like all women, but she wasn't a coward. He put his arm around Rogan's shoulders. "We'll find you another wife. We'll find you a beautiful one this time, and if you want one that'll set your bed on fire, we'll find her. As soon as—"

Severn wasn't prepared when Rogan whirled on him, slammed his fist in his jaw, and knocked him to the ground.

"You stupid bastard," Rogan said, straddling his brother's legs and glaring down at him. "You never understood anything. You with your high-born slut locked away, you fought her all the time. You made her life hell."

"Me?" Severn put his hand to his bloody nose. He started to rise, but one look at Rogan's face made him decide to stay where he was. "I wasn't the one who slept with other women. I didn't—" He stopped because the anger had left Rogan's face. He turned away and walked into the forest.

Severn got up and went to stand behind his brother. "I didn't mean to insult her memory. I liked her, but she's gone now and there are other women. At least she didn't betray you with Oliver Howard as your first wife did. Or did she? Is that why you're so angry?"

Rogan turned to his brother and, to Severn's horror and disbelief, there were tears that were beginning to roll down Rogan's cheeks. Severn could not speak. Rogan had not shed tears at the death of his father or any of his brothers.

"I loved her," Rogan whispered. "I loved her."

Severn was too embarrassed to watch this. He could not bear to see his brother cry. He backed away. "I'll leave the horse," he mumbled. "Come back when you're ready." He left very quickly.

Rogan collapsed to sit on a rock, his face buried in

his hands, and began to cry in earnest. He had loved her. He had loved her smiles, her laughter, her temper, the pleasure she received from the smallest things. She had brought laughter to him after a lifetime of hatred. She had given him clothes without lice or fleas, food that didn't grind his teeth down. She'd brought that arrogant bitch Iolanthe out of hiding, and she didn't know it but she'd made Zared ask Rogan to buy her some women's clothes.

And now she was gone. Killed in the feud with the Howards.

Perhaps her death should increase his hatred of the Howards, but it didn't. What did he care for the Howards? He wanted Liana back, his soft, sweet Liana who threw things when she was angry and kissed him when she was pleased.

"Liana," he whispered, and cried harder.

He didn't hear the footsteps in the soft bracken, and his grief was so deep that he didn't move when the soft hand touched his cheek.

Liana knelt before him and pulled his hands away from his face. She looked at his tear-stained face and tears came to her own eyes. "I am here, my love," she whispered, and kissed his hot eyelids, then his cheeks. "I am safe."

Rogan could only gape at her.

Liana smiled at him. "Have you nothing to say to me?"

He caught her and pulled her into his lap, then went rolling with her to the forest floor. His tears turned to laughter as he rolled over and over with her in his arms, his hands running up and down her body as if to reassure himself she was real.

At last he stopped and lay on his back, Liana on top of him, holding her so close she could barely breathe.

"How?" he whispered. "The Howard bitch—"

She put her fingertips to his lips. *"Jeanne,"* she said pointedly, "saved our lives. She knew one of her women was a traitor, and moments before she came to me, she overheard something that made her believe she knew which one it was. She sent me one way and took her traitorous maid the way you went. The woman thought Jeanne, shrouded in a cloak, was me and tried to stab her. Jeanne killed the woman while I was safe further down the wall. She had to tell you I was dead because she knew that otherwise you'd never leave the grounds."

She caressed Rogan's cheek. "I saw you swimming. If the Howard men hadn't been so interested in you, they would have seen me. Jeanne had horses waiting, so I was never far behind you, but you traveled so fast I could not catch you."

Her peasant's hood had fallen away in their tumbling and her hair had come down. It lay softly on her shoulders. Rogan touched it. "Do you find it ugly?" she whispered.

He looked back at her, love in his eyes. "There is *nothing* ugly about you. You are the most beautiful woman in the world and I love you, Liana. I love you with all my heart and soul."

She smiled at him. "Will you let me judge the courts? Can we add on to Moray? Will you stop fighting with the Howards? What should we name our son, my love?"

Rogan's anger began to rise, then he laughed and hugged her to him. "The courts are men's business, I'm not adding on to that heap of stone, Peregrines will always fight Howards, and I shall name my son John, after my father."

"Gilbert, after my father."

"So he can grow up to be lazy?"

"You'd rather he spent his life impregnating the

peasant girls and teaching his children to hate the Howards?"

"Yes," Rogan answered, holding her and looking up at the sky. "We may disagree on most things, but there is one we seem to agree on. Take off your clothes, wench."

She lifted her head and looked at him. "I am always obedient."

He started to speak, but she kissed him and he didn't say another word for hours.

The Conquest

Chapter One

England
1447

The old castle, even from a distance looking run-down and in need of repair, stood surrounded by a clean, deep moat. Outside on the grounds many men trained, practicing with swords and lances. Some fought on foot, some on horseback.

Overseeing the training were two men, both big, both muscular, both wearing looks of intense concentration on their handsome faces. These were the two remaining Peregrine brothers, the others having long ago been killed in the three-generations-old feud with the Howards.

"Where is Zared?" the older Peregrine brother, Rogan, shouted. Sun glinted off his dark hair, showing the red he had inherited from his father.

"Inside," Severn, the younger brother, shouted back, and he met his brother's eyes. "I saw Zared go," he said, not using the feminine pronoun "she," not letting the men around him know Zared was female.

1

JUDE DEVERAUX

Rogan nodded and looked back at the men fighting near him. He had already lost four brothers to the sneaking treachery of the Howards, and two years before he'd almost lost his wife. He did not mean to lose his little sister to the skulking rats, and so he checked often on her whereabouts.

He glared at the men near him. "Are you women that you fight so softly? Here, I will show you." He took a pike from a knight and attacked. Within minutes the knight who'd tried to fight against him was on his knees. Disgusted, Rogan glared down at the man. He raised the pike as if to strike but instead tossed it to the ground and walked away.

How could he protect his family, protect what little land the Peregrines had left, when the men who fought for him were so weak?

He mounted his horse and started toward the castle, but Severn halted him.

"You mean to see to her?" Severn asked belligerently when they were alone. He was angry that his brother had not taken his word that their young sister was safe.

"She is disobedient," Rogan answered, scowling. Three weeks earlier Zared had decided to go swimming and had ridden out alone, unescorted, unprotected. At seventeen she had a youth's belief that she could come to no harm.

"I will see to her," Severn said, trying to relieve his older brother of at least one responsibility.

Rogan nodded, and Severn reined his horse away. Severn knew all too well how his sister felt, for he, too, had felt the weight of his family's hatred of the Howards on his shoulders. Over the years he'd watched the Howards kill his family one by one. He'd seen his older brothers killed, his father and step-mother starved to death by the Howards. He'd seen

2

Rogan's agony when his first wife and later his beloved second wife had been held captive by the Howards.

Since the birth of Zared, the only girl born to their father, the family had bonded together to protect her. From the first they had let no one know that anything as fragile and as vulnerable as a female had been born to the Peregrines. They had spread the news that a seventh son had been born.

After Zared's mother had died, starved in a castle besieged by the Howards, Zared had been raised by her six older brothers. They raised her as they would have another brother, dressing her as a boy, giving her her first sword when she was four, laughing when she'd fallen off horses. Never had they allowed Zared the luxury of believing herself to be a weak, delicate female.

But now the brothers seemed to be paying for having raised her as a male. Zared acted as independently as any boy of seventeen. She felt that if she wanted to leave the castle grounds, she had that right. She strapped a sword to her belt, hid a dagger in her boot, and thought she could protect herself from an army of Howards.

Both Severn and Rogan had tried to reason with Zared. As much as the girl liked to think she was strong and skillful with weapons, she was, in fact, merely a puny girl. Rogan's wife, Liana, had had something to say about Zared, but then Liana seemed to have something to say about everything, Severn thought.

"How could you raise her with a sword in her hand and then one day tell her to sit in the solar with her sewing and think that she would be content to do so?" Liana had asked. "She is the hardheaded know-it-all that you have raised her to be."

Severn grimaced in memory and thought for the

thousandth time that Rogan ought to take a hand to his wife. Her tongue was too sharp by far.

So now, as if he and his brother didn't have enough to worry about, they had constantly to see about Zared, to make sure she had not taken it into her head to wander about the fields alone.

As Severn's horse clattered across the drawbridge he smiled. Two days past he'd had an idea about how to get Zared away from the danger of being watched constantly by the enemy Howards, and how to win himself a rich wife at the same time. He had already told Rogan of his plan, and all that was left was telling Zared. He smiled more broadly when he thought of Zared's reaction. For all that she dressed as a boy and swaggered like one, she had a girl's way of showing her pleasure over the smallest things. And Severn knew that what he had planned would give his little sister pleasure.

Of course, first he had to tell Liana what he intended. She would, no doubt, give him some difficulty, but he knew he could handle her. "A sight better than Rogan does," he muttered, for he thought his brother much, much too soft on the woman. "Ask Liana," Rogan had said when Severn told of his plans for Zared. *Ask* a woman? "I shall *tell* her," he said firmly as he dismounted and started up the stairs to Liana's solar.

Zared stood to one side of the doorway, her cheek against the rough stone and silently watched Liana's women. They laughed and giggled and whispered to one another while sliding dresses of gorgeous silks and velvets over their heads. Now and then Zared could catch a whispered word as they talked about the men of the castle. Zared stood a little straighter when she

4

heard Ralph's name mentioned. He was a young knight her brother Rogan had recently hired, and never had a man affected her as Ralph did. Just walking past him made her heart beat faster and the blood rush to her face.

"Would you like to try this gown?"

It took Zared a moment before she realized the woman was speaking to her. She was one of Liana's prettiest ladies, her hair encased in a net of gold, her body corseted and wrapped in velvet, and she was holding a gown of emerald satin toward Zared. Although the secret of Zared's femininity had been kept from her brothers' men, Liana's women knew the truth—that Zared was a girl.

Zared almost reached for the gown, but she drew her hand away sharply. "Nay," she said, with as much disdain as she could put in her voice. "I have no need for frivolities."

The woman, instead of looking as if she'd been put in her place, gave Zared a look of pity.

Zared tried her best to look haughty and turned away. What did she care for women's finery? For women's gossiping chatter?

Zared ran down the steep stone stairs and then paused at the second level, stepping back into an alcove when she heard Liana's voice. Zared held her breath as Liana passed.

In the two years since her oldest brother had taken a wife many things had changed in the Peregrine household: The food was better, the beds cleaner, and there were women all over the place. But Liana had not changed Zared. No amount of arguing with Zared's brothers had softened them into allowing Zared to change. For her own protection Zared must remain disguised as the youngest Peregrine son.

5

Of course, Zared told herself, she wouldn't want the confinement of being a woman. She wouldn't want to be like Liana, always confined within the castle grounds, never allowed to ride free, to gallop across a field. Women such as Liana and her ladies had to sit and wait, wait for a man to come to them. But Zared didn't have to wait for anything. If she wanted to go riding, she did so; she didn't have to wait for some man to help her on a horse and then accompany her.

But sometimes, just sometimes, she wished she could have a woman's wiles. She had been in sword practice with Ralph when one of Liana's ladies had walked past. Ralph had turned away to watch the woman. Zared had been so angered that she'd struck Ralph on the side of his head with the flat of her sword. He'd fallen to the ground, and the men around them had laughed. After that Ralph wouldn't practice with her. Nor would he sit with her, nor, if he could help it, would he remain in the same room with her. Severn said Ralph might think Zared was a boy, but she bothered him just the same.

After a week of Ralph's hostility Zared had considered asking Liana for a gown, but she couldn't bring herself to ask. If she wore a dress, she might get Ralph's notice, but her brothers would be mightily displeased. If she wore a gown she knew her brothers would no longer allow her outside the castle walls. Was gaining Ralph's favor worth the loss of her freedom?

She was thinking so hard that at first she did not realize that the voices in the next room had grown much louder.

"You cannot think to do this," Liana was saying in a voice filled with exasperation.

Zared knew her sister-in-law had to be talking to

Severn, for the two of them were always butting heads. Liana had a way of getting anything she wanted from Rogan, which was one of the things that enraged Severn. Whenever Severn spoke to Liana there was an undercurrent of hostility in his voice.

"She is my sister, and I will take her," Severn said with anger. "I do not need your permission."

Zared's ears perked up as she listened.

Liana's voice grew calmer, as if she were reasoning with the village idiot. "You are barely able to keep her safe here, yet you mean to expose her for all the world to see?"

"She will be my squire. *I* will protect her."

"While you court the Lady Anne? Will Zared sleep with the other squires? Or in your tent with you while you take your whores to bed? Zared is no Iolanthe to stand by and watch while you bed other women."

Zared sucked in her breath. Liana had gone too far. Iolanthe was the beautiful woman who had lived in the rooms above the kitchen. She had been married, but her old, senile husband had let her live with Severn—or maybe he hadn't known where his wife was. When the old man died Severn had asked Iolanthe to marry him, but she'd refused. She said she loved Severn, would always love him, but he was too poor for her to marry. She'd returned to her husband's house and within a year was married to a fat, stupid, but very rich man. She'd asked to see Severn again, but he'd refused to see her. Now Iolanthe's name was never mentioned.

Zared couldn't see Severn, but she knew he was no doubt trembling with rage.

"Severn," Liana whispered pleadingly. "Please listen to me."

"Nay, I do not listen to you. I must go to get a wife. I

7

do not want a wife, for I have seen how a wife can change a man, but the coffers must be filled if we are to win the war against the Howards, if we—"

"Cease!" Liana shouted. "I can bear no more. It is always the Howards. I have heard of little else since I married into this family. I eat with the Howards, sleep with them. They never leave me. How can you risk your sister's life in your hatred of them?"

Zared held her breath. Severn wouldn't strike his brother's wife, would he? If he did, Rogan would kill him.

Yet how could Liana speak so lightly of their enemies? How could she dismiss what the Howards had done to them over three generations?

Zared released her breath when Severn spoke again. At least he could control himself enough to refrain from striking Liana. Zared knew what her brother was talking about. A month before a herald had come issuing an invitation to a huge tournament to be held in honor of the marriage of Lady Catherine Marshall. There were rich prizes to be won, including a large emerald, but the herald had hinted that the richest prize was the younger daughter, Lady Anne. She was eighteen, just returned from years spent at the French court, and her father was seeking a good English husband for her.

At supper, after the herald had left, Severn had announced his intention of going to the tournament and returning with the rich Lady Anne as his wife. That had started a loud argument between Liana and Severn. Liana had said he thought a great deal of himself if he believed he could win a lady of manners and education merely because he could unhorse a few brawny, battle-scarred men. Severn had said Rogan had gotten himself a rich wife, and he planned to do so, too. Liana pointed out that *she* had chosen Rogan,

8

not the other way around, and she doubted very much if Anne would choose an unshaved, dirty, full-of-himself knight like Severn who also happened to be in love with another woman. Severn dived across the table, going for Liana bodily, and Rogan had had to leap on his brother to prevent him from harming Liana.

There hadn't been much peace in the Peregrine household after that, and Zared thought the continuing battle was Liana's fault. Ever the organizer, Liana had started to prepare Severn for the tournament. She ordered new garments, embroidered hangings for his horses, planned Severn's tent, planned even the decorations for his helmet. But the more Liana planned, the more Severn dug in his heels and refused to comply with her wishes. After three weeks of arguing he told Liana that if he had to, he'd sling the Lady Anne over his horse and force her to marry him.

"You'll have to do that," Liana said. "Force is the only way you'll get her to marry you after she gets near enough to smell you."

So Severn was planning to leave in two days for the tournament, and he was refusing to take the finery Liana had had made for him. "She will take me as I am."

"She will not have you at all," Liana had snapped.

But now he was telling Liana that he planned to take Zared as his squire. Zared smiled in anticipation: to see the world, to hear the music, taste the food, to . . .

"She can *not* go," Liana was saying. "Do you forget that for all her disguise she is a female? What if her sex were discovered? What is to keep some drunken man from her body? She will not be much of a marriage prize without her virginity."

Marriage? Zared thought. No one had mentioned marriage to her.

Liana's voice lowered. "What of the Howards? They will know that two of the Peregrines attend the tourney. Will they not try to take one of you? And will it not be the younger, smaller one?"

"Even the Howards would not offend the king, and he will be there."

"On the journey there and back, then," Liana said angrily. "Severn, please listen to me. Do not endanger the child's life. Do not let your anger at Iolanthe cause the death of your sister."

Zared realized that her hands were made into fists, her short nails cutting into her palms. She wanted to show herself to Liana and shout that she could take care of herself, that if any man tried to touch her, she'd use a knife on him. How could Liana think she was so weak that she must be protected like the puniest female? She was a man, not a woman!

"I mean . . ." Zared whispered, and to her horror she felt tears coming to her eyes. She was *female,* but she could take care of herself.

"She will go with me," Severn said, and his tone made Zared know that he meant to discuss the subject no further.

Zared pushed away from the wall and ran down the stairs before Severn saw her. Damn them all, she thought. One minute she was on the training field with Rogan yelling at her to hold her sword higher, and the next she was hearing Liana say she was too weak to fend off some drunk's advances. Was she a knight or a puny female? Was she a man or a woman?

She kept running down the stairs until she reached the courtyard below, and there stood Severn's stallion saddled and waiting for him. Cursing her whole

10

family for confusing her, she jumped on his horse and thundered across the drawbridge, ignoring the shouts behind her.

She rode as hard and as fast as she could, not caring where she was going. The castle and the Peregrine lands disappeared behind her, and she spurred the horse harder and faster. She was some miles from home when the three men fell in behind her. A quick look back showed that they wore the Howard chevron and the Howard colors.

Her heart leaped to her throat. Rogan had warned her that the Howards watched them, that the Howards sat in wait for one of the Peregrines to go unprotected.

All her life she had been warned about the Howards. From the time she had been born the treachery of the Howards had been drilled into her. Generations earlier a Peregrine duke, old and half senile, had taken for his second wife a young, pretty woman from the Howard family. The woman was ambitious, and she had persuaded her old husband to change his will to leave all—the money, the title, the estates—to her weakling of a son, a son that many whispered was not the duke's get.

The only way the Howard woman could persuade the old man to disinherit his grown sons was to make him believe he and his first wife had not in truth been married. The old man, his mind clear one day and foggy the next, had requested that the parish registers that recorded the marriage be brought to him, as well as the witnesses. But no registers were to be found, and all the witnesses had died—some of them all too recently.

The old man, dying and in great pain, had declared the sons of his first marriage bastards and had given everything to his wife's waiting family.

Since that time the Peregrines and the Howards had fought for the wealthy lands that the Howards controlled. Over the years the losses on both sides had been heavy, and the hatred was very deep.

Zared looked back at the Howard men chasing her, then rode harder than she ever had in her life, her head down to the horse's neck, the mane whipping at her eyes. The horse's hooves pounded on the hard, rutted dirt track, past people and carts and animals. But it wasn't long before she could feel the tired horse losing ground and feel the Howard men gaining on her.

"Come on, boy," she said to the horse. "If we make it to the king's forest, we'll lose them there."

She spurred the horse on, her heart beating hard with the horse's.

They almost made it, but moments before they reached the forest, when Zared could see the concealing safety of the trees ahead, the horse stepped in a hole and went down. Zared hit the ground and went rolling head over heels across the dusty road. When she stopped rolling and looked up three men were standing over her, swords pointed at her throat.

"It's the youngest Peregrine," one man said, as if he didn't believe his luck. "We'll be paid well for this."

"Stop counting your money and tie him up. I don't want him escaping before we can get him back."

One man grabbed her arm and pulled her up. "Little thing, he is," he said, feeling Zared's arm.

She jerked out of his grasp.

"Don't fool with me, boy, or I'll give you a taste of my knife. I don't guess Howard will mind whether a Peregrine is delivered to him dead or alive."

"Quiet!" the first man said. "Put the boy on your horse, and let's leave before his brothers come."

The mention of the elder Peregrines sobered the

12

men, and one threw Zared up into a saddle and mounted behind her.

All Zared could think of was that now the feud would start afresh, and before it ended she would lose more of her brothers. She closed her eyes against tears of regret. As long as possible she must make them continue believing her to be a boy. She didn't like to think what could happen were men like these to discover she was a female.

Tearle Howard stretched his long, muscular legs, gave a great yawn, and leaned back on the sweet grass by the side of the little stream. The sun was warm on his body, and the flies droned lazily. To his left he could hear the low murmur of his brother's three men.

Tearle meant to fall asleep, meant to idle the day away dozing in the sun, but the men's voices kept him from sleeping, for the voices reminded him of his brother's obsession.

Until two months ago Tearle had lived in France, had spent time at the court of Philip the Good. Under his mother's direction Tearle had lived a life of education and refinement. He'd learned the finer aspects of music, dance, the arts. His life had been one of ease and plenty, spent in a place where conversation was an art.

But six months earlier his mother had died, and with her death Tearle's main reason for living in France disappeared. At twenty-six years of age he'd found himself curious about the family he'd never known and rarely seen, so when Oliver demanded his young brother's return Tearle had been pleased and intrigued. Tearle had made the journey back to England in the pleasant company of friends and had greeted his brother and sister-in-law warmly.

The warmth had soon cooled when Tearle found

that Oliver wanted him to wage war on a family named Peregrine. Oliver had been horrified to find that Tearle had not been taught from an early age to hate the Peregrines. According to Oliver, the Peregrines were devils on earth and should be eradicated at all costs. Tearle was just as horrified to discover that the elder Howard brothers had been sacrificed to this long-running feud.

"Isn't it time to cease all this?" Tearle had asked Oliver. "Isn't the cause of the feud that the Peregrines believe our estates to be theirs? If we own the estates and they do not, would it not make more sense for the Peregrines to attack us instead of our attacking them?"

Tearle's words had so enraged Oliver that his eyes had glazed over and spittle had formed at the corner of his mouth. It was at precisely that moment that Tearle began to doubt his brother's sanity. Tearle could never get a full answer regarding the true cause of Oliver's hatred of the Peregrines, but after piecing together bits of castle gossip he suspected Oliver's hatred had something to do with his tired-looking wife, Jeanne.

Whatever the cause, the hatred was far too ingrained in Oliver for Tearle to be able to dislodge it. So while Tearle did his best to stay out of his brother's way, life with Oliver was dull at best. As far as Tearle could see, all of his brother's energies went into his hatred of the Peregrines, and nothing was left over for the finer things in life like music or pleasant society.

So there he was, idling the day away, sent out on a fool's errand by his obsessed brother.

"Go and watch them," Oliver had said, as if when Tearle saw the Peregrines he'd see not men but devils with red scales for skin. "Go with my men and see them."

14

"You post men outside the Peregrine castle?" Tearle had asked. "You watch them on a daily basis? Do you count the cabbages they buy?"

"Do not sneer at what you do not know," Oliver had said, his eyes narrowing. "Two years ago the oldest one went with his wife alone into the village. Had I but known, I could have taken him. I did take that wife of his, but she . . ." He stopped and turned away.

"She what?" Tearle asked with interest.

"Do not remind me of that day. Go and see what I fight. If you see them, you will understand."

Tearle was beginning to become curious about the Peregrines, so he went off with one of the four groups that Oliver planted about the Peregrine castle.

Tearle had not been impressed by the sight of the crumbling old castle. Some effort had been made to patch the worst of it, but nothing could disguise the poverty of the place. Tearle sat on a hill some distance away and watched through a spyglass as the three remaining Peregrines trained daily with their men. The youngest was a mere boy.

For three days Tearle sat there and watched the Peregrines training. By the end of the third day he felt he knew them all. In addition to the two men and the boy there were two illegitimate brothers who were awkward with their training, as if the weapons were new to them.

"Their father's by-blows," Oliver had said in contempt. "Had I known—"

"You would have killed them," Tearle said tiredly.

"Beware you do not try my patience too far," Oliver warned.

The Peregrines in their poverty took in illegitimate brothers, but Oliver, with all his riches, constantly threatened to toss Tearle out. Wisely, Tearle did not make that observation to his brother.

By the fifth day Tearle had no more interest in watching the Peregrines. He was itchy for exercise and wished he could join the training. "I could take the blond one," he said to himself as he watched Severn down yet another man. He gave the spyglass to one of the men and walked away. He had to figure out a way to get away from his duty as spy.

He wasn't aware that he was drifting into sleep until the thundering hooves of horses woke him. Oliver's men were gone. Tearle was on his feet instantly. He grabbed the spyglass from the ground where it'd been tossed and looked. The Peregrine men were in confusion, the oldest, Rogan, shouting as he mounted his horse. The slightly younger brother was already galloping away. But no one seemed to know exactly which way to go, so they split off in four directions.

"The boy," Tearle said. Once before he'd seen the boy ride away from his protective brothers, but Tearle had not told Oliver's men. Let the boy meet his village sweetheart, he'd thought, and then he worked on keeping the men's attention until the boy was safely returned.

Tearle ran to his horse and rode after Oliver's men. Obviously they had seen the direction in which the boy traveled. It took Tearle a while to find the men, and at first he thought he was too late. A stallion he knew to be Severn's led behind them, the men were already heading toward the Howard lands.

Tearle's heart sank. The capture of the boy would mean open warfare—and the Howards would be at fault. Damn Oliver and his obsession, he thought.

The men reluctantly halted when they saw Tearle. Their ugly faces were shining with triumph in having captured one thin, weak boy, and they looked at Tearle in expectation of praise.

Before one of them, sitting rigidly in the saddle, was the boy. Tearle could hardly bear to look at him.

When at last Tearle could meet the boy's eyes his mouth dropped open in shock. For he didn't look into the proud face of a boy, but into the fiery eyes of a girl.

In astonishment he looked back at the men.

"We caught him, my lord," one man said. "Do we take the boy to your brother, or do we kill him here?"

Tearle could only gape at the men. Couldn't they see that they held a girl? Couldn't they tell the difference between girls and boys?

"My lord?" one of the men asked, his voice anxious. "The Peregrines will be here soon."

Tearle regained his composure. He didn't think those Peregrine brothers would stop to talk when they saw their little sister held captive.

"I will take the . . . child to my brother," Tearle said. And get the girl out of the hands of these louts, he thought.

The men hesitated.

Frowning, Tearle tossed them a bag of coins. "Here, take this. I will deal with this Peregrine myself."

The men's eyes laughed. They had what they wanted, and they couldn't care less what Tearle did with the boy, or what happened to Tearle, for that matter.

One of the men rode beside Tearle and half shoved, half dumped Zared into his saddle. Tearle winced when he saw how tightly the girl's hands were tied. "Go!" he commanded the men. "Before they find you."

17

They hesitated not a second longer before they spurred their horses toward the Peregrine lands. Tearle fastened his arm around the girl's slim waist, hugged her body close to his, and rode hard and fast into the king's forest.

Chapter Two

Tearle lost himself in the forest, leaving the paths
that centuries of villagers' feet had carved, and
slipped deep into the dark recesses between the giant
oak trees. As he rode he held the girl before him,
feeling her slim back against his chest, her slim, strong
legs against his. Once a low-hanging branch threatened to hit her, and he put out his hand to protect her,
the branch painfully cutting into the back of his hand.
Another time, as he leaned forward to duck a branch,
he put his face in the curve of her neck, her soft hair
on his face.

He smiled as they rode. Oliver thought he knew all
there was to know about the Peregrines, yet he'd never
guessed that the youngest son was actually a girl. The
Peregrines were right for keeping her gender a secret,
for Oliver seemed to be particularly fascinated by the
Peregrine females.

He pulled his horse up sharply when he entered a

secluded glade. He dismounted, then pulled the girl down before him. Her hands were still tied behind her back, and she was alone with her enemy, but her eyes showed no fear.

He put his hands on her shoulders and looked down at her. Her worn, dirty tunic reached to mid-thigh, and from there down her legs were encased in tight knit hose, her little feet in soft boots that reached to her knee. Her dark hair, showing red even in the shadows of the forest, was shoulder-length, curling under at the ends, and she wore a jaunty little cap with a feather on one side.

For the first time since leaving France he was feeling some interest in life. What an intriguing female she was, he thought, remembering watching her train with her brothers. He suddenly felt an overwhelming urge to remount his horse and take her back with him to his brother's estate. The place was so big he could no doubt hide her there.

Zared looked at the man who held her by the shoulders, a big man with dark hair and eyes—and the unmistakable look of a Howard about him. The men who had captured her had called him lord, so he must be the long-missing youngest Howard brother.

Zared had heard stories of this younger brother, so evil he'd had to be sent away to France with his she-devil mother when he was just a boy. Looking at him she could believe all the stories about him. On the ride into the forest he'd felt her body as though to see if she were plump enough for roasting. And his beady little black eyes were glittering as though he meant to have her for a feast.

Lunatic, she thought, and she would have crossed herself in protection if her hands hadn't been tied.

While he stood there looking at her as a starving

man might look at a meal, she tried to make a plan. She could never have escaped three of the Howard men, but she had a chance with one madman. If she could get him to untie her hands, perhaps she could get to the knife hidden in her boot. With a weapon she could, perhaps, fight him off. He was big, true, but he might be as lazy as his brother, and his large size could be attributed to fat instead of muscle.

"What is your name?" he asked.

"Peregrine!" she hissed at him. If he did not untie her, if he meant to kill her, she would not disgrace her family by dying a coward.

"Your Christian name," he said softly, his eyes gentle.

What trick is this? she thought. Did he think to make her believe there was anything but evil in him? "My brothers will kill you," she said. "They will take you apart piece by piece."

He smiled a bit. "Yes, I imagine they would." He took a jewel-handled dagger from his belt, and Zared took a step backward involuntarily.

"I don't mean to hurt you," he said, talking to her as though she were a frightened wild animal.

He was stupid as well as crazy if he believed she'd ever trust the word of a Howard, she thought.

He took her by the shoulder and turned her around, then used his knife to cut the cords that bound her hands. As he turned her back around, in one deft movement she had practiced many times, she pretended to stumble, went to the ground on one knee, removed the knife from her boot, and slipped it inside her sleeve.

"Are you hurt?" Tearle asked, helping her to her feet. "I fear my brother's men were over-rough with you."

21

He had his hands on her shoulders again, and, not seeming able to help himself, he pulled her to him and kissed her gently on the mouth.

Zared was outraged! No man had ever kissed her before, and that this man, this evil, hated enemy of hers, should dare to touch her was more than she could bear. She dropped the knife from her sleeve into her hand and plunged it into his ribs.

He stepped back from her, looked down at the blood forming on his tight-waisted velvet tunic, and looked back at her in surprise.

"Death to all Howards," she spat at him, and she ran to the horse nearby.

"You are free," he whispered. "I never meant to keep you a prisoner."

She mounted the horse and glanced at him. He was growing pale, and the blood at his side was spreading wider. She kicked the horse forward and left the glade, putting her head down as she and the horse raced through the forest.

She had to find her brothers and tell them she was safe. She had to prevent them from attacking the Howards. At all costs she must stop what could become open war.

It was when she was at the edge of the forest that she realized that there could yet be war between the Howards and the Peregrines, for she had, perhaps, just killed the youngest Howard.

She rode on. Of course she hadn't killed him. She had merely wounded him. She had not hit vital organs. Had she? The image of his pale face swam before her. What if he lay there and bled to death? Oliver Howard's three men would know that once again a Peregrine had attacked a Howard. The Howards would attack, and because of Zared more of her brothers would be killed. Perhaps this time Oliver

22

Howard would succeed in wiping out all of the Peregrines.

At the edge of the forest Zared halted. She had to go back. She had to see that the man didn't die. But what if he regained his strength enough to hold her captive and take her to his brother?

Zared put her hands to her head as though to still her thoughts. All her life her brothers had made decisions for her. She knew that both Rogan and Severn would be so enraged at a Howard taking their sister that they would joyfully destroy the youngest Howard. Should she go to her brothers and tell them what had happened? Should she add fuel to their hatred? Renew all the old hurts and rages?

Yet it was her own fault for having been taken. Both Severn and Rogan had warned her again and again that the Howards' men lurked just outside the grounds.

She *had* to return. She had to keep the man from bleeding to death and thus causing a war. She would take his sword and, if need be, tie his hands and feet to prevent his overpowering her. She had to do what she could to prevent a war.

Tearle watched the girl go with regret. He guessed he'd never see her again. Peregrines and Howards rarely socialized, he thought with a bit of a smile.

He looked down at his side, at the spreading blood, and pulled up his tunic to examine the wound. His ribs had deflected her blade, and he was glad she wasn't experienced enough at knifing humans to have known how to injure him more severely.

He looked about the glade, realizing she had taken his horse. Was he supposed to walk back to his brother's? He calculated how long it would take the three men to get to Oliver, then how long it would take

Oliver to mount a body of men and come in search of Tearle and his Peregrine prize.

Four hours, Tearle thought. Within four hours his brother would be there. Until then he might as well rest and give the wound time to stop bleeding. He stretched out under a tree and was asleep very soon.

Zared dismounted and left the horse some distance from the glade. Then, knife in hand, she crept back to where she'd left the man.

Dead, she thought when she saw him stretched on the ground. He was already dead, and she was too late to save him.

Tearle heard her coming from some distance off, knowing by the lightness of her step that it was she. He had to prevent himself from smiling. So much for the cruel, inhuman monsters his brother spoke of. This Peregrine, at least, had a much softer side to her. Whatever he did, he must not frighten her away. He must seem helpless and keep her near him as long as possible, he decided.

He moved just a bit and gave a groan of pain.

Zared jumped at the sound, then gave a sigh of relief that he was still alive. Cautiously she moved forward, creeping nearer to him. With her knife at the ready she nudged him with her foot. He gave another little groan.

"A priest," he murmured. "Get me a priest."

Zared lost her caution at that. She had to save him. She went to her knees beside him, slit his tunic away, and examined his wound. She had hit his ribs, but she couldn't tell how deep her knife had gone. There wasn't much flesh over his ribs, just skin and muscle, but he seemed to have lost an extraordinary amount of blood.

She glanced at his face and saw that his eyes were closed and that he wore a pained expression. Were

24

Howard men so weak that they died from such slight wounds? She'd seen her brothers hurt that way and continue fighting for a full day before the wound was dressed. Yet the man was calling for a priest because of a mere cut.

She cut away more of his tunic and sliced a long strip of his linen shirt away. She wadded a piece of his shirt against the wound, then tried to wrap the linen strip around his big body.

He was an inert weight, and lifting him was impossible. She could have as easily lifted a dead horse. She leaned across him and tugged. She put her arms about his neck and tried to lift him. She heaved against him with her shoulders, but he just lay there, oblivious even to her presence.

"Wake up!" she commanded.

He stirred but didn't open his eyes.

Zared gave him a few sharp smacks on his cheeks, and at last he opened his eyes. "I am trying to get this bandage about you. You must lift yourself up."

"You must help me," Tearle said in a hoarse whisper.

She gave him a look of disgust, then leaned over him and helped to pull him up. He was very weak and ended in clasping her to him, his body heavily against hers. Zared had difficulty reaching around him to pull the bandage about his ribs, and holding him up was straining her back, but she managed to dress the wound.

"Lie down now," she said. The man really did seem to be quite stupid. She had to tell him the simplest things. She eased him back to the ground, but he had to have Zared's help all the way, and she had to peel his arms from around her body when he was lying flat once again.

"You will be all right now," she said. "The wound is

25

not deep. Stay here and rest. Your brother will come soon. He is never far from Peregrine lands." She started to rise, but he caught her hand.

"You would leave me? I will die here alone."

"You won't die," she said in disgust. Perhaps the Howard had been sent away as a child not because he was evil but because he was such a weakling that his family was embarrassed by him.

"Wine," he whispered. "There is a bottle of wine on my horse."

Zared gritted her teeth. Her brothers were no doubt frantically searching for her, yet she was playing nursemaid to a sniveling Howard. Reluctantly she went to the horse, removed the hard leather bottle, and handed it to him. But he was too weak to sit up without Zared's support; he couldn't even hold the bottle to his lips.

This is the enemy? Zared thought. This cowardly, weak, trembling, oversized child is something to fear?

She took the wine bottle from his lips. "I must go," she said. "I will leave the bottle here and—"

"Stay," he said, clasping her hand in his. "Please stay with me. I am frightened."

Zared rolled her eyes skyward. She was sitting on the ground, and he was leaning against her as though he could not support himself.

"I will die if you do not stay."

"You won't die," she snapped. "You ought to at least try to have some courage. The bleeding's stopped, and besides, I have to leave. My brothers will be searching for me, and it's best if they don't find me . . . here."

"Ah. You mean with a Howard. Do you know that I am a Howard?"

"We know much about the Howards. You are our enemy."

He sighed and leaned limply against her. "Surely *I* am not your enemy."

"If you are a Howard, you are indeed the enemy of all the Peregrines."

"Yet you returned for me."

"I came back to prevent a war. Had you died, your brother would have attacked my brothers." She tried to move out from under him, but he had her trapped by his weight.

"You returned only because of your brothers?"

"Why else?" she asked, genuinely confused.

He lifted her hand to his lips. "Perhaps you know all of us, but it seems we do not know all about the Peregrines. We did not know the youngest was a daughter and a lovely young woman." He kissed first one fingertip and then another. "Did you not perhaps return because of our kiss?"

It took a moment for the words to sink in, but then Zared began to laugh. Still laughing, she squirmed out from under him, stood, and looked down at him. "You think I care for a kiss? You think a kiss from a Howard could make me forget my four brothers your family has killed? You think me shallow enough to betray my family for anything a Howard could give me? I could slit your throat now, but your death would mean open war, and that I do not want."

Her laughter was changing to anger. "You Howards are less than nothing to me. Did I not show you what I thought of your kiss?" She nodded toward the bloody bandage on his side.

She stepped away from him and gave him a look of contempt. "I would feel a kiss that was from a *man,* but not from a spineless weakling such as you. Oliver Howard is no doubt greatly ashamed of his youngest brother—and well he should be."

She crossed to the horse and mounted. "I will free

27

your horse at the edge of the forest, for I do not want my brothers to see me on a Howard animal. I will not tell them of your men's skulking treachery or of your touching me. My brothers have killed men for less."

She gave him one last look. "Even the Howards do not deserve such a half-man as you."

Tearle was on his feet by the time she'd turned the horse, but she was out of the glade before he could catch the bridle.

Rage gave color to his pale face. Half-man?! His brother should be ashamed of him? A spineless weakling?

He? He, Tearle Howard, a weakling? In France he had won tournaments since he was a boy. He beat all comers. Women threw themselves at him. Women begged him for his kisses, yet this . . . this boy-girl had said his kiss was not that of a *man!*

As though she knew one kiss from another. As though she were such a lady of sophistication that she knew anything about kisses—or anything else, for that matter. All she knew were swords and warfare and . . . and horses. She'd have to be a *woman* to know if a kiss came from a man or not. She'd have to—

Abruptly he stopped his silent tirade and began to chuckle. Perhaps he had appeared to be a little too helpless. But it had been nice having her lean across him in an attempt to lift him. When her chest had been against his he had felt a hard padding and guessed she must bind her breasts down in her attempt to appear a boy.

And what a futile attempt that was, he thought, for her every movement screamed that she was female. How anyone could believe her to be male was beyond his understanding.

A boy wouldn't have come back to see if his enemy

was all right. Of course, Tearle wouldn't have kissed a boy and thus prompted the stabbing, but either way, a boy would not have returned.

He leaned against a tree and closed his eyes for a moment. What an intriguing girl she was, all passion and fury, yet softness underneath. She was so unaware of how she could affect a man. She was so different from other women who were coy and flirted and gave promises. The young Peregrine would never flirt, never tease. She would always say what she meant.

He moved away from the tree. He would probably never see her again, he thought.

He started walking. Maybe, he thought, he'd see his brother's men soon. If anyone knew what the Peregrine family planned, it was his brother. Oliver would no doubt be pleased when at last his young brother began to take an interest in the enemy family.

Zared stared out the small stone-cased window and watched the people on the grounds far below. Two days locked in the tower room with nothing but bread and water was her punishment for scaring her brothers half to death. Severn had yelled at her for a solid hour after she'd come limping back home. Rogan's anger had been worse, for he'd looked at her in such a way that she felt small enough to slide between the stones of the fireplace.

At least Severn's yelling had made lengthy excuses unnecessary. Zared had merely mumbled that she'd wanted to ride, Severn's stallion had thrown her, and she'd had to walk back. She much regretted the loss of Severn's horse, but only she knew how very much worse it could have been. All considered, two days locked away was a slight punishment. Her biggest fear was that her brothers wouldn't allow her to go to the tournament.

29

"If the Howards keep me from that pleasure," she muttered, "I will kill that whining, cowardly worthnothing with my bare hands."

She jumped when she heard the door open behind her. Turning, she saw Liana enter with a cloth-covered basket. Zared repressed a smile, for Liana, underneath her efficient exterior, was as soft-hearted as a human could be. No doubt she feared that Zared would starve in two days without meat and wine.

"I have brought you something to eat," Liana said. "Not that you deserve it, for what you did endangered all of us."

"And I am most sorry," Zared said, reaching for the basket. "You are more than kind to bring me food when I do not deserve it." She moved to sit on the edge of the filthy bed.

"I couldn't let you starve," Liana said, taking a seat on the one chair in the room and looking about. "This place is not fit for humans."

Zared didn't think the room was so bad—a few fleas here and there, a few rats, but not unlivable. Speculatively she looked at Liana. She knew that Liana had power over whether or not she went to the tournament, for Rogan listened to his wife, and if Liana said Zared should not be allowed to go, then Rogan would forbid it.

"Do you not think it is time for me to have a husband?" Zared asked as she bit into a thick piece of pork.

Liana looked startled. "I have thought so, but I did not think you or your brothers gave much thought to the idea."

"I have been considering it lately," Zared said. "Perhaps I should have my own home, children. Perhaps I should get away from this." She waved her hand. "And the Howards."

"Oh, Zared, I could not agree more. Your life would change so much if you had your own family. Perhaps it would help your brothers get over their hatred of the Howards if they were allied with another family."

"Ah," Zared said. "Then you have someone in mind for me to marry?"

"No," Liana said slowly. "We are so isolated here that we see no one. But perhaps my stepmother would know of someone." She was quiet a moment.

"Perhaps Severn will meet someone at the tourney," Zared said, as though it didn't matter to her. "Or perhaps *I* could look the men over there."

Liana didn't say anything, and when Zared looked at her she was smiling.

"I see," Liana said. "Perhaps if you, say, went to the tournament as Severn's squire, you could find yourself a husband?"

Soft-hearted, true, Zared thought, but awfully clever. "Liana, please. Please allow me to go. I have never been anywhere in my life but here. I should like to meet some people who are not my relatives or hired by my family."

Liana's face showed her agony of indecision. "It's so dangerous for you. The Howards—"

"Bah!" Zared said, standing up. "The Howards! Those spineless cowards! They aren't worth considering."

"What do you know of the Howards to call them cowards? What happened when you rode away on Severn's horse? There was blood on your hose but no cut on your leg."

"Must have been the horse's from when it fell," Zared said quickly.

"I'm not sure I'm hearing all of the truth."

"What else could there be? Do you think I was captured by the Howards?" Zared gave a little laugh.

"They captured me, but out of the goodness of their hearts they released me. Very amusing idea."

"I've seen you use a knife," Liana said softly. "Perhaps you could have escaped were you captured."

Zared walked across the room, grabbed a chunk of bread, and filled her mouth. "This is *delicious* bread. When I'm married I hope I can be half the housewife you are. That is, if I can find a husband, or, rather, if Severn can find one for me. I'm sure he will pick a good husband for me."

"All right, keep your secrets," Liana said. She'd lived with the Peregrines long enough to know that they revealed nothing about themselves unless they had to. She sighed in resignation. "Severn will no doubt choose a man who is best able to help fight the Howards, some man with years of war experience." She looked at Zared. "You need less war and more love."

"Love?" Zared said with a snort. "I have my brothers, I have God, I need no more love."

Liana looked up at her pretty young sister-in-law. She was sure Zared would someday love a man. If she knew nothing else about the Peregrines, she knew they were people of passion: They hated with passion, fought with passion, loved with passion. Zared seemed to think it didn't matter who she married, but were she bound to a man she couldn't respect, or worse, one she held in contempt, she would hate him until, if the man had any sense, he would fear for his life.

Liana also knew that all she had to do was tell Rogan that Zared should not go to the tournament and Zared would not be allowed to go, but something held Liana back. Zared would be safer at home, true, but what if Zared's passion should turn to hate: more hate for the Howards, who prevented her from leaving her home-prison, and possibly hate for Liana as well.

"You will stay near Severn?" Liana asked softly, wondering if she'd ever see Zared alive again.

"Yes, oh, yes," Zared said, her face filled with joy.

"How I wish I could go with you! I'd order some gowns for you, greens and blues. You could be quite pretty if your hair weren't always in a snarl. Oh, Zared, a tournament is so lovely. You give your favor to a man, and he—"

"I'd rather fight," Zared said. "I'd rather mount a horse, hold a lance, and knock a man off his horse. I would not like to sit and watch."

"No, I guess you wouldn't." Liana put her hands on her big belly. She was too soon due with her second child to be able to leave. Perhaps it was better if she didn't see her husband's young sister acting as a squire, mucking out stables, currying horses, running between combatants to deliver fresh lances.

Liana stood. "I do not feel it is the best thing to do, but perhaps you will be safe enough. Perhaps Severn is right and Oliver Howard will not dare attack while the king is there. I will tell Severn he has his squire." She started for the door.

"Liana," Zared said. "When you met Oliver Howard, what was he like? Is he a very great fighter?"

Liana smiled. "Not at all. He's much older than your brothers and gone to fat. But then he does not have to fight, for he's very rich and can hire as many men as he needs."

"And what of his brother?"

"Brother? I heard nothing of a brother. I'm afraid I don't know the Howards as well as your family does. Zared, what do you know of a brother?"

"Nothing. Nothing at all. It's just that . . ." She

33

looked at Liana. "I have not seen much of the world and know only of my brothers. They are such fine men." She smiled proudly. "They are strong and handsome. No one could beat them on a battlefield. Are they such unusual men? Or are there many men like them?"

Liana took a while to answer. "I don't believe there are *any* other men like your brothers, but Zared, there is more to a man than a strong right arm. You do not choose a husband by physical strength alone. There are other qualities such as kindness and unselfishness and whether he will love you and your children or not."

"And protect his family from enemies."

"Yes, that's important too, but . . ." She didn't know how to explain to this girl that there was another way of life besides what she'd known. All her life Zared had lived in a private war with another family. She'd been raised as a boy to protect her. She knew nothing of sitting in the sunshine with a handsome young man while he played a lute and sang to her. She'd never had a man kiss her hand and tell her how lovely the sunlight in her hair was. Zared had never giggled with the maids or flirted with a boy, or done any of the things other girls did. Zared knew swords and horses and could sing all the vulgar songs with the men. But she didn't know satin from brocade or ermine from sable. Worst of all, she knew no men except her brothers.

"You'll find no husband like your brothers," Liana said softly.

"Then I shall never marry," she said with all the confidence of youth. "I shall remain a virgin until my death."

That made Liana laugh and the baby kick. A Peregrine remain a virgin? That was a good one. She knew, much better than her brothers did, that when Zared discovered sexual feelings she was going to be impossible to restrain. If Severn did not keep close watch on her at the tournament and she met some splendid man who took her fancy . . .

Liana did not like to think of the possible consequences, for Zared's brothers would kill any man who touched their little sister. "I am sure I am making a mistake in allowing you to go."

"I will be good," Zared said. "I will obey Severn and stay near him, and I will get into no trouble. I swear it, Liana. You have my word as a Peregrine."

Liana smiled and sighed at the same time. "Peregrines were born to be in trouble. I'm sure both you and your brother will get into a dreadful mess. Swear to me that you will not allow Severn to kill anyone and you will not come home with child."

Zared's mouth dropped open. "With child?"

"Swear to me. You cannot go otherwise."

Zared grimaced. Her sister-in-law understood nothing. Severn was going to get a wife, not to kill anyone, and she was going to see the sights. Besides, people thought she was a boy, so no man was going to try to impregnate her. A brief memory of the youngest Howard kissing her crossed her mind. He'd known she was female, but that was probably because he was half female himself, fainting over a little cut!

"I swear," Zared said.

"I guess that shall have to do. Now get a good night's sleep, because tomorrow you leave with your brother."

Zared grinned broadly. "Yes, I will, and thank you, Liana, thank you. I will do the Peregrine name proud."

"Don't say that or I'll think you mean to return with a dozen heads on pikes. Goodnight, Zared. I will pray

35

for you every day." Liana left, shutting the door behind her.

Zared stood where she was for a moment, then jumped high, her hands hitting the cracked plaster ceiling. She felt as though the next day her life would truly begin.

Chapter Three

For two days Tearle listened to Oliver rant about the Peregrines. Most of what he heard was useless information, but Tearle listened just the same. He found out that the girl's name was Zared, and it was Oliver's opinion that the "boy" would never be the equal of his brothers.

On the afternoon of the second day Oliver received the news that Severn Peregrine was to enter the Marshall tournament, and it was rumored that he was going to try for the Lady Anne's hand in marriage.

Oliver had been quite jovial at the idea. "I shall take him prisoner while he is there."

"With the king watching?" Tearle asked, yawning. "I don't imagine Anne's father would like this feud of yours taken onto his land."

"Anne, is it?" Oliver asked, his ears perking up like a hunting dog's. "You know the woman?"

"Only by sight. She lived in France for a while."

"Then you shall go."

"To the tournament? To spy on the man as he goes courting?"

"Yes." Oliver's eyes were feverishly bright. "You will see what they do, watch them, report to me about—"

"Them?" Tearle sat up in the chair. "Who is to go besides the second son?"

"The boy is to be his squire." Oliver snorted. "He cannot afford a true squire, so he has to use his own brother. He will be a laughingstock, for they are a dirty, crude lot, and the Marshalls are people of great refinement. Would that I could see the Peregrines' humiliation."

"I will go," Tearle said.

Oliver grinned. "You will fight him. I shall *have* to go. I must see this. On the jousting field a Howard will down a Peregrine. The king—the world—shall see that a Howard—"

"I'll not fight him," Tearle said. He knew that he would never have an opportunity to spend time with the youngest Peregrine were he to announce himself as a Howard. "I shall go in disguise." Before Oliver could open his mouth Tearle continued. "I shall spy on them," he said, feeding Oliver's obsession. "No one in England knows I have returned. I shall attend the tournament as . . . as Smith. I shall watch and learn more about the Peregrines than I could if I announced myself as their enemy."

Oliver looked at his brother, and his expression changed. "I was not sure you understood," he said softly. "But I should not have doubted our blood."

Tearle smiled at his brother. He did not feel the least bit guilty for deceiving his brother, for Oliver's hatred of that family did not deserve respect. I shall protect them, he thought. I shall see that no harm comes to the Peregrines, no misaimed arrows, no pieces falling from the roof, no cut saddle cinches. I shall see that for once they are safe from Howard hatred.

"No, you should not have doubted me," Tearle said. "I have always been as I am. I have never changed."

Oliver frowned a bit at that but then smiled. "Yes, I see. You have always been a Howard. When do you leave?"

"Now," Tearle said, and he rose. He wanted to hear no more of Oliver's venom, but most important, he wanted to get to Anne Marshall. He hadn't told his brother the truth when he'd said he barely knew Anne. He'd tossed her on his knee when she was a child, had kissed her tears away when she'd fallen, had told her ghostly stories at bedtime and then received tongue-lashings from her mother for causing Anne to wake screaming in the night. An adult Anne had comforted Tearle when his mother had died.

Tearle knew that if he was to appear at the Marshall tournament in disguise, he had to get to Anne first and tell her of his plans.

Tearle sat on top of the garden wall and watched Anne and her ladies walking. One lady was, as usual, reading aloud. Tearle had often teased Anne for her scholarly ways; she seemed forever buried in a book.

He leaned back against a branch of an old apple tree and smiled at the sight. The women in their bright gowns, their elaborate headdresses trimmed with jewels and gauze veils, were a beautiful sight, but Anne stood out even from those women. Anne was a beauty among beauty. She was tiny, barely reaching a man's shoulder, and she was vain enough that she always surrounded herself with tall women. She looked like a precious jewel, and the towering women were a setting for that jewel.

As she and her women moved forward he had no doubt that Anne would see him. The other women would probably never look up, but Anne didn't miss anything. If possible, her brain was even brighter than her face was lovely. And, Tearle thought with a wince, her tongue could be as sharp as a blade. Too often he'd been on the receiving end of her barbs, and he knew how they could sting.

When Anne glanced up and saw him, only for a second did she look startled. Startled, but not fearful, for it would take more than one mere man to frighten Anne Marshall. Tearle gave her a smile, and she looked away quickly.

Within moments she had dismissed her women, sending them all away on errands, and she stood below Tearle, looking up at him.

He jumped lightly to the ground, took Anne's small hand, and kissed it. "The moon has no beauty compared to you. Flowers hide their faces in shame when you walk past. Butterflies close their wings; peacocks do not dare show themselves; jewels cease to sparkle; gold—"

"What do you want, Tearle?" Anne asked, pulling her hand away. "What causes you to skulk about my father's garden? Are you in love with one of my maids?"

"You wound me," he said, his hand to his heart as, stumbling as though he had been stabbed, he sat on a stone bench. "I have come merely to see you." He looked up at her with a bit of a grin. "I would forgive your accusations were you to sit on my knee as you used to do."

Anne's beautiful face relaxed its sternness, and she

40

smiled as she sat beside him. "I have missed your silver tongue. Do you not find these English a sober lot?"

"*Most* sober. My brother is . . ." He didn't finish.

"I have heard. My sister has filled my ears with naught but gossip. Your family is at war with another family."

"Yes, the Peregrines."

"I have heard much of them," Anne said. "My sister attended the wedding of the eldest son to Lady Liana." She gave a delicate shudder.

"They are not so bad." He was on the point of telling Anne about Zared but stopped himself. It would not do to tell anyone she was female. If a person could not tell by looking at her, he did not deserve to be told. "The second son is coming to the tournament and means to win your hand."

Anne turned to look at him, astonishment on her beautiful face. "To win *my* hand? A Peregrine? For all your family's feud with them, you must not know much of those men. They are a filthy, ignorant lot. The oldest brother did not attend his own wedding feast. He was too busy counting the gold his bride brought him. When Lady Liana's stepmother was justifiably so angry she threatened to dissolve the marriage, he took his virginal bride upstairs and . . . and . . ." She stopped and looked away. "He is more animal than man."

"All hearsay," Tearle said in dismissal. "I have seen the men fight. The one who comes will do well in your tournament."

"He can beat you?"

Tearle smiled. "I don't plan to find out. I do not enter the games. I have come to ask a favor of you."

"Ah, so you have not come merely to see the flowers bow down in shame at my beauty?"

41

"Of course that was my first reason." He reached for her hand, but Anne pulled away.

"I would think more of your compliments if I hadn't heard you use the same ones since I was eight years old. Really, Tearle, you are too easy in your lovemaking. You need a woman who will not give in to you at hearing your same old tired flattery."

"A woman such as you? I could be happy if you would marry me."

"Ha! I shall marry a man who uses his brain instead of his brawn. I want a husband to whom I can talk. If I tried to speak to you of something besides armor and lances, you would fall asleep snoring."

He smiled at her sweetly. She didn't know him at all if that was what she thought most interested him. "I swear I would not fall asleep were I married to you. And I would give you something to do besides talk."

"Your bragging is wasted on me. Now tell me what favor you have to ask of me."

"I plan to help the Peregrines, and I do not want them to know I am a Howard. I shall pose as a man named Smith."

Anne gave him a cool look. She had dark hair, mostly hidden under her headdress, dark brows, and dark eyes that could burn a man when she chose to do so. "You ask me to endanger a man who will be a guest at my father's house?" She rose, glaring at him. "I had thought better of you than this."

He caught her before she'd gone two steps. "I said I meant to help them, and I am telling the truth." He said no more, just looked at her, praying she would believe him.

"Why?" she asked. "Why do you wish to help filthy beasts like these Peregrines? Isn't it true that they believe all your lands to be theirs? You wish me to believe you would help men who would make you a pauper?"

"It is difficult to believe, but it is true. I do not even know these brothers. I've seen them only from a distance, but I have no hatred for them as my brother does. I merely wish to . . ." He couldn't tell her more and couldn't think of an excuse for why he wanted to help the Peregrines without telling her of Zared.

"There is a woman involved," Anne said.

Tearle blinked. Clever brat, he thought. "A woman? How could a woman be involved? There are two brothers coming—an older one to compete and a younger one to be his squire. Can I not do something out of my love of mankind? My brother hates these Peregrines, and I am sick of the talk of hatred. Could I not merely wish for the end of this hatred? Perhaps I wish only to make peace between our families."

"What is her name?"

Tearle narrowed his eyes at her. "I recant my marriage proposal. I have known you since your birth, yet you doubt my good intentions. You dishonor me and my family."

Anne smiled at him in a knowing way. "Are you in love with her as much as you loved that young count's wife?"

"That was something altogether different. She was a woman married to a boy. And I told you, this has nothing to do with a woman." Tearle vowed to go to confession as soon as possible. "I am hurt that you think so little of my character."

"All right," Anne said. "You win. I will keep your secret, but I swear to you that I will find out why you wish to dupe this poor stupid Peregrine man."

Tearle didn't answer her because he had no answer to make. He had no idea why he was interested in a

43

girl who dressed as a boy, a girl who was the daughter of a house that had been at war with his family for generations. Her brothers had killed his brothers. By rights he should hate the girl, should have been glad his brother's men had captured her.

But he hadn't been glad, and later, when she'd tried to dress his wound, he'd wanted her to remain with him.

He looked back at Anne and smiled. Perhaps it was merely that the Peregrine girl was a novelty. He'd had many beautifully dressed women, so perhaps it would be different to bed a woman who might fight him for his clothes in the morning.

"There is nothing to find out," Tearle said, looking innocent. "I but want to help some poor, misunderstood people."

Anne gave an unladylike snort. "You may keep your secrets, but keep those Peregrines from me. I do not wish to be the fool Lady Liana was. Now leave here before someone sees you and tells my father."

Tearle gave a nervous glance toward Hugh Marshall's big house. "Thank you," he said, quickly kissing her hand and bounding over the garden wall out of sight.

Anne sat on the bench after Tearle had left and smiled. It was so good to see a person who could laugh, a person who could take life less than seriously, people such as she had known in France. Anne's mother had taken her daughters home to France when Anne was only five years old and her sister Catherine six, and Anne and her sister had grown up with their mother's family. They'd been surrounded by laughter and learning and beauty. Their mother's family's household had been a place where they'd felt free to say whatever they wanted, where they were encouraged to use their wit and intelligence. They were praised for their beauty, their skill at cards, their talents on a horse or when they read aloud. It was almost as though they could do no wrong.

Looking back, Anne knew she had not been appreciative enough of those wonderful years of freedom and happiness. They seemed so long ago and far away.

When Catherine was seventeen and Anne sixteen Hugh Marshall had demanded that his wife bring his daughters back to England, saying it was time to get them husbands. Since neither Anne nor her sister could remember their father, they felt no fear. Instead they looked at their journey with anticipation, and they whispered excitedly about the idea of husbands.

But Hugh Marshall's demand had sent their mother into a decline. Overnight her face had lost its sparkle, her hair its sheen. At first the girls were too caught up in their own excitement to notice their beloved mother's misery, but by the time they boarded the ship for England they saw that their mother was wraithlike in her thinness, and her face had no color in it.

It didn't take two weeks at their father's house to learn the cause of their mother's misery. Hugh Marshall was a humorless, uneducated bully of a man who ran his rich estates by terror and brute force. He also tried to run his wife and daughters that way.

After the women returned to England there was no more laughter, and certainly no more praise. Hugh Marshall made no attempt to hide his disappointment in how his wife had reared their two daughters.

"You give me nothing but daughters," he bellowed at his wife, who seemed to lose weight daily, "and then you fill their heads with books. They try to *defy* me!" he yelled.

When Catherine had told him she didn't like his choice of husband for her he'd blacked her eye, then locked her in a room for two weeks. Tearfully Catherine had finally agreed to the odious old man her father had chosen for her. Her father, already a rich man, wanted more riches, but more than that he wanted power. He had visions of grandsons who sat at the king's right hand. So he was marrying Catherine to an earl who was a distant relative of the king and enjoyed some society at court.

Six months after they'd returned to England their mother had died. Hugh Marshall had shown no regret at the loss, saying she was never a wife to him, that she'd been able to bear only worthless daughters. He'd allowed her to go to France when he was told she could bear no more children. She was useless to him as a wife if she couldn't give him sons. Since she was dead he planned to get himself another wife, one who could give him a dozen sons or more.

Anne had stood at her mother's grave and felt deep, deep hatred for her father. He had killed her mother as surely as if he had taken a knife to her throat.

After her mother's death and her sister's betrothal Anne had declared war on her father. There was a part of her that didn't care what happened to her, so she dared to defy him and to make some demands of her own.

Anne knew that her father would use her as a pawn in his life game, just as he'd used Catherine, but Anne planned to do better than her sister had. Anne used all her knowledge, used everything she'd ever learned, to talk Hugh Marshall into giving a tournament at Catherine's wedding. At the tournament Anne planned to choose her own husband and to use her powers of persuasion to get her father to marry her to a man who would make her a proper husband. She was not going to allow him to marry her off to a man like himself, as he was doing to Catherine.

She looked up at her father's house and narrowed her eyes. From that point on it would be a battle between her father's brawn and her brain. And how she fought the battle would determine the rest of her life. If her father had his way and married her to a man like himself, she would spend the rest of her days in an even worse hell than she'd known since she had returned to England.

At the tournament she would see what England had to offer, and she would find a man who would please both her father and herself.

She turned when she saw her ladies returning, and she remembered Tearle's visit. She was glad Tearle wasn't going to enter the tournament. Her father would no doubt like Tearle. He was second in line to his brother the duke, and his family was very, very rich.

But Anne had no desire to marry Tearle. He was young, handsome, rich, and suitable, but he was too glib for her, too much a ne'er-do-well. Were they to marry they'd probably kill each other within a year.

"My lady, you have had bad news?"

Anne looked up at her maid. "Nay, I have heard nothing I have not heard before. Come, let us walk. Or better yet, we shall ride. I feel in need of exercise to clear my brain."

Zared stood to one side and watched her brother's men straining to push the big cart out of the mud. They had been traveling since the day before, and now they were within hours of reaching the site of the tournament. Zared was so excited she hadn't been able to sleep and had, instead, pestered Severn with hundreds of questions. Usually he would have snapped at her to be quiet, but he didn't seem able to sleep either. At one point Zared thought perhaps he was excited, too, but she knew that couldn't be. Severn had been to lots of tournaments—hadn't he?

"Did you win the others?" she'd asked.

"What others?"

"The other tournaments you've entered. Have you won all the prizes?"

Severn looked at his little sister's eager face in the moonlight. He'd never attended a tournament in his life. His youth had been spent fighting the Howards. "Of course not," he said, and he watched Zared's face fall. "Rogan won some of them."

Zared laughed. "They must be wonderful, with all the men in armor. They must look splendid."

"No more of that!" Severn commanded. His voice lowered. "How am I to keep you safe and to prevent others from knowing your gender if you look calf-eyes at every strutting ass whose armor catches your eye?"

"I have more sense than that," she hissed. "I would never—"

"And what of Ralph?" he asked mockingly. "The poor boy thought he was beginning to lust after my brother."

"Lust? Are you sure? What did he say?" She stopped at her brother's infuriating chuckle. "His lust is not my concern," she said haughtily. "He is naught to me."

"Umm hmm," Severn said smugly. "You are to behave at this tournament. Do not make a fool of yourself, and do not dishonor the Peregrine name."

"You honor our name on the fields, and I will do my part," she said, a bit angry that he'd think her capable of dishonoring their family name, but then she relaxed. "Tell me of a tournament. Are there many people there? Liana said the people wear beautiful clothes, that even the horses are garbed most wonder-

48

fully. Perhaps we should have taken the garments she had made for us."

"Ha!" Severn said. When Liana had shown him an embroidered cloth that his horse was to wear he'd scoffed at her. What did it matter what a man wore when he fought? What was important was whether he knocked his opponent to the ground or not. "I want them to see me, not my horse," he'd told Liana, and he walked away. He wasn't going to let a woman tell him how to dress, *nor* was he going to let her know he had no idea what a knight wore to a tournament. And he wasn't going to let his little sister see his ignorance.

"The men who can't fight need to dress up their horses," Severn said firmly. "I do not need to wear cloth of gold to make me a man." He took a breath and expanded his chest. "It is my experience that the better a fighter a man is, the less he has to dress as a peacock to impress others."

Zared was thoughtful for a moment. She was sure her big brother was right—Severn and Rogan seemed to be right about most things—but there was still doubt in her mind. "If the other men's horses are dressed, will not the Peregrine horses look plain?"

This had crossed Severn's mind, too, and a couple of times on the journey he'd wished he had taken the pretty garments Liana had offered him. The helmet with the plume on it or that black velvet cloak might have looked good on him. He caught himself. No, he thought, he was a fighter, not some London playactor.

"The Peregrines will stand out as a haunch of beef on a table loaded with fancy sweets." He smiled as he said that, liking the image. "You will see, people will remember the Peregrines."

Zared smiled in the darkness. "We need only Hugh Marshall to remember us so he will award you his rich daughter. Do you think your wife will be like

Rogan's?" Her voice was hopeful, for she liked Liana very much and especially liked all the things she'd done to horrible old Moray castle in the past two years.

Severn grimaced at his sister's words, for he hated what Liana had done to his older brother. He didn't like the way marriage had changed Rogan, the way it had softened him. Before marriage Rogan had been a man of fire, a man ready to fight, but since then he constantly preached caution. Instead of fighting he'd rather sit with his wife and listen to ladies singing. Now he found more pleasure in his little son's first steps than he did in training. Severn was sure that someday the Howards were going to attack and kill them all while Rogan was tickling his wife.

"My wife will *not* be like Rogan's!" Severn snapped. "Now let me go to sleep, and no more of your foolish questions. You'll find out what a tournament is like when we get there."

Zared didn't ask him any more questions, but it was a long time before she could go to sleep.

The next day she stood watching the men pushing at the mud-jammed cart. They traveled with four knights, and four servants to do the mundane work, and two big carts full of armor and weapons and a couple of tents. Grazing under trees were Severn's precious warhorses, as well as the riding horses and the nags to pull the carts.

Severn and the men had been working for an hour to clear the carts, and Zared watched them impatiently. They were very near the Marshall estate, and she was eager to get there and set up their tents. During the three days of the tournament all food was to be provided by Hugh Marshall. In the morning the procession would be held, and all the knights would ride their splendid horses before the stands to greet Hugh Marshall and his daughters.

Zared wondered what the Lady Anne was like and how she would fit in with Rogan and his wife. It never crossed Zared's mind that Severn would fail to win Lady Anne's hand. She believed that whatever her brother wanted, he would get.

Zared was the first to hear the rider approaching. She knew what she had to do. She gave a low, piercing whistle to Severn as she ran for a nearby tree. Grabbing the lowest branch, she swung herself upward.

Sometimes it annoyed her that her brothers made her hide at the least sign of danger, but after her recent encounter with the Howards she was not about to be disobedient.

Zared was high off the ground by the time the rider came by, and she gave a look of disgust to see some fool of a lady tearing below her. She'd lost the reins to the horse and was hanging on for all she was worth. Zared would have climbed down, but she didn't dare until Severn had called that it was safe.

She looked through the branches at Severn and the men, swords drawn, ready to fight.

Severn was muddy from head to foot, but Zared could see the way he looked at the approaching woman. That idiotic look he wore could only mean that the woman was pretty. She rolled her eyes, thinking she'd probably be up in the tree all afternoon while Severn wooed the woman.

Zared watched without much interest as Severn ran straight at the horse. The horse reared, but Severn ducked the hooves to catch the reins.

"He'll be killed!"

Zared was so startled at the sudden voice from beneath her that she almost fell from her perch in the

51

tree. Below her were three ladies and two men, all dressed in velvets and furs. She had been watching Severn so intently that she hadn't heard them approach, and she cursed her lack of wariness.

"What does it matter?" one of the men said. "He's only some farmer."

The other man turned. "His death will matter very much if . . ." He paused. "If my lady's gown is splattered with blood." They all laughed.

Before she thought, Zared slipped the knife from her boot and prepared to jump. Some tiny bit of common sense stayed her. She sat rigidly and glared down at the people, trying to see their faces and memorize them.

"Oh, look," one of the women said, "he has caught the reins. He's braver than any farmer I have seen. Do you think Lady Anne will reward him?"

Zared looked through the leaves to the woman on the horse, but her back was to her. Severn's face looked even stupider than it had a moment before, so she guessed this Lady Anne was quite something to look at. She wished her brother's face didn't have quite so much mud on it because, from the way Lady Anne was leaning away from him, she didn't seem to find Severn exactly appealing.

"Thank you," Zared heard Lady Anne say.

"It was a pleasure to save such a beautiful neck."

"Why, the insolent dog!" the man below said. "I'll teach him—"

"He doesn't look as though he'd take kindly to a whipping, and have you not noticed those four buffoons lurking in the trees?" the other man said.

Buffoons! Zared thought. She very much hoped the soft-spined men would face Severn on the tourney field the next day. They would find out he was no farmer!

"Come to me on the morrow at the tournament, and I will reward you," Lady Anne said.

"I shall be there, and I shall collect my reward," Severn answered, eyes twinkling.

She reined her horse away, and Severn went back to his men. Lady Anne rode back to the people under the trees.

"Fine lot of help you are!" Anne snapped. "You left me unprotected with that . . . that . . ."

"He seemed much taken with you, my lady."

"I do believe he would have touched me if I had given him any encouragement." She shuddered. "As it is, I shall have to boil the reins to rid them of his touch."

"He did save you, my lady," one of the women said softly.

"I am aware of that!" Anne snapped. "And now I must reward him. What shall I give him?"

"A bath?" one of the men said, laughing.

Lady Anne did not laugh. "Perhaps, John, I should let *you* bathe him. You seem more fit for women's duties than for men's when you cannot help a lady in danger of falling to her death." She kicked her horse forward.

Zared stayed in the tree and stared after the people for a long while. So that was the Lady Anne, the woman who was to become her sister-in-law. She didn't seem very promising as a woman who would make the Peregrine lives easier, as Liana had done. In fact, the woman seemed like a real shrew, a mean, ill-tempered shrew.

"Can you not hear me?"

Startled, Zared looked down at her brother as he grinned up at her.

"I have called you, but yet you sit there." He turned away to lean against the tree as Zared climbed down.

"Did you see her? She is beautiful. She is as beautiful as a rose."

Zared dropped to the ground. "Roses have thorns."

"What does that mean?"

"I was but stating a fact. You said she's like a rose, and I said roses have thorns. Maybe beauty isn't all there is to a woman."

"And you know so much of women and life?" He was smirking at her.

"More about women than you seem to."

He looked as though he would get angry, but then he ruffled her hair and grinned. "I forget how young you are. Come, help us make camp."

"Camp? But tonight we go to the tourney grounds, and tomorrow we ride in the procession."

"We will ride in the procession as planned, but I do not want the Lady Anne to see me before we enter. She will be most surprised when she sees that it is I who saved her."

"Hope she has her reins washed by then," Zared muttered. "Are you sure?" she asked, louder. "Maybe she won't be so glad to see you. Not as glad as you think."

Severn put his hands on her shoulders and wore the expression of an older, much wiser man talking to a simple but well-meaning child. "You could not see her face. The way she looked at me . . ." He chucked her under the chin. "There are things men and women share—a look, a gesture—things you do not know, but which I as a man of some experience do know. The woman—ah, well, how can I put it? The woman wants me."

"For what? Scrubbing her horse? Look you at yourself. She could not see your face for the mud. She will not recognize you in the procession if you are clean."

Severn dropped his hands and his patronizing expression. "Do not talk to me of things you do not know. I know what I saw in the woman, and I saw lust. Now get to the camp as I said."

Zared obeyed her brother. Maybe he was right. Maybe Lady Anne had looked at Severn with lust, and she only said those things to her people to make them believe she didn't like a man who was covered with mud. She shrugged. She was sure Severn knew much more about ladies and tournaments and lust than she did.

Chapter Four

Zared sat on her horse with her back utterly rigid. She was sure that if she didn't remain absolutely stiff, she would fall into a heap of tears.

Before her, on his war horse, sat Severn, wearing sixty pounds of armor, and she couldn't tell what he was thinking or feeling. Around them, huddled close, were the men who had come with them, but outside their group was a laughing, jeering crowd of peasants.

That morning Zared had ridden proudly behind her brother, proud to carry the eight-foot-long Peregrine banner, but as they neared the Marshall estate and the field for the tournament they had halted.

Before them rode long lines of gorgeously attired knights. Their armor, partially covered with fur-trimmed, richly embroidered garments, was painted with beautiful designs, or else had been dipped in silver and flashed in the sunlight. Plumes or models of beasts and fowl decorated the knights' helmets.

Zared gaped at the men and boys before her, then looked at the Peregrine group. Severn's armor was dented and rusted, and his horse wore only a saddle, no sparkling cloths. The armor his men carried was in even worse condition, and as for Zared, her old tunic was threadbare in places and dirty most everywhere else.

"We cannot enter the procession," she whispered to Severn.

He threw up his face guard and glared at her. "Fine clothes do not make a good fighter. You are a Peregrine—remember that." He slammed down his guard and turned away.

Yes, I am a Peregrine, she thought, and she straightened her spine. Severn would beat them all in battle, so what did clothes matter?

Severn raised his hand, and the Peregrine knights fell in behind him as they started riding toward the tournament grounds. Along the road the peasants, who had come from many miles away to see the spectacle, had stopped to gape in awe at the sumptuously clad men.

When they saw the Peregrine knights they pointed and laughed. Zared kept her eyes straight ahead, not daring to look at them. What did they matter? she thought. Only the coming games mattered.

At the entrance to the grounds all the participants halted, and a Marshall herald called off the name of the first challenger to go before the Marshall family and the king.

Zared had assumed that the procession was just that, a parade of men riding before the Marshalls. But what she saw made her mouth fall open. She was as awed as the peasants.

The first knight to enter was named Grenville. He was dressed in black velvet over armor painted gold, and he was surrounded by half a dozen young pages also wearing black and gold. Before him went four trumpeters announcing Grenville's arrival. Behind the trumpeters were fifteen pretty young girls wearing saffron-yellow gowns, baskets in their arms as they spread rose petals on the ground for Grenville's horse to tread upon.

"The horses will make a mess of the roses," Severn said, and Zared joined him in his ridicule. She wanted some way to feel superior, but as Zared looked about and saw merchants dressed better than the Peregrines she wished she had not been allowed to attend the tournament.

As the procession continued Zared realized that Grenville's show had been one of the tamest. Some men entered with plays being performed before them. Others had entire orchestras. One man had a long, flat wagon pulled by six beautiful black horses, and on the wagon was a man dressed as St. George who was trying to slay a twenty-foot-long green dragon that hissed at him.

With each entry Zared sank a little lower in her saddle. Perhaps if she closed her eyes and wished hard enough she would find herself safe at home, away from the humiliation she was going to face. The people in the stands were applauding each entrant as he rode past. Would they laugh when the Peregrines came by?

"You!"

Zared turned to see a boy near her own age looking up at her. He was holding a lovely tunic of red velvet up to her. "What is this?" she asked.

"It's from my master," the boy said angrily. "He said to give it to you."

Charity, Zared thought, and the steel returned to her spine. "Tell your master I want nothing from him."

"From the look of you, you need everything."

Zared didn't think what she did, but she took her foot out of the stirrup and hit the boy in the chest, sending him sprawling.

"Behave yourself!" Severn bellowed at her, taking his anger about the procession out on her.

"But he offered me—" she began, stopping when she saw a man bend to help the boy from the dirt. He was the most beautiful human she'd ever seen: blond hair, white skin, blue eyes, armor of silver that was draped with white silk embroidered with silver roses.

Zared's mouth fell open as she stared at the man.

"Forgive my squire," the man said, and his voice flowed over Zared like hot honey. "I sent the tunic. I thought perhaps, through an accident, all of your garments were lost. I meant only kindness."

"I . . . we . . ." Zared could only gape, not able to say a coherent word. She didn't know men could be so beautiful.

"We need no charity!" Severn bellowed at the stranger. "We have all we need to fight. I am no popinjay who must wear flowers in order to fight," he said sneeringly.

The boy whom Zared had knocked down turned into a fighting cat. "You know not who you speak to!" he yelled. "This is Colbrand. He will knock you off your horse before you enter the lists."

"Jamie!" Colbrand said sharply. "Leave us."

The boy Jamie gave Zared a defiant look, then turned away. "Forgive him," Colbrand said to Severn. "He is young, and this is his first tournament."

Severn didn't answer, just glared.

Colbrand smiled at Zared, and she nearly fell off her horse. His smile was like a ray of sunshine on a rainy day. "I did not mean any offense. Good luck to you all."

She watched as he turned away. He bolted into the saddle of a white horse that was clothed in white that had been embroidered with more silver roses.

She was still gaping at him, her chin down about her waist, when Severn hit her on the shoulder so hard she almost fell out of her saddle.

"Get that look off your face," he growled.

Zared tried, but it wasn't easy. She watched Colbrand enter the procession. Before him went six men carrying hand-held harps. Behind them came six more men with trumpets. Then came six knights on white horses carrying Colbrand's weapons. Colbrand rode alone, his squire and more retainers behind him.

All of Colbrand's people, from musicians to knights, wore white and silver. Zared thought his group stood out splendidly from all the colorful spectacles that had gone before him. She sighed, for not only was he beautiful, but so were his horse and his clothes and his—

"We ride," Severn said, and Zared could tell from his voice that he was angry. She straightened. It was better to get it over with, she thought.

Severn was indeed angry. Theirs were the last name to be called to enter the procession, and already he could see that some of the people in the stands were beginning to leave. It was time for dinner, and they'd looked down the line, seen that the Peregrines lacked the sumptuous attire of the others, and decided they were not worth seeing.

Anger raged through him. People were judging men on the sparkle of their clothes and not on their skill at arms. Since when was a man's worth based on what he wore instead of how he acted?

The act of charity from that man, that Colbrand, had been the final straw. Severn couldn't wait to flatten that softling on the lists. He imagined standing over him and laughing.

Severn motioned for his men to fall in behind him, and he waited for the herald's signal that the Peregrines could at last go before the stands. Severn saw the herald watching the stands and saw that he was waiting for the Marshall family to leave before he allowed the Peregrines to go.

It was when Severn saw Lady Anne rising to leave that he decided he wasn't going to wait. Even if no one else wanted to see him, he knew she did. Hadn't she promised him a reward for saving her?

He tossed his helmet to the ground, then spurred his horse forward, ignoring the shouts of the herald, ignoring the laughter of the people around him, concentrating only on getting to the beautiful Lady Anne.

At the sound of the thundering hooves of his war-horse everyone halted and turned to look. Severn had an impression of a man standing beside Lady Anne, but he didn't look at him. Severn bent to the right, his thighs holding onto the horse as his armor-clad right arm caught Lady Anne about the waist and pulled her to him. He tried to kiss her, but he was so sweaty from sitting for hours in the sun in his helmet that his face merely slid across hers.

At the far end of the grounds he halted his horse, then triumphantly set her on the ground. "I have taken my reward," he said loudly to all the people that he knew were watching.

Lady Anne's eyes were alive and bright, and she looked as though she wanted to say something, but he didn't give her a chance before he rode away. Later there would be time for her to whisper love words to him. He rode away without looking back to see the impression he'd made. But there was no laughter. He had shut them all up.

As Zared watched her brother break the rules and gallop ahead and snatch the Lady Anne from beside her father she prayed to be struck dead on the spot.

Her prayer was not answered.

What was Severn about? She knew next to nothing about tournament etiquette, but she could see that what he'd done was awful, truly awful. They could have quietly paraded past the stands, and perhaps their worn, dirty clothes would have caused little comment, but after that . . .

She looked at Lady Anne, standing where Severn had left her, her hands in fists at her side. Zared knew fury when she saw it, and Lady Anne was murderous.

All around her the people were silent, too stunned to make a sound. Then, to her left, came one loud, sneering laugh. Zared turned and saw it was the boy Jamie. He was standing there in his white tunic and hose, so clean and neat, and Zared's own rage came to the surface.

She reined her horse toward the boy, lowered the staff of the Peregrine banner as though it were a lance, and charged. The boy's eyes widened in horror as he began to run.

Zared never reached him, for the long banner trailed on the ground, tangled in her horse's feet, and made it stumble. Zared, leaning forward in her charge, kept going forward even when the horse stopped. She went flying over the horse's head, landing flat on her back. For some moments she could neither breathe nor think. She just lay there looking up at the sky.

The first thing she heard was the roar of laughter.

Standing over her was Jamie, his hands on his knees

as he looked down at her and laughed. To her right she could hear hundreds more people laughing.

She was too dazed to move, or to do anything but lie there.

"Cease!" she heard someone say, and she looked up to see Colbrand bending over her. In his white and silver he looked like an angel.

"Are you hurt, boy?"

Zared managed to shake her head, and when he held out his hand to help her up she smiled at him.

"Good," Colbrand said, smiling back. "Let me look at you."

He put his hands on her shoulders and turned her about, dusting off the back of her. Zared thought she might die from the pleasure of his touch. She looked at his face, at his blue, blue eyes, and felt her knees go weak.

"I think you *are* hurt," Colbrand said, and to Zared's disbelief, he swept her into his arms.

It was too much for Zared. She fainted.

Anne Marshall bathed her face in cool water and looked in the metal mirror on the wall. Her face was still red from the scrubbing she had given it when she'd tried to remove that man's sweat from her body. Her ribs still ached from where he'd pulled her off the ground, his armor digging into her, bruising her skin.

For a moment her ears seemed to ring with the laughter of the people after that . . . that . . . She could think of no name for him. He had humiliated her, made her an object of ridicule before hundreds of people. Even that odious old man who had married Catherine that morning had laughed at her.

She looked in the mirror and saw her eyes change from rage to tears. If only she could have remained in

France with her mother . . . If only she had never come to the barbarous land where men were little more than animals. If only—

She didn't finish the thought, for the door to her chamber burst open, and her father entered. He didn't bother to knock, never bothered to show the least respect to either of his daughters.

"People are below eating, and they want to see my unmarried daughter," he said.

"I am not well," Anne said truthfully. "I cannot eat."

"You will eat if I have to force you. I'll have no daughter who sulks because a man touched her."

Anne's self-pity left her. "A *man!* That barbarian, that pagan! You call that animal a man? I have encountered dogs with more sensibilities than that one."

"You don't know a man from a dog." Hugh snorted. "You women took tournaments, these preparations for war, and turned them into showings of fashion. Were it up to you, the man with the most feathers or gold embroidery would win the prizes. The Peregrine boy isn't—"

"Peregrine!" Anne gasped. "Is that who he was? I should have guessed. He is brother to that man who married poor Lady Liana. It is no wonder—"

"Married two years and she's given him one son, and another due any day. The father of these Peregrines bred nothing but sons."

"There is more to life than sons!" Anne spat at him.

Hugh Marshall took a step toward his daughter, but Anne didn't allow herself to flinch. "I would not look down my nose too much at him. You will perhaps join this Lady Liana in breeding Peregrine sons."

"No," Anne said under her breath. "Please . . ." she began, but she stopped. She wasn't going to beg her father for anything. She straightened her shoulders. Remember, she thought, it was her brains against his power. "If you wish grandsons who are stupid, then by all means marry me to the man. No doubt the king will want one of these Peregrines at his table. What I saw today assures me of the suitability of a Peregrine at court. But perhaps that means naught to you. You would no doubt like to see your grandsons jeered at when they parade before the king. Perhaps you should ask His Majesty if he plans to invite this Peregrine knight to sit above the salt with him."

Hugh glared at his daughter. He hated clever women, hated it when a woman said something he had not considered. Her mother had been like that, her tongue moving twice as fast as his brain. When she'd asked to leave and return to her people in France he had been more than happy to let her go.

But at no cost was he going to allow his too-clever daughter to know that her words had confused him.

"If I see you show your displeasure to this man, you will regret it," he said, then he quickly left the room. If he had no other considerations, he'd marry the witch to the roughest man he could find, he thought. She needed a man who'd curb her tongue. But she knew that Hugh wanted grandsons. He'd not been able to get sons on a woman himself, so he must look to his puny daughters to give him grandsons. Much as he hated to admit it, the girl was right. He did not want grandsons who would be laughed at at a tournament. Even the king had chuckled at the sight of the dirty Peregrines.

Hugh grimaced. Damn the girl. If there was anything he hated more than a clever female, it was a female who was right. He stormed down the hall to the stairs. In the next three days he'd find a husband for the girl and get rid of her. He wasn't going to put up with her sharp tongue and sharper brain. Let another man deal with her.

After her father left Anne breathed a sigh of relief. She was going to be able to handle him—for the moment, anyway. But even as she hurriedly finished dressing she knew she would not always have the words to control him. He was as stupid as he was mean, and at one point he would forget about reason and act only on instinct. What Anne knew she had to do was to choose a man and get her father to approve of him. She had to find a man who could replace that filthy Peregrine in her father's mind.

She lifted the three-foot-long cone-shaped henna and slipped it on her head, arranging it at the perfect angle so it was tipped far back. The heavy wire loop on her forehead that held the weight of the henna cut into her skin, but the pain soon lost its bite. She adjusted the soft, transparent silk veil over the henna and gave herself one last look in the mirror. She wanted to look her best because she was going hunting. Hunting for a man.

When Zared awoke she was lying on a cot in her brother's tent, and through the open flap she could see that the sun was low in the sky. Feeling groggy, she didn't try to sit up. The last thing she clearly remembered was Colbrand picking her up in his strong arms.

She smiled up at the tent roof and remembered the look of him, the smell of him, the sound of him, the—

"So, you are awake."

Languidly she turned her head to look at the man standing over her. But the light was behind him, and she couldn't see him very well. "Is there anything to eat? I'm hungry," she said.

The man snorted. "It is, no doubt, hard work making a fool of yourself."

"A fool of myself?" In puzzlement she squinted at the man. He seemed somewhat familiar, but she couldn't quite place him. He moved out of the bright light, his back to her, and she absently listened to dishes clattering and a noggin being filled. Her mind was full of Colbrand. Perhaps she had dreamed him. Perhaps no man alive could be as he was.

"Eat this," the man said, and he thrust a wooden platter of meat and bread before her.

She took the food, sat up on her elbow, and began to eat. The man sat on a stool beside the cot. Outside a clash of arms sounded. "It has begun!" she said, sitting up. "The fighting has started. Colbrand will need me." She started to get up, but a big hand pushed her chest just below her throat, and she sat back down.

"What do you think—" she began, then her eyes widened as she looked at the man before her. It was the youngest Howard! "You!" she said under her breath, and immediately she reached for the knife hidden in her boot.

"It isn't there," he said calmly. "I have removed all your weapons, and I must say I enjoyed looking for them."

She put her head down and rammed him in the chest. He made a little *woof* sound, but then he caught her in his arms and easily held her.

"Severn!" she shouted.

He put his hand across her mouth. "Your brother is on the field." He paused. "As is Colbrand, the weakling."

Zared stopped struggling against him. "Colbrand is not a weakling."

"And you know so much, do you? Seen him fight a hundred times, have you?"

"Let me go. My brother will chop you into little pieces. He'll—"

JUDE DEVERAUX

"Yes, yes, you've said this."

Zared realized that he was toying with her as she struggled against him, as a child and a parent might play. But his hands were roaming over her hips and thighs. With a push she shoved away from him to land back on the cot. She put her chin up and looked at him.

"Take *me*, but do not sneak up on my brother. I will go with you and be your prisoner if you will not harm my brother. I will . . . do whatever you want if you will but keep your army from attacking my brothers."

Tearle looked at her a long while, knowing she meant every word she said. For all her boy's hair and clothes, there was a woman underneath, a woman capable of sacrificing all for love.

"I am here to harm no one. Your brother believes I am called Smith and that I have been sent here by Lady Liana."

Zared gaped at him, her mouth opening and closing like a fish. "Liana sent you?" she gasped.

"No, of course not. Eat your food, and I'll tell you all."

"I'll eat nothing a Howard gives me."

"That is your choice, but you will perhaps get hungry, as I am to care for you and your brother for the next three days."

"Care for? A Howard care for a Peregrine? You mean to poison us." She started to get up, but he pushed her down again, and she didn't fight him. "Where is Severn?" she whispered. "If you have harmed him, Rogan will—"

"You are a bloodthirsty wench. I have harmed no one. Your brother is on the fields waiting his turn to knock some fool off his horse."

"As he will knock you down," she said. "You have

68

seen what a Peregrine blade can do," she said, referring to the cut she had given him.

"And it still pains me. You owe me much for that, as well as for saving your brother's name."

"No Peregrine owes a Howard," she said. There was a noise outside, and as Tearle turned to look Zared leaped from the cot and headed for the door. Tearle's foot tripped her, but he caught her before she fell.

"Where are you going?"

"To get my brother. To escape you. To fetch the king. Anyone!"

"If you call your brother and he kills me, an unarmed man, then my brother will attack that heap of stones your brothers own and kill all the Peregrines." Tearle gave her a bored look. "Go. You are free to call your brother. Get my death over with, but please, beg him to use a very sharp sword. I do not wish to die a lingering death."

Zared stood there blinking at him and felt as though she'd lost the war before the first battle. Everything he'd said was true. If Severn did kill the man, it could mean the deaths of all the Peregrines.

Feeling very heavy, she sat down on the edge of the cot. "What do you want?" she whispered. "Why are you here?"

"I have come to help," he said brightly. "From what I had heard of your family, I correctly guessed you would come to the tournament in rags."

"We do not wear rags," Zared said indignantly.

He curled his upper lip as he looked at her worn and greasy tunic. "Rags," he repeated. "Days ago I sent one of my men to my brother to fetch clothing. I regretted he did not return in time to prevent this morn's disaster, but now your brother wears more suitable clothing."

Zared was beginning to recover from the shock of waking to find a Howard bent over her. She went to the tent doorway and looked out. Standing near the lists was her brother, and he was wearing a black tunic over his armor. She could not be sure from a distance, but it looked to be embroidered in gold.

"My brother," Zared spoke slowly and evenly. "My brother is wearing clothing given him by a *Howard?*"

"Yes, but he doesn't know that. He believes it comes from his lovely sister-in-law."

Zared sat down again. "Tell me all," she whispered.

"After you made a fool, an ass, a laughingstock of yourself yesterday over that colorless, weak, simpering Colbrand, I—"

"When I want a Howard's opinion, I will ask for it. Tell me what treachery you have done."

"Treachery? I? I have been kind and generous while your Colbrand— All right, I will tell you. After you lost your senses I came to your rescue and took you from that spineless—"

"*You* touched me? A *Howard* touched me?"

"I have been touching you since I met you."

"I shall have to bathe."

"Whatever accomplishes that is worth it."

"Continue!" she spat at him.

He smiled at her. How easy she was to provoke to passion. "There was no Peregrine tent, so I took you to another."

"To Colbrand's?" she asked eagerly.

"Nay, not there. I would rather have thrown you into a pit of vipers than take you there."

"With a Howard I would rather go into a pit of vipers."

Tearle snorted. "I knew I had much to do and you would be a hindrance to me, so I gave you a draught of—"

70

"You have poisoned me," she whispered. "How long do I have to live? I must go to warn my brother. Does he die also?"

She was almost outside before Tearle caught her. He grabbed her shoulders and put his nose to hers. "Do you not hear? No one is hurt. I have not come to hurt you. I gave you a drink to make you sleep so I could do my work without your hindrance."

"Without my sounding an alarm," she said, jerking out of his grip.

"That, too." His voice softened. "Come, sit down. Eat."

"I would never eat what a Howard touched."

He took her plate from the cot, tore away a piece of bread and ate it, then cut off a piece of meat. "The food is not poisoned."

Zared was still not convinced even though she was very hungry. "Why are you here?" she repeated.

"I came . . ." He trailed off, for he didn't know why he was there. Some part of him said he wanted an end to the hatred, but another part knew that if it weren't for that angry young woman, he wouldn't care what happened between his brother and the Peregrines. He had no idea why he was so interested in her. There were many other women prettier. Others who were richer. Nearly all women were sweeter-tempered than she was. Yet there he was, and he didn't think he could leave if he wanted to.

"I came to end the feuding," he said at last.

"To end . . ." Zared was so stunned she sat on the cot.

"You see, my brother is obsessed with the hatred between our families. Your entire family is concerned with little else. No, do not deny it. It is all you talk of, and I have seen the way you are prisoners in that falling-down castle of yours."

71

Zared was amused at the idea of ending the feud. She knew him to be cowardly and weak-fleshed, but was he stupid also? "How do you propose to stop the fighting? To give us back the land your family stole from us? Will you give my brother Rogan the title of duke that should be his?"

"Why, no," Tearle began, and at that moment he had an idea. "I shall end the feud by marrying a Peregrine to a Howard. We will join our families."

"Do you have a sister hidden away who you plan to marry to Severn? Some drooling idiot of a sister you will try to foist on my handsome brother?"

He smiled at her. "I thought perhaps I would marry you."

Zared made the mistake of trying to breathe and laugh at the same time. She choked rather spectacularly.

Tearle pounded her on the back and handed her a mug of watered wine. She gulped the wine while trying to move out of his reach.

"Me?" she said at last. "Marry me? Me marry a Howard?"

Tearle stiffened. "What better could a Peregrine hope for? You have no dowry." He looked her up and down. "You are not even a full woman."

"Woman enough to want a man," she shot back at him. "Do you know how my brothers would take my saying I was to marry a Howard? My brother Rogan would—"

"Yet you considered Severn marrying a sister, if I had one, which I do not." He had talked of the marriage on impulse, but since he'd said it, he didn't like her laughing at him. After all, it was an excellent idea, the best part being that he'd get his hands on her slim little body.

Zared knew the man was stupid. "If my brother

72

married a Howard, the woman would come to us. If I married you, a mere second son, I would go to live under your brother's rule. Do you think Oliver Howard would treat me well? Or do you think he would enjoy having a Peregrine to torture?"

Tearle blinked at her. He could see his brother laughing in glee at the prospect of having a Peregrine under his roof. What he would do to Zared would increase the feud, not dampen it.

"So you came to marry me," Zared said, still laughing at him. "How did you get past my brother?"

"I have told you. I brought clothes." Tearle didn't feel jubilant any longer. He'd never proposed marriage to a woman before, and he had certainly never been turned down. What more did a woman want? He was the brother of a duke, he was handsome, he was—

"Surely you did not think I would be fool enough to agree to marry you," she said. "It would be the same as turning myself over to you as a prisoner. I want the truth of why you are here."

Tearle tried to recover his self-esteem. He grinned and shrugged. "You cannot blame me for trying. I told the truth when I said I wanted to end the feud. I am tired of hatred, and I thought perhaps I could befriend your brother and stop the hatred."

"Befriend? How can a Howard be a friend to a Peregrine?"

"I have made progress already. I brought clothes, and I brought your brother a splendid suit of silvered armor. It is mine. We are nearly the same size." He meant to point out to her his own strong, muscular body and to let her know he wasn't the weakling she seemed to think he was. But she didn't seem to hear.

She stood and walked to one side of the big tent. "You came bearing clothes and armor—Howard clothes and armor—and my brother accepted it all

73

without question?" Zared was having some doubts
about her brother. Severn had said he'd been to lots of
tournaments, yet he hadn't known about the procession. He said he knew all about women, yet he hadn't
known Lady Anne would hate being picked up in
front of everyone.

"It was easier than I'd hoped. Your brother seemed
to be expecting clothes from Lady Liana."

"Not expecting them, but Liana . . ." She stopped.
She wasn't going to tell that man, that enemy, anything. It wasn't like Severn to believe a stranger, but
perhaps he had been embarrassed this morning, too.

Zared's head came up. "So you are to be a servant
to my brother? Is that what you told me? He is to call
you Smith, and you, a rich man—falsely rich, for your
land belongs to my family, but a rich man nonetheless
—you are to fetch food for us? Shall you empty the
chamber pots?"

"I'll see that those lazy servants of yours do the
work."

She didn't believe him, not one word he said. "Now
that the Howards know there is a Peregrine female, is
it I you plan to take?"

"I have told no one that you are female. I have told
no one that I am a Howard."

"Someone will recognize you. Someone will point
you out as a Howard, and then my brother will kill
you and your brother—"

"Cease!" he half yelled. "I am not the evil monster
you portray me to be. I am a simple man who does not
want to spend his life hating. I saw a way to befriend
the Peregrines, and I took it. No one knows me here
except Anne, and she—" He stopped because he'd
said far too much.

"Anne? *Lady* Anne? The woman Severn is going to
marry?"

"Anne marry your uneducated lout of a brother? She'd rather—"

Zared slapped him across the face, and it was a good, hard slap.

"Why, you little—" he said, going for her.

"You are awake," Severn said from the doorway, his eyes adjusting to the dim light. "Have you met Smith? Liana sent him." He walked toward the cot and picked up Zared's plate, but before he could get a bite to his mouth Zared grabbed the food from him.

"That's mine," she said. "I mean it was meant for me."

Severn looked puzzled. "All right. Smith, get me food."

"No!" Zared yelled, dropping her plate. Food fell to the ground as she ran to put herself between Tearle and the food that stood on a little table.

"What is wrong with you?" Severn asked, frowning.

"Uh . . . uh . . ." She couldn't seem to think quickly enough.

"I believe the boy is concerned that this food isn't as good as what the Marshalls are serving. This is cold and greasy, while in the hall hot soups are being served."

Severn still looked puzzled. It wasn't like Zared to care about food. As long as the meat didn't have maggots on it and the weevils in the bread had been baked and weren't still crawling, the Peregrines didn't pay much attention to food.

"I want you to have the *best*," Zared said. "To keep up your strength for the fighting."

Severn rumpled her hair. "All right. I'll go up to the hall. You stay here with Smith and sort out the clothes Liana sent. See if there's something in there for you."

"My clothes are more than suitable for a Peregrine." She looked at Severn's tunic of thick black silk.

There were gold and silver dragons embroidered along the edge. "We need not all look like peacocks."

Severn gave her a hard look. "Do not disgrace me. Smith, see to my squire." With that, he turned on his heel and left the tent.

Zared turned to look at Tearle. "Once in my life I get to see the world, and I am put in the care of a Howard. Now I shall have to stay with you every minute to see that you do no harm to my brother."

"Every minute?" Tearle smiled, liking the prospect.

Chapter Five

Zared watched as the Howard man went outside and rummaged through the cart that contained the clothes and weapons he had brought. Her belly growled with hunger, and in the distance she could hear the clash of weapons and the shouts of the crowd as the combatants met one another in the joust. Had Severn fought yet? Who had he fought? Had Colbrand fought yet?

She didn't know because she had been drugged by a Howard and had slept the day away.

Watching the man with his black hair and black clothes, she knew that what was to have been a pleasurable time for her was going to be a nightmare. Do Howards mean to ruin *all* my life? she thought. Was she to have no time when she was free of them? On her own land she could not ride out alone without being snatched by a Howard. And it

looked as though she wouldn't even be allowed to enjoy herself at the tournament.

She watched him pull out a garment of ruby-red velvet, the hem trimmed in gray fox.

He had proposed marriage to her. Marriage between a Howard and a Peregrine. How absurd the idea was. Her brothers would never allow her to live under Oliver Howard's power. Not to mention the fact that the Howards would probably chain her to a wall and starve her.

As she watched the Howard she knew he would not have strength enough to fight his older brother. A marriage to him would mean being a prisoner to his brother. The weak man who had nearly died from a small cut was not man enough to stand up to someone like Oliver Howard.

"This," he said, holding out the dark red tunic to her. Across it was draped a pair of finely knit hose.

"I will—" She started to say that she would not wear anything a Howard gave to her, but then Colbrand went striding by. He was as beautiful as she remembered, perhaps even more beautiful. Again he was wearing white. A white as pure and as clean as a mountain lake. His hair shone in the sunlight. Rays sparkled off his armor. His eyes—

Tearle shoved the tunic into her chest so hard that Zared took a step backward. "Put it on," he growled.

She felt the velvet, looked at the fur. Perhaps Colbrand would like her better in pretty clothes. "I will wear them, but not for you," she snapped at Tearle, turning back into the tent. "Stand here so that I can see where you are," she ordered.

With one eye on her enemy's back she quickly changed into the new clothes. She stretched out her leg, pleased that there were no holes in the hose, no

grease stains. There was soft fur about the neck, and she rubbed her cheek against it.

"Are you dressed yet?" Tearle asked impatiently from outside. "Your brother rides against his first opponent."

Zared shoved past him to go outside and ignored the way he looked at her. "Come, I would see my brother. You are to stay near me."

"I will force myself to do so," Tearle said, chuckling.

But Zared never made it to the lists. Not far from the dilapidated Peregrine tent she could see a tent of white sendal, a white banner embroidered with silver leopards flying from the crown. As though she had no control over her feet, she turned toward the tent.

"Your brother—" Tearle said from behind her, but Zared kept walking.

Before the tent sat Colbrand's squire Jamie, ineptly trying to sharpen a sword on a round, pedal-powered whetstone.

"You," Jamie said, looking up at Zared with the hovering black shadow behind her. Jamie had decided he hated the Peregrine boy because he had been the cause of a severe tongue-lashing from Colbrand. "What do *you* want?" Jamie sneered.

Zared opened her mouth to reply, but then Colbrand came out of the tent. He no longer wore his armor, but his big, muscular body was covered in a short white tunic, his legs encased in pale gray hose. She could only stare at him speechlessly.

Colbrand did not at first see the Peregrine squire. His eyes were on Jamie. "That is not the way to hold the blade," Colbrand said in a tone, as though he'd said it a hundred times. "You have not your mind on the task. I will show you."

"I can do it," Zared said, and she walked to Colbrand, her eyes big as she gazed up at him.

Colbrand smiled at her. He was used to young boys hero-worshipping him and this boy was no exception, he thought. He was always kind to the boys, for who knew if in a year or two he might not meet one in a joust. But then Colbrand was kind to most people because it was his nature.

"I would be pleased if you would show my squire," Colbrand said.

Zared took a step forward, but a big hand clamped on her shoulder. "He has to attend his brother."

"Oh, then you must go."

Zared turned and narrowed her eyes at Tearle. "My brother can take care of himself. *All* the Peregrines can take care of themselves, including *this* one." She jerked her shoulder from his grip, then turned and smiled back at Colbrand. She was still looking at him as she took the sword from Jamie.

"I'll get you for this," Jamie whispered as he relinquished Colbrand's sword.

Zared ignored him as she sat on the stool before the whetstone. When she'd been growing up her brothers had despaired of making her as strong as a boy might have been, so they gave her many peripheral tasks, such as sharpening swords and banging dents from armor. She was good at putting an edge on a blade, and she used all her knowledge to put a perfect, sharp edge on Colbrand's sword.

When she was finished she held it up to him, looking at him as a puppy might when it hoped for praise from its master.

Colbrand took the big sword and ran his thumb along the edge. "Excellent," he said, and he smiled so warmly at Zared that she was sure she was going to faint again.

At that moment a vendor came by, a big tray on a ribbon about his neck.

"Work such as this must be rewarded," Colbrand said. "Are you boys hungry? No," he said, laughing, "boys of your age are *always* hungry." He gave the vendor a coin and told Zared and Jamie to choose the tarts they wanted.

Zared chose a cherry tart, and for a moment she just stared at it. It was from Colbrand, and she had an urge to save the tart, to keep it forever. But hunger won out, and she ate it, but slowly.

"Have you fought yet?" she asked Colbrand.

"Once," he answered, smiling fondly at the boy who looked up at him with such naked worship. The boy had no doubt heard of his reputation, of the many prizes he had won over the years.

"And he won," Jamie said belligerently to Zared. "He scored four times. Colbrand has *never* been knocked from his horse."

"Now, Jamie," Colbrand said. "We should not tempt fate. Perhaps at this tournament I shall be downed. There are some new men here, such as your brother. He is good with a lance?"

Zared bit down on a cherry pit, and instead of spitting it on the ground she sucked it dry, then slipped it into the top of her hose. "He is very good," she said. "But perhaps with your skills and practice you will show yourself well against him."

"Show himself well!" Jamie said, coming to his feet. "Colbrand will knock your brother to the ground." Jamie didn't like the way his beloved master was paying attention to the too-pretty boy. He was angry that the boy could sharpen a sword better than he could. He didn't like the way people were saying that for all their dirt, the Peregrines were brilliant fighters. He knew Colbrand expected him to display good

81

manners at all times, but the bragging of the Peregrine brat was too much for him. He leaped on Zared.

Tearle's first instinct was to let the two of them fight it out. Zared had been making a fool of herself over Colbrand, and he didn't like it one bit. How could she be so starry-eyed over a man who was too stupid to see that she was a girl? How could she be so dumb as to fall for a pretty face on top of some shiny armor?

Neither Colbrand nor Tearle had time to interrupt the brawl because Severn, wearing armor, his hair plastered to his head with sweat, came storming up to them and grabbed both Jamie and Zared by the necks of their tunics and pulled them apart. He didn't so much as look at Jamie but flung him aside as though he were a used rag. Zared he held on to, and he pulled her with him as he hauled her through the tents, past the watching eyes of the many people on the grounds, and led her to their tent. He shoved her inside, shoved her so hard she nearly went through the other side.

She knew Severn was angry, and when one of her brothers was like that she knew better than to open her mouth.

"You are my squire," he said in a low voice that Zared knew meant he was really, truly, deeply angry. "Your duties are to bring me fresh lances, to care for my horses, to give me drink when I need it. Yet you sleep the day away, and when you wake, do you come to help me? No, you make an ass of yourself over that puffed-up, strutting—"

"Colbrand isn't—" Zared stopped herself. It was not the time to argue with her brother.

He advanced on her, and she stepped back in fear. While her brothers often pummeled each other, they'd never hit her in the same way, but she didn't trust him to hold his temper. "I am most sorry, Severn," she whispered.

"I've a mind to return you to Liana."

"Oh, no, please don't," she whispered. "I will help you. I swear it."

"How? By playing the fool to that Colbrand? Don't you realize that he also tried for the Lady Anne's hand? At dinner it was said that she favors the man, as does her father."

"I didn't mean any harm. His squire is stupid. He doesn't even know how to sharpen a sword. I had to show him all that you have taught me, and—"

"You sharpened *his* sword?" Severn's eyes were popping, he was so angry. "A sword he is to use against *me?* Has your loyalty changed so completely? Do you wish to see him shed my blood?"

"No, Severn, please, I meant no harm. I was only trying to help. His squire cannot even sharpen a sword."

"And *my* squire cannot even get out of bed. What is it you want from this Colbrand? Do you wish to see him beat me?"

"No, Severn, of course not. I just . . ."

"What?" he demanded.

"I . . ." What could she say? That she found Colbrand beautiful beyond words? That when she was near him her skin tingled?

"I believe she desires him in her bed," Tearle said calmly from behind Severn.

"I do not!" Zared bellowed. "What do you know of my wants? What do you know of anything? You are—"

"She?" Severn asked. "You told someone of your sex?" He sat down on a stool, his head in his hands. "Liana was right."

"I didn't tell him anything," Zared spat. "He knew."

Severn looked up at Tearle questioningly.

83

Tearle was quite calm. "Look you at her. Would *you* believe her to be male? She is so hot for this Colbrand she can barely stand when he is near, yet the fool thinks her to be a boy. She argues as a girl; she speaks as a girl; she walks as a girl; her voice is that of a girl. How could I not know?"

Severn's mind was reeling. If it became common knowledge that Zared was female, that knowledge was sure to get back to Oliver Howard. He seemed to have taken a vow to capture all Peregrine females, and Zared would be no exception. How could Severn possibly protect her if he was always on the jousting field? That day, when she should have been where he could see her, she was instead dallying with a man who was competing with him for a woman's hand. How was he to know that perhaps Colbrand wasn't paid by Oliver Howard?

"You must return to Rogan," Severn said at last. "You are in danger."

"No!" Zared and Tearle said in unison.

Tearle knew that if she left now, he'd never see her again. "I will see to her," he said quickly.

"You?" Zared said, sneering. "You, a—"

"A what?" Tearle asked, daring her to tell Severn he was a Howard.

Zared looked at her brother. "He's a coward and a weakling, and he can't look after anyone."

At another time Severn might have been puzzled by his sister's animosity toward the stranger, but he had too much on his mind. "Liana sent him; she chose him." His opinion of his sister-in-law was rising by the hour. He should have listened to her and taken the clothes and left his sister at home, he thought.

"Liana didn't—"

"Didn't what?" Severn asked.

"Didn't know what he was like. He's too weak to

protect anyone. If the Howards attacked, he'd probably deliver me to them." That was as close as she could come to telling her brother the truth.

Severn looked at the man Liana had sent and couldn't reconcile his sister's words with what he saw. The fellow Smith was a bear of a man: big, thick, muscular. While Zared had slept Severn had seen just how strong the man was when he'd helped unload weapons and armor. And twice Severn had seen him hold a sword in a way that told Severn the man had had some training.

"Will you pledge your life to protect her?" Severn asked.

"I will," Tearle answered, and there was truth in his eyes.

"No! Oh, Severn, no, you cannot do this to me."

"You have done it to yourself," Severn said, rising, feeling much better. "See that she does not let the world know she is female. Keep her out of fights, and for the sake of all of us, keep her out of men's beds. I promised Liana I'd return her with her virginity intact."

"I will protect her always," Tearle said. "You have my word."

"Good," Severn said, standing. "She is yours to guard. See that no one knows the truth of her. Now I must watch the jousts. I must weigh my opponents' abilities." He turned and left the tent.

Zared stood where she was, staring after her brother. Never in all her imaginings could she have conceived of where she was. Her brother had just put her under the care of their family's sworn enemy. A Howard was to protect her from the Howards.

"Do not look at me so," Tearle said when Severn was gone. "I have told you again and again that I will not harm you. I will protect you."

"Your family has killed mine for three generations, yet I am to believe that a Howard is now my friend? No," she said tauntingly, "you are to be my husband."

Tearle winced at her words and again asked himself why he did not leave. Perhaps her words weighed on him, and he felt the sins of his ancestors and his brothers on his shoulders. Perhaps his ancestors *had* stolen the Peregrine lands.

"It is time for supper," he said, "and you must serve your brother and his men."

"I must what?"

Tearle smiled at her. She carried the title of squire, but she also bore the name of Peregrine. Usually when a boy reached about seven years of age he was sent to foster with a family other than his own. People had known for centuries that a boy would gladly take lessons from strangers but would learn nothing from his own family. Zared, who was used to eating beside her brother, was balking at fetching his meat and wine.

"I have told your brother I will care for you, and I mean to see that you do your duty. If you have more work to do, you will have less time to make a fool of yourself over Colbrand."

"I have had more than enough of your orders." She strode to the open tent flap. "I am going to supper by myself."

Zared had to elbow her way between two squires to get the hunk of meat Severn had told her to fetch for him. She was trying to keep her temper, but it wasn't easy. Severn had very much liked the idea of his little sister serving him, and he also wanted to punish her a bit for having neglected him earlier in the day. He'd point to joints of meat on other tables and command her to get him a piece.

"Get your brother a napkin," the Howard man told her.

"Why? He will not use it," Zared had retorted.

Of course Severn had then decided that the thing he wanted most in life was a napkin, so Zared had had to run and find one for him.

With every move she made she glared at the Howard man. Severn had seated him at his right hand, and they looked for all the world to be old friends. Friends who had a common enemy, she thought. Me.

It was a long meal, and Zared was so busy she never had a moment even to look about her. She'd had such dreams about going to the tournament with her brother, and so far all of it had been a disaster.

At long last the meal was over, and the men, the Marshall family, the king, and the guests began to file out of the enormous hall and go about their evening's entertainment. Some of the young men invited Zared to go whoring with them, but she declined. She tore off a big chunk of beef, took half a loaf of bread and a flagon of wine, and left the hall.

"I have waited for you," Tearle said as soon as she was outside.

Zared nearly dropped the wine. Was there no reprieve from the man? "Leave me," she said.

"I have sworn to your brother to protect you."

"From what? From yourself? Can you not see that I do not want you near me? Go and find another to inflict yourself upon. Leave me to myself."

Tearle looked at her, and quite suddenly he wondered why he was forcing himself where he was not wanted. His brother wasn't going to come after her, not while Tearle was at the tournament. He looked around, and there were hundreds of people milling about, and groups of boys teasing groups of girls. There were ladies in their long gowns being escorted by gentlemen in fur-trimmed tunics. There were vendors hawking goods, acrobats climbing on top of one another, singers and musicians.

"Go," he said. "Go, but do not stay so late that I have to come looking for you."

Zared practically ran from him, hurrying into the crowd to get away from him as fast as she could. She ate her food as she walked about and looked at what was for sale, at the performers, at a dog baiting a chained bear. The sights were all wondrous and new, and they kept her attention for quite some time.

But her good mood fled when a pretty young village girl began flirting with her. Zared glared at the girl, but instead of leaving she came up to Zared and asked if she'd like to go for a walk. Zared turned on her heel and left the girl.

Some other girls, daughters of rich merchants, walked by in their lovely gowns, jeweled headdresses twinkling, and Zared tried to memorize everything they wore. She'd like to wear something like their gowns with their trailing skirts, she thought. She watched the girls glance over their shoulders at a group of boys, and the boys follow like dogs answering a whistle.

"Come with us," one of the boys called to her.

Zared stepped back and shook her head.

"He's one of those Peregrines," she heard one of the boys say, and they all laughed.

Zared turned away, feeling as though she didn't belong anywhere. She didn't belong with the girls, and she didn't belong with the boys. And their entrance into the tournament had made the Peregrine name a source of laughter.

"Tomorrow Severn will fix that," she whispered to herself, vowing to help her brother in any way that she could. She wouldn't allow the Howard man to drug her so she slept the next day away.

The people and the commotion had lost its appeal to her, and all at once she wished she were at home. She would go up on the battlements of Moray Castle and look out across the fields to the trees in the distance. She wished she could sit in Liana's solar and listen to one of her ladies sing.

She wondered where Severn was. "Probably with some woman," she said in disgust. Her brother never seemed to have trouble acquiring women.

She kept walking away from the noise until she reached the stream in the trees that ran near the Marshall estates. There seemed to be a couple of grunting people under every bush, and as Zared sidestepped them she felt lonelier than ever. She couldn't go with the girls and didn't want to go with the boys, so there was nowhere for her to go.

She followed the stream, stepping over bracken, moving around trees. It was almost full dark, but the moonlight was bright. Ahead of her she heard splashing and stepped through the trees expecting to see a deer. Instead, what she saw halted her and made her draw in her breath.

Standing in ankle-deep water, his back to her, was Colbrand, and he wore not a stitch of clothing. A warmth flooded her body as she looked at him, his white skin looking silver in the moonlight. Her mouth grew dry as she looked at him, and her knees grew weak.

He turned to look at her over his shoulder and smiled. "Young Peregrine. Come and wash my back."

Zared tried to swallow the lump in her throat as she waded into the icy water. She didn't bother to remove her shoes for, truthfully, she didn't remember that she wore shoes. Her eyes were only on Colbrand's bare body.

She took the soap he handed her and lathered his back. Her hands spread out over the muscles in his back, down his arms, to the small of his back and lower.

Colbrand laughed. "It seems you are better at many things than my squire. Why is it you are not out kissing girls as Jamie is?" he asked.

"I . . ." She couldn't speak when she was touching him. She seemed to change from a thinking person to one who could only feel.

He turned toward her, and Zared gulped. Would he realize she was female? Would he kiss her?

"Fetch the bucket that I may rinse," he said, and Zared obeyed him.

He had to kneel before her so she could pour buckets of water over him, and as she did so her heart pounded in her ears. He was so close to her.

"My thanks to you," he said, standing and walking to the bank, where he began to dry off.

Zared just stood in the water and gazed at him. Was there any other man on earth as splendid-looking as he? Golden hairs glistened on his muscular forearms.

"Will you stay in the water all night?" Colbrand asked, smiling.

"Ah, no." She left the water and didn't notice that her feet were half frozen. She just stood there and watched as Colbrand began to put on his clothes. "You . . . you are seeing someone?" she managed to ask. I will rip out her eyes, she thought.

"The Lady Anne," Colbrand answered. "Her father has invited me to talk with him of the morrow's games, and I believe the Lady Anne is to be there."

"She is beautiful," she said, and there was resignation in her voice.

"And rich," he said, laughing. "Now I must go. If you see my squire, tell him to sleep some tonight, as I'll need him fresh on the morrow." He gave Zared a little wave, and then he was gone.

She stood staring after him for a while, then sat on the cold bank and looked at the water. How did she have a chance with Colbrand when her competition was Lady Anne? She couldn't offer more beauty, more money, more anything than Lady Anne. "Except maybe a sweeter temper," she said aloud, remembering Severn's encounter with the woman.

She sat there for a long time, completely lost in her thoughts, and didn't hear the man behind her.

"I have searched for you," Tearle said.

Zared was feeling so low that she didn't even curse at him. She just kept looking at the stream.

Tearle had tried to occupy himself at the tournament but, unlike Zared, he had been to many a similar gathering in France, and there was little to hold his interest. A few women had cast their eyes at him, but he'd looked away. For some reason it seemed that only red hair interested him. It was no doubt the challenge Zared represented to him. After an hour or so without her he'd begun to search for her and had become concerned when he couldn't find her.

He had at last swallowed his pride, found Colbrand, and asked if he had seen the young Peregrine squire. Colbrand had said that Zared had helped him bathe, and that news had sent a current of rage through Tearle. It hadn't taken him long to find her after that.

He wanted to lecture her, wanted to tell her again that she was making a fool of herself, but there was a look on her face that stopped him. He sat down beside her.

"It is time for bed," he said. "Your brother will be on the lists early tomorrow."

Zared kept looking at the water. "I will be there."

"What plagues you?" he asked softly.

She turned toward him, her eyes sparkling. "You!" she snapped. "Why do you know I am female if no one else does?"

"I do not know. If you refer to Colbrand, he does not know because he is stupid. He's like an animal, clever enough to fight but not clever enough to think."

"Why do you hate him so? Because he can do manly things that you cannot? Are you jealous of all men who are *men?*"

She started to rise, but he caught her arm and made her sit back down.

"What defines a man to you? Fighting skill? You fainted for Colbrand before you ever saw him fight; you have not yet seen him fight. How do you know him to be a man? You step into the water with him, run your hands over his nude body, and he is not smart enough to know that a woman touches him—a woman who lusts for him. Is stupidity what makes a man to you?"

"You are jealous," she said in wonder. "You are jealous of Colbrand. Why? Because he can have all the women, and you can have none?"

"None?" He looked at her, then stood, looming over her. "Can you not see me? Can you not forget that I am a Howard long enough to *look* at me?"

She looked up at him, but he was right. The fact that he was a Howard blinded her to all else.

He turned away, his hands in fists, for he saw that his words made no difference to her. What did he care? he asked himself for the thousandth time. What did it matter what this one young woman thought of him? Why wasn't he enjoying himself? He could be laughing and drinking, with a buxom wench on his lap and another beside him, but instead he was standing in the dark trying to make one hardheaded imp of a girl see that he was as handsome as an idiot like Colbrand. He, Tearle, was handsome, rich, strong, educated, yet this girl treated him like a farrier's son.

He turned back to her. "Come, we will return to your brother's tent. He will worry if you are not there."

"Severn will not spend the night alone. He will spend it with a woman."

She said this with such heaviness in her voice that he smiled, realizing that she had been sitting there feeling sorry for herself, no doubt because Colbrand hadn't known she was a female.

He could not bear to see her feeling sorry for herself, and he knew enough about her to know that her pride was stronger than her self-pity.

"Peregrine," he said with mock severity, "were you to don the most beautiful gown on earth, Colbrand would not notice you. You could not be a woman no matter what you wore. You could not entice any man."

She reacted as he'd hoped. She shot up to stand in front of him. "I could have any man I wanted. Liana says I'm pretty."

"A woman has told you that, but not a man?" He was chuckling at her.

But Zared didn't realize he was teasing her, and she felt herself close to tears. He was saying all the things she'd felt. "A man would tell me that if he knew I were a woman. Lots of men would like me if—"

Abruptly Tearle's teasing spirit left him. She *could* entice any man she wanted, but whom would she want to entice? "Such as Colbrand?" he said with some anger. "He doesn't even notice you when you run your hands over him. Why do you think he would notice you if you wore different clothes?"

"I hate you," she whispered. "Hate you." She turned away from him and started up the bank.

He stopped in front of her. He had not meant to make her cry, but her lust for Colbrand was more than he could bear. "Would it mean anything to you if *I* said you were pretty and as feminine as any woman I have met?" he asked softly.

She looked away from him. She would not let him see her cry. "Your words mean less than nothing to me." She stepped around him and walked away, trying to keep her shoulders back.

Tearle watched her go and felt rotten as he followed her back to the tent. In his teasing of her he had only hurt himself.

Chapter Six

There were three cots in the main Peregrine tent, with Severn's men sleeping in the secondary tent. Zared was already on one cot, the light blanket pulled up to her chin, when Tearle returned. He didn't say anything, just undressed down to his loincloth and got into bed.

He didn't go to sleep right away but lay awake and looked at the tent ceiling. The girl was doing something to him that he didn't like; she was making him into someone he didn't know. Where was the man who could kiss and caress a woman, the man who teased and laughed with women? The girl, somehow, made him feel little except anger.

He went to sleep vowing that he would not get angry again, that no matter what she did, he would not become angry. He woke only slightly when Severn came in and fell facedown on his cot.

Just before dawn Tearle awoke, his eyes wide, his

senses alert, and he knew that something was wrong. He lay there quietly, listening to the silence outside the tent, trying to sense if there was some danger. His first thought was that his brother was outside, and his hand slipped down to the sword he kept by the cot.

After a moment of listening he realized that the apprehension he felt came from inside the tent and not outside. He threw back the cover and went to stand over Zared. She made no sound, but he knew she was crying. He sat on the edge of her cot and pulled her into his arms, realizing as soon as he touched her that she was still asleep. Did she often cry in her sleep? Did she always cry so silently?

He held her body, wrapped only in one thin layer of linen, against his bare chest and cradled her to him. Like the child she was not far from being, she snuggled against him, her hot tears wetting the mat of hair on his chest. If he had not felt her unbound breasts pressing against him, he would have thought her to be a child.

He held her securely while she cried, stroking her hair and wondering what made her weep so in her sleep.

Severn had awakened before Tearle. He knew his sister cried, for she often wept in her sleep, just as her mother had done, but he didn't go to her. He lay awake, silent, ready to go to her if she needed him, but he did not try to stop her weeping.

When he heard the man Smith stir, then saw him rise from his cot, Severn put his hand on the sword by his cot. What was the man doing sneaking about at night? When Smith went to Zared Severn almost drew a knife on him, but he hesitated and watched as Smith pulled Zared into his arms.

At first Severn gaped in astonishment. How had he heard Zared's weeping? No one except Severn knew how she cried in her sleep. None of her other brothers had ever been aware of Zared's tears, yet that man had heard.

Severn relaxed against the cot as he watched the two shadowy figures. Liana, he thought. His sister-in-law knew more than he had given her credit for. She had chosen Smith, perhaps knowing he was the right man for Zared.

Severn watched Smith hold his sister, and he remembered all too well those years when Zared's mother had cried. His brothers had hated hearing the woman's loud unhappiness, and in their way they had tried to comfort her. For a year or so they had allowed her to cry and had not complained, but in the second year of her marriage to their father they had told her to cease. Their words seemed to make her cry more.

It was Severn who had made an effort to stop the woman's tears. He was already a big, sturdy boy of ten years, and his own mother was long dead, but his stepmother's tears awakened a need within him. At night he would creep down the stairs and go to her room and climb in bed with her. Her own child, Zared, the only daughter born to his father, had been taken from her at birth. She used to cling to Severn, hold him so tightly he thought she might break a rib or two. But in the end she did not hurt him; in fact, he found he slept better on those nights when he slept near her.

He had been very afraid of what his older brothers and father would say when they found out that he had gone to comfort a crying woman, but his stepmother had never told anyone, and during the day, on the rare occasions when he saw her, she made no reference to the fact that sometimes he came to her.

Yet sometimes he'd find a piece of fruit in his room, or perhaps a sweet beside his bed. And in 1434, when he was so ill, she had sat up day and night nursing him, feeding him mugs of hot broth and spoonfuls of vile-tasting herbs. He hadn't fully recovered his strength when she went off with his father and his oldest brother William to Bevan Castle.

The Howards had laid siege to Bevan Castle, and she had starved to death there. His stepmother, his father, and William all dead at the hand of the Howards.

Afterward Severn and his remaining four brothers had decided to raise Zared as a boy to protect her from the Howards. Perhaps it was the memory of that poor, crying woman starving to death that had influenced them. They could not bear to think of their failure to protect one weak female. Perhaps Zared's pretty face with its long lashes, her bright hair, her smiling ways, reminded them too much of their failure.

There were times when Severn knew they were working Zared too hard, but a year after Zared's mother was starved by the Howards Rogan's first wife was taken prisoner. Severn shut his eyes in memory, for the fight to get her back had killed both Basil and James.

When there were only three brothers left Rowland, then the eldest, had doubled his vigilance against the Howards, and the brothers' training had also doubled. Rowland intensified his watch over Zared, forcing her to train as hard as her brothers. If he saw even a hint of softness in her, he stamped on it.

When Rowland was killed by Howard's men four years before, both Rogan and Severn had been devastated. Rowland had been their guiding light, the foundation of what was left of their family.

It was after Rowland's death that Zared began crying, just as her mother had done. The first time

Severn had heard it he'd thought it was the ghost who haunted Moray Castle, but on the second night he got up to see who it was. Zared, half asleep, half awake, lay in her bed on a wet pillow. She was thirteen years old, but she felt frail to him when he pulled her into his arms. She had begged him not to tell about her crying, and he'd sworn he would not.

After that she didn't cry aloud, but sometimes he went to her and saw that she cried while she was sleeping. At first he thought her tears were from grief—she had seen many deaths in her short life—but he came to realize there was more than grief. He suspected that Zared didn't know why she cried, but he guessed that she was lonely, as deeply lonely as a person can be.

Severn had once mentioned to Rogan that he thought perhaps it would be all right to allow Zared to show that she was female. But while Rogan pondered the idea Oliver Howard had kidnapped Rogan's wife Liana, and the Peregrine vigilance had been renewed.

For Zared's own safety she had to remain in disguise.

Looking at Smith holding Zared, Severn smiled. To him, Zared was so obviously female that he could never believe that others believed her to be male. He and Rogan always teased her because she got angry like a wet cat, all claws and hisses. Yet the men who worked for them never seemed to question who the young lad was. As far as he knew, no one had ever guessed that Zared was a girl. Even Liana, his smart sister-in-law, had had to be told.

Until Smith. The man said he had known from the beginning that Zared was female, and Severn believed him. He knew Liana would not tell anyone outside of her ladies. She knew too well the danger the Howards posed to Zared's safety. Yet the man had known.

99

Severn watched Smith put Zared back in the bed and then go to his own cot. If Zared were to marry and go away with her husband, she would be out of the Peregrine–Howard war. She could live elsewhere in peace and contentment. She could wear pretty gowns and let her hair grow down her back as it had when she was a child. Severn thought he'd like to see his sister as a sister, with a fat baby on her hip and a smile on her lips. It would be pleasant to see her doing something other than beating boys at sword practice.

He smiled again. It looked as though Liana had chosen well.

Tearle awoke early, but not as early as the Peregrines. They were already out of the tent, and he could hear low voices outside and the splash of water. The sound of water reminded him of Zared washing Colbrand the evening before. Already, before he was even fully awake, he could feel his anger rising. He pulled on his stockings and started to pull his linen shirt on over his head, but he paused. Perhaps it might do Zared some good to see another man besides Colbrand.

He went outside the tent, bare from the waist up, yawning and stretching. Severn was sitting on a low stool just outside the tent, also bare from the waist up and Zared was washing his back.

"Good morn," Severn said to Tearle, and he smiled at him.

Tearle didn't look at Zared but instead smiled at her brother. "You are ready to fight this day?"

"I fear I have not brought enough lances to cover all that I will break this day," Severn said, boasting.

Zared poured cold water from a basin over Severn to rinse the soap away as he ran a rough and not-too-clean cloth over his body.

"Have a seat, Smith," Severn said as he stood and motioned to the stool. "My squire will wash you."

"I will *not!*" Zared said, but then she looked at her brother, saw the way his eyes narrowed.

I should have stayed at home, Zared thought once again as the Howard enemy sat on the stool before her. She soaped her hands and ran them over his back. She was cursing him to herself, cursing all men everywhere, since it was her brother who had made her do the disagreeable task, when he spoke.

"It is like bathing Colbrand?" Tearle said softly over his shoulder. "I hear that you washed him also."

"I washed him, but I *enjoyed* that," she said under her breath.

"And you do not enjoy touching me?"

"How could I? You are my enemy."

"But first I am a man."

"If man you can be called. A weak-limbed, puny thing like you."

"Puny? I?"

Zared hated when he taunted her, but then she hated everything about him. He *was* a weak-limbed . . . She looked down at the body under her hands. There was nothing small or weak about the muscles that moved under his skin. He wasn't quite as large as Colbrand . . . or maybe he was. Maybe he was even more muscular.

She straightened and moved away from him. Perhaps he had the look of a man, but she knew he was but a soft, weak, spineless demi-man. All his muscle was fat. He was—

"Do you waste my time dawdling?" Severn snapped at her. "Have you no armor to clean? No horse to see to? Do you sharpen only the swords of my enemy?"

Zared threw cold water over Tearle, threw a dirty drying cloth in his general direction, and began to run to get ready. She was not going to be accused of being a laggard.

Within an hour she had Severn dressed in his armor and mounted on his war-horse, ready to go. All morning he was to face competitors at the lists.

A low wall of wooden planks had been built before the stands, and the jousters were to run at each other, wooden lances tucked under their right arms, and try to break the lances against each other. Points were awarded to each man according to where he struck his opponent's body (no hitting below the waist), the number of lances broken, the number of courses each man ran, and the number of times a man was struck, whether the lance broke or not.

Severn, riding toward his first opponent, had to move aside to miss being struck at the same time that he broke his lance giving a clear, solid hit to the other man's body. If at all possible, it was best to maneuver so that your opponent's lance struck your saddle or your horse, for demerits were given then.

A cheer went up at the first loud thwack of lance hitting steel. Severn rode to the far end, and Zared was waiting with a fresh lance as Severn rode again.

Severn rode again and again and again, knocking men from their horses and breaking several lances against his opponents' armor.

"He is good," Tearle said to Zared. "The people like him."

"Yes," she said, her voice full of pride. "They care not that he wears no plume on his helmet, and they do not remember the procession. He is heroic now."

Tearle had to agree with her as, with each pass Severn made, the cheers of the crowd grew louder. Only Colbrand received as much attention.

"Who will you want to win when your brother fights Colbrand?" Tearle asked.

"My brother, of course," she said, but only after a moment's pause. She looked away.

There were other jousters besides Severn, and between turns he would stand by Zared, downing huge mugs full of beer, while he watched the other men, trying to ascertain their weak and strong points.

"He will not win the Lady Anne," said a spiteful voice in Zared's ear.

She turned to see Colbrand's squire, Jamie, sweaty, just as she was, from running to fetch lances and help his master.

"My brother may not want the woman," Zared said haughtily, too well remembering Lady Anne's words about Severn.

"Ha!" Jamie said. "The lady's father approves of my master. He does not care for the filth of a Peregrine."

Zared's anger that had built up over the last days came to the surface. Severn's sword lay propped against a nearby post, and she grabbed it, going after the boy as though she meant to kill him.

Tearle caught her about the waist and lifted her off the ground. "Release it," he said.

"I have had enough of his taunts and mean to silence him," she yelled.

Tearle's big arm squeezed her waist until she could no longer breathe. With his other arm he took the sword from her. He dropped her so that she barely caught herself before falling. "Go back to your master," Tearle growled at Jamie, and the boy scurried away.

Tearle turned to Zared. "Do you always greet anger with a weapon? Do you not know how to think?"

"As well as you do," she snapped. "That child—"

"Is just that," Tearle interrupted, then he sighed. "I

should be grateful you did not agree with him and hope for Colbrand to win."

"Over my brother? Colbrand will no doubt beat the other men, but he will not beat a Peregrine."

Tearle was glad Zared was not ready to betray her brother for the stupid Colbrand. He didn't say more as he turned back to the field.

At noon the jousting was halted, and all the participants were to leave the grounds to go into dinner. Zared knew it would be another long meal serving her brother. "You are ready?" she asked Severn.

He looked down at her, then at Smith behind her, and he remembered the way the man had held her in the night. Severn wondered if Zared remembered what had happened. He ruffled his sister's hair, knocking her cap askew. "Go you with Smith and see what the merchants have to sell," he said.

"Leave? But who will serve you? Who will—"

"I will not starve. Now go before I change my mind."

Zared didn't waste a moment in making up her mind. She turned and was off the tournament grounds almost before Severn had finished his sentence. She almost ran into a man who had two dead pigs slung across his back.

Tearle's hand clamped on her shoulder.

"Leave me," she snapped at him. "I do not need a keeper."

"Will you enjoy this visit among the people as much as yesterday? You left early to go and sit alone in the woods."

"I wanted to do that," she said, her chin stuck out. "I was tired of the crowds, and . . . and . . ."

"Mmmm," he said, obviously not believing her. It didn't take a great deal of work on his part to figure out why she cried at night. Were he made to dress as a woman he would do more than weep.

"If you will allow me, I will accompany you."

Zared didn't want to agree to go with him, but she, too, remembered the night before, when she'd felt so alone. Perhaps a Howard was better than nothing—not a great deal better, but better than being alone. "All right," she said. "You may come with me."

"You are very kind to me, Lady Zared," he said softly.

"Lady" Zared, she thought, and she rather liked the sound of the words.

She hated to admit it—oh, very much hated to admit it—but she enjoyed the Howard man's company. He led her through the tents of vendors set up near the tourney grounds and showed her everything. At a booth selling religious objects she stared in awe at bloodstained splinters from Christ's cross. The Howard man showed her that some of the blood wasn't even dry yet, and he pointed to a wooden tent post that was suspiciously missing some large splinters.

He took her to a goldsmith's booth, and when Zared would have stood to one side to look at the beautiful objects the Howard man bade the goldsmith show them all his wares. At a cloth merchant's booth he had the man pull down all the luscious fabrics so that Zared could see and feel them. At another booth he showed her children's toys, bidding the merchant to demonstrate each one.

The few hours they had before the tournament began again went by much too quickly, and Zared was reluctant to return.

"A woman at heart," Tearle said, laughing. "How have you resisted purchasing? If nothing for yourself, then a gift perhaps for your lovely sister-in-law."

105

"The Howards stole our fortune," she said, hating being reminded of her poverty.

Tearle's handsome face lost its smile. He had only meant to tease her, not to remind her of her family's poverty. "Here," he said. "See what this man sells."

Zared lost her anger when she looked at the man with the big tray suspended from around his neck. On the tray were beautiful embroidered gloves. They were of white or tan leather, or of colored silk, and the embroidery was so bright it flashed in the sunlight.

"You may touch them," Tearle said, smiling. "Smell them."

"Smell?" she asked, and she picked up one soft, beautiful pair. The gloves smelled of roses. She turned to him, delight on her face. "How?" she whispered. In her experience leather smelled of horses and men's sweat.

"Before the gloves are cut the leather is buried for months in flower petals. Do you have jasmine?" he asked the vendor.

The man, watching the strange pair, dug through the pile and took out a pair of yellow leather gloves heavily embroidered with gold thread. For all the world, he thought, these people talked as a man and his lady, but what the vendor saw was a big, handsome, obviously aristocratic lord and a pretty red-haired boy who had a smudge of dirt on his cheek.

"Choose the one you want and one for Lady Liana. Or perhaps a pair for each of her ladies."

"Liana would love these," Zared said, looking at the colors, feeling the softness of them. She put the gloves down and stepped back.

"Choose," Tearle urged her.

She glared at him. She didn't want to admit before the vendor that she had no money and couldn't afford

106

something as frivolous as one pair of gloves, much less several pairs as gifts.

Tearle understood her thinking. "I mean to purchase all that you want."

Her fists clenched; her back teeth locked together. She was so angry she couldn't speak but turned on her heel and stalked away.

Tearle grimaced. He was beginning to understand the Peregrine pride. He lifted his tunic edge, felt for the drawstring bag hanging from his waist, and pulled out a gold coin. He flipped it to the gaping vendor, then took the gloves—all of them—shoved them down the front of his tunic, and went after Zared.

She was walking so stiff-legged that it was easy to catch her. He didn't try to reason with her but grabbed her arm and pulled her into a narrow place between a thatch-roofed hut and a stone wall. He blocked the exit with his big body.

Zared glared at him, her arms crossed over her chest. "Peregrines do not take charity from a Howard. We do not take charity from anyone. Even though our lands were stolen we—"

She broke off because he kissed her. He didn't pull her into his arms but just leaned forward, head turned, and kissed her firmly. When he stood upright Zared could only look at him, blinking. It was a moment before she could recover the use of her senses. She wiped her mouth with the back of her hand and stared at him.

"It is good to see you have no words," he said.

"I have words for you," she answered, and tried to push past him to get out of the confined area. "Let me pass."

"Not until you listen to me."

"I will hear nothing you say."

"Then I shall kiss you again."

Zared stopped and looked at him. His kiss had not been unpleasant. In fact, it had made her feel a little warm. "I will listen if it puts an end to such degradation."

He smiled at her so knowingly that she looked away. "Say what you must."

"First, see this," he said softly, and he pulled a pair of red silk gloves out of the inside of his tunic. They were embroidered with bumblebees and yellow buttercups.

In spite of herself Zared took the gloves from him. Before, in front of the vendor, she couldn't try the gloves on, but now she did, slipping her small hand into the silk. They were beautiful, soft and bright, glistening as she turned her hand to look at them. "I have never seen anything as beautiful," she whispered.

"Not these?" he asked, withdrawing another pair. "Or these?"

She took them one by one, but as he pulled more and more pairs from his tunic she began to laugh. "What have you done? Stolen them?"

"I gave him a gold Howard coin," he said, watching her.

Her face lost its laughter. "Take them. They are yours."

He made no effort to take the gloves, and he could see that Zared wasn't about to drop them in the dirt.

"I take no charity."

"If Howard lands belong to the Peregrines, then perhaps the gold I gave him is, in truth, Peregrine gold. You have purchased the gloves yourself."

Zared had to think about that a moment. Was he jesting with her? But then there was some truth in his words. The Howard lands *did* belong to the Peregrine family. She shifted her arms, and the leather gloves sent up a heavenly scent. A wave of longing went through her. She would like to own something as beautiful, something as feminine as a pair of the gloves, and she would very much like to give gifts to Liana and her ladies. Liana's ladies had often looked in pity at Zared, for they knew she was female even if her brothers' men didn't. If Zared gave the ladies such lovely gifts as these gloves, their faces would change.

Tearle could see her thinking the matter over and had to work to keep from laughing out loud. For all her boy's clothes and hair, she was feminine throughout. "Which pair is your favorite?"

"I . . . I do not know," she answered, looking at them. The pair on top was white leather embroidered with black and yellow butterflies.

"Perhaps you should keep them all. We will purchase another gift for your sister-in-law."

"Oh, no, one is enough, as I cannot wear them."

"Can't . . . oh, yes, I see. What will you do with your pair?"

"Hide them. I have a . . . a secret place, a loose stone in the wall. I shall wear them when I am alone."

He frowned, guilt flooding him, for it was his own brother's obsession with the Peregrines that made the young woman have to hide away a pretty garment. At that moment he had an idea. Perhaps later at the tournament he would have an opportunity to give her what she so clearly wanted.

He reached out to touch her cheek, ran his finger down the side of her face. "I should like to see you wear the gloves."

She should, she thought, spit in his eye, but she didn't. Was it her imagination, or was he better-looking than when she had first met him? She remembered him as having beady little eyes, but his eyes were rather nice, actually, she thought.

"I . . . I think I'd better get back," she said softly. "Severn will need me."

"Yes," he said, and he moved his hand down her cheek to her shoulder, then pulled away from her. "Here, I will take the gloves. Were you to tuck them away you would add to what you work so hard to conceal."

It took a moment for her to realize that he was referring to her breasts. She could feel the blood rushing to her face, and she ducked her chin down to keep him from seeing her red cheeks, but when he'd taken the gloves and she looked up he was smiling at her in an especially infuriating way.

"Let me pass, Howard," she hissed at him.

"Aye, my lady," he said under his breath, then he bowed to her as she pushed past him.

As they started back to the tournament grounds Zared walked ahead of Tearle. Something had happened in the few hours since they'd left the grounds, and she wasn't sure what it was. When they'd left she would have as soon put a knife in the man as look at him, but at the moment he seemed part human to her. He had been very kind to her as they'd looked at the merchants' wares. He'd explained everything to her, and never once had he acted annoyed or been impatient with her lack of knowledge.

He certainly was different from her brothers, she thought. Severn and Rogan always seemed to be impatient with her, as her other brothers had been. They grew angry when she would stand in one spot and watch a sunset. They ridiculed her once when she'd made a crown of flowers and put it in her hair. They had no patience with her when she was too slow. They had no time for anything but war and training for war.

Since Liana had come into their family their lives

had softened, but still neither Severn nor Rogan had much time to give to her. Rogan spent his time with his wife, Severn with his mistress, and Zared had been alone.

She turned to look back at Tearle, walking backward as she went. "In France, did the women wear such gloves as these? Is that where you learned about their scent?"

"English women wear them also. I would think Lady Liana has a pair or two of scented gloves."

"I do not know. I have not smelled them." She looked at him not as her enemy, but as a man. He did not look feminine, but how did he know so much about women's clothes? Her brothers knew nothing of women's clothes, she thought. Wasn't that how men were supposed to be? "Did you spend your time in France with the women? Is that why you know of women's goods and not of men's?"

"I know of men's goods," he said, puzzled and somewhat defensive. She always made him feel as though he were defending his masculinity.

It was very confusing to her. She recalled that Liana had said that there was more to a man than his fighting ability, but was this the kind of man Liana had meant? This man knew of women's gloves and fainted from small wounds. Were men divided into two categories? Men like her brothers and Severn on one side and men like the Howard on the other?

"Why do you look at me so strangely?" he asked, pleased that she was looking at him at all.

"You are not a man, yet you look to be one," she said thoughtfully.

"Not a man?" He was aghast.

"No. You do not fight as men do. You faint from the smallest of wounds. You are large, yet I, much smaller than you, fought you and won."

"Fought me and won?" he said under his breath, at first having no idea what she was talking about. Then he remembered the first time they'd met, when she'd drawn the knife on him. He'd planned to release her from the moment he saw she was female. Yet suddenly he knew she thought she had "forced" him to release her.

"Yes, I fought you. Had someone pulled a knife on my brother, he would have destroyed his attacker."

"Even a bit of a female?"

"Perhaps not a female, but he would not have been beaten so easily. No, not my brothers or"—she thought for a moment—"nor do I think Colbrand would have been beaten so easily."

"But then Colbrand would not have the brains to know you were female," he said tightly.

"Perhaps not. You do have a mind, it seems. You seem to know about . . . about unmanly things such as women's gloves, and how to tell the quality of emeralds. It is just men things you know nothing of."

"Oh?" He was trying to keep his temper. "And what assures you I know nothing of what men do?"

She looked surprised. "You would be entered in the tournament if you could. You would not spend your time playing nursemaid and servant if you could hold a lance. Liana said Oliver Howard was so rich he could hire men to fight for him. Perhaps in France you hired men to joust for you while you sat with the ladies." Her face brightened. "Yes, that is it. That is how you know so little of men and so much of women."

Tearle could not speak for a while. She was still, like a kid, walking backward, and she was smiling as though she'd figured out some great problem. She had decided that because he knew so much about fabrics and jewels and ladies' clothes that he could not be a man. It had not occurred to her that there were more men like him than men like her brothers, who cared *only* for warfare.

He opened his mouth to tell her—as though words could change a lifetime of her ideas of what men should be—but he saw a man behind her trying to control an unruly horse. The horse, angered by several strokes from its master's whip, broke free, running and kicking toward Zared, who had her back to the animal.

Tearle didn't think; he just leaped for Zared and flattened her to the ground, his big body completely covering hers. As the horse ran at him, hitting him again and again with its steel-shod hooves, he tucked his head down, trying to protect his head and neck by hunching his shoulders.

Within seconds there were shouts, and men scared the horse away, but not before it had done a great deal of damage to Tearle. He lay still a moment, taking deep breaths. He couldn't yet tell if his ribs were broken.

Beneath him Zared began to squirm as she tried to push out from under him so she could breathe.

"You are hurt?" a man above them yelled.

"Fetch a cot," another man yelled. "We will carry him."

Tearle painfully rolled away a little to let Zared out from under him, and as he looked at her face he knew he could not allow himself to be carried away. He could give her no more reason to think him less than a man.

He took a deep breath and rolled onto his side.

"I will fetch Severn," Zared said. She could think of nothing else to say, but she knew that a Howard had

113

probably just saved the life of a Peregrine. She would fetch Severn, and he would know how to deal with an injured man.

"I am well," Tearle said, speaking with difficulty. The right side of his body felt as though it had been crushed. "I have merely had the wind knocked from me."

"Severn can—"

"No!" he said, closing his eyes against the pain. Using all the effort he could muster, he sat up.

"You are hurt," Zared said. "I will fetch help."

"No!" he said again.

By then there was a crowd around them, all of them gaping at the man who had been brutally kicked by a horse but was rising as though he had not been injured.

It took all Tearle's effort to come to his feet. He slowly took a couple of deep breaths, and as far as he could tell, his ribs were unbroken. "We must return," he said to Zared.

"You have to—"

"To what?" he asked, glaring down at her.

"Nothing," she said angrily. "There is naught I want you to do. If you were hurt, you would no doubt cry to high heaven for relief. I have to return to help my brother."

She turned away from him, leaving him to follow or not. She hated the way her knees felt a little weak after what had happened. The Howard man's body had so completely covered hers that she had been able to see nothing of the horse, but she had felt the impact of the hooves on his body as the horse hit him.

Yet he had shielded her. Why? What did that Howard want of her?

She glanced back over her shoulder to see him following her. He was walking, but stiffly. He said he was unhurt, yet how could he be? Should she go to him and demand that he let her see his wounds?

She, a Peregrine, demand to help a Howard? Yet he had saved her. *Why* had he saved her? Why hadn't he allowed the horse to trample her? It would have eliminated one Peregrine on earth.

There had to be something that he wanted. There must be a reason that he wanted her alive. He had talked of marriage between them, a marriage that would join their two families. What if the documents saying the Peregrines were true owners of the lands the Howards held had been found? Perhaps Oliver Howard had found the papers and sent his young brother to court the only Peregrine female. That would explain why the man so much wanted her to stay alive. If the only Peregrine female were dead, the families could not be united, and if the papers were found, Oliver Howard would lose all he had killed to keep.

The weakness began to leave her knees. Everything was beginning to make sense to her. The Howard man wanted her alive and well, and he wanted her to marry him willingly. That explained why he had purchased the gloves for her. The gloves were an attempt to endear himself to her.

It will not work, she thought. He will not be able to win me no matter what he does. And if he is hurt, it is because he has his own selfish motives. She straightened her shoulders and hurried toward the tournament grounds. She no longer felt guilty because a Howard had protected her.

Chapter Seven

Tearle managed to walk back to the tournament grounds keeping his head high and his back straight. What kind of woman was she? he thought. A man had just risked his life protecting her, and she did not so much as acknowledge the deed.

He went back to the tent only long enough to leave the gloves, then went to the field. On the grounds Severn was dressed for the joust, and he was in a foul mood, obviously angry about something that had happened at dinner. He snapped at Zared for being late, and the first man to run against him was hit so hard by Severn's lance that he went sprawling in the dirt. The crowd cheered, but Severn's mood didn't lighten.

Tearle stood to one side and watched as Zared scurried to and fro fetching lances and trying to do enough to please her brother. Only once did he try to speak to her, and for his attempt he got a tongue-lashing.

"Do you think to impress me, Howard?" she hissed at him. "Do you think I will marry you now and unite our families? Do you hope to assure yourself of keeping the lands that belong to my family?"

Tearle stood there, the entire right side of his body screaming in pain from having saved her underdeveloped little body, and she was talking to him of land and estates. He could only gape at her as she went running off to help Severn as he mounted to ride against Colbrand.

He watched Zared smile sweetly at Colbrand even as she helped her brother. "I nearly die for her, and I receive not even thanks, but Colbrand receives all ⬛her for doing naught," he muttered.

⬛ stood to one side and watched Severn and Colbrand run at each other. They were both excellent fighters, and he could see that unless one of them had luck on his side, the match would be a draw. By the fourth run Tearle was sick of watching Zared hold her breath at each pass, her eyes on Colbrand, afraid he might be harmed. "She cares naught for horses' hooves on my back but all for a light wooden lance against his steel-covered body," he muttered.

When Severn broke his fourth lance against Colbrand just as Colbrand had broken his fourth lance against Severn, Tearle waved Zared away and took water and a lance to Severn.

"He lowers his lance too much," Tearle said to Severn while he drank. "And he holds it wide to the left. If you were to swing in to your left and lift your lance, I think you might take him."

Severn gave Tearle a hard look. "My sister watches this Colbrand. Do you have a wish to see him downed?"

"I should like to see his guts in the dirt," Tearle answered with feeling.

Severn grinned, then lowered his faceplate. "I will do my best," he said, adjusting the lance Tearle handed him.

It was the only run in which Severn's lance broke but Colbrand's did not, thus giving Severn the higher score.

Tearle could not resist gloating to Zared. "It seems your invincible knight can be brought low," he said smugly.

"By my brother," she said, "but only by a Peregrine. There is no other man here who could beat him. No other man in England."

"I—" Tearle began, then he stopped.

"You what?" she asked, glaring. "You wer■ about to say that *you* could beat him." She smil■ him. "Howards can only hide and kidnap. Howards do not make open fights."

She turned away from him and went to Severn as her brother went back to the Peregrine tents. Suddenly it was all too much for Tearle. He had always had more women than he knew what to do with. Never had obtaining the affections of a woman been a hardship for him, yet this scrap of a girl was beginning to make him doubt himself.

He stopped a boy passing by, gave him a copper coin, and told him to deliver a message to Lady Anne in the stands. Moments later he saw Anne listen to the boy, then say something to her father before leaving the stands. Tearle followed her at some distance as she went back into the house. He watched as she mounted the stairs, and he was soon behind her. On the second floor he saw the edge of her skirt disappear inside a doorway. He followed her into the room and shut the door.

"You are in danger?" Anne asked.

"Danger of killing a woman," Tearle said.

"And I a man," Anne answered.

"Colbrand?"

"Nay, it is your enemy, that Peregrine."

"Severn?" Tearle asked as he unbuckled his belt and began to remove his tunic.

"What do you do?"

"A horse stepped on me, and I would have you look at the wound. What has Severn done?"

Anne began to help her friend undress. "Do you know he plans to marry me? To him there is no question. Today at dinner my father seated him next to me, and this Peregrine told me he had journeyed here for the express purpose of marrying me. He seemed to consider this a great honor for me—as does my father, now that he has seen this man on the field."

Tearle felt sympathy for Anne, for if her experience with a Peregrine was as bad as his was, she deserved sympathy. When Tearle pulled off his linen shirt Anne gasped.

"You are black and blue and bloody. Tearle, no horse merely stepped on you, you have been kicked— and hard. How far does this extend? Get the rest of your clothes off. I would see all of you." She went to the door and told a passing servant to bring rags and hot water.

Behind her Tearle smiled. This was how a woman was *supposed* to act, he thought. Women were supposed to be sweet, gentle creatures. They were supposed to stroke a man's brow and murmur soothingly to him when he was in pain. Proper women did proper things. They knew about gloves and satins, and they did not sharpen swords.

Tearle removed all his clothes except his breechcloth and stretched, facedown, on the bed in the room. Anne, beautiful, sweet, proper-woman Anne, bathed his wounds and applied salve to them.

"Tell me of her," Anne said softly.

Tearle started to say he could not, that there was too much danger, but he knew he could trust her. After all, he was already trusting her with his life. If Anne told who he was and Severn heard, Tearle had no doubt that Severn would kill him instantly.

The whole story came tumbling out. Tearle told Anne everything from the beginning, about Oliver's men kidnapping the youngest Peregrine and Tearle realizing they held a girl. He told her about Zared cutting him, about his obsession with her and how he'd arranged to be near her.

"But she has fixed on Colbrand," he said bitterly. "I throw myself over her body and protect her, yet still she does not acknowledge that I am a man."

"You could beat Colbrand. You could take Severn also. How I'd like to see him fall," she said, her eyes glittering. "After dinner today he tried to kiss me." She smiled. "I applied my knee to his brain."

Tearle snorted. "It seems we have opposite goals. Your father would not force you to marry a man who could not win the tournament." He smiled. "And I would love to beat Colbrand; I should greatly love to see him brought low."

"Were it not for this silly disguise you've adopted you could fight them. You could bring them both down. I have seen you fight, and you are better than either of them."

"Yes," Tearle said sadly, sitting up so Anne could bind his ribs. "If only I didn't need to remain as Smith—" He broke off and stared at her. "I could fight now."

"Yes," she said eagerly, "there is no reason you

120

cannot be seen. Announce yourself as a Howard and enter the next two days. That Peregrine would not dare harm you while under my father's roof."

"No," Tearle said thoughtfully. "I will not stoop to my brother's level. Too many people have seen me with the Peregrines, and they will see them as fools for having had a Howard in their midst."

"They *are* fools," Anne said vehemently.

Tearle looked at her exquisite face. Was she protesting too much? "Severn does not strike me as being unattractive to women."

"He is a boor, an unmannered boor who believes a woman is his for the taking—not for the asking, mind, but for the taking."

"But not unpleasant to look at," Tearle said. "He sits a horse well."

"I should like to see him fall to the ground. I should like to hear him laughed at. I should like him seen as the fool he is. I should—"

"I understand," Tearle said, unable to keep the amusement from his voice.

"If you dare to laugh at me, I will—"

"I?" Tearle said in innocence. "I, a man sorely wounded in the cause of the Peregrines, laugh at another's ill wishes for them?"

Anne's lovely face relaxed. Tearle had known her too long and well, she thought. When that awful man, smelling of sweat and horse, had pulled her into a dark corner, she had at first responded to his kisses. There was something so very basic about the man. He seemed to take it for granted that she would be willing, even eager, to marry him. Throughout dinner he had talked easily to her father, as though they were already kin, and her father had responded in kind. Anne had sat between them, ignored. The Peregrine

man had repeatedly reached across her for food, and
she'd had to lean away from his elbows. He had talked
across her and over her as though she weren't there.
And all the talk had been of weapons and warfare.
As far as she could tell, there wasn't a finer sentiment
in the man's body. At least Colbrand, the other man
her father favored, had beautiful manners and had
noticed when her gown matched her eyes. There were
no compliments from the Peregrine. He had looked at
her once as though appraising her, and as far as she
knew, he hadn't glanced at her again.

After dinner he'd gone off with her father. Anne
would have left them, but her father had ordered her
to accompany them to the mews where he had some
hawks to show the Peregrine. Anne and a couple of her
ladies had followed the men, not speaking or being
spoken to.

It was at the mews that the man had pulled her
behind a shed and kissed her. Perhaps it was because
she was so full of anger that at first she kissed him
back, but it didn't take long for her to recover her
senses. She'd raised her knee and brought it up
between his legs. He had pushed her away from him,
his face furious. Anne didn't want him to know how
much he frightened her, so she had stood her ground.

He didn't say anything to her for a moment, then
said, "Go back to your father," and he turned and left
her. She had to admit that his reaction wasn't what
she would have expected, but she was pleased she had
made him so angry. Perhaps he would drop the suit
for her hand.

"I shall appear in disguise," Tearle was saying.

"In disguise?"

"Yes, as . . . as the Black Knight. Can you find
armor for me and have it painted black? I will
challenge the men who have the most points so far."

"That will be Colbrand and this Peregrine. No one seems able to touch them."

Tearle remembered the way Zared looked at Colbrand each time the man came within sight of her and felt a surge of strength flow through him. "I will beat them," he said softly. "For you I will beat Severn, and for myself I will make Colbrand sorry he was born."

Anne smiled at him. "I will find the armor. Come to the garden tonight at midnight, and I will see that you have what you need. And I will see that all is arranged with my father. He will like a mystery knight to act as his champion."

Tearle rose, his wounds feeling much better. "And what if he gives you to me as my prize?"

Anne, sitting on the edge of the bed, looked up at him. He was wearing only the smallest piece of white linen, and as he moved muscles played under his skin. "I would accept," she said softly.

He turned to look at her. She was so lovely, so perfectly featured, and he knew her dowry would be enormous. Uniting the Marshalls and the Howards would be a very wise thing to do, and he knew his brother would heartily approve the match. Oliver could use Anne's dowry to buy more weapons to try to destroy the Peregrines.

As he looked at Anne's face, at her perfect loveliness, he began to see Zared's face, her prettiness nothing to compare with Anne's beauty, but there was an innocence to Zared that Anne could never have. Tearle remembered the look on Zared's face when she'd tried on one of the gloves. There was a world of new and different things he'd like to show Zared.

Perhaps it was her lack of experience that fascinated him, he thought. Perhaps because he had seen and done so much in his years on earth, Zared's freshness was a delight to him. Even the open, adoring way she looked at Colbrand intrigued him. Anne, and women like her, who were used to courts full of handsome men, would never show their feelings so openly. Tearle knew that if Anne loved a man she would not tell him so unless it was suitable for her to do so. But Zared, Tearle thought, smiling—if Zared loved a man, she'd protect him with her life.

"Then I should be most honored," Tearle said, smiling as he lied.

Anne smiled, too, knowing he lied. "Get dressed. I will leave first so no one sees me alone with a half-dressed man—even if you are old enough to be my father."

Tearle smiled at her knowingly. He was pleased to have her look at him as a man. After Zared, it was pleasant to have any woman look at him. "At midnight, then," he said as she reached the door.

She nodded and left the room.

Zared left the tournament grounds more confused than ever. Too many things were happening to her. She kept remembering—feeling—the Howard man on top of her as the horse stomped on him. She could feel the blows through his body to hers. Yet later he had refused any help from her.

Had he saved her for some ulterior reason? Did he want to unite the Peregrines and the Howards? If his brother had found papers proving the Peregrines owned the land held by the Howards, Oliver Howard would merely have burned the papers. He wouldn't need to send his brother to join the two families.

She put her hands to her ears as though to stop the raging thoughts. What did the man want from her? Why didn't he just go away and leave her to herself and to . . . to Colbrand?

At the thought of the beautiful man Zared decided to go to his tent. Perhaps the sight of the blond man would make her forget the dark one who was beginning to haunt her.

But at Colbrand's tent she was greeted with abuse from Jamie, his squire.

"Do you come to gloat?" he sneered at her.

"No, I . . ." What? she thought. Just wanted to see Colbrand?

"Your brother had luck on his side. My master's horse slipped."

"It did not. Severn is just a better fighter, that's all."

"He is better at naught than my master!" Jamie shouted. "My master fights better. He is a better man. Colbrand will win in the end, for he will win the Lady Anne."

Zared was too upset by the day's events to control her tongue. "My brother is to marry Lady Anne."

Jamie smiled nastily. "The Lady Anne hates your brother. She sneers at him when he does not look, but others see. Today after dinner she struck him."

Zared glared at the boy, knowing that what he said was true, but at the same time hating him for saying what he did. He was a scrawny thing and quite young. She thought she could quite likely beat him to a pulp.

She made a move toward him, but Colbrand put a hand on her shoulder.

"Fighting again?" he asked, bemused.

"I have told him of your intent to marry Lady Anne," Jamie said smugly.

"Ah, yes, the lovely Lady Anne. Her father wants a strong man for her husband."

"Then her father will want a Peregrine," Zared said evenly.

"Then he will have made a good choice in your brother," Colbrand said.

125

Zared smiled at him. Beautiful, kind, as well as gracious, she thought.

Zared would have answered him, but at that moment Severn came by, angrily grabbed her ear, and pulled her toward their tent. "What are you doing?" she demanded, but he wouldn't answer her.

Once inside the tent he released her. "Where is Smith?"

Zared was rubbing her painful ear. "I do not know. He is my keeper, not I his."

Severn poured himself wine. "I have heard what happened today, that he saved you, and in protecting you he was trampled by a horse."

Zared turned away. "He had his reasons for what he did."

"Aye. He believes himself in love with you."

Zared looked back, wide-eyed. "In love?" she gasped. "With me?"

"You are no more surprised than I, but he looks at you with lovesick eyes just as Rogan looks at Liana." And I vow never to look that way at a woman, he thought.

"Your brain was knocked from your head," she said. "The man cares naught for me."

"He has known always that you are female. He goes to you when you weep at night, and now he has saved your life."

Zared was horrified by the conversation. She had never spoken of love—or any emotion, for that matter—with her brothers. "What would you have of me?" she asked suspiciously.

"I believe Liana means for you to marry the man. She must have sent him here to court you."

"Liana did not—"

"Did not what?"

"Does not mean for me to marry him," she said, unable to tell him any more of the truth. "What matter is it to you who I marry?"

"The man knows weapons. He gave me advice so that I beat Colbrand."

"I see," Zared said coolly. "You want me to marry him so you can have someone to help you beat other men in tournaments."

"To help our family beat the Howards."

"He'll not help you there!" she snapped, then, to cover herself, she attacked. "Why do *you* not marry to help our family? Are you pushing me to marry because you think you may not get the Lady Anne? I hear she struck you."

Severn's face turned red with anger. "What I do with a woman is not your concern."

"And my life is yours? You cannot get a wife, so you are foisting me on some man you know nothing of?"

"I know he wants you, which no other man does," Severn snapped.

It was true, all so painfully true, she thought. Only one man desired her, and he was her family's sworn enemy. She pushed past Severn, jerking from him when he tried to hold her, and left the tent. As soon as she was outside she started running, and she didn't stop until she reached the stream.

She sat down on the bank, put her head on her arms, and began to cry. Why couldn't life be simple for her as it seemed to be for everyone else? Of course, other people seemed to be sure whether they were male or female.

She didn't know how long she sat there crying as quietly as possible, but the moon rose, and still she stayed there.

At one point, when she wiped her nose on her

sleeve, she jumped to see the Howard man next to her. "Have you no work to do?" she snapped.

He stretched out on the bank beside her. "Nay, I have none. I am of the worthless Howards, do you not remember?"

Zared looked at him. Severn said the man desired her, she thought.

"I remember how your brother took Rogan's first wife, Jeanne, and later he took Liana."

"You could have been no more than a babe," he said. "How could you remember Jeanne? She is the best there is about Oliver."

Zared looked at the moonlight on the water. "Liana speaks highly of her." Her voice lowered. "Does she love your brother Oliver very much?" Zared had never told anyone before, but the story of Rogan's first wife fascinated her. Her oldest brothers had chosen Rogan as the one to take a wife because they needed the dowry a wife would bring. Rogan had married a young woman named Jeanne, but mere months after the marriage Oliver Howard had taken her prisoner.

The Peregrine men had fought long and hard for the return of Rogan's wife—so hard that two of their brothers had been killed. It was after their deaths that the Peregrines found out that the captive Jeanne had fallen in love with Oliver Howard and was carrying his child.

A child herself then, Zared only remembered the quiet rage of her three remaining brothers. Her parents and her brother William had died the year before, and Zared remembered being afraid that one by one her brothers would leave her.

"I believe that Jeanne loved him once," Tearle said, bringing her back to the present. "But I am not so sure now. My brother is bitter at having no sons to pass his wealth to."

"Rogan has a son," she said, smiling in memory of the baby with red-gold curls.

He didn't say anything for a moment, then, very softly, he said, "Why do you cry? Why do you weep in your sleep and now, here, alone, as well?"

Zared was on her feet instantly and starting back to the camp. But he came to his feet quickly and caught her by the shoulders. "Release me or I will make you regret your hold of me."

"Oh?" he said, smiling at her. "Will you draw a knife on me again? Will you call for your beloved Colbrand?"

"He is not my—" she began, then she wrenched away from him and took a step forward before he caught her again.

"So this is why you cry? Did he ignore you? Did you again make a fool of yourself before him? Did he again fail to recognize you as female?"

She tried to twist away from him, but he wouldn't release his grip, and after a moment she stopped struggling. "What do you want of me?" she hissed at him. "Why do you not go and leave me to myself? Are there no other women to interest you? We are enemies! Do you not understand that? Since you cannot conquer us in battle, do you mean to conquer us with your pretense of friendship?"

Her eyes were blazing, and he was so close to her. "Nay, I do not want friendship," he said in a husky whisper before drawing her into his arms.

At first she struggled against his lips touching hers. She pushed against him, tried to turn her head away, but his hand held the back of her head, and she could not move away. Realizing that it was no use fighting him, she allowed her body to go limp, thinking that as soon as he lightened his grip she would escape him.

But when she stopped struggling the oddest thing

happened. He loosened the hold on her head, and his lips on hers softened, and the feeling was . . . was something Zared had never felt before.

She just stood there, her eyes wide open, as he kissed her, and she could feel her body growing warmer by the second. He used his hand to turn her head sideways. Zared felt her body being pulled against his, and it was as though she melted into him, her head going against his thick, hard shoulder.

His lips opened over hers, tempting her into opening them. She closed her eyes and leaned against him as his body covered hers, and she felt as though she were drowning. He moved his lips off of hers to kiss her cheeks, her temple, her neck, moving down to her throat.

Zared leaned against him, her body a mass of sensations. Her life had been entirely without affection. To be touched so gently, to be held, to be kissed was almost more than she could bear.

Tearle leaned back from her and looked at her in his arms. She was leaning on him fully. If he released her she would no doubt fall to the ground. No woman had ever put herself into his care so completely. He touched her hair, smoothed it back from her temple. When she loved a man, she was going to love him with all her being—and he meant to be that man.

"My name is Tearle," he whispered as he kissed her forehead, and the old name, meaning one who is without tears, sounded like a caress.

"Tearle," she whispered against his neck.

He smiled down at her, for there was the softness he'd always known she possessed. "I should like to take you away with me," he said softly, touching the hair at her temples. "I would make love to you all night and into the morning."

She moved closer to him and put her face up to be kissed again.

Tearle kissed her slowly, softly, a gentle kiss for a virgin. "Now, my love, I must return you to your brother."

"Mmmm" was all Zared could say as she put her face in his neck, her lips on his skin. She'd had no idea that touching a man could be so pleasant.

Tearle pulled her away from him, and the look on her face made his body grow hot. He could take her if he wanted; he knew that. "We have to return," he said. For leaving her a virgin that night he was sure that in heaven he would be given a crown of gold.

He put her hand in his and started leading her back toward the tents.

They had gone only a few yards when Zared's senses returned to her. She shook her head as though to clear a fog from it, then jerked her hand from his. She had just given herself to the enemy. Instead of remembering that she was a Peregrine and the man her family's enemy, she had lost all memory and allowed him to touch her. Allowed him? She would have allowed him much more if he'd wanted it—which he had not. He had broken from her when she would have gone on.

She drew the little eating dagger from her belt, turned, and held it out as though she meant to thrust it into him. "If you ever touch me again, I will kill you," she said.

He, the hideous, odious man, smiled at her.

Zared lunged at him, but he easily caught her wrist and pulled her into his arms again.

"I have a half-healed knife cut and a bruised side because of you. I do not want more wounds."

"I will cause you a great deal more pain if you force yourself on me again."

"Force?" he said, still smiling, then he bent his head as though he meant to kiss her again.

Zared turned her head away. "No," she whispered.

He released his hold on her, and when Zared ran from him she could hear him laughing behind her.

Chapter Eight

She ran all the way back to the tent, and when she arrived she was shaking. Severn was lounging on his cot eating an apple, and he turned to look at her when she entered.

"Someone chasing you?" he asked. "Colbrand's squire after you again? I do believe the boy senses your sex. He seems to have the brains his master lacks."

"Haven't you something to do?" she snapped. "No swords to sharpen? No women to court?"

"I have won all the women," he said smugly.

"Except the Lady Anne."

He finished his apple and swung his feet to the floor. "Where is Smith? Did you see him with another woman—has that put you in an ill temper? Beware, little sister, that you do not play *too* hard to get."

"You know *nothing!*" she yelled at him. "Nothing!"

He chuckled at her as he left the tent.

133

Zared sat down on her cot, her body stiff with anger. She was angry at her brother for being able to see nothing, at the Howard man for coming into her life, and at herself for the way she had acted.

"It would have happened had any man kissed me," she whispered aloud. "Had Colbrand touched me . . ." She trailed off, remembering the way it had felt to be touched by the Howard man. By any man, she corrected herself. It would have felt wonderful to have been held and kissed by any man at all.

"Yes," she said, standing. She was a Peregrine, and as her brothers liked lots of women, she, no doubt, liked many men. It was a shame, perhaps, that her family's sworn enemy could make her react, but that was the way of the world.

She just had to keep her wits about her and not allow the man to make her lose sight of what was really important, she decided. He was a Howard, and he had put himself in the Peregrine camp for a reason. Since Zared was the only one who knew who he was, did he mean to seduce her so that she would begin to believe him?

She didn't yet know what he hoped to gain from his disguise, but it was her duty to protect her family.

"And that does not mean succumbing to his kisses," she told herself. It won't happen again, she thought. She wouldn't allow him to touch her, and if he did happen to touch her, she was *not* going to fall against him like some peasant girl. "I'll take my knife to him before I allow him to touch me again," she said, chin in the air.

Hours later she was in bed, her eyes tightly closed as her brother and her enemy came to the tent. From the way they laughed and staggered she thought they must have shared about half a hogshead of beer.

"Sssh," Severn said loudly. "Can't wake my little sister."

"I'll take her back to bed," Tearle said even louder, and both men dissolved in laughter.

Zared slammed her fist into her pillow and turned onto her side. Her anger and indignation kept her from sleeping—and if anger hadn't kept her from sleeping, the drunken snores of her brother and that man would have.

She was just about to go to sleep when she heard the Howard man rise very quietly from his cot and leave the tent. She looked at Severn and saw he was still sleeping, so Zared got out of bed, slipped her tunic on over her head, and followed the man.

Severn was awake the moment Tearle put his foot to the floor, and he lay there watching as the man took his sword and left the tent. For all that Severn liked the man, he was always cautious, and Zared's continued animosity made him less trustful of Smith than he might normally have been.

He and Smith had gotten drunk together—or at least Severn had pretended to get drunk. He hoped to pry some secrets out of Smith, to find out how he knew of weapons yet didn't fight, and where Liana had found him. But Severn had discovered nothing about the man. He was very good at not answering questions and at revealing nothing about himself.

When Severn saw his little sister slip out after the man he relaxed. He was glad Smith liked Zared, and Severn knew he could trust Smith to protect Zared, just as he had when the horse had nearly trampled her. He lay back on the cot and went to sleep.

Zared followed Tearle as he made his way through the people who were still awake. She watched as he slipped in and out of shadows; it was easy to see that he did not want to be seen. Twice Zared had to slip into darkness to keep him from seeing her.

After many twists and turns he slipped through a door in the stone wall that surrounded the Marshall castle. Zared could not follow him without being seen, and it took her a while to find a tree that she could climb to see over the wall. She had to climb slowly to keep from being heard, and when at last she was high enough to see she gaped in openmouthed astonishment.

The Howard man hugged Lady Anne, then he whirled her about, her pretty skirt belling out around her. He set her down and soundly kissed both her cheeks.

Zared wanted to see no more. She climbed down from the tree.

For a while, as she walked back to the tent, she couldn't think clearly. She had discovered the reason for the Howard man's interference in the Peregrines' lives. He wanted to prevent the Peregrines from marrying into the wealth of the Marshall family. He wanted to make sure the Peregrines were never wealthy enough to conquer the Howard stronghold.

She went back to bed, but she did not sleep. When the Howard man at last returned to the tent her body grew rigid, and she lay there awake all night, not sleeping until nearly dawn.

In the morning two things happened: one, the practical jokes started, and two, the Howard man disappeared.

Severn overslept, and when he awoke to find Zared still asleep and the other cot empty he was annoyed with Zared, saying she had done something to anger Smith. Severn said he needed Smith to give him advice on the day's fighting, and he was sure Zared had done something to make Smith leave.

Zared had no way to defend herself. She had kept too many secrets for too long to begin to reveal them. Her only consolation was imagining telling Severn the truth when they were once again at home. She hoped her brother would have the courtesy to apologize to her for his accusations.

But for the time being all she could do was clench her fists at her sides and repeat that she had no idea where "Smith" was.

It was once they were on the tournament field that the "jokes" began. Severn put on his helmet and found that the inside of it had been coated with mud. At his first charge his lance broke away in his hand before he ever reached his opponent. Someone released bees from a hive, and while the bystanders swatted at them they came to land on Severn because parts of his armor had been coated with honey. When the Peregrine banner had been unfurled, instead of a white falcon on a red ground the banner had been replaced with cloth that was painted with a picture of a satyr chasing a nubile young girl—and the satyr looked remarkably like Severn.

With each of these harmless but mean little jokes the crowd laughed, and their laughter increased until at midday the mere sight of a Peregrine caused gales of laughter.

Zared looked into the stands and saw Lady Anne and her father laughing and pointing. Zared was glad the king had left the day before, but she had no doubt he would hear of how the Peregrine knight had been made to look the fool.

Severn instructed one of his men to stay with his armor at all times to see that nothing more was done to it. Zared had to ask other knights for lances, for all of Severn's had been sawed nearly through during the night. Colbrand sent his smirking squire over with an armful of new lances, and Zared forced herself to say thank you to the boy.

Severn took it all quietly, never saying a word as Zared washed mud off his face and out of his helmet. But the fact that he would not bend down to her, so that she had to climb on a short barrel to reach him, showed how enraged he was. He said nothing while she scrubbed honey off his armor. He did not comment while she frantically rerolled the banner that should have been the proud Peregrine falcon.

With each new thing that made the crowd laugh Zared was more and more sure that the Howard man was behind the jests. It would suit him, she thought. He seemed to like to spend most of his time laughing at her, and he was making everyone laugh at her brother as well.

And this laughter, she thought with anger, would assure that Lady Anne would not marry a Peregrine. She doubted if an old war-horse like Hugh Marshall would allow his daughter to marry a man who was the butt of such jokes.

"He has what he wants," she whispered to herself, watching as Severn knocked another man from his horse. It looked as though the Howard man would be able to keep the Peregrines from using the Marshall wealth to regain their lands.

Would he marry the lovely Lady Anne himself? she wondered. Again she remembered seeing him kiss her. What would he have done if Zared had accepted his marriage proposal? Added something else to his list of what there was to laugh at the Peregrines about? Would he sit with his fat older brother and laugh that the youngest Peregrine had agreed to marry him?

"That is one pleasure I will deny him," Zared said under her breath.

When the games were halted for dinner Severn did

138

not go to the castle to eat, and he would not allow Zared to go either. Not that she wanted to, for she could not bear to hear more laughter. Severn sent one of his men to fetch food, and Severn and Zared sat alone on stools outside the tent and ate without speaking.

At one point Zared asked her brother who he thought was playing the tricks.

"I will kill whoever it is," Severn said softly, and he continued eating.

Zared knew he meant just that. Were she to tell him she was sure that the man he seemed to think so highly of, Smith, was actually a Howard, and that he was making the Peregrines look like fools, she knew that Severn would kill the man. And then what? Would Severn be executed? Would Oliver Howard retaliate by laying siege to Rogan and Liana and their child?

Zared just kept eating and said nothing.

After dinner Severn did not return to the lists. He was not due to fight again until late in the day, and he did not care to see the men he had beaten earlier. He went into the tent and stayed there.

Zared decided to go to see the other jousters. As she neared the lists she straightened her back, preparing herself to be the object of ridicule.

As she drew closer to the lists she realized that something new had taken the crowd's attention, for no one even glanced her way. All eyes were on the jousting field. She could see the people in the stands, saw the way their eyes were wide, their bodies leaning forward.

She moved through the crowd of spectators and found herself near Jamie. He barely glanced at her and showed no sign of even remembering the Peregrine humiliation of the morning.

139

"What is it?" she asked. The crowd was quiet, as though waiting for something.

"There," Jamie said, pointing to the far end of the field.

At the end of the field was a man on a black horse draped in black silk, wearing black-painted armor, his face covered, a black plume on top of his helmet. It was not at all rare to see black armor, and she could find nothing unusual about the man.

"That is what you gape at?" she asked.

Jamie gave her a look of contempt, as though she were too stupid to comprehend even the smallest thing.

"He is the Black Knight. No one knows who he is, and he has come to challenge all. So far he has knocked every man from his horse."

"So has my brother," Zared snapped.

Jamie snorted. "Your brother is likely to smear them in honey and the bees knock a man from his horse."

Zared put her hand up to smack the boy, but Colbrand stepped between them and smiled down at her. Zared's anger melted away as she looked up at him.

"The man is a mystery," Colbrand said.

"Who is?" Zared asked, smiling up at him. His golden hair waved back divinely from his temples and his eyes were very blue.

"The Black Knight," Jamie snapped. "Is all your family stupid as well as foolish?" he hissed across Colbrand so only Zared could hear him.

"I will make you eat those words," she said, and she started for him, but the shout of the crowd got her attention. The Black Knight was about to ride against his opponent.

His heavy horse thundered down the field, and the

man kept his body tilted forward, his lance held low. When he hit the armored man on the other side of the low fence the blow was so hard that the man fairly lifted out of his saddle and hit the ground, landing with a crash of armor.

"He is good," Zared said under her breath.

"Better than anyone except Colbrand," Jamie said, but there was doubt in his voice.

"Who is he? Where does he come from? What does he want?" she asked.

"He was announced as the Marshall challenger, to fight all comers, and his identity is to be kept a secret."

"People have reasons for keeping secrets," Zared said with some bitterness. "What does he want?"

"To win the emerald," Colbrand said above their heads. "What else could he want?"

"All that the Lady Anne possesses," she snapped. "Power. The notice of the king."

Colbrand looked down at her with vacant blue eyes that had no understanding in them, and suddenly she didn't think they were such handsome eyes.

She shrugged and turned away. She had more to think about than whether or not Colbrand was handsome, for there was something wrong. Why had the man waited until the second day to enter the games? Why keep his identity a secret?

She moved away from Colbrand and Jamie and made her way to the Black Knight's end of the field. There were half a dozen boys crowding around the knight, handing him new lances, wetting his horse's nose, and in general worshiping the mysterious man who was such a good fighter.

Zared watched the man through two more runs before she realized there was something familiar about him. At first she thought he might be her oldest brother. He was the same size as Rogan, but he did not

move as Rogan did. Nor was he one of her father's illegitimate sons, for she knew them well.

She stepped closer to watch the man, and when she did so he turned his head toward her. She could see none of his face through the grid of his face mask, but the way he moved his head, even when it was encased in steel, made her draw in her breath.

Howard, she thought, and she knew without a doubt who was inside the armor.

She turned away before he could see the expression on her face. She walked back to stand by Colbrand and watch the man joust, but she looked with new eyes.

There was the man who had nearly died when her knife had grazed his ribs. *Had* nearly died? Or had just pretended to? He had lain there on the grass and told her he was afraid to be alone, and she, fool, had believed him. She had left him, yet she had returned because she feared he was dying.

Lies, she thought. The man was composed of lies. He pretended to be a weakling; he pretended to be who he was not; he pretended to want to marry a Peregrine; he pretended to be a friend.

"Do you think your brother can take him?"

It took her a moment to realize that Colbrand was speaking to her. And it was another moment before she realized that her body did not vibrate at being so near the beautiful man. Beautiful, yes, but so were the gloves Tearle had bought her, and Colbrand's eyes looked as though they held as much intelligence as the gloves. She would have very much liked to talk to someone about the mysterious knight, but as she looked up at Colbrand's handsome face she knew he would not be the one. She sensed that he would not be able to understand the finer points of a conversation that involved logic and deduction.

"My brother will kill him," Zared said softly.

"With mud or honey?" Jamie said, smirking.

She did not react to his words at all but turned a blazing face to the boy. "Go and fetch my brother."

Jamie didn't hesitate, for he knew a command when he heard it. He turned and started running.

Zared stood beside the field and watched as the Black Knight downed one man after another. Her ears rang with everything she'd said to the Howard man, how she'd taunted him about being soft, about knowing of women's clothes yet not knowing of men's weapons.

How he must have laughed at her, she thought. How he must have chuckled over her every word. Did he laugh at Zared while Lady Anne was in his arms? He had admitted that he knew her in France, so perhaps they had planned their marriage while there. What had happened? Did Lady Anne's father dislike the notion of having a Howard son-in-law—and had he forced his daughter to choose another man? Had Hugh Marshall chosen Severn?

But the Howard man had eliminated Severn from competing for Lady Anne's hand. The crowd laughed whenever they saw a Peregrine, laughed even at the Peregrine banner. So now the Howard man caught the crowd's fancy by dressing as a mysterious knight. He fought no better than Severn had, but in the end, when he revealed himself, he would not be a man the crowd had laughed at. With the glory of the Black Knight strong Hugh Marshall would no doubt listen to a Howard petition of marriage.

Zared watched the man who called himself the Black Knight with increasing concentration. Severn *must* beat him, she thought.

It was a while before she realized Severn was standing behind her.

"What do you think?" he asked softly.

"You can take him," she said. "He has intimidation on his side. Half these men *expect* to be knocked down by him. He scares them. He has weight and strength on his side, but he is no larger or stronger than you."

"You seem awfully sure."

She turned to glare up at him. "I *am* sure." She saw something in her brother's eyes and realized that the laughter of the morning had hurt him. "He is the one who put the mud in your helmet, the one who released the bees."

Severn stared at her. "You are sure?"

"Aye," she said with conviction. "It is not skill he uses as much as fear. Why else appear in disguise? He knew he could not beat you, and he knew he could not make you afraid, so he tried to break your spirit with laughter."

She could have told her brother that the man in the black armor was Smith, the man Severn had believed to be his friend, but she did not. She wasn't sure why she didn't tell Severn the truth; perhaps from fear of his rage at such a betrayal, or perhaps because if she gave more than the necessary information, it might lead to more questions, and Severn would discover Tearle's true identity.

Severn straightened and looked at the man on the black horse, and as Zared watched his eyes changed. Her brother was returning. She saw again the man of supreme confidence, and no longer were his eyes filled with doubt.

"Aye, I can take him," Severn whispered.

Knock him down for me, Zared thought. Beat him to repay him for his humiliation of me. She turned and went back to the tent with her brother to help him dress.

An hour later she walked with her brother to the

lists. Upon seeing Severn the crowd began to smile and poke one another in the ribs. Zared soon found out that the Black Knight had knocked Colbrand to the ground and had then challenged him to fight on foot with axes. Colbrand had refused the challenge.

"If the Black Knight can beat Colbrand, he can beat anyone," the people said as Severn walked past, clanking in his armor.

"Remember the bees," Zared said as she handed Severn his lance once he was mounted.

Severn nodded and slammed his face guard down. When the herald blew his horn he thundered forward.

Both men broke lances at the first pass. Even score.

At the second pass both lances broke. Still even.

"Remember the mud," Zared said.

Severn broke his lance against the Black Knight at the third pass, but he managed to dodge the knight's lance. A point scored for Severn.

"I believe he means to have Lady Anne," Zared said, giving her brother water. "He wants to make people laugh at you so he can gain her hand and her money."

Severn's eyes blazed as he slammed his faceplate down. He charged the Black Knight as he would charge a man on a battlefield. He was out for blood. He sat firmly in his saddle, leaned forward, held his lance in his gauntleted hand, and charged.

Everything happened too quickly for Zared to understand. One moment her brother was charging, and the next he was on the ground. The crowd's roar of approval for the Black Knight's win was deafening as she ran under the barricade to help her brother.

Severn, humiliated beyond words, pushed his sister away and stomped back to the tent. Zared followed, carrying his helmet.

"What happened?" she asked once they were alone.

"He bested me," Severn answered. "The better fighter won."

"I do not believe that. You are better than he is."

Severn picked up an apple from the little side table and crushed it in his strong fingers. After a while he turned to Zared, his handsome face showing his rage. "My saddle cinch slipped. He never touched me. *I fell off my horse.*"

Zared swallowed. The Howard man would pay for this, she thought. She would make him pay if she had to die trying.

Chapter Nine

Tearle swam underwater, only coming up to the cold surface of the lake when his lungs were bursting. He swam on his back for a while, smiling as he moved. He doubted he'd ever felt so good in his life. He was tired, sore, hungry, and he wasn't sure he'd ever be able to replace all the water he'd sweated out, but he felt very good.

He had done exactly what he'd set out to do: He had proved to Zared that he was a man. He was sure she'd recognized him, for he'd seen her eyes widen. He wondered what had given him away, but perhaps she just sensed who he was, as he had known she was female the first time he'd seen her.

He turned onto his stomach and swam easily across the lake. She would change toward him now, he thought. No longer would she doubt him. No longer would she think him less than a man.

He swam to the edge of the lake and walked onto

the shore. Two of his brother's men were hidden in the trees. Throughout the tournament they had stayed dressed as merchants, and Tearle had paid them well to keep his secret. They had helped him dress and undress, and they had hidden his horse and armor.

He dried himself and began to dress, smiling all the while. It had not been easy beating all the contestants. By the time he got to Severn his body was screaming with pain. The bruises where the horse had kicked him, combined with the jarring his body took when his lance met steel, was almost more than he could bear.

But any amount of pain was worth it, he thought, for he had beaten them all. Colbrand had been difficult, and only sheer will power had kept him on his horse. By the time he got to Severn he wasn't sure he would succeed. Severn was good, very good, and after Severn's lance broke Tearle had been sure Severn was going to beat him. But on that last run, almost by magic, Severn had flown out of his saddle and landed on the ground.

It had been a bittersweet moment for Tearle because he could not savor his triumph. He could not remove his helmet and show the roaring crowd who he was. He had only a moment to watch Zared run to her brother before the crowd reached him. The people meant to see who the mystery man was. Tearle had turned his horse and thundered away before they could reach him.

He had ridden into the forest a few miles, his brother's men behind him, then tiredly dismounted at the side of the lake. He'd stood while the men unfastened his armor, then he'd removed his sweat-soaked clothes and waded into the water.

An hour later he was feeling better. He was eager to

see Zared's pretty little face. She placed so much importance on skill at arms, unlike most women who liked soft words and flowers, and now he had shown her he was even better at arms than her brother.

As he mounted his horse he smiled again. At last the woman was going to look at him as something other than an enemy.

Zared had no experience at soothing a melancholy man, for in her lifetime her brothers had mostly been full of rage. She had seen them overcome with grief when death struck their family, but that grief was usually tinged with anger, for most Peregrine deaths had been caused by Howards.

However Severn's anger was different this day, for his confidence seemed to be broken. She had never known her brothers when they were not utterly confident. The way Severn sat silently inside the tent, not speaking, eating alone, seeing no one but Zared, caused her more concern than anything she'd ever experienced.

When the Howard man entered at sundown she turned to look up at him, and for a moment she could not keep her hatred for him from her face. For what he had done to Severn she could easily have killed him. She looked away quickly. She would not let him see her hatred because she planned to revenge herself on him. She didn't know how she was going to do it, but she was going to make him pay.

"There was an illness in my family," Tearle said, looking from one to the other. He had carefully rehearsed the excuse for his absence, but the look in Zared's eyes made him forget everything. If he'd thought he'd seen hatred from her before, that had been nothing compared to what was there now.

"You missed the final humiliation of the Peregrines," Severn said, sitting on the cot.

Tearle looked from Severn's ravaged face to the back of Zared's head and knew that something was very wrong. Did Severn take one defeat so hard? he wondered. Tearle had thought more of the man than that.

Tearle filled a plate with food, then sat on a stool to eat. Zared didn't look at him. "I hear there was some excitement today," he said, his mouth full. "Something about a mystery knight."

Severn, after one angry glance at Tearle, left the tent. Zared, glad she had not identified Tearle as the Black Knight to her brother, left quickly to follow Severn.

"Return to our camp," Severn said to her when they reached the edge of the forest.

"People should be told," she said. "They should know that that man did not knock you from your horse. Had not the cinch been loosened, you would have beaten him."

Severn turned on her. "I am to cry foul play? That will cause more laughter." He turned away. "You do not understand. I have failed."

"You have *not* failed! You have an enemy at this tournament, and he has taken the victory from you."

"Aye, we Peregrines have an enemy, but Oliver Howard is not here. Do you not see that this is the end of our hope to regain what we have lost?"

"What do you mean?" she whispered.

"I had hoped to show myself well at this tournament and catch Hugh Marshall's eye. And after the humiliation of this day no man would give his daughter to a Peregrine. The word of this tourney will spread from one end of England to the other. If I do not get a rich wife, we will never be able to afford what is needed to beat the Howards. We will never get back what they have stolen from us."

Zared could not bear to hear the words, for all of this was her fault. If she had told Severn from the first that the man he trusted was actually a Howard, this would not be happening. She remembered all too well seeing the Howard man with the Lady Anne.

"You shall marry her," Zared said softly. "If it is possible, you shall marry the Lady Anne."

She turned away and left her brother. She had some serious thinking to do.

As Zared walked back through the crowd to the Peregrine tent many people stopped to look at her and smile. Everyone was once again laughing at the Peregrines.

Once inside the tent she saw the Howard man asleep on his cot. She did not hesitate as she picked up Severn's sword in both hands and prepared to bring it down over the man's neck.

Tearle rolled away as the sword swung downward. He hit the floor and came to his feet in one movement, then leaped across the cot to land heavily on Zared, throwing her to the ground and pinning her under him.

"You could have killed me," he said into her face.

"I meant to," she spat at him. "Even if I die for ridding the world of you, it would be an honor."

He looked down at her. She had always looked at him with anger, but there had also always been an underlying softness. Now there was no softness. Had he been fully asleep when she attacked, he would not be alive, for she would have severed his head from his neck.

"What has happened?" he asked softly, easing his weight off of her but still pinning her with his arm, a leg thrown across hers.

"What your brother could not do, you have done. Yet he uses a *man's* weapons, while you use treachery and deceit. My brother thinks you are a . . . a friend." She nearly choked on the word.

He didn't dare release her, for the look in her eyes told him she'd attack again. "What do you know?"

"I know all. You want the Lady Anne for yourself. You—"

"Anne? I want Anne?"

"You conspire with her. You—"

Tearle could only look down at her. She was saying he wanted Anne. If Anne was angry at a man, she wouldn't grab a sword and try to behead him, she'd dress in some beautiful gown and seduce him into doing what she wanted. No, Tearle did not want Anne. He'd much rather have Zared, who spoke and acted honestly, with no hidden meaning, no hidden treachery.

He had not heard all of what Zared was saying. "Why would I want Anne?"

"She is a rich wife for a second son."

"True." He moved his hand down her arm and moved closer to her.

"Do not touch me!" she yelled, fighting against him, but he held her easily, although he grunted when she hit a sore place.

"I do not want Anne," he said, and he put his face against her neck.

Zared let her body go limp. Then, when the man relaxed, she rolled away from him, and as she did she kicked him hard between the legs.

Tearle groaned and grabbed himself with one hand and Zared with the other. "Sit!" he commanded, shoving her onto a cot. He hovered over her, trying to recover from the pain, and when he could at last breathe again he bent over her. "I want to hear all. I want to hear all that is in your head."

"I will tell you nothing," she said, firm-jawed.

"If you do not tell me, I will tell your brother who I am."

"He will kill you!"

"As he did today?" he asked mockingly, then he wished he hadn't. He had not meant to admit he had disguised himself.

"You loosened his cinch," she screamed at him. "You humiliated him! You want the Lady Anne!"

Tearle had to hold her to keep her on the cot while he thought about what she'd said. Perhaps there had been no "magic" to Severn's being unhorsed. Perhaps he had slipped. After all, Tearle's lance had barely touched him.

"Someone loosened Severn's cinch?" he asked softly, fearing his brother's hand. Since the king was gone, Oliver might dare much.

"*You* should know. You put the mud in his helmet, the honey on his—"

"What?" Tearle straightened and looked down at her. "I put mud in his helmet?" he asked indignantly.

"The people laughed at Severn," she said, and misery at the memory of that laughter was replacing her rage. "Severn will not get his rich bride now, and it will be my fault. If I had told him about you at the beginning, he could have killed you. Better that he was executed than suffer this humiliation."

Tearle couldn't seem to think for a moment. He had meant merely to dress in black armor to impress a girl, but instead of impressing her he had somehow caused her family humiliation and dishonor.

"What would you have of me?" he asked softly.

153

"Shall I go? Shall I leave here and never see you again?"

"Yes," she said, putting her face in her hands. "You have ruined all. Severn will never marry his rich bride."

He put his hand lightly on her hair. "You must believe that I meant only good for you and your brother. I never meant—"

She jerked away from his touch. "Go! Leave me. I never want to see you again. You have ruined all for my family."

Tearle turned away from her, not really understanding, but hearing the deep sorrow in her voice. He left the tent and intended to leave her life, but first he wanted to find out what she meant when she talked of mud in a helmet.

It didn't take Tearle long to hear the story, for it was all the people on the grounds could talk of. As he listened to each recounting of the story of bees and mud and broken lances a suspicion began to grow inside him.

"Hugh Marshall won't be giving his lovely daughter to a Peregrine," one man said, laughing. "He wouldn't want a fool for a son-in-law."

"The Black Knight is who Marshall wants. I hear he's offering a reward to anyone who can tell him who the man is."

"The reward being the Lady Anne," someone else said, laughing.

Tearle didn't listen to any more but walked away. He paid a boy to go to the hall and deliver a message to Anne that he would meet her in the garden at dark.

A few hours later, when he arrived in the garden, Anne was there waiting for him, and her beautiful face was radiant in the moonlight.

"You were magnificent," she said, holding his shoulders and kissing both his cheeks. "Really magnificent, and Tearle, it worked so well. My father no longer speaks of that Peregrine man. Now all he talks of is the Black Knight, who, of course, will never be found."

"And this pleases you, that Severn is no longer considered by your father for marriage?" he asked softly.

"It pleases me very much. He is a dreadful man, and I could not bear to spend five minutes' time with him."

"Have you done so? *Have* you spent five minutes with him?"

Anne stopped smiling and gave him a hard look. "What is on your mind? Are you not pleased with your victory?"

He turned away from her. Pleased? He had meant to show Zared he was not the weakling she believed him to be, but instead he had made her hate him and had caused a good man like Severn great humiliation.

He looked back at her. "Who put the mud in Severn's helmet?"

Anne looked away, but not before he saw her smile.

He grabbed her shoulders and turned her to face him. "Who, Anne? Who made the people laugh at him?"

She jerked away from him. "I will *not* marry him. He has humiliated me publicly. Did you see what he did to me at the procession? He picked me off the ground in front of everyone. Twice he has tried to kiss me."

"He wasn't like the fawning men at court, was he?" he asked softly. "Severn wrote no love poems to your beauty. He did not woo you with words."

155

She glared at him. "I do not like your tone," she said, lifting her skirts and starting to walk away.

Tearle caught her arm. "Severn is a good man. His manners may have little polish, but he is a good man. He cares about his family and his honor. He is a man with a great deal of pride."

At that Anne broke. She put her hands over her face to hide her tears. "And I have no pride?" She looked up at him as she tried to control the tears. "Yes, I humiliated him. Yes, I made people laugh at him. But tell me, what else could I do? What other ways of fighting are open to me? I have told my father I do not want to marry this man. I have told Peregrine I do not want to marry him, but no one listens to me. Don't you understand that I had to *do* something?"

Tearle had no answer for her. He gave a sigh, and when he spoke it was softly. "Who does your father favor now that Severn has been made to look a fool?"

Anne sniffed. "My father chose my sister's husband based on his connection to the throne. For me he says he wants a strong man."

"A wise father," Tearle mumbled.

"He favors Colbrand or—"

"Colbrand!" Tearle gasped. "The man is an idiot. He has no sense."

"He has lovely manners and is beautiful to look at."

"And easy to manage," Tearle answered. "If you married Colbrand, you'd eat him alive. He is no match for you."

"And who is?" she snapped, recovering herself. "That filthy Peregrine?"

"A better match for you than anyone else I've seen. Severn wouldn't allow you to control him."

"I have no desire to control him or even so much as look at him." She put her hand on Tearle's arm. "This Peregrine may be a friend to you, but to me he is rude.

He never speaks to me. At dinner he talks to my father, not me."

"And wisely so—as you have just said, he must court your father and not you."

She gave Tearle a look of exasperation. Could he understand *nothing?* "Colbrand spoke to *me.* He—"

"Colbrand!" Tearle said through his teeth. "I have heard enough of the man to last all my life. He is too stupid to tell girls from boys. Within a year of marriage you'd hate Colbrand."

She glared at him. "I do not need a year to hate this Peregrine. If you love them so much, you marry them, but not I. I thank you for helping me rid myself of my father's urging me to marrying one of them, but I do not feel I owe you any reward. You got what you wanted."

"What I wanted? Pray tell me, what did I want?"

She looked at him in astonishment. "Why, the same as I wanted: to humiliate the Peregrines. All of England will laugh at them after today, and when it is known that it was a Howard who beat this Severn even the animals in the fields will laugh. You will have no more worries of war with them, for they will be too afraid to stick their noses out their doors." She smiled. "You and I have done a fine job indeed. Your Severn will be hard pressed to find a bride at all, rich or poor."

She lifted her skirts and left him alone in the garden.

Tearle was too stunned to move from the dark garden. Every word she'd said rang in his ears. He had meant merely to impress a bit of a girl, but instead he had helped to make the Peregrines a laughingstock.

He knew that Anne was right; the identity of the Black Knight would eventually be found out. Too many people knew for it to remain a secret forever.

Some of his men knew, Anne knew, and Zared knew. Before long word would get out, and as Anne had said, all of England would laugh that a Howard had beaten a Peregrine.

Tearle thought of his brother Oliver and knew that Oliver would be filled with glee at the knowledge of what Tearle had done. Oliver would see to it that the news of a Howard beating a Peregrine was spread all over the country.

Tearle sat down heavily on a stone bench. Zared was correct: He had destroyed the Peregrine family. Through good intentions he had accomplished what three generations of his family could not do with their weapons.

He lay back on the bench and looked up at the stars. Was there any way he could right the wrong he had done?

Zared didn't sleep much that night. She lay awake trying to figure out a way to keep her promise to Severn and make Lady Anne marry him. She thought of going to Anne but remembered too well the way the woman had reacted when Severn had caught her runaway horse. She thought of going to Hugh Marshall and pleading Severn's case, but as Severn said, it would not look good to plead foul play. She doubted she'd be believed anyway.

She lay there and listened to Severn thrash about on his cot. No longer did he spend half the night carousing and teasing the women. He remained in the tent, not even spending time with his men—which was good, since the men weren't exactly proud of riding under the Peregrine banner.

Morning came, and Zared went to get them some food. Severn was not to joust until afternoon, and she did not think either of them would leave the tent until then. At midmorning she went outside to the privy, and as she was leaving a hand was placed over her mouth and nose.

She kicked and clawed at the arm about her waist but could not escape. When she thought she was going to die from lack of air the hand moved away from her face, and she gasped for air. As she did a cloth was stuffed into her mouth, then a cloak thrown over her body.

She was picked up, thrown across the saddle of a horse, and taken away. Howard, she thought. Once again she had been captured by a Howard.

They rode for some while before he stopped the horse and pulled her down, then removed the cloak from over her body. She was not surprised to see *him*.

"Do not look at me that way," Tearle said. "I mean you no harm."

Once the cloak was gone Zared started running, removing the gag as she ran.

He caught her within a few yards, grabbing her and landing hard on the ground so that she fell on him. He held her against him as she struggled.

"Do not kick me, I beg of you," he said tiredly. "You have stabbed me, I have been trampled by a horse while protecting you, I have nearly killed myself on the tourney field, you tried to cut my head from my body, you have perhaps removed all hopes of my having children, and last night I slept not at all. Please, I beg you, give me a moment's rest."

He sounded so genuinely tired that Zared nearly laughed. She didn't laugh, but she lay still on top of him. He was so very warm and comfortable, and she, too, had not slept much for two nights.

"What is it you want of me now?" she asked.

He pulled her head down against his chest. "Please do not struggle. I am too weak to protect myself from your knives and your swords . . . and your feet."

"Weak!" she snorted. "You downed Colbrand."

"Easy," he said. "Very, very easy."

"Release me," she said, pushing against him, but he wouldn't let her go. "I shall scream for help."

"I shall kiss you then."

"No!"

He smiled at the fear in her eyes. "Will you marry me if I get Lady Anne to marry your brother?"

She lost her lethargy at his words and began to struggle against him in earnest.

With a sigh he released her, but when she tried to stand he put a big hand on her shoulder and made her sit by him.

"I would not marry you were you the last man—"

"Even to bring Anne's riches into your family?"

"I wouldn't marry you . . ." She looked at him stretched lazily before her. "Her father will not allow her to marry a Peregrine. You have seen to that. You have made all of England laugh at us."

"I did not make anyone laugh at your family. I did not put honey on Severn's armor or remake your family's banner. If I want to beat a man, I do so with a sword or lance." He smiled at her. "You have seen that."

"I know you could not beat my brother, so you loosened his cinch to make it seem that you could beat him."

"I could beat your brother were I to lose an arm."

Zared's face turned an unbecoming shade of purple, and she leaped on him, ready to strangle him.

He chuckled and rolled with her, tossing her back and forth in his arms, moving his head when she tried to claw him.

160

After a few moments Zared realized he was playing with her, and her body went rigid. When his hands loosened their grip she moved off of him.

"I will not marry my enemy." She looked away from him.

"I thought you cared for your family name," he said, rolling to his feet. "I thought it mattered to you whether the Peregrine name is a great source of humor." He started walking toward his horse, but Zared put herself before him.

"You know *nothing* of family pride," she spat at him. "You live on stolen land. Your brother is insane. If you fight, you must do so in disguise."

"I disguised myself to protect your family name," he said, aghast. "I did not want people to know a Howard beat a Peregrine."

"*You* beat my brother?" she yelled. "You had to loosen his cinch to—"

He bent and kissed her.

Zared turned her head away, hating the way he made her feel. "It is because I love my family that I would not marry a Howard," she whispered.

"A marriage alliance would end the feud."

She looked back at him, recovered again. "Your brother would—"

"I would live with you," he said. "Wherever you wish. I will go with you to live with your brothers."

She blinked at him. "Rogan would kill you," she whispered.

"I doubt he can."

"You are a fool."

"Probably," he answered, shrugging. "I may be a fool, but I am not without honor. I did not loosen your brother's cinch. I can beat him without such low tricks."

"Ha! You could not—" She stopped because he

161

looked as though he might kiss her again. She turned away. "It matters not. It is done now. Lady Anne will not marry a man who causes laughter."

"Then you will not do what you can to stop the killing, or to help your family bring a rich bride into the family. I understand." He took the reins of his horse.

"I would do all that I could to protect my brothers. I would do *anything.*"

"Oh?" he said, one eyebrow raised. "It does not seem so to me."

She looked at him, eyes narrowed. "How do you plan to get Hugh Marshall to allow his daughter to marry a Peregrine?"

"You leave that to me."

She gave him a slow, humorless smile. "Do you plan to throw a cloak about her head, put a gag in her mouth, and kidnap her? Howards are masters at kidnapping defenseless women. Will you force her to marry my brother? Do you mean to start a feud between the Peregrines and the Marshalls? Do you plan to unite with the Marshalls to wage war on us?"

For a moment he was quiet, just standing there and blinking at her. "Do you think of naught but war? Do you believe there exists no other motive for a deed besides war? I do not plan to force Anne Marshall to do anything. Her father will give her in marriage to your brother."

"And you are sure of this?"

"As sure as one can be about the future." He smiled at her. "But I will not go to the trouble to arrange your brother's marriage if I am not to get what I want in return."

"And you want a Peregrine," she snapped. "You will not go to my brothers' house to live as you have said. You will force me to go to the Howard house.

What then? Torture for me? Or do you use me as a hostage to force my brothers to do your bidding?"

"I have told you I will not take you to live with my brother. I will live with you and your family, just as I do now, as Smith."

Zared could only stare at him. Was he stupid? "The Howards watch us. They will see you with my brothers, and they will betray your identity. When my brothers know who you are they will kill you. And your brother will—"

"Yes, I know," he said, his voice full of disgust. "There is no more use in our talking. Go back to your brother. Ask him to propose marriage to Colbrand for you. Marry him. See if on your wedding night he can tell that you are a woman." He mounted his horse and looked down at her. "Give my farewells to your brother."

As she saw him start to ride away all she could think of was that her worries were at last over. She was at last free of the hideous burden of keeping his identity a secret.

But as he turned his horse away she called after him. "Wait!"

He halted and looked down at her.

"What of Lady Anne?" she asked. "How do I get her to marry Severn?"

"The problem is that your brother is an object of laughter, and Hugh Marshall will not allow his daughter to marry him."

"And you can change his mind?" she asked nastily.

He turned his horse away, but she caught the reins.

"Tell me how!" she demanded. "You owe me this after the way I have kept your secret."

"And you owe me for saving you from my brother's men, and you owe me for saving you from the horse, and you owe me for—"

163

"Tell me!" she yelled, smacking him on the calf with her fist. "It is all to my family and nothing to you."

"You know my price," he said quietly.

She put her forehead against the neck of the horse. "I cannot marry you," she said slowly. "You are my enemy, and I hate you."

"If you think you hate me, it is nothing compared to what Anne Marshall will feel when she's made to marry your brother."

Zared smiled at that and looked at him. "Before the games her horse bolted, and though Severn saved her, she sneered at him. She said she needed to boil the reins before she could touch them again."

"That sounds like Anne."

"You know her well?"

Tearle wasn't sure, but he thought he detected an undercurrent in her voice. He didn't dare hope it was jealousy he heard. "Well enough," he said.

He took a deep breath, for he meant to make her decide. No longer could he bear the indecision about his future, and since it was the last day of the tournament, it was now or never.

"I will get your brother the wife he wants," Tearle said. "Hugh Marshall will give Lady Anne to Severn, but I will not do it nor tell you how unless you agree to marry me."

"You will not succeed," she said. "Hugh Marshall will not do the bidding of a second son."

"Then you have no cause for worry, do you? If I fail, you will not have to marry me." He looked at her. "But I will not make the attempt if you do not swear to what I want."

She dropped the bridle and walked away to look at the forest. To marry him? To marry a Howard? How would her brothers react if they discovered that their new brother-in-law was actually a Howard? Severn

164

might hesitate in killing him since he liked him, but Rogan wouldn't blink before running him through. And then Oliver Howard would bring an army to kill them.

On the other hand, all of England was laughing at the Peregrines. Only Severn's marriage to Anne Marshall would stop the laughter.

Zared put her hands to her ears. He was like the devil tempting her, and he looked like the devil, too, sitting atop the big horse with his black hair and eyes. Marry him? she thought. Marry him and live forever under the rule of a family that her family had hated for generations?

"I cannot," she whispered.

Tearle reined his horse away.

"Stop!" she screamed. Not looking at him, her fists clenched at her sides, she said, "I will."

"I did not hear you."

She didn't look at him. "I will marry you," she whispered.

"I still didn't hear you."

She looked up at him, her eyes sparkling with anger. "I will marry you," she shouted. "If you can get Lady Anne to marry Severn, I will marry you." Her lips tightened. "But I will *never* go to live at your brother's. I will *never* be put under Oliver Howard's rule."

He looked down at her, and his face softened. "I will live wherever you do until you are willing to follow me wherever I go."

"Ha!" she said. "Ha!"

But Tearle just smiled at her, turned his horse, and rode away.

Chapter Ten

Zared walked back to the tents, her body shaking with both anger and fear. What in the world had she done?

"You were gone long enough," Severn snapped at her.

She almost let him have a piece of her mind. How could he be ill-tempered with her after what she'd just done for him? Agreed to do for him, she corrected herself. So far none of the horror that *could* happen *had* happened.

The thought cheered her a bit. Perhaps nothing bad was going to happen. Perhaps she and Severn could stay in the tent until his last run on the tourney field, then they could go home and pretend nothing had happened. Perhaps people would forget all about the mysterious Black Knight, and about the mud in Severn's helmet, and about the banner with the satyr on it.

Sure, she thought, and God will give me angel's wings tomorrow.

Severn dropped his dagger, and Zared jumped half a foot.

"What ails you?" he asked.

"Nothing. I am fine. I have no problems. My life is a joy."

Severn smiled. "Missing Smith, are you?"

"It is good you have bone in your head, for you have no brain to hold your helmet off your neck."

"I'll brook no such insolence from you," he said, and in one lunge he was across the tent after her.

Zared didn't try to escape him as she usually did. Instead she felt like having a good, rousing fight, so she put her head down and rammed Severn in the stomach. He grunted, then grabbed the back of her clothes and pulled her away.

"What the hell's wrong with you?" he asked just before she swung her leg and kicked him in the shin.

"Why, you little—" he gasped, tossing her to the cot.

Severn had every intention of teaching his little sister a much-needed lesson, but in walked Smith, a tearstained, richly dressed woman held firmly to his side. Severn looked up from Zared and caught both her elbows in his ribs. With a grunt he cuffed her one across the head and sent her rolling off the cot.

"What is this?" Severn asked, rising.

Zared rolled away from the side of the tent, shook her head to clear it, and stood, narrowing her eyes at the Howard man as soon as she saw him.

"Tell him," Tearle said to the woman.

She began to cry, then she lowered her head and shook it no.

Tearle tightened his arm about her waist. "I will give you to him," he threatened.

The woman gave a quick look at Severn, and there was fear in her eyes.

"My brother is not—" Zared said, meaning to say that he was not to be used as punishment, but Tearle cut her off.

"Tell him!" he ordered.

The woman sniffed. "She will kill me."

Tearle didn't say another word to the woman, but then he didn't have to. His look was quite enough for the woman.

Zared watched the woman cry a bit more. When she spoke, at first her words were so soft she could barely be heard.

"Lady . . . mud . . . armor . . . banner."

Zared looked in puzzlement to Severn and saw he also was straining to hear.

"Louder," Tearle said.

The woman put her chin in the air and glared at Severn as one might glare at the face of the devil.

"My lady does not want to marry you. She arranged for the mud in your helmet, the honey on your armor. She paid a man to paint your—"

She stopped because Severn was advancing on her, but Tearle protectively put the woman behind him.

"She is not the one," Tearle said. "Lady Anne played the tricks on you."

"Anne?" Severn asked in wonder, and Zared knew what he was thinking. Usually women liked him, usually women did what he wanted and were pleased to be allowed to do so. By any reckoning Severn was a handsome man. Were he not her brother, Zared might even believe him to be as handsome as Colbrand, so the news that Anne had done those things to him was shocking.

"Lady Anne did these things?" Severn asked.

"Aye," Tearle answered. "She has her heart set on

Colbrand, but she knew her father favored you, so she made sure you were no longer a contender for her hand. She made everyone laugh at you."

Severn looked at Tearle. "A woman did this?" he whispered. "This was no Howard trick?"

"I can guarantee it was no Howard trick." Tearle glanced at Zared. "Perhaps Lady Anne thought it was a great joke."

Zared could see blood staining Severn's neck as his anger seemed to rise from somewhere deep inside himself.

"A joke?" he said. "I have been made to look like less than a man, and she believes it to be a *joke?* She has made even the lowest of the low laugh at me. *Me!* A Peregrine. Who is *she?* Naught but the rich daughter of a trumped-up merchant, while I . . ." He trailed off, no longer able to speak.

"Where is she?" Severn managed to croak out after a while.

"Eating dinner, I believe," Tearle said cheerfully. He released the woman from his grip, but she did not move.

"I will show her what it means to be laughed at," Severn said.

"My lord," the woman cried, "you cannot—"

Severn pushed past her and left the tent, the woman following him, begging him not to harm Lady Anne.

"What have you done?" Zared hissed at Tearle.

He smiled innocently. "I do not yet know what I have done, but based on your brother's temper, I can guess."

Zared didn't waste more time talking to him but ran after her brother. Maybe she could stop the worst of whatever Severn planned to do. Maybe she could prevent him from making the Peregrine name more of an object of ridicule.

Zared ran, Tearle right behind her. "I'll kill you for this," she yelled over her shoulder at him. Why in the world had she ever believed him when he'd said he could get Anne Marshall married to a Peregrine? After Severn made his accusations to Hugh Marshall people were going to laugh at them even more than they had.

She reached the Great Hall just as Severn reached the high table where Hugh sat, his daughters on either side of him. Hundreds of men and women ate and drank at the long tables set up in the hall.

Zared started to run to her brother to stop whatever foolishness he intended, but the accursed Howard man grabbed her about the waist, put his hand over her mouth, and pulled her into a shadow. No one would have noticed had he torn her arms off, for *all* eyes were on Severn, his handsome face enraged as he glared down at Anne.

Severn didn't look at anyone else in the hall except her. He leaned across the table, grabbed her by the shoulders, and pulled her up. She screamed at him, and more than a dozen men drew their daggers and started for Severn, but Hugh Marshall put his hand up to halt the men. He was fascinated and eager to see what the big man was planning for his daughter.

When Anne was halfway up Severn caught her waist and dragged her across the table. When Anne saw that her father was going to allow no man to rescue her she began to fight for all she was worth. She beat Severn with her fists and kicked out at him, trying to hit him, but she succeeded only in knocking over wine pitchers, goblets, platters of meat, trays of vegetables.

"Unhand me!" she screamed. "Father!"

When the guests realized the performance was sanctioned by Hugh they sat back down and began to enjoy the spectacle.

Once Anne was on Severn's side of the table he

170

tucked her, screaming, kicking, clawing, under his arm and hooked his foot over a bench. He pulled the bench to the middle of the space between tables—the space left for acrobats and other such performers—and sat on it.

"Help me!" Anne screamed. "Someone, I pray you, help me."

Severn tossed Anne across his knees, flung all but one of her petticoats over her back, and applied his hand to her firm little buttocks.

Whack! "That is for the mud in my helmet," he said. Another *whack!* "And that is for the mud on my face."

It was at that moment that the diners began to understand what it was about. They knew enough about the slovenly Peregrine ways, and they had had ample time to observe the too-fastidious ways of the beautiful Lady Anne, and all they had to do was put one and one together.

Hugh Marshall was the first to laugh. It was a joy to him to see his too-clever daughter brought low in such a way.

"And for the sawed lances," Severn said, applying his hand at each sentence he spoke. "And the honey. And the banner."

Anne stopped struggling at the first sound of laughter. Her fear was replaced by anger and hatred. She clenched her fists, gritted her teeth, and refused to cry at her humiliation. For humiliation it was. He was not hitting her hard, just enough to sting—and that, if possible, made her even angrier.

The huge old Great Hall echoed with laughter, the laughter of everyone: guests, servants, entertainers, children, even the dogs started scampering about.

At long last Severn pulled Anne's skirts down and stood her upright before him while he still sat on the bench. The crowd quieted as they waited to hear what Severn had to say.

"That should teach you to play tricks on men."

With him sitting and Anne standing they were nearly at eye level. He wore a smug look of triumph. She spit in his face.

The crowd hushed.

Severn, after a second's anger, grabbed her by the back of the neck and pulled her to him, and after a second to look at her he put his mouth on hers.

The crowd began to laugh and applaud, and when Severn continued holding Anne and didn't break the long, hard kiss they began to stamp their feet in approval.

Anne fought him throughout the kiss, but she was no match for his strength.

When at last he pulled away from her Severn picked her up in his arms, walked toward the table, and proceeded to drop her, bottom first, onto her father's half-eaten plate of food.

"I suggest you keep closer watch on your daughter," Severn said loudly, then he turned to leave the hall.

The people were laughing again, but now, he thought, they weren't laughing at *him*.

Throughout Tearle had been holding Zared against him. He hadn't had to hold her mouth to keep her quiet, and he probably hadn't had to hold her at all, but he refused to release her.

As Severn started to leave, the beautiful Lady Anne left behind on a large plate of pork, Zared jerked away from him. "Now Hugh Marshall will *never* allow his daughter to marry a Peregrine," she hissed.

"Halt!" Hugh Marshall shouted, and the entire hall grew quiet instantly.

Severn stopped where he was, his hand ready to go

to his sword in order to defend himself. Zared stepped from the shadows, ready to fight beside her brother.

Slowly Severn turned to look at Hugh Marshall.

Hugh stood, and when Anne tried to get off the table he pushed her back down.

"I have something to say to you, Peregrine."

"I can hear you."

There wasn't a sound from any of the hundreds of people in the big room. They held their breaths. Would the fierce old Hugh declare war on the poor Peregrines for the way his daughter had been humiliated?

Anne turned and glared in triumph at Severn, her arms across her chest, her bottom in pork roast, her feet in cabbage stew. She hoped her father would order a particularly vile death for the man.

"It is my wish," Hugh said into the silence, "that you . . ." He took a breath and looked about the room. "I would be honored, sir, if you'd take my daughter in marriage."

The roof nearly fell in at the explosion of laughter.

Zared's mouth fell open as she watched her brother's chest swell in pride. Swaggering, Severn made his way to the high table, then leaned across Anne as though she weren't there, tore a leg off a roast pig, sat on the table near Anne's head, and began to eat.

"How much gold do you give me to take the wench off your hands?"

The crowd was laughing so hard they could hardly stay on the benches, and how Severn loved it! He was going to take his time in the wedding negotiations and enjoy this moment when the crowd wasn't laughing at his family.

Zared stood where she was, watching as Severn bargained with Hugh over Anne's dowry, and she

knew that the Peregrine reputation would not suffer from the bargaining. She could see men's heads nodding in approval as Severn asked for more and more gold if he was to take on the burden of Lady Anne.

Zared had some sympathy for Anne, but not much when she remembered how hard everyone had laughed at Severn. But one look at Anne's face, red with rage, and she sensed that perhaps Severn wouldn't have the last laugh, for she doubted that Anne would be an easy person to live with.

After a while she grew tired of the noise and left the hall. There would be much to do to prepare for Severn's wedding.

Outside there were very few people, for they'd all heard of the excitement and jammed into the hall to hear Severn bargaining for the uppity Lady Anne.

A hand clamped on Zared's shoulder. "Do you forget our bargain?"

Zared turned to see the Howard man, and she remembered everything.

"What bargain?" she said, stalling for time. Her mouth was growing dry.

Tearle smiled at her. "I have given your brother his rich bride."

"*You* gave her to him? You had nothing to do with it. My brother got the woman by . . . by . . ." Humiliating her? By making people laugh at her? "You had nothing to do with it," she finished.

"I caused it all. I told your brother that Anne played those tricks on him."

"Yes, but that is not what made Hugh Marshall offer his daughter. My brother did that on his own, without your help, so there is no bargain between us." She turned away, but he caught her shoulder and turned her back.

174

"I arranged all. I know your brother's temper, and I know that when he is angry he has no control, he—"

"He can control a sword, and if he were here now, he'd control it through you!"

"Oh?" Tearle asked, not at all perturbed. "He could not control his temper today, as I knew he would not be able to. Had Anne another father, not one such as Hugh who values strength above brains, I would not have told Severn what Anne did. But I rightly guessed that Severn would do something such as he did, and that Hugh would be pleased by it. I, little wife, arranged their marriage."

"Wife?" she said under her breath. "I am not your wife and will never be. I cannot keep a bargain that was not fulfilled. You could not have known what would happen. Severn could have killed the woman— he was angry enough to do so—and then where would we be? Or her father could have—"

"I took note that Severn does not hurt women. If he did, you would have bruises aplenty, for I have never seen a woman deserve chastising as much as you do."

"You know *nothing*. Hugh Marshall could have ordered Severn killed for what he—"

"It is a sad but true fact that Hugh cannot abide his younger daughter. She has more brains in one foot than he has in all his body, and he resents that. Also, I have heard it rumored that he was not her father. He's the sort of man to want to repay Anne for rumors she could not help."

"You mean for me to believe that you knew all this, and that this is why you brought the maid to Severn?"

"No, I brought her to Severn to give him the wife he wants so that I may have the wife I want."

She could only look at him, unable to say a word. After a moment she recovered herself and turned away. "You could not have known what would happen, therefore you did not bring about this marriage, therefore my bargain with you is void." She started to walk away.

She walked about ten yards before she stopped. What would he do now? she wondered. Go to his brother and raise an army to attack the Peregrines? Challenge Severn to a combat to the death? Tell Severn who he was and cause a war?

She looked back and saw that he was walking in the opposite direction. She ran after him. "What are you planning now?"

"Planning? I plan? You have just told me that I am incapable of planning."

"What are you going to do to us?" she asked, teeth clenched.

"Do to you? Why should I do anything to you?"

"Because I'm not keeping my bargain. I mean," she said quickly to cover her error, "what are you going to do to my family because I won't marry you because your bargain was false?"

"I will do nothing," he said, smiling.

"Oh, I see. Your *brother* will do all. Do you go to him to plan war now? Will you use what you know against us?"

Tearle's eyes widened. "I would never tell my brother or anyone else that a Peregrine refused to fulfill a bargain. I would want no one to know that a person who bore the proud, ancient name of Peregrine was so lacking in honor."

"We Peregrines do *not* lack honor," she screeched at him.

"I know that to be true of one brother, but you . . . Tell me, is your brother Rogan like you or like Severn?"

She tightened her fists until the skin turned white. "We are *all* honorable. I am most honorable."

"If you say it, it must be true."

She wanted to kill him, to run a sword through him and watch him bleed. "I will marry you," she shouted.

"No," he answered, moving away.

She stepped in front of him. "No? But our bargain was for me to marry you if you got Anne to marry Severn."

"Severn did that himself. I did not have the pleasure of paddling the beautiful Lady Anne; he did that himself."

"But you told him Anne had played the jokes."

"What did that have to do with paddling her lovely bottom?"

The man was truly stupid, she thought. "If you had not told him, Severn wouldn't have known, and if he hadn't known, he wouldn't have gone to Hugh Marshall's Hall and taken Lady Anne—" She stopped.

"Yes? Are you saying that if I hadn't told Severn, he wouldn't be betrothed to Anne now?"

She refused to speak to him.

"So if I did have something to do with the betrothal taking place, then perhaps I did fulfill my part of the bargain."

She refused to speak, but she gave a tiny, curt nod.

"So it seems that I kept my end of the bargain, but you do not wish to keep yours. I understand now. Good day, Lady Zared." He smiled at her and started walking.

She caught his arm. "Where are you going?"

"Home to the evil brother you so fear." He smiled. "You seem concerned that I plan some revenge because you will not keep your word. It is my idea that breaking an oath is revenge enough. You must live with this on your conscience the rest of your life. Were it me, I could not bear myself, but then you are a

Peregrine, not a Howard, so perhaps your name means less to you than mine does to me. However, it is your choice. I will not force you to honor your own word. It is my belief that one has honor or one does not. In this case it seems that you do not. There-fore—"

"Cease!" Zared yelled at him, her hands to her ears. "I will marry you."

"I could not ask that of you, for you seem to doubt that I kept my end of our bargain."

"You kept it!" she hissed. "I have told you so. Do you wish me to shout it from the rooftops?"

"It might be pleasant were you to tell your brother you wish to marry me."

"*Wish* to marry you? You are the last person I would *wish* to marry."

He started to walk away.

"All right! I'll tell Severn I"—she swallowed—"that I wish to marry you. He would be suspicious otherwise."

"How kind of you," he said, smiling. "Shall I meet you in the church in two hours?"

"Two . . . two hours?"

"Of course, if you would rather not fulfill your part of the bargain, I can leave now. If you can live with your dishonor, I am sure I can."

"I will be there," she said, then she angrily turned on her heel and left him.

Tearle smiled at her back. He was *very* happy.

Chapter Eleven

Zared sat rigidly on her horse, trying not to look at the man who rode beside her, the man who was her husband. They had been married for two days, and she was still a virgin. She was glad, of course—glad that the Howard man had not touched her—but some part of her, some part deep within her, resented the fact that he had not made her his wife.

But then she had said a few things to him that seemed to make him quite angry.

After she had agreed to marry him he had lost no time in going to her brother to ask his permission for the marriage. Severn, still involved in his own marriage negotiations, had not wasted much time in thinking about giving his permission. He liked Tearle, and he thought Liana had sent him, so Severn quickly consented. Zared had been hurt at how little attention her brother had paid to the matter of her marriage. Severn had given her a perfunctory kiss on the forehead and gone back to counting coins with Hugh Marshall.

Zared hadn't said a word to Tearle as they walked to the church, and her mumbled replies to the priest in answer to his questions could hardly be heard. After the ceremony she had stood rigid as Tearle had bent and kissed her cheek. There were others in the church, and they were snickering, for it looked as though the big man was marrying a slim boy. Zared kept her head up, refusing Tearle's arm as they left the church and went to their waiting horses.

She mounted and then tried to still her growing fear. What did the Howard plan for her? Did he mean to take her back to his brother's place, to the place for which Peregrines had died? Would she turn her over to his brother to use against her brothers?

"I am not the devil," Tearle said as he mounted his horse. "You need not look at me as though I mean to torture you."

She hadn't answered him. She didn't ask him where he was leading her or what he planned to do with her. Of course, he had said that he was going to take her back to her brothers and that he would live with the Peregrines, but she was not sure she believed him.

They left the Marshall lands, taking only what they could carry on their horses, and outside the grounds they were met by three men—Howard men.

Zared knew then that she had been betrayed by him. She cursed herself, for she knew that her marriage was going to cause the deaths of her two remaining brothers. She rode beside the man who was her husband, but she did not speak to him. Several times he tried to talk to her, but she didn't answer him. It took all her strength and all her courage to hold back her tears. She tried to think of ways to kill the three knights who rode with them, but she didn't think she

180

could do it. She had to face what she knew was going to happen.

It was on their wedding night that all her fears and misery came out. The Howard man hired a room at an inn. At supper Zared sat silently by him. She did not speak, and she ate very little. Several times she glanced at Tearle and saw that he was looking at her with gentle eyes, almost as though he understood what she was feeling, but she wasn't going to let herself soften toward him.

When it was time to go to bed she braced herself, but instead, with a polite concern, he sent the landlady up with her. But Zared didn't undress. Instead, she sat rigidly on the bed and waited for him.

Some time later Tearle came to the room, and by the light of a single candle she stared at the bed hangings while she heard him undress. She heard the loud rustle of the straw-filled mattress as he climbed into bed beside her. And then he reached out to touch her.

At his touch all of Zared's fears and rage came leaping to the surface. Later she couldn't remember exactly what she had said, but she used words that would have earned her a beating had she used them around her brothers. She told the Howard man what she thought of his treachery, of his lies. She told him that the souls of the Peregrines would come back to haunt him. She called him every name she could think of and said that she would shed her own blood if he so much as touched her.

Days later she could still remember the look on his face. He seemed to be stunned by her accusations, stunned by her hatred. He got out of bed and pulled on his braes, then he turned to look at her.

"I was in error. I thought perhaps that—"

"You thought what?" she spat at him.

"I thought that we could be a man and a woman. But I seem to be wrong."

"We are a Peregrine and a Howard," she said. "How could we be anything else? Did you expect me to love you because a few words were spoken by a priest? Did you expect to wipe out three generations of hatred with a few moments in a church? I told you I hated you. Did you not believe me?"

He was silent for some time as he looked at her. "I do not think I did. I have had . . . feelings for you since I first saw you. It was vain of me to think that those feelings would ever be returned." He pulled on his linen shirt, then gathered his other clothes over his arm and went to the door. "I will see you in the morning," he said, then he left the room.

For a moment Zared was too stunned to speak. She sat on the bed and stared at the closed door. What manner of man was he? Had a woman spoken to one of the Peregrine men as Zared had just spoken to Tearle . . . well, her brothers would have done just what Severn did to Lady Anne. But when she had cursed the Howard man he did not return her rage but instead left his bride on her wedding night.

She didn't sleep much that night, and in the morning she went downstairs to where the Howard men were already waiting for her. Her husband did not help her onto her horse as he usually tried to do, nor did he speak to her during the day.

That night they stayed at another inn, and he did not so much as come to her room. Zared was too tired to stay awake, but when she awoke in the morning she tried to stamp down the resentment that she felt. She rode beside him and found his silence as annoying as she'd once found his constant talking.

"Where are we going?" she asked, and the words came out more belligerently than she meant them.

He gave her a hard look. There were dark circles under his eyes and whisker stubble on his cheeks. Had Zared not been so caught up in her own misery she would have wondered at the look of him. She had no way of knowing that Tearle had spent the previous two nights alone and awake, drinking and cursing himself. He had congratulated himself in being so clever in persuading the woman to marry him, but he'd not thought beyond the ceremony. Perhaps he'd been foolish enough to believe that after the words were said she'd turn to him in love. But the mere ceremony of marriage had not changed her. Even knowing her as he did, he had been unprepared for the vehemence with which she had attacked him on their wedding night. He had won her, true, but what had he won? A woman who hated him with all her heart and soul.

"I am taking you to my brother so that he can throw you in the dungeon and torture you. I am going to allow him to use you in his war against your brothers. I, like he, have a great desire to own that decaying castle of yours. It is my greatest wish to see your brother Severn dead and to be married to a woman who hates me."

She looked away from him. "Where are we going?" she asked in a much softer tone.

"To my house. I do not often stay with my brother. The house was owned by my mother."

She gave him a look of surprise.

"Does it surprise you that I had a mother? Or have you been taught that all Howards come directly from hell?"

"I have never thought about your mother. Your brother starved mine to death in a siege when I was but a child."

Tearle looked away from her. "Yes, Oliver would do that."

183

She didn't speak for a while, and then she asked him about his mother, saying that she thought he had grown up in France. He told her of living with his mother in France but added that every other year she would come back to the place that had been her father's house to see to the people on her land. Tearle would travel with her.

There was another long period of silence, then he looked at her. "Do you know why I wanted to marry you?"

"No," she answered honestly. "I do not know."

"Part of the reason is that I want to end this feud. It has gone on too long. Unlike you, I have not been raised with this hatred between the Howards and the Peregrines. I know that there is a dispute about who should have the title and the land. My brother has no children, and from looking at him, I would guess that he has not long to live."

"Then you will be the duke," Zared said softly.

"Yes, I will become the duke. I thought that if I were to marry a Peregrine and a son were to come from that union, then the child could one day inherit the title and the lands. That way both the Howards and the Peregrines would own what they both want."

"No!" she said sharply. "It is Peregrine land. It has always been Peregrine land. My brother Rogan should be the duke, and his son should rule after him. No Howard should own the land or the title."

He arched an eyebrow at her. "It would be your son who became the duke. Would you not want that?"

There was no decision for her to make. "My son would not deserve the title. Nor do you. It belongs to my brother Rogan." She looked at him. "You married me to ensure the title for yourself and your son?"

At that Tearle sighed and shook his head. "Will you forever believe the worst of me? I am not my brother. I saw a way of ending the feud, and yet you believe only that I want power. What can I do to prove to you my worth?"

"When you inherit, turn it all over to my brother."

Tearle's eyes widened. "Your grandmother was never legally married. It is only legend that they were married. Your family is a lot of bastards. Even the king declared it so."

"That's not true!" she yelled at him. "My family is the true owner of all that your brother holds. Why do you think he fights us so hard if it isn't true?"

"It might have to do with your brothers killing my brothers," Tearle said softly, then he paused a moment. "If our marriage and our producing a child will not settle the feud, then I see no reason for our being married."

"Nor do I," she answered, looking straight at him.

Tearle looked at her a while, and then he smiled. "I have done foolish things in my life, but nothing like this. Lady Zared," he said, sweeping off his cap, "I apologize for having forced you into marriage with me. I apologize for thinking that I could make you care for me. I see now that I was a fool. The Peregrine hatred is stronger than the Howard love. Since there seems to be no way to compromise in this feud—since both sides ask for complete surrender—then I suggest that we end this marriage."

"H-how can we do that?"

"I shall petition the king. I am sure that with a little land deeded to him he will allow the marriage to be annulled. Then we can all go back to where we were. Your people can spy on my people, and mine can spy on yours. Does that suit you?"

"I'm not sure," she said hesitantly.

"Not sure? What alternative is there? You hate me, and you'd rather die than allow me to touch you, so there can be no hope of children. For myself, I would like to have a few brats. My proposal is that we stay at my mother's house until we have heard from the king. I do not think that I would like to stay with you and this formidable brother of yours, nor do I think that you would like to stay with my brother."

"No!" she said quickly. "I don't want to stay with the Howards."

"Then it is settled. That is, if this is all right with you. I no longer want to be accused of forcing you—of forcing you to marry me, of forcing you to go to bed with me. As you said, you'd rather mate with a . . . what was it you said? A three-legged hunchback with the mark of the devil on his cheek. Do I have it right?"

Zared looked away, her face red. She had said many things on their wedding night and didn't remember half of them. She would have said *anything* that night to keep him from touching her. She nodded.

"Good, at last we seem to agree on something. The sooner we get the marriage annulled, the sooner we can get away from each other, and the sooner I can find myself a few willing women." He smiled in a way that Zared had not seen before. His whole face softened. "At the tournament there was the prettiest little green-eyed blonde. She had hair . . ." He stopped and cleared his throat. "Well, then, it's settled. Shall we clasp hands on the bargain?"

Zared took his hand and quickly and firmly clasped it, then she looked away, frowning. She had what she wanted, but for some reason she wasn't happy at all.

The sight of the house owned by her husband's mother made Zared even more unhappy. It was a house—not a fortress protected by high walls, but a beautiful, large house made of pink stone. There were

186

trees in the large park surrounding it, and she saw deer roaming under the trees. Everything was clean and tidy and utterly beautiful.

Part of her said that the house was useless in defense, that it could be taken by anyone who wanted it, but another part loved the beauty of the place.

When they rode up to the courtyard their horses' hooves clattering on the cobblestones, people came out of the house to greet them. There were three older women, all exquisitely dressed in brocade, their head-dresses sparkling with jewels.

Tearle introduced her to the ladies who were kind enough and polite enough to make no reaction to her boy's clothes. Zared had planned to dismount and curtsy to them, but she bent only a little before Tearle caught her arm and held her upright. He told her that the lovely women were to be her maids, that they were to care for her just as they had for his mother. She was to go with them, and he would see her at supper.

As Zared looked at the women, looked at their beautiful gowns, she felt something akin to fear. Until that moment she hadn't considered what it was going to mean to her life to dress as a woman. She had been so involved with her anger at her husband that she had not considered the issue. She thought of wearing a silk gown and felt some excitement, some part of her wanting to feel the fabric against her skin, but another part of her was terrified. With longing she looked back at the Howard men. They were no doubt going to the stables or to the men's quarters to drink beer and brag to one another about the tournament. How she would have liked to have gone with them! She would feel more comfortable with those bragging, belching, scratching men than with the ladies.

She looked from the men to Tearle and saw that he

was watching her. For the first time she didn't look at him as though he were her enemy; he was the most familiar person to her. She gave him a little smile.

He didn't return the smile and seemed to be puzzled by hers.

"This way, Lady Zared," one of the women said to her.

Zared gave Tearle a look of pleading, silently asking him to help her, to allow her to go with the men.

Gradually he seemed to understand her meaning, and he smiled at her. "I will come to you soon," he said.

The words made Zared blush, for they sounded as though she couldn't bear to be parted from him. She put her nose in the air and followed the three ladies. She'd show him that she didn't need him.

Upstairs it was worse than she had feared. The women seemed to think that she was dressed in boy's clothes for protection and that she was dying to put on a silk gown. They apologized for not having made her room ready.

Zared looked at the large oak-paneled room and wondered what could have been done to make it more ready. There was no room in her family's castle that was half as nice. She went to the big four-poster bed and tentatively touched the hangings.

"Shall we help you bathe and dress, my lady?" one of the women asked.

Zared did not want to show her ignorance. "No, I . . . I will do it myself." She saw the women look from one to the other and knew that she had done wrong.

"Very well, then, we shall have your bath sent to you."

Zared gave a silent nod, and the women left the room. Within minutes four men carried the big wooden tub into the room, and women followed with hot water, soap, and towels.

The bathwater felt good, and Zared was glad that Liana had shown her enough about bathing so that she wouldn't look to the Howard maids to be more of a fool than she already did. She soaped her body and her hair, then ducked under the water to rinse. When the water was cool she stepped out of the tub onto the cold stone floor and picked up the drying towel. It was of a finer quality than she was used to, and it was warm from the fire. For a moment she buried her face in its softness and smelled it. No matter how much her home castle had been cleaned, she thought, it could never smell as good as this house and everything in it.

When she was dry she looked for her clothes, but they were nowhere to be found. Instead, on the bed was a clean linen shift and a long, soft velvet robe. She put the shift on, then slipped her arms into the robe. It was of a deep blue with tiny gold fleurs-de-lis embroidered on it. She hugged her arms about her and closed her eyes for a moment as she rubbed her cheek against the lush softness.

At that moment there was a soft knock on the door, and then one of the maids entered. Zared thought her name was Margaret.

"My lady," the woman said, and it took Zared a moment to realize that the woman was speaking to her. "Lord Tearle asks that you join him below for supper."

Zared opened her mouth to say that she would be there soon, for she was quite hungry, but then she realized that she had no clothes. "I would like my clothes returned to me," she said as haughtily as she could manage.

"If you would be so good as to tell me where your

baggage is, I will see that your garments are sent to you straight away."

There was nothing to reply to that, for Zared had no baggage. "Tell him"—she wasn't sure what to call her husband—"that I am not hungry and will not eat with him."

"Then I will help you into your nightdress."

Zared knew that she didn't have any nightclothes either. In her family night apparel had been an unnecessary expense. Her brother bought her a suit of clothes, and she wore them night and day until they either wore out or she was too tall for them. "No," she told the maid, "I will see to myself." She breathed a sigh of relief when the woman left her alone.

With a sigh she looked at the bed. There didn't seem much else to do except to go to bed with her stomach rumbling. She was startled when, a few minutes later, four men came and took the tub of dirty water away.

Moments later, when she was standing by the fire warming her hands, running them across the velvet of her robe, another knock sounded. This time, again before she could speak, the door opened, and her husband entered.

"You carry this too far," he said to her. "Do you hate my company so much that you will starve yourself?"

"Why, no," she said in surprise. "I do not—"

"Ah, then you plan to have all your meals alone in your room."

"I did not request a meal in here." The truth was that she didn't know that she could request a meal brought to her room. It was not something that had ever been done at her brothers' house.

Tearle went to her and put his hands on her shoulders. "You cannot do this. You cannot starve yourself. If it is my company that you so despise, then

I will see that you have your meals here alone. No one will bother you, but below I have music and entertainment. Can I not persuade you to sit with me at supper?"

She gave him a look of disgust. "I have no clothes, you fool. What am I to wear while I sit at your table? Those maids of yours have taken my clothes."

It seemed to take him a moment to understand what she was saying, then he smiled at her. He turned away and went to a large carved chest against one wall. "You should have asked. I had you put in this room because it was my mother's. Her clothes are here."

Zared stood back as he rummaged in the chest and withdrew a gown of dark reddish-brown velvet. There was fur of a darker brown on it, and she very much wanted to touch it, but she held back. "How could I ask your maids for clothes? Am I to let them know that I am a pauper? My sister-in-law came to my brother with wagons full of dresses." She wanted to let him know that if she didn't have the proper clothes, she at least knew what she was supposed to have.

Tearle saw the pride in her face. "I will tell them that all you had was lost in a flood. Yes, that you had eight—no, twelve—wagons full of the finest clothes from France, but they were all lost, so now you must make do with my mother's old things." He held out the dress to her. "It is indeed old, but I think it might be a near fit, and the color will suit you."

Zared put out her hand to touch the fur that edged the neck of the dress. "Mink," she said, and she looked up at him and smiled.

"You'll wear the dress?"

She could only nod.

"Then I will call a maid to help you with your hair and help you dress."

"No!" she said, looking down at her hands. "I will

dress myself." She didn't want to look like a fool in front of the maids. She knew that they would laugh when they saw that she had no idea how to put the dress on or what to do with her hair. Zared had heard Liana's maids ask Liana hundreds of questions about braids and headdresses and ribbons and stockings, and Zared knew that she would know none of the answers.

Tearle put the gown on the bed, then took her hand and led her to sit down on a bench before the fire. He took a beautiful tortoiseshell comb from the top of a small table and gently began to comb Zared's hair.

"I can do this."

He pushed her hands away. "You and I will not be together long. Do not deny me what pleasure I can find."

She didn't answer him but closed her eyes as he gently combed the tangles from her hair. As a child she had never combed her hair; only when she grew older and began to notice the handsome young men who trained with her brothers had she taken a comb to her hair, and then she had merely dragged it through, tearing at the knots.

"Such a beautiful color," Tearle said. "And as soft as thistledown." He ran his hands up the back of her neck, then over her scalp, massaging it. "There is no silk to compare with your hair."

When he stopped caressing her head she opened her eyes and saw him standing between her and the fire. There was a warmth in his eyes that she hadn't seen before. "It's only hair," she said gruffly, trying to hide the fact that his words had pleased her.

"Will you get dressed now?"

Zared looked at the gown lying on the bed. Surely she could figure it out by herself. Before she could decide what to do Tearle came up behind her and put his hands on her shoulders and began sliding the robe off of her. Instinctively she clutched it to her.

"I will play the lady's maid tonight," he said. "I will help you with the fastenings." He smiled. "Unless you'd rather I called Margaret."

"No, I . . ." She swallowed. "Perhaps I could have supper in this room."

"Zared," he said sternly, "you are going to have to leave this room at some time. You cannot stay in here forever wearing only that one robe. If you do not want me in here, I can call a maid."

He was her enemy but at least he was familiar to her. She had spent days in his company. She released her hold on the robe, and he took the robe from her. Zared snatched the gown off the bed and held it in front of her body.

"Now," he said with the sound of efficiency in his voice, "over the head. No, not that way, the other way. Here, turn this around so the front is this way."

Zared held the gown to her, clutching it so that it did not gape across her bosom. Never in her life had she gone into the light of day with her breasts unbound, and putting on the dress—her breasts without their painful binding—made her feel rather strange.

"Hold still," Tearle said from behind her as he drew the laces down the back of the dress tightly together.

Zared was used to tight lacing, but it usually covered her breasts. This tightness was lower, pulling in her waist. She looked down and saw that her breasts were quite exposed in the deep V of the neckline. She put her hand up to cover herself.

Tearle finished with the lacing then turned her around to look at her. "I think it is a perfect fit. My mother was always very slender." He stepped back to look at her. "Put your hand down. Go on, hands to your sides."

Zared obeyed him, but she didn't look at him until his silence was more than she could bear. Slowly she lifted her eyes to look at him. He wore an odd expression that seemed to make her body grow warmer.

Tearle cleared his throat and dragged his eyes away from her. "Shall we go down to dinner?" He held out his arm for her to take.

Zared took two steps toward him and promptly fell face forward. She would have hit the floor except that Tearle caught her.

"It's the train," he said.

Zared looked behind her and saw that the dress had a great deal of fabric flowing out the back of it. How, she wondered, did one walk with that dragging?

"I think you throw it over your arm," Tearle said, and when Zared gave him a look of disbelief he tried to demonstrate. "I think you do it like this."

She watched as he took a few mincing steps, then made a sweeping bend as though reaching for something. He flipped the imaginary object over his arm. Zared did everything that she could to keep from laughing. *This* was the Black Knight? This was the mysterious knight who felled all comers?

She gave a little frown. "I still do not understand. Will you show me again?"

"I told you that I'm not completely sure how it's done, but the ladies seem to do it with ease. Now walk like this."

She watched as he did his imitation of a lady taking tiny steps.

"Then bend—do this gracefully—pick up the train, and drop it over your arm. There, that wasn't so difficult, was it?"

"I shall try it." Zared took two steps, trying to imitate his walk, then she bent and purposely missed catching the fabric of the train. She looked up at him. "I think you will have to show me again."

He sighed. "All right, but watch carefully this time. Walk. Bend. Lift. Drop." He demonstrated each word, then turned back to her. "Now you try it."

Again Zared made a mess of trying to toss the train over her arm, and she managed to conceal her smile at his frown.

He moved to stand behind her, then put one hand about her waist. "Walk," he ordered, then he bent forward, forcing her to bend also. He took her right hand in his. "Now pick up the damned thing and throw it over your arm."

Zared again managed to drop the train. She stepped away from him and gave him an innocent look. "I seem to be a fool at this. Perhaps you should try on the gown and show me that way."

The look on his face made Zared's laughter erupt.

"Why, you little minx," he said, lunging for her.

With a motion that was almost expert Zared grabbed the train and flung it over her arm before she began to run from him. At first she began to run in earnest, immediately making for the door, but he reached it before she did and put his arm across it so that she couldn't open it. For a moment she was afraid of him. Had she teased her brothers as she had him, making fun of their masculine abilities, they would have made her pay. But when she looked into the eyes of the man she saw that he was amused by her.

She ran from him, holding her train with one hand and slipping around the bedpost with the other. At first it seemed odd to her that she knew he could catch her but that he didn't. She ran toward a table and put it between them, and when she dodged one way he blocked her exit, so she went the other way, and he blocked that way, too. She smiled, and then she laughed and moved back and forth as quickly as possible. But he was always faster.

Zared pushed a chair to the floor and made a leap across it, and he reached for her, but she ran before he could catch her. She ran toward the window seat, and when he made a lunge at her she gave a squeal of laughter and jumped to the floor. He was inches behind her, and twice he caught her, but his hands were loose on her body, and she could easily escape him.

By the time she jumped on the bed she was breathless from laughter and from running, and from something else that she didn't quite understand.

He caught her on the bed. He rolled her about, tickling her until she was dying of laughter, his hands running up and down her body.

"Do you beg me for forgiveness?" he asked, his hands at her ribs. He stopped moving his fingers as he looked down at her. She was on her back on the bed while he sat over her, his thighs straddling her hips.

"Never!" she said, but she was smiling. "I will never beg forgiveness from a Howard."

She had meant no harm by what she said—she hadn't even thought of the meaning of her words—but his face lost its good humor, and he moved off of her. She caught his arm before he left the bed. "I meant no . . ." She didn't know how to finish her sentence.

He sat on the edge of the bed for a moment, then he turned and looked at her. Zared held her breath. Actually, she thought, he wasn't a bad-looking man at all. She smiled at him.

He grinned at her, and Zared thought that perhaps he was the opposite of bad-looking.

He grinned more broadly and made a lunge across

the bed for her. "You'll be the death of me," he said as he caught her in his arms.

Zared squealed, her arms together, then stopped moving and looked up at him. His eyes were soft, and she didn't understand the expression.

"You're very pretty, you know." He tucked a strand of hair behind her ear.

"I'm not," she said softly. "I look like a boy."

At that he gave a snort of laughter and lay down beside her, then pulled her into his arms, her back to his front. "I never saw anyone look less like a boy."

"But no one even questions that I—"

"That shows how stupid people are."

She relaxed against him. No one had ever held her like that. There was no physical affection between her and her brothers, and there were few women in her brothers' home. Some part of her brain told her to move away from him, but it felt so good to be held that she didn't move.

His big hand smoothed the hair off of her face. Her hair was still damp from washing, and she felt him bury his face in it. She closed her eyes for a moment.

"You're not beautiful like Anne Marshall," he said softly. "You're more like . . . a two-day-old colt or a pup."

She pushed at his arms, but he didn't release her. "A horse? I look like a horse? Or is it a dog?"

"You know very well what I mean," he answered, and he put his face further into her hair, smelling it. His lips reached her neck and kissed her a few times.

"Mmmm. I understand," she said, her eyes closed. "Men like Anne Marshall. My brother did. He liked her even after all the terrible things she did to him." She moved her head so that he could have better access to her neck. He was placing little nibbling kisses down it. "I wager that you wish you could have had Lady Anne."

Tearle stopped kissing her and pulled her closer to him. "She was offered to me, but I turned her down."

Zared was astonished by that, and she wanted to look into his eyes to see if he was lying. She turned over in his arms so that they were facing each other. "You would not have turned down Lady Anne. She is beautiful, and she is rich. Any man who was offered her would have taken her."

"I was, but I did not." Again he began to touch the hair at her temple. "What fine red stuff this is. Like a spider's web."

"Spiders' webs are sticky. Why would you have turned down Anne Marshall?"

"Because I did not want her. She has a sharp tongue on her, and she is much too clever to live with."

"But what does that matter? Severn will not care for her tongue. He will make her obey."

"As your older brother Rogan has made his wife obey?"

She started to ask him how he knew of her family, but then she remembered that he was a Howard, and that his family spied on hers. But she also remembered that he had been out drinking with her brother Severn, and Zared knew that there were no gossips like men with a keg of beer to share. Instead of cursing him, as was her first inclination, she smiled. "Did Severn tell you of our brother?"

"In detail. He does not know whether to hate his sister-in-law or love her." Tearle ran his hand down her shoulder, his eyes lowered. "However did you hide all of that under your boy's clothes?"

Zared looked down at her breasts, which were pushing out above the velvet of her dress. She put her hand up to cover herself and at the same time started to move away from him, but he held her where she was.

He moved her hand away. "If I cannot touch, at least allow me to look my fill."

She felt herself blushing, and her body tingled all the way down to her toes. "Cannot touch?" she said, her voice catching.

"If our marriage is to end, if I ask the king to annul our marriage, then I feel that I must leave you a virgin. If you are to get another husband, then I would think that he'd want the pleasure of taking your virginity."

"Oh," she said. "Of course." She couldn't breathe very well because his hand was running over the exposed skin of her breasts.

"I hope he is a good lover to you."

"Who?"

"The man you marry. The man who has the right to give you children. The man who has the right to take his pleasure with your beautiful body."

"I am not beautiful. You have just said so. And you said that I was not clever."

"But you have never heard me say that you were not the most desirable female I have ever met in my life, have you?"

"No, I have not." Her voice was very soft. His fingers were slipping down the front of her gown.

"In all the French court I saw no woman more desirable than you."

"A-and how am I d-desirable?" Her eyes were closed. She could smell the strong masculine scent of him, feel the heat of his body so near hers.

"There is an innocence about you. Too many women know all there is to know about men and women before they spend the night together. But you, you are an unmarked slate. A man may teach you what he wants you to know."

Her eyes flew open, and she stiffened in his arms. "I know how children are conceived," she said with some anger in her voice. "I am no ignorant country girl. I may not be a clever beauty like your Lady Anne, but I know a great deal about men and women."

He gave her an infuriating smile. "You know only of the act. You know nothing of what goes before."

"Before what?"

He ran his hand over her bare shoulder. "There is what happens between a man and woman that produces children, and there is lovemaking. A world of difference exists between the two of them."

She was still feeling hurt by his saying that she knew nothing. "Perhaps you should tell me the difference, and I will tell you if you are correct."

He gave a little laugh. "Ah, my little falcon, would that I could show you the difference, but there is my sanity to consider. I think we have had enough of this and that we had better go to dinner."

He dropped his arms from around her and started to move to the other side of the bed, but she caught his shoulder.

"You would tell Lady Anne, wouldn't you? She would be clever enough to understand you, wouldn't she?"

He looked over his shoulder at her. "I imagine that Anne knows all there is to know of what goes on between men and women. If your brother does not please her on their wedding night, Anne will no doubt complain to him and to anyone else who will listen."

Zared moved away from him and leaned back on the pillows, her arms crossed over her breast. "Then I shall complain also. When I have a husband who takes me to bed, if he does not please me, I shall tell him so."

He turned back to smile at her. "And to what will you compare his lovemaking? To your other lovers?"

"Why no, I . . ." Her eyes widened. "Do you think the Lady Anne has had other lovers? Severn will not like that."

"Your hotheaded brother may kill her if she isn't a virgin, and Hugh Marshall will no doubt praise him for it."

She didn't understand at all. If Anne Marshall was a virgin, too, then how could she know so much of lovemaking? Zared wasn't sure what the man was saying, but she knew that she felt insulted. Her brothers had always treated her like a child, and this man was treating her like a child as well.

She turned her head away from him and started to get off the bed. She was not going to humiliate herself further by asking more questions.

"Zared," he whispered, pulling her to him.

She started to fight him, struggling against him. She didn't like the way he smirked at her and talked of other women.

He pinned her to the bed with his big body, but her arms were free, and she began to beat him on the back and shoulders. "Release me!" she demanded. "I hate you. I hate having you near me."

He caught her head in his hands and held her steady while he began to kiss her lips. She kept them closed for a moment, but the sensation was very pleasant, and she couldn't resist him for long. He nibbled at her lower lip, and the tip of his tongue very sweetly ran along the crevice between her lips. He kissed her eyes and her cheeks.

It was as though no one had ever touched her before—and in truth very few people had—and she was hungry for physical contact. She forgot that he was supposed to be her enemy, and she opened her mouth to his. It was she who turned her head sideways so that she could kiss him more deeply. Her arms stopped beating on his broad back, and they went around him to hold him as tightly as possible.

Her life had been spent in very physical ways. She was no prim and proper miss who had spent her youth behind an embroidery frame. Instead she had grown up on the back of a horse with a sword in her hand. She was used to exuberance and a great deal of movement.

When she felt desire pouring through her she acted on it with all the enthusiasm that she had been allowed to express in her life. She put her tongue in his mouth and wrapped her legs about his hips, locking her ankles together.

When he seemed to want to pull away from her she went with him, hanging onto him when he rolled over so that she was on top of him.

Tearle had to take her by the shoulders and pull her away from him. He lay on his back looking up at her, and there was an expression of amazement on his face. "Where did you learn that?" he said, and there was barely concealed rage in his voice.

It took her a moment to remember who she was, where she was, and who he was. She was on top of him, her legs straddling his hips, the position he had taken with her earlier. It felt good to be on top of him, rather as though she had wrestled him to the ground and was holding him there. "Learn what?" She smiled down at him.

He did not return her smile but instead threw her to the other side of the bed and got off of it. "Some man must have taught you that. Was it Colbrand? When you were with him in that pond did you do more than bathe him?"

She was taken aback by his words, and she could feel anger rising in her, but then she relaxed against the pillows. "He taught me nothing. I know what I know."

At that he caught her about the waist, pulled her off the bed, and stood her before him. "You may not want to be my wife, but if I so much as catch you looking at another man I will—" He broke off.

"You will what?" she whispered.

He released her and stood there looking at her for a moment. "Put your shoes on and come downstairs. Supper grows cold."

When she was alone in the room Zared hugged herself and twirled around the room, the heavy velvet skirt whirling about her.

"You will have supper now, my lord?"

Tearle gave a start and looked up from his goblet of wine. "Oh, Margaret, I didn't see you. Has she come down yet?"

"No," Margaret said slowly. "I imagine that she will find it difficult to dress herself."

"You do not miss much, do you?" He smiled at the woman who had come to his mother when they were both girls. Tearle's mother had died in Margaret's arms.

"I could not help notice that you are mad in love with her."

"She hates me," he said gloomily.

Margaret nearly laughed aloud at that. "The girl who gave you such a look of longing in the courtyard does not hate you."

"You have not heard her speak to me. Ah, sometimes she desires me, if I kiss her enough and tell her that she is pretty, but she desires that from any handsome man." He snorted. "She desires that even from me, who she thinks is ugly." He looked up at Margaret. "She is a Peregrine."

Margaret's face lost its laughter. She went to Tearle and put her hand on his shoulder. "You were always a good boy. That you'd marry this boy-girl to settle a feud is very noble of you."

"I tricked her into marrying me," he snapped. "And I didn't marry her to settle a feud. I married her because I wanted her."

"Ah, could you not just have bedded her?"

Tearle didn't speak for a while. "Perhaps." He didn't say more but just sat there looking at his wine goblet.

Margaret sat on the chair next to him. He was as near to being a son as she was ever going to have. "I have heard about these Peregrines. Are they as rough as I have heard?"

"Worse."

"Then perhaps some softness in the girl's life would do her good. Perhaps soft music and soft words would win her. Perhaps if you let her see you as you are, she would come to love you."

"I have told her I will petition the king for an annulment. I mean to keep my word."

"Did you tell her when you would send the messenger?"

Tearle smiled at her. "No, I did not. But I did say I would give her an annulment, which means I am not to touch her."

Margaret laughed. "Do you not know that there is much more sensuous pleasure than what goes on in the bed?"

Tearle gave her a look to say that she was half mad.

"The girl moved from me when I but meant to touch her arm," Margaret said. "And she looked at my gown with lust in her eyes. For all her boy's clothes, I think she hungers for what a woman has and wears. I think that roses might win your lady."

"Roses?"

"And music and tales of love and silk and gentle kisses placed behind her ear."

Tearle looked at the woman for a long while, his mind racing with his thoughts. He remembered the way Zared had reacted to his kisses. Perhaps she did not hate him as much as she said she did. If he had not allowed his jealousy to overcome him, what might have happened? Perhaps it was possible to win her with a bit of courting. He smiled at Margaret.

Chapter Twelve

Nothing that Zared had ever experienced had prepared her for life in the Howard house. At supper she sat at a clean table and ate delicious food, and her new husband treated her as though she were fragile and precious.

The calmness of the servants, the general peace of the whole house was new and interesting to her. In her own home it wasn't unusual for her brothers' knights to come storming into rooms demanding that someone come and settle a fight. Her brother Rogan regularly slammed his battle ax into tables to make a point. But at Tearle's the questions were whether she had enough wine or whether her soup was hot enough.

After supper a handsome young man came and played a lute while he looked at Zared with liquid eyes.

"What is he saying?" she asked, since the man was singing in French.

Tearle looked at her across a silver wine goblet. The whole room glowed with the light from the fireplace. "He is singing of your loveliness, of your beauty, and of the beautiful way you move your hands."

Zared looked startled. "My hands?" Her brothers had always complained that she had no strength in her hands, that she could barely lift a sword. She held her hands in front of her and looked at them.

Tearle took one in his own and kissed her fingertips. "Beautiful hands."

"What else is he saying?" she asked, looking away from her husband to the handsome young man.

"He says only what I have told him to, for I wrote the song," Tearle answered, an edge to his voice.

She looked back at him in wonder. "You? You can write songs in another language?"

"Songs and poetry. I can play the songs as well. Should I demonstrate?"

"If you can write, then can you read? Liana can read. Could you read me a story?"

Tearle stopped kissing her hand and smiled at her, then signaled the man to leave them. Another soft command from him and a servant brought five books into the room. "Now, what shall you hear?" When Zared looked blank, Tearle smiled. "I know. I shall read you *Héloise and Abelard*. That should appeal to you."

An hour later Zared was sitting in front of the fire trying not to cry, for the story he had read to her was very sad.

"Come now, it happened long ago, and there is no need to cry." When she kept sniffing he pulled her into his lap and stroked her hair. "I did not know you had such a soft heart."

"I do not think you have any heart at all," she snapped.

He kissed her forehead, then, still holding her, he stood and began to carry her up the stairs. "I think it is time you were in bed."

Zared snuggled against him. He was still her enemy, of course, but at the thought of spending the night with him her skin began to tingle. But when they entered the room he kissed her forehead and left her alone.

She didn't know whether to be glad or enraged. In the end she was just puzzled. She undressed and went to bed and lay awake for a while, thinking about the odd man she was married to. She knew of his idea to keep her a virgin until he could petition the king for an annulment, but how could he keep his word? Her brothers would not have allowed a wife to remain a virgin no matter what the woman said. The more she thought the more puzzled she became. The Howard man was not like any man she had met before.

She woke to find him sitting in her room, a rose on the pillow beside her. He helped her dress in riding clothes, a shorter skirt with no train, but he did no more than kiss her neck as she held her hair up for him to fasten the ties at the back of the gown.

They went down the stairs together, and there were horses waiting and servants bearing trays of fresh bread and cheese and goblets of wine. They rode together, and he talked to her not of war or weapons, but of the beauty of the day. He pointed out pretty birds and once even imitated a bird's call.

They stopped at a lake, and he asked her to go swimming with him. Zared said that she did not like to swim and that she didn't really like the water. She sat under a tree and watched as Tearle stripped down to his loincloth and slowly walked to the water. She looked at him for as long as she liked without his watching her. Over the past few weeks each time she looked at him he seemed to have grown larger. She remembered thinking that he was a puny man, a weak man. There had been that time when she had first met him and thought that he had nearly been killed by a slight knife wound. Then she had thought him to be very weak.

But she looked at him and saw how broad his shoulders were, how thick the muscles in his legs were. There were scars on his body, scars just as her brothers had, scars made by weapons. She wondered if he had been injured in battle or if all the scars had come from practice or tournaments.

She leaned back against the tree and watched him swim. It was all a waste of time, of course. She should be training as she usually did, she thought, but then she smiled. Her training had always been to prepare her for fighting the Howards, but she had married a Howard and was watching him swim in a pool.

He lay on his back in the water, and Zared could not help but notice the deep muscles on his chest. He wasn't as big as her brothers, of course, but he was certainly larger than Colbrand.

She was lazily watching him as he raised his arm to wave at her. She smiled at him, then saw him dive under the water. She sat still and waited for him to resurface. A minute went by, and she sat up. He had not come to the surface.

She waited a few seconds more, and still she did not see him. She got up and walked to the edge of the lake. "Howard!" she called, but there was no answer. She called louder. "Howard!" Still no answer, and still no sign of him.

She didn't think about what she did. She ran into the water. She could swim, her brothers had seen to that, but she had never liked doing it. But she didn't think about like or dislike, she just reacted.

She took a deep breath and dived under the water, her eyes wide as she looked for him. It didn't take her long. He was easy to see, as he was curled under the water, his face against his knees.

Her lungs were already beginning to hurt, but she stayed under long enough to pull him up, putting her arm under his chin and dragging him to the surface of the water. She heard no intake of breath as he came to the surface; in fact, a quick glance at him showed him to be as pale as death.

She swam to the edge of the pool with him, then had to drag him to the shore. He was as heavy as a draft horse, and she had to strain every muscle to get him onto land.

When he was on land, his lower half still in the water, she looked down at him, as pale and cold as death. What should she do? she wondered. "Howard!" she yelled into his face. "Howard!"

He didn't respond. She straddled his stomach and began to slap his cheeks, but it had no effect on him. "Damn you, Tearle," she said, and there were tears of frustration in her voice. "Don't you dare die just when I have begun to think you are worth something."

On her knees she leaned over him, put her hands to his cheeks, and shook his face.

At that Tearle spewed a fountain of water from his mouth. Zared, her face dripping, leaned back from him and stared in astonishment.

Tearle opened his eyes and smiled at her. "I could always hold my breath longer than anyone."

She knew then that he had been playing a joke on her. She sat down hard on his stomach, but he didn't so much as flinch. "You are a horrible man," she said, and she struck him on the chest with her fists.

He caught her fists and rolled over on top of her. "You were worried about me."

"I was not. I only cared that your death might cause a war between my family and yours. Not that that brother of yours deserves the name of family. I care only for my brothers and Liana and maybe Rogan's son, but not for you." He had her pinned to the ground, her hands above her head. She knew that she wanted him to kiss her. She had indeed been frightened for his safety, but she didn't want to admit that to him.

He rubbed his cold, wet face against hers, which was also cold and wet, then he nuzzled her neck. When he released her hands she put her arms around him— and when she did that he rolled off of her.

Zared frowned, for somehow she felt rejected.

"You will freeze if you do not get dry," he said, and there was a smugness in his tone that angered her. It was as though he had wanted to know something and had found it out.

He stood, then pulled her up with him, and when she wouldn't look at him he put his hand under her chin. "Would it be so awful if a Peregrine came to care for a Howard?"

"It cannot happen," she said with as much sincerity as she could muster, but even to her the words sounded false.

He laughed, then picked her up in his arms and whirled her about until she was dizzy. She clung to him, and before long she, too, was laughing.

He stopped twirling her and held her close to him. "Come, my little enemy, and let's get dry. There's a crofter's cottage nearby. Let's see if they can feed us."

She stood by while he dressed, and she allowed him to help her on her horse when they left the lake.

After that things between them began to change. Zared wasn't sure what it was that changed, but she knew that something had. It was as though her attempt to rescue the man had answered a question for him and had freed him from whatever had been holding him back.

She didn't know what he was really like, for she had known him only under the most unusual circumstances, but after that afternoon at the lake she sensed that he began to relax around her. No longer was he afraid of whatever he had been afraid of before, and she began to see the man he really was.

He was as unlike her brothers as night and day. Whereas her brothers tried to get as much work out of each day as they could, Tearle seemed to want to get as much pleasure out of each day as was possible. He trained, just as her brothers did, but he didn't train for many hours at a time, and he had a lighthearted spirit about his training. He laughed when he could. He wagered with his men and paid them when he lost. There was no life-or-death feeling to his training.

At first Zared was annoyed at that attitude of his. She said that he did not understand that training was very important, that men needed to be trained for war. She said that he was so frivolous that even she could beat him with a knife. She knew that she had no chance of winning against him with a heavy sword, but she figured she was faster than he was and more agile.

It didn't take her but minutes to realize that she was wrong on both counts. For all his playfulness he was a very good opponent. He toyed with her, teasing her, making her think that she was winning, then he'd sidestep and take her off balance. As with all the Peregrines her anger rose to blazing in just moments. And when her anger came to the surface Tearle easily took her knife away from her.

"I hope you have learned that a cool head can think faster than a hot one," he said, then, when she meant to try to strike him, he caught her in his arms and kissed her soundly. Zared was embarrassed because of the laughter of the men around them.

Later he came to her and tried to make up. He teased her and handed her a bouquet of flowers and told her she was pretty and that her eyes sparkled more than any jewel. She told him that he was absurd, but she couldn't help smiling. He was an easy man to be near.

The next day he took her to a fair in a town ten miles away. Zared had never been to a fair, for at home she had never been allowed out of her castle, and besides, her brothers did not believe in such frivolity.

The fair was a wonder to her. At the tournament she had not been able to enjoy herself, for she had been under such strain with her brother and her enemy being in the same camp, but at the fair things seemed to be different. Nothing had actually changed, but it seemed that it had. She was still with her family's enemy, but as she glanced at him on his big horse he didn't seem like much of an enemy. In fact, she was beginning to think that he was as big and strong and handsome as her brothers.

The day at the fair was wonderful. All the merchants were glad to see the lord and his pretty lady. It was so different from the tournament, when she had been sniggered at for being one of those dirty Peregrines.

Tearle bought her everything. After having grown up in a household where every penny was treated as though it were gold, it was heavenly to be able to buy pretty things. She ate some of everything that was for sale until Tearle warned her about having a stomachache. When the juice from half a dozen cherries ran down her chin he leaned over and licked the sweet liquid off. She turned red to her toes, but he just laughed at her.

When he saw her watching a beautifully made wrestler bragging that he could beat all comers, Tearle stripped and wrestled the man. When her husband won Zared was bursting with pride, and she held the prize, an ugly knot made of cheap ribbons, as though it were a jeweled ornament won in a tournament.

Tearle stood behind her, his hands on her shoulders as she laughed at a puppet show. When a fight broke out between half a dozen men who'd had too much wine he swept her into his arms and carried her to safety.

There was a booth where a man was selling fabrics from Italy, and Zared paused to look longingly at a bolt of dark green brocade. Tearle ordered the man to show it to them. It was expensive beyond belief, and Zared told the man to put it away. Tearle bought the entire bolt for her. "You can make bed hangings from it," he said.

Some part of her said that she should remember that the money he was spending so freely actually belonged to her family and not his, but all that seemed far away.

He stood with her and watched as she hid her eyes while a man walked across a rope stretched tight between two poles. "That is not so hard. I could do that," Tearle bragged.

"You could not," she answered, and when she saw him moving toward the man she caught his hand and begged him not to do it. It was one thing to wrestle a man, but quite another to walk a narrow rope ten feet above the ground. He could be killed doing that.

She had to beg and beg and beg him to keep him from getting on the rope. In order to stop him she had to tell him that she believed that he could walk the rope and therefore did not have to prove it to her. She had to tell him that he was the best and the bravest knight in all the kingdom. He wanted to know if she thought he was better than Severn, and she said she was certain that he was. He asked if she thought he could beat Rogan, and she assured him that he could. Then he asked if she thought he could beat Colbrand.

"Not in a pig's eye," she said, and then she had the wisdom to start running.

He caught her and tickled her until she admitted that maybe, perhaps, possibly he was better than Colbrand.

When night fell he told her that they had to return to his house, for he was sure that unsavory types came out at night, and he didn't want to risk injury to her. She protested, but she was indeed tired. He mounted his horse, and then one of the five Howard men who had been with them all day handed her up to him, and she rode the ten miles home held in Tearle's arms.

Once they were at home she undressed and waited for him. She was sure that he would come to her bed, but he didn't. As he always did, he kissed her goodnight and left her. As tired as she was, she couldn't sleep, and so she got out of bed and sat before the fire.

She leaned back against the chair and felt the warmth of the fire on her face. Sometimes she wished she could go home, for there everything was exactly as it was supposed to be. She knew who were her friends and who were her enemies. She had grown up knowing that she was to hate the Howards, yet her mind was cluttered with a thousand images. She remembered Tearle in black armor knocking all challengers from their horses. She remembered his laughing and teasing her. She thought of his reading to her and smiling at her across the light of a single candle.

She put her hand to her head. Was he the enemy or

her friend? He was a Howard, so he could not be her friend, and yet . . .

In the last two weeks they had been together almost constantly, and she had talked to him as she'd never talked to anyone before. In her family, all talk that did not concern war with the Howards was considered a waste of time, but Tearle did not seem to think that any talk was a waste of time.

They talked about things that had happened to them as children, what they liked and disliked, what they hoped would happen in the future. They always managed to avoid talking about the hatred that was between their brothers. In fact, they managed to avoid that issue so well that it was almost as though they weren't sworn enemies.

Tearle had shown her plans he'd had drawn for renovating the dwellings around his mother's house. He took her to meet some of his tenants. At her brothers' house the tenants were not known by their names. Her brothers considered men who could fight to be the only men of importance. But during the many visits Tearle and his mother had made to her home in England Tearle had gotten to know the people who farmed his acres, and he asked about their children, and when there was sickness he saw that the people were cared for.

How could she hate a man who was so kind and who laughed so often? At first she thought that he was pretending to be a man who thought of other people, but the men and women who worked for him were unafraid of him. And the children ran to him, expecting the sweets that he carried in his pockets.

Zared began to ask him more questions about his life, about what he did when he'd returned with his mother to England. "Did you see your brothers when you returned?"

216

"No," Tearle had answered softly. "My mother felt that she had done her duty and given her husband sons that he could kill in his battle with the Peregrines, so she owed him no more sons and no more of her time. I was the youngest, and she took me with her to France. I lived with her and rarely saw my father or my older brothers."

It took Zared a while to realize that he had not been raised to participate in the feud, that the hatred between the Howards and the Peregrines meant nothing to him.

The more she thought, the more confused she became. If he wasn't interested in the hatred, why had he married her? He had suggested an annulment readily enough when she'd said that she didn't want him to touch her, but he seemed to like her well enough.

She got out of her chair and walked to the fire. *Like* her, did he? She closed her eyes for a moment and tried to think about going back to her brothers' house to live. She would have to return to a place where no one laughed or made jokes, where everything was of the utmost seriousness.

She thought of her oldest brother Rogan and the way his wife had to fight him for every bit of freedom she had. Rogan loved his wife, but it wasn't a love that allowed her to say and do what she pleased. And then there was Severn, who was married to the beautiful Lady Anne. Zared wondered if Lady Anne's temper had caused her brother to kill the woman yet.

She moved back to the chair and sat down hard, her head in her hands. God help her, but she didn't want to go back to her brothers. She wanted to stay with this man, this man who was her enemy, the man her family hated. The blood that ran through him had killed her older brothers, had stolen everything that belonged to them. He was a man she should hate, yet she didn't.

On the table beside her was the ribbon knot that he had won for her. She remembered how proud she had been when she had seen him wrestling that man, how much prouder she had been when he had won. She put the ribbon to her cheek.

What was she going to do? Was there any way that she could have both her family and the man?

She went to bed, but she had a restless night, and in the morning she found herself snapping at people. She was already at the table when Tearle came downstairs. Unlike her, he had no circles under his eyes from lack of sleep.

He greeted her cheerfully, smiling and happy.

Zared looked at him over her mug of watered ale and said, "When will you hear from the king?"

Tearle sat down at the head of the table and cut a large piece of cheese to put on his bread. "You are anxious to have the marriage ended?"

She looked up at him, and for a moment her heart was in her eyes, but she looked away. "It would be best to have it over with."

Tearle was quiet for a moment, so she looked at him. His face showed no expression. When had he grown so handsome? she wondered. When had he changed from being a frog of a man to being the most handsome man she had ever seen in her life? If their marriage must end, it was better that it should end sooner than later. She could not allow herself to grow any fonder of him than she already was.

At last Tearle shrugged. "Who can say what the king will do? I am sure that he will take his own time." He looked at her over his mug. "Perhaps he will deny my petition."

218

"Deny it?" She held her breath. "W-why would he do that?"

"All in all I would say that ours is a good marriage. We unite two warring families. Perhaps he will not allow us to separate."

Zared's first reaction was to smile. Maybe they could stay in the house forever. Maybe she could have an herb garden. Maybe she could have some new gowns made. Maybe they could breed a few children.

She caught herself and gave a good imitation of a frown. "My brothers will not like my being married to a Howard. Perhaps I should go back to my brothers' house. Perhaps the king will more likely sign the petition if I am home again."

She looked at him and realized that she wanted him to say that he wanted her to stay with him forever, that he wanted her never to leave him. She wanted him to beg her to stay with him.

"As you wish," he said. "Shall I have my men guide you to your home?"

She felt like throwing her food in his face. "If my brothers were to see me riding under the Howard banner, they would attack before questions could be answered."

"Ah, then," he said slowly, "perhaps you should remain here for as long as it takes the king to reply."

It took her a moment to understand him, but then she smiled. "Perhaps that would be best."

They went riding that day, traveling far into the countryside and leaving the men behind them. Tearle took her to see a circle of enormous standing stones that had been built by the ancients. He told her a scary story about human sacrifices being made on the stones, then he lunged at her, pretending that he was about to sacrifice her. She squealed and giggled, but then stopped when he paused with her on the stone, his big body hanging over hers.

He will kiss me now, she thought. He will forget about this talk of annulment and hold me.

But he didn't. He turned away from her and walked to another stone, and when she got down from the stone where he had placed her he didn't look at her. She walked to him, but he kept his face averted, and only after some moments had passed did he look at her.

"It grows dark," he said softly. "We should return."

It was after that day that he began to stay away from her. In such a short time she had become so used to spending time with him that she found that she missed him. She saw him in the courtyard training with his men, so she borrowed some clothes from the cook's boy, dressed in them, and went to join him.

She smiled at him, but he did not return her smile. "You are my wife. You are not to display yourself before my men that way," he said, looking down at her legs, which were covered with no more than thin knit hose.

"What am I supposed to do all day?" she spit at him. "And I am *not* your wife!"

She meant that she was his wife in name only, but he took what she said the wrong way. "You will be free soon enough," he said, and his voice was hard.

Zared turned away from him and from the men around them, who were watching with a great deal of interest in their eyes, and she went upstairs to her room. Her single, lonely room. She had been alone most of her life, and she was alone again, but why did it seem so much worse? It was as though she'd found a friend and lost him.

She flung herself on the bed, wanting to cry but not

220

able to do so. She should be glad that he was staying away from her, she thought. Who wanted the company of a Howard anyway? She was a Peregrine, and she hated all Howards.

Didn't she?

She thought of what her brother Rogan was going to say when he found out that his little sister was married to a Howard. Rogan would go to the king himself and demand that an annulment be given. Rogan never trusted anyone—he'd probably demand that a midwife examine Zared to be sure that she was a virgin and that the Howard man had never touched her.

"I'm still a virgin," she whispered. "As clean and as untouched as the day I was born." And after Rogan had the annulment papers in his hand he'd no doubt hate the Howards more. He'd probably think that his sister had been rejected by a Howard.

"There must be something that I can do," she thought. "There has to be something that can be done to prevent more hatred."

"My lord," Margaret said softly to Tearle. He was at the well scrubbing off the sweat he had raised while training with his men.

"Yes?" Tearle turned to her. He hadn't been in the best of spirits in the last few days. Night and day his thoughts plagued him. He was falling in love with the brat who was his wife. Maybe he had been in love with her since he had first seen her struggling with his brother's men, men who didn't have sense enough to know that she was a female. But his feelings for the girl were not returned, for she still talked of returning to her brothers' house and of the annulment. He thought that someday soon he should consider sending a message asking the king to annul their marriage.

He looked at Margaret. "What is it?"

"Lady Zared has gone into the village."

He frowned. "She is not a prisoner. Did you send an escort with her?"

"Yes, but she eluded them."

Tearle was immediately alarmed. Had she run back to her brothers?

Before he could move Margaret put her hand on his arm. "She has been found. One of the men saw her going into Hebe's place."

"Why would she want to see that old woman?"

"It is said that she is a witch." Margaret's voice lowered. Like all servants, she knew much more about what was going on between the master and his mistress than they would have liked.

"Why would she go to a witch?"

Margaret hesitated. "Hebe rids women of unwanted children."

At that Tearle's face lost its color. "Tell John to saddle my horse."

An hour later it was an enraged man who burst into the old woman's dark, dirty hut. Tearle's first instinct was to kill the woman, and after that he was going to kill the woman he'd married. He had no doubt that it was Colbrand's child she was carrying. No wonder Zared had wanted to go back to her brothers'. There she could pass the child off as belonging to a Howard and perhaps use it to try to gain the Howard lands. He cursed her and himself and all women and marriage and everything else that had to do with men and women.

"My wife was here," he said to the terrified old woman. "Did you rid her of her child?"

"Nay, my lord," she said, her voice quivering. "She carried no child."

"Do not lie to me. I will burn you if you lie to me."

The woman was thin with age, and she cowered back against a wall covered with drying batches of herbs. "I do not lie. Please, my lord, I do not yet want to die."

Suddenly Tearle's rage left him, and he sat down on the only stool in the hut, his body deflated. It was not the old woman's fault that his wife had wanted to get rid of her child. Perhaps Tearle should be glad that Zared wanted to do away with the child rather than keep it. Considering how she felt about Colbrand, it was a wonder that she did not want to put the child on the throne of England.

"What did my wife want?" Tearle asked sadly.

"A love potion."

Tearle's head came up. "A what?"

"Your lady wife asked for a love potion. A potion to drive a man insane with lust."

"Who?" was the only word he could get out. He had thought that he had given her little time in the last weeks to form an attachment to another man. But perhaps she planned to see Colbrand later, and—

"You, my lord. She wanted the potion for her husband."

Tearle blinked a few times, not understanding.

The old woman saw the way Tearle relaxed, and she began to gain some courage. She stood up straighter, not slouching against the wall. "The Lady Zared asked me to make her a potion that she could give to her husband so that when he drank it he would be so overcome with lust that he could not resist her."

Tearle stared at the old woman for some minutes. "You are sure of this?" he asked softly. "She said it was for her husband?"

The woman managed a bit of a smile. "I did not get

this old by being a fool. I was not going to give a
potion to the wife of a powerful man who planned to
use it on a man other than her husband. Were she a
farmer's wife I might have done so, but not her. I told
her that, should she lie to me and use the potion on a
man other than her husband, she would suffer ill luck
all the rest of her life. She said . . ."

"Yes, out with it. What did she say?"

"She said that her husband—you, my lord—
looked upon her as a child, and a boyish one at that.
She wanted to give you something to drink that would
make you see her as a woman."

Tearle got off the stool and took two steps so that he
was standing at the far side of the hut. His head grazed
the underside of the thatched roof. With his back to
the woman he allowed himself a smile. She thought he
did not desire her, did she? And all the while he had
thought she was pining for that fool Colbrand. She
had certainly changed her affections easily, hadn't
she? But he wasn't going to quibble about that. If he
could get her to go to bed with him willingly, that was
the first step toward making her return the love he
bore for her.

He looked back at the woman. "What did you give
her?"

The woman could see that Tearle was amused. She
had seen him since he was a boy and suspected he was
not a violent man. She straightened. "My potions are
a secret known only to me." When Tearle frowned she
continued. "I told her to invite you to supper in her
room. There was to be a fire and candles, and she was
to boil water with sweet-scented herbs in it, and she
was to wear her lowest-cut gown. She was to put the
herbs in her husband's ale, and when he drank it he
would be unable to control himself."

Tearle could no longer repress his smile. "It is to strike me as a bolt of lightning?"

The woman was offended by his tone. "I do not cheat my customers. The potion will work."

"I can guarantee that," Tearle said with good humor. "I shall be the most thunderstruck of lovers." He reached under his tunic and withdrew a small bag of coins. He started to open it and give the old woman a coin or two, but on second thought he gave her the whole bag. It was doubtless more money than she had earned in all her lifetime together.

The old woman was speechless as she held out a trembling hand and took the bag.

When Tearle left the hut he was whistling.

Zared had had some trouble getting Margaret to do what she wanted her to do. For the first time since she arrived the woman seemed to be snubbing her. She answered all Zared's questions curtly and supplied little or no information beyond what she had to.

Zared wanted a special gown, and she had to ask repeatedly where Tearle's mother's gowns were kept. Margaret evaded her as best she could until Zared was ready to take a knife to the woman's throat. At last Zared was taken to a storeroom, and there, amid bolts of fabric that were waiting to be cut and sewn, was a large wooden box. Reluctantly, with a look of great distaste on her long face, Margaret opened the box to reveal a dress that, even in the dark room, glowed. It was made of cloth of gold.

Zared had never seen such fabric. She took the gown, still in its box, to the doorway and held it to the light. "What is it?" she whispered.

Reluctantly Margaret told her that the fabric had come from Italy. Solid gold was drawn out into extremely thin wires, then wrapped about a strong fiber of silk. A loom was then warped with silk, and the gold thread was woven into it. Margaret also informed her that the fabric cost over thirty-eight pounds a yard.

Gingerly Zared lifted the gown from its box. There was much cloth in the gown. She had no idea how to add, but she knew that the gown cost almost as much as her brothers' castle was worth.

Zared took a deep breath and tried to look as though she wasn't frightened as she lifted the gown from its box. She was doing it to save her family from going to war, she told herself. Perhaps her husband had been right and they could create a child together, and that child would inherit the lands that the Howards held. It wouldn't be right, of course, because the lands should go to her oldest brother, but at least there would be Peregrine blood in the owner of the estate.

"I will wear it," Zared said. The gown was very heavy, and it was stiff. She smiled as she draped it over her arms. Men thought women were weak. Her brothers said that no woman could ever wear a suit of armor, but the stiff, heavy gown was another type of armor. Zared smiled, for she was, in a way, waging a war, a war that she meant to win, and the golden dress was the armor she needed.

She turned to Margaret. "Shall we suit me?" she asked, and she saw a hint of humor in Margaret's eyes, as though she understood what Zared meant.

An hour later Zared had her room prepared just as the old witch-woman had said it should be. It glowed with candlelight, and it was fragrant with herbs boiling in a pot. There was a table with succulent food waiting. It hadn't been easy to arrange, since Margaret

226

had questioned everything that Zared wanted. She had also asked her young mistress repeatedly if she felt well, if she was ill in the mornings.

Zared found all the questions annoying, but she answered them as best she could, for the answers seemed to put Margaret in a better mood.

At last all was ready. "Do I . . . do I look all right?" Zared asked, smoothing down the gold of the dress. The silk that had been used in the weaving of the gown was red, and the red-gold of the gown combined with Zared's fair skin, her reddish hair, and the glow of the fire to make her a breathtaking sight.

Margaret looked at her young mistress and smiled. She didn't know why she had gone to the old witch-woman's place, but she was convinced that it was not to rid herself of another man's child. (All the castlefolk and half the villagers knew that his lordship had not slept with his young wife since their marriage.)

"You are beautiful," Margaret said.

"I do not look like a boy?"

Margaret could only laugh at that. Zared's hair was pulled back and draped in a sheer white sheath, and there were rubies along her forehead. "You could not look less like a boy." On impulse, because she was so much older and because it was easy to tell that Zared had no idea what was wrong and what was right for servants to do, Margaret kissed her young charge's cheek, then smiled at her and left the room.

A few minutes later Tearle knocked and entered her room. She could instantly see that he was in a bad mood. "What has happened?" she asked, afraid that it had to do with her brothers.

He sat down heavily on a chair before the fire. "My horse stumbled and threw me in a bog. One of my

227

men knocked me down in sword practice, and I seem to have a rash growing on the right side of my body. And when I came in I was told that I could not have supper at a table but must go to your room. What do you want from me, Zared? To tell me that your brothers have come for me? It would be a fitting end to an ugly day."

Her first impulse was to tell him what he could do with his dinner, but instead she smiled. "I am wearing your mother's gown."

He turned as though he were glancing over his shoulder, but he didn't really look at her. He gave an enormous yawn. "Yes, so you are." He looked at the table laden with food. "Call someone and tell them to serve me. I am hungry and I am tired."

"I will serve you," Zared said quickly. "We need no one with us."

She went to the table where the food was, lifted the silver covers, and began filling a silver plate for him. When it was heaping she handed it to him, then took a seat on a stool at his feet.

He used his spoon to shovel in a large mouthful of carrots and then talked to her, his mouth full. "What is it you want?" He pointed at her with his spoon.

"I want nothing. I am not used to all the servants, and I wanted to be away from them."

"You never could lie." He narrowed his eyes at her. "Have you had some message from your brothers? Is that why you went to the witch?"

Her eyes widened.

"You will find that my people are loyal to me. They will tell me all that you do."

"I have not had a message from my brothers. I did not invite you here for talk of war."

"Ah, but what else can you talk of? What other reason would you have for visiting the witch?" He put his plate in his lap, and his voice lowered. "She rids women of unwanted children."

Zared gave him a look of disgust. "It is not possible that I carry a man's child, if that is what is in your mind."

"Not even Colbrand's?"

"You are a hateful man," she said, rising from her stool.

"I am a Howard. How do I know what you have done with another man? You seemed to have found the man more than desirable. You thought him the strongest, bravest, most handsome knight in all of England."

"You downed him," she said, some exasperation in his voice. "You downed *all* the men at the Marshall tournament."

At that Tearle leaned back in his chair and smiled at her. "Are you saying that Colbrand is not the best knight in all of England?"

She realized then that he had been teasing her. "You are a dreadful man. Are you never serious?"

He held out his empty plate. "I am serious about needing my bed. I have never been so tired in my life." He stood up and gave a great stretch and another yawn. "There is nothing tonight that could keep me from my bed. Were the king himself to come to me, I would not tarry from it."

Zared did not want to have to use the witch's potion. She wanted to think that she herself had enticed her husband to her bed. "You did not say if you liked your mother's gown."

He was yawning again. "I have always liked it. She wore it in France. Even the king remarked on it."

"It is heavy. Feel the skirt."

He stretched some more. "I have felt cloth of gold often, as well as cloth of silver. I have even removed a

JUDE DEVERAUX

few of those gowns from court women." He scratched at his side. "I must get to bed. I find that my clothes are beginning to itch. Perhaps it is just my great desire to get them off."

She didn't know what to do to get him to look at her. The hard corset inside the dress pushed her breasts so flat that they ached, but they swelled above the gown's neck as though they were overripe melons. As far as she could tell, he hadn't yet seen them.

"Your mother's corset hurts me," she said. "I do not think your mother had as much to fill the dress as I have." She held her breath to see what he would say to that remark.

"I do not remember looking at my mother in that way," he said stiffly, as though she had offended him.

"I did not mean—"

"Yes, yes, apology accepted. Now, are you sure that there was nothing that you had to say to me, other than telling me that my mother was an ugly creature?"

"I did not say—" She cut herself off and turned away from him. "Oh, go on, go to bed. It no longer matters what I wanted. You are tired, and you must have your rest."

She expected to hear the door open and close, but when it did not she turned to look at him. "Go on, I will keep you no longer."

He sat back down in the chair. "You are upset about something. Has the message from the king come so soon? Is that why you have dressed in my mother's best gown and planned this dinner? You want to celebrate the good news?"

"I have heard nothing from anyone. I have not heard from my brothers, or from the king, or from the Peregrine ghost, for that matter. No one has talked to me all day."

He smiled at her in a knowing way. "Ah, so that is

230

it. You desire company. Come, then, talk. I will try to stay awake long enough to listen."

She turned away from him. "I had a purpose when you came, but now I do not know what it was," she muttered.

He was so silent from behind her that she turned to look at him. His head was back against the chair, and he was asleep. She felt anger when she looked at him, then she felt a bit like crying. Why were other women so able to entice men when she was not?

She walked to him and put her hand on his cheek. He was better-looking than her brothers, better-looking than Colbrand—in fact, better-looking than any man in the world.

He awoke with a start. "I was dreaming," he said.

She smiled at him. "What were you dreaming?"

"That I was at court and Lady Catherine was coming to my room. I think it must be the gown. She had a blue cloth-of-gold gown."

Zared stiffened and moved away from him. "I would like for you to leave now."

He stood and ran his hand over his eyes. "I must go to my room and finish this dream." But before he left he walked to the mantel and lifted a fine silver goblet. It was filled with ale, and there were herbs floating on top.

"I am dying of thirst," he said before he downed the entire drink.

"Do not drink that!" Zared shouted.

Tearle finished the drink, then looked at her in surprise. "You would deny me something to drink when I am so thirsty? Come now, I would have thought more of a Peregrine, not to mention a woman who is my wife." He paused. "Or, as you shouted at my men, one who is not my wife. Why are you looking at me so strangely?"

"I am not looking at you at all," she said softly, but she was looking at him so intently that she didn't even blink.

He gave another little stretch. "I must go now. It's time for bed for me." He suppressed a yawn, then leaned over and chastely kissed her forehead. "My mother's gown looks good on you. I daresay that she did not look any better in it than you. Now you really must excuse me."

He turned away toward the door, Zared's eyes following him. He had drunk the potion, yet nothing had happened! Tomorrow, she thought, she would go to the witch and demand her coin back. She would not pay for a useless spell.

It was as Tearle put his hand on the door latch that he paused. For a long moment he didn't move. Then slowly, very slowly, he turned to look at her. His eyes were wide, as though he'd had some great shock. For a moment he looked at her face, his eyes dropping to her lips, then his eyes fell to the floor, and he looked from her hidden feet up to her face, his eyes lingering a long time on her exposed bosom.

Out of instinct Zared put her hand to her bosom and took a step backward. Tearle stepped toward her, his eyes hot and full of longing.

Zared looked at him, and immediately her heart began pounding. That was how she'd wanted him to look at her. That was why she had bought the potion. But she began to feel afraid. He had always been kind and gentle with her, but would the potion turn him into a monster? Would it make him into someone that he was not?

She backed away from him until she was pressed against the bed. He was stalking her slowly, like a large animal going after its prey and knowing that the prey was cornered.

"I . . . I think that . . ."

She couldn't finish as he reached her and put his hand on the side of her face. "I have never seen you this beautiful," he whispered. "I have never seen any woman as desirable as you. Not in all the courts of France or Italy or England have I seen another woman to rival you. I desire you above all others."

She looked up at him and blinked. Those were the words she had wanted to hear, the words that she had purchased when she bought the love potion.

Very gently he kissed her lips, and Zared felt her knees weaken. He caught her about the waist and lifted her to the bed, where he lay her gently on the coverlet. He stretched out beside her and kissed her face and neck and then moved to her breasts, exposed above the gown. Zared closed her eyes and enjoyed the sensation for a moment, then looked down at his hair. He had such thick, dark hair. She ran her fingers through it.

He leaned on his elbow and looked down at her, his hands running over the skin of her chest, playing along the swell of her breasts. "I do not seem able to help myself. It is as though some outside force has taken over my body. I must have you or I will die."

He pushed her to her stomach and began to unlace the back of her gown, his fingers slipping inside to touch her skin through her linen undergarment. Zared closed her eyes at the sensation. It was what she had wanted for so long. Too bad that she'd had to resort to using a love potion to make him desire her.

Easily and with more knowledge than Zared wanted to think that he had he unfastened her gown, then expertly slipped it off over her head. She was wearing only her undergarments, and he made quick work of relieving her of them.

It wasn't long before she was unclothed, wearing

only her stockings, fastened at her knees with pretty ribbon garters. For a long moment Tearle lay beside her and looked at her, then he sat up and looked at her some more until she began to become anxious.

"I do not please you?"

"I have never seen a woman such as you," he said softly, and he meant it. He had seen many women unclothed before, but with the exception of a few peasant girls, they had lived soft lives. Zared's life had not been soft. From the time she could walk she had carried a sword and had been taught how to use it. She had worn demi-armor. She had learned to ride before she could walk. All her training had given her a body of firm, hard muscle. There was no fat on her body except for her soft, rather large breasts.

Zared was not experienced enough with men to know that the way he was staring at her was with lust. She started to roll away from him, but he caught her and pulled her back.

He looked at her as one might look at an unknown species of animal, and as he looked his eyes grew hotter and hotter.

"Zared," he whispered, and he moved his body on top of hers and began to kiss her with an ardor she had never felt before.

She was by nature an enthusiastic person, and she began to kiss him back with passion. He didn't so much as break the contact of their mouths as he began to fling his clothes off. She knew that he was a man who cared about his clothing, and she almost laughed when she heard a seam rip. But tearing cloth didn't slow him down in his urgency to get out of his clothes.

His mouth moved down to fasten onto her breast, and Zared stiffened in surprise, then seemed to melt in desire. It was better than she had imagined, and she buried her hands in his hair as she arched her back so that he could have better access to her body.

"You are the loveliest woman I have ever seen. Had I known what was under your clothes I would have torn them from you sooner," he said as his mouth moved down to her stomach.

It was those words that made Zared open her eyes. He would not have torn her clothes from her body because he had not drunk the potion. The potion was what was making him desire her. It was not Zared he wanted. His desire was caused by the spell of the witch.

She pushed at him. "Let me up! Release me!"

She pushed and pushed at him, but he did not move. He kept kissing and nibbling at her hips, moving down to her legs. Zared lifted her leg, put her foot on his shoulder, and gave him as hard a shove as she could manage.

Dazed, befuddled, Tearle looked at her as she moved to the far corner of the bed. "I have hurt you?"

"You do not want me."

Tearle was too stupefied to understand her words. He could not take his eyes off her body: those legs, that stomach with the two muscles running down the sides of it. She looked like a woman, but she also looked like the sleekest racing animal in the world. He reached for her.

Zared eluded his hands. "It is not me you desire. You are under the spell of a witch."

"Aye, that I am," he said, leering at her. His palms were beginning to itch from wanting to touch her. In another moment of looking at her he would not be able to control himself; the man in him would flee, and he would become the animal that he felt like.

When he lunged at her again Zared left the bed and

went to stand behind the post at the corner of the bed. "You do not want me. You have never wanted me. It is a trick. Go to your Lady Catherine."

Now that her body was hidden behind the curtains of the bed his mind cleared a bit, at least enough to begin to understand her. "I do not desire you?" He reached out a hand to touch her. "I will show you how much I desire you."

"No!" She moved out of his reach and grabbed a pillow from the window seat, making an attempt to hide her nudity. But the pillow only tantalized him more, leaving her legs bare as well as the swell of her breasts at the sides.

Tearle knew enough about women to know that words were going to be needed before he could get what he wanted. "Do you wish me to tell you that I love you?" he asked. "Do you wish me to make up a poem to your beauty?" At that point he would have done *anything* to get her to come back to the bed. His voice lowered. "Do you wish me to swear to give my brother's estates to your brother?"

At that Zared sat down on the window seat, her face a study in dejection. The potion was indeed a powerful one if it would make him agree to such a thing. "I have done a dishonorable thing," she said.

Tearle sat up straight on the bed. "If it is another man, I will kill him. No man will have what is mine."

"Will you stop talking?" she half shouted. "Do you not understand that what you are saying is not what you mean? It is the witch's brew that is talking."

Tearle's concentration was on her body, so he had difficulty understanding what she was saying. "You are a witch," he murmured, and he got off the bed to go to her.

Zared jumped off the window seat and ran to the

other side of the room. On the floor in an untidy heap were his clothes, and on top was his thin-bladed, jeweled-handled knife. She picked it up and held it as though to protect herself. "Do not come closer to me," she said.

There were times when a man could cry, he thought. Her red hair was hanging down her back and falling across one shoulder. The knife somehow added to her beauty. "Zared, I will give you anything. Tell me what it is you desire. Jewels? Estates? What do you want?"

Zared looked at him. He wore not a stitch, and he looked even better without clothes than in them. She wanted him to hold her, to touch her, but she did not want him to do so only under a spell. She tossed the knife on top of his clothes. Even when he was driven by the uncontrollable lust of a witch's spell he was not a violent man. He still was not forcing her to lie with him.

Going to the witch had not been an honorable action on her part, but she would save her honor by fulfilling her part of the spell. She walked past him, not touching him, and climbed onto the bed. She lay rigid, her hands at her side, her legs held closely together. She looked up at the underside of the canopy. "I am yours to do with as you will," she said regally.

Tearle wouldn't have thought that his passion could have been killed, but it was. Some men found unwilling women desirable, but he did not. He stood by the side of the bed and glared down at her. "You are the most infuriating woman. You desire me so much that you are willing to risk poisoning me with some filthy witch's potion, yet when I touch you you draw a knife on me. How am I to understand this?" He raised his

hands in a gesture of helplessness. "Would that someone would explain women to me. Or is it just my wife
I am unable to understand?"

Zared turned to look at him. "You know of the
potion?"

He grimaced, then bent and fumbled among his
clothes and withdrew a small bag, which he tossed on
the bed. "There is your potion."

Zared turned on her side and picked up the bag. "I
put the potion in the mug of ale. This cannot be it."

"I was not going to drink that filth. For all I knew it
contained roasted frogs' eyes. Or worse."

Zared opened the little bag, looked inside, and
sniffed. The contents smelled as awful as she remembered. She looked back up at Tearle. "If this is the
potion I paid the witch for, then what did you drink?"

"Mint, I think. I would not recommend it. It does
not go with ale, but I daresay it tastes better than that
mess you would have given me."

Zared held the bag. "If you did not drink the
potion, then what has inspired this . . . this newfound
lust of yours?"

At that Tearle did not know whether to laugh or yell
at her. He did neither. He sat down on the edge of the
bed and talked very slowly. "I do not know how you
came to the conclusion that I have not been eaten alive
with desire for you from the moment I first saw you.
Why else would I have made myself your brother's
lackey? Do you think that I enjoy slogging in mud up
to my knees to carry lances to him? Did I remain with
him because I enjoyed his company? Or yours? At the
tournament, did you so much as say a kind word to
me?"

She sat up on the bed, oblivious to the way Tearle
was looking at her. "But I thought you disliked me. I
thought you wanted to . . . to . . ."

"Get my hands on the Peregrine wealth?" He leaned toward her, his nose almost touching hers. "I have always had one objective: to get my hands on the body of the Peregrine daughter."

Zared blinked at him. "Really? You do not think I look like a boy?"

He looked down at her bare body, then back up at her face. "I am the only man who has known from the beginning that you were *not* a boy."

Zared looked back down at the pouch. "But if you did not drink the potion, then why did you react so?" Her head came up. "And why have you not come to me on your own before now?"

He had to control himself to keep from yelling. "Do you not realize that I have been courting you?"

"Courting me?"

"Aye, courting you. I realize, after having spent some time with your brother, that the Peregrine idea of courting consists of turning a woman over one's knee, but in other households going with a girl to a fair is a much more acceptable method of courtship."

"But what of the annulment? What of the message to the king?"

He gave a bit of a smile. "What message? What annulment?"

"The one we—" She smiled back at him. "You did not send the message? I called you some awful names."

"I felt that they were temporary. I hoped that if I could get you away from your brother, you might see that I was not the monster you had been told of." He picked up her hand and kissed it. "I have wanted you since I saw you struggling against my brother's men. And I have cared for you since you came back to see if I were dead, even though I was a Howard and you had been taught to hate me."

She watched him as he began to kiss her fingertips. "I was afraid that if you bled to death, it would cause more harm to my family. I cared nothing for you."

He looked back at her with hot eyes. "Perhaps I can change that. Perhaps I can make you care." He put her small hand on his side and then moved toward her. Zared lay back on the pillows. "I do not believe that you can. No Howard could make a Peregrine squeal in delight."

He stopped kissing her ankle and looked up at her. "What do you know of squeals of delight?"

"I have heard many of them from my brothers' women, and you cannot wring such cries from me." There was challenge and daring in her eyes and a bit of a smile about her lips.

"Oh?" he said, accepting the challenge. "Let us see about that."

He began to kiss her then, and since he was not burdened by having to talk he could give himself over to his lust for her body. He kissed her and fondled her until he thought he might go mad. When he entered her he expected her to cry out in pain, but she did not.

"I liked that," she said later as Tearle was dozing in her arms. "Shall we do it again? Can it last longer this time?"

Tearle lifted one eyebrow and looked at her. "Perhaps. In a moment."

"Ah," Zared said. "I understand."

Had another woman said such a thing Tearle would have thought she did understand, but given Zared's experience in life, he doubted if she understood anything. "What do you understand?"

"That you are a weak and puny Howard, while

240

I have the blood of falcons running through my veins. Do you think our children will be weak like you?"

At that he caught her and pulled her down beside him. "I will see who will cry 'enough' before this night is through."

Chapter Thirteen

Zared sat down gingerly on the chair that was pulled up to the table. Her husband looked at her smugly and with such a superior look that she grimaced. But she was happy, very, very happy.

Tearle smiled at her. "What say you we do today?"

"Teach me to read," she said before she thought, and he smiled more broadly.

What followed for Zared were two weeks of heaven on earth. She seemed to crave affection. It seemed that she wanted to make up for all the years she had been forced to act and look like a boy, and all she wanted to do were the most feminine things. Tearle, so unlike the men she had known all her life, was glad to show her all the most feminine arts.

He helped her choose gowns that he thought would look good on her. Each night he brushed her hair, both of them hoping that the brushing would make it grow faster.

They played games with each other and with the other people of his household. They rode and hunted and sometimes did nothing. He started teaching her to read, and he showed her some of the notes on a lute. Together they wrote a few poems, and Tearle told her she had a talent for poetry.

And through all of it they made love. Everything seemed to have some sexual connotation to them. The sight of a baby made them think of creating their own. Music made them retire to their chamber. Reading was lusty to them, especially since some of the poems that Zared created were quite bawdy.

Zared showed Tearle how to use a knife, and her demonstration nearly drove Tearle wild with desire. It wasn't that she was teaching him anything that he didn't know, but that she wore no clothes while demonstrating.

They played hide and seek for one whole day when it rained, and whoever found the other made love to the other on the spot, wherever they were.

Tearle, who had in the past made love to women mostly in secret, was fascinated with the freedom he had. He could have his wife any time he wanted her.

He was also fascinated by Zared. She had not been told what "ladies" should and should not do, so she was willing to try anything. Also, she was so athletic that sometimes she made him feel old and decrepit. She scampered up trees with the agility of a lizard. He followed her and then made love to her on a forked tree branch.

She had none of the fears that he had always assumed ladies were born with. She was not afraid of high places or of weapons or of charging boars or of his men.

One night as they lay together, sweaty and satiated, he asked her about her exuberance.

"Do you not see that I am free?" she said. "I have never been free before. You have had a life of such ease that you cannot understand what being a prisoner is like. You are so soft."

"Perhaps I am now, but I am not always soft," he said, some hurt in his voice.

"No, you goose, I do not mean that. I mean that you are soft inside. You are gentle and kind, and you are not driven by hatred."

"You make me sound as though I am less than a man. You can see the scars on my body. I can fight."

"You can fight in mock battles, true, but can you kill? Could you look a man in the eye and kill him?"

He held her hand in his and looked at it. "I would kill whoever touched you."

"Yes, you probably would." She sighed, for she didn't have any idea how to explain what she meant. He didn't understand hatred. He had no idea what it was like to feed off hatred—to have hatred consume the souls of those around you.

"Could you look into a man's eyes and kill him?" he asked.

"If he were a Howard," she said before she thought, then she turned to look at him, a feeling of horror growing inside her.

"I am a Howard," he said softly. "Could you look into my eyes and kill me?"

She didn't know what to say to him. She knew that she could not kill him. Or could she? If he were to threaten one of her brothers, what would she do?

She shivered, then looked at him. "I have many times looked into your eyes and killed you. You have no stamina. You are a weak and puny thing who cries 'Enough' after only a few hours of coupling. We

Peregrines are—" She didn't say any more because he started kissing her again.

It was in the middle of the third week that Zared's happiness came crashing down about her head. It was barely dawn, and since living with Tearle she had grown so lazy that they were still in bed when the door burst open.

One of Tearle's knights hurried into the room, his face red from exertion, veins pounding in his forehead. He was so out of breath that he could barely speak. "He comes."

Zared looked up, rubbing her eyes. She had been safe for so long that danger seemed a long-ago experience to her. She saw her husband nod at the man.

"How many?" Tearle asked.

"Hundreds. They come armed for war."

Again Tearle nodded. "Prepare the men. Remember they are to aim no weapon. These men are now my relatives. I will have no blood shed this day."

At the mention of blood Zared came fully awake and sat up, clutching the top sheet to her. "What has happened?"

Tearle dismissed his man, then turned to his wife. "Your brother has come with an army. I believe he means to kill me and take you to his home."

Zared didn't say a word, but felt as though the blood drained from her entire body. She started to roll to the far side of the bed, but Tearle caught her arm.

"Here, what is this you plan to do?"

"I will go to my brother. I will not allow him to kill you. You have been good to me."

His hand tightened on her forearm. "In spite of the fact that I am a Howard, I have been good to you." There was sarcasm in his voice. "And now you plan to leave me."

"I mean to stop a war!" she shouted.

"*You* mean to take care of this?" he asked softly.

"Aye." Her mind was working quickly. "I will tell my brother that I wanted to marry you. I will tell him that my lust overcame me. He might understand that. Although Rogan is a man of great honor. *He* would never allow his lust to make him do such a dishonorable thing as I have done. He would have died rather than marry the enemy, and *he* would have hated the enemy until the end of time. He would have not done as I have and come to . . . to care for the enemy."

Through this long speech Tearle had been silent, just looking at her.

"Do you mean to stay there all day?" she snapped at him. She didn't want to think that it was the last time she would probably ever see him again. She had no doubt that her brother would never allow her to remain with a Howard. Rogan would have the marriage annulled, saying that his sister did not have her brothers' permission to marry. "Why are you looking at me so strangely?"

"You still see me as a Howard, not as the man that I am. You still think that I am a weakling and that your brother, with his violent ways, is all-powerful. Can you not yet see that violence is not always the answer?"

She shook her head at him. "I will see if you say that when my brother's sword is moving toward your head." She went to the chest by the window, withdrew the clothes she had taken from the cook's son, and began to put them on.

"No!" Tearle said, bounding out of the bed. "You are no longer a boy. You are not a Peregrine boy, you are a Howard woman."

"I am not!" she screamed at him, throwing the clothes on the floor. "I will never, never, never be a

246

Howard. I cannot be a Howard. Howards are my enemy."

Tearle pulled her into his arms. "Sssh, love. Be quiet. There is no reason for this fear you have. Your brother cannot take you from me."

She pushed away from him. "He will fight you. Do you understand nothing? My brothers hate the Howards. Rogan will die trying to kill you. Only if I go with him will he not declare war on you."

He smiled at her. "Then by all means you must go with him. But you will not dress as a boy. Those days are over. You will wear the cloth-of-gold dress. You will let your brother see that you have become a woman."

"I will let my brother see that the Howard money can buy dresses that cost more than the yearly rents of all the Peregrine wealth," she muttered. She was hurt, deeply hurt that he didn't seem to care that they would never be together again. She would go to her brother and her brother . . . Heavens, but she hated to think of what her brother would do to punish her for what she had done.

"What shall I wear?" Tearle asked.

"What do I care what you wear? I will not be here to see it." I will not be here to see what you wear or do not wear. Now I will never learn to read, she thought. Now I will never have children, or have a husband who holds me and makes me laugh.

"What do you think will impress your brother? Do you think riches impress him, or should I wear a suit of armor? I do not know whether to wear the cloth of silver or the armor. We will look a fine pair with you in gold and me in silver, will we not? But I fear that your brother will want me to prove myself to him, and I think that the silver is too fragile for that. And it is difficult to get blood from it."

She put her hands to the side of her head. "My brother is marching toward us with an army, and you stand there talking of clothes. You have no sense to you. Do you not realize that I will never see you again? That today I must return to my brother?" She was trying not to cry. "I knew that this soft life could not last. I knew that there could be no life such as this for me. I knew that it would end."

At that Tearle took her wrists in his hands. "Look at me and listen to what I have to say. You may think that your brother is the most powerful man in the world, but he is not. For all that you remind me every hour, you seem to forget that I am a Howard. I have men and riches at my disposal that could take your brother and his puny army at any time."

Zared's eyes widened in horror, and she stepped away, but he pulled her back to him.

"I am telling you what I *can* do, not what I plan. What I plan is to give myself to your brother."

"You cannot," she whispered. "He will kill you."

"Will he? You said that he was a man of honor. Will he kill a man who is not only a cousin by blood but is now a brother by marriage? Will he kill a man who surrenders himself?"

"You cannot give yourself to him. I will go. He wants the return of me. You do not know Rogan. His family is all to him."

He moved his face close to hers. "And you have become all to me. Do you think that I will allow you to go? Do you think that I will let you walk away from me after I have fought so long and hard to get you?"

"I . . . I do not know. I do not know what to think. My brother will kill you, that is all that I know."

"Your puny brother would have difficulty killing a Howard." He laughed at her look. "*That* is the woman

248

I know. Now get dressed, or your brother will be here and we shall be wearing nothing. I shall wear the silver. With your brother's temper he might think that a Howard in armor is an invitation to a fight, and I am tired today from a brawl in bed last night with another Peregrine."

"You could not beat my brother Rogan. He is as—"

"Yes, yes, spare me the details of the glories of your brother. Would that some day you would speak of me as other than a weakling who can barely summon the energy to get out of bed in the morning." He turned her around and smacked her bare bottom. "Now get dressed and prepare yourself to greet your brother with all the graciousness of a Howard lady."

Every time he called her a Howard her heart sank a little further. She was hardly aware when he left the room and when Margaret entered and began to help her dress.

It wasn't much later that Tearle came to get her. He was resplendent in cloth of silver that had a blue silk background. It made his dark hair seem darker, and she had never seen a more handsome man in her life.

He smiled at her look. "At last I seem to please you in something that I do." He held out his arm to her. "Shall we go to meet your brother?"

Zared found that she was trembling as they went down the stairs together, and for the first time she looked at the house not for its beauty but as a place to defend. For defense it was worthless. There were no walls to protect it, no gates to shut against intruders. And the building was not stone but wood. One flaming arrow could set the whole place ablaze. The house no longer seemed so beautiful; it seemed a useless place.

She stopped on the stairs. "Leave now and I will tell

249

my brother that I will go with him if he swears not to harm you."

He kissed her sweetly on the mouth. "No," he said softly. "For all that you seem convinced that I am a coward, I am not."

He put his arm tightly about her waist, and they began walking again. "And for all that you think he is, your brother is not a god on earth. He is merely a man, as we all are. Now do try to look less frightened. Your brother will think that I beat you."

Yes, she thought, she had better keep her chin up. Rogan was terrifying enough. She did not need to give him more reason for his anger than he already had.

When she realized what her husband planned to do she thought she might faint from fear. She thought he meant to meet her brother's army with his own, but instead he walked with her, alone, to the front of the house, to the little courtyard where fragrant flowers grew. They stood there, his arm about her, supporting her, the sun flashing off the brilliant fabric of their clothes.

"You cannot do this," she said frantically as she felt the ground tremble from the stamp of Rogan's men's horses. "Rogan will run you through."

"I cannot believe that your brother would be that stupid. The king would have him drawn and quartered. Now be still and smile at him. Are you not glad to see him?"

The man is crazy, Zared thought, absolutely crazy. If she had been strong enough, she would have carried him to safety, but as it was she could only stand beside him, her heart pounding in her ears, her body trembling, her hands and feet cold from fear, and watch her brother approach.

Rogan rode at the head of what must have been

three hundred men, and she wondered where they had all come from. Some of them she recognized, but most she did not. She tried to straighten her back, but it seemed to be made of gelatin.

Rogan and his men rode straight for the front of the house, their horses trampling over the pretty walkways and the flowers and the shrubbery. In spite of the seriousness of the situation she found herself frowning. Rogan would not think flowers meant anything in life.

"Good morn to you, brother," Tearle said cheerfully. "Will you come inside and eat with us?"

Rogan, atop his horse, his red hair making him look angry even when he wasn't, looked even bigger than Zared remembered. "I have come for my sister," he said in a voice that Zared had always obeyed.

She started to pull away from Tearle, but he held her fast.

"We will be ready soon," Tearle said. "Our garments and household goods are being packed now. But come and rest with us while we wait. I have ordered a half dozen cows killed, and they will be set to roasting soon. Your horses must be hungry, too."

Zared looked up at her brother and knew that Tearle must sound as insane to him as he did to her.

Rogan ignored him as he looked at his sister. "Mount and ride."

Again Zared tried to obey, but Tearle held her.

Rogan drew his sword. "Do you force her? I will kill you now."

At that Tearle released Zared, thrusting her behind him as he reached for the small knife at his side. Zared jumped between the men.

"He does not hold me," she said as loudly as her powerful lungs would allow. "No man holds me. I am free. Oh, Rogan, do not kill him. I have come of my own free will. Do not harm him."

She looked from one man to the other and knew in that instant she had insulted both men. She knew that Rogan had thought that she was honorable and that the only way she would have gone with a Howard was if she had been forced, but now he knew that she was not honorable, that she had betrayed the ancient Peregrine name. And she had insulted her husband by, in essence, saying that a woman must fight his battles for him.

It was Tearle, as she knew it would be, who made the first move toward peace. He sheathed his knife. "I do not wish to fight you. We are related now, and I wish this feuding to stop. You must come and eat with me, and we will discuss the future."

Rogan sneered down at him. "How many men do you have hidden in the house, Howard? Do you plan to take us once we are inside and befuddled with drink?"

"We can eat outside and drink water if that is your wish," Tearle said.

At that there were many groans from the men behind him.

"He will not attack you," Zared said. "He believes in peace." She said this with some wonder in her voice. How could one think of peace when looking at three hundred armed men?

At that Tearle put his hands on her shoulders. "I think you should leave us. Your brother and I have matters that we must discuss."

Zared turned pale at that. "I cannot leave the two of you alone."

Tearle looked up at Rogan as he sat on his big horse. "Your brother may hate me, but he is not a fool. He

knows that if he kills me and takes you, now that you are my legal wife, then my brother will wipe what is left of your family from the face of the earth. Is that not right, brother?"

"I am not your brother," Rogan muttered, but he looked at his sister. "Go. I will not kill him—not now. Ready yourself to return with me."

She nodded at her brother, then took one more look at her husband and went back into the house.

"What are they doing now?" Zared asked Margaret.

"The same as before. The men are eating, and your brother is sitting at the table in silence, but he is listening. Lord Tearle is doing all the talking."

"Yes, yes, I know that he is a talker. He could talk until a dead man would leave the room to get away from him." She remembered the way Tearle had been able to twist everything she had said to him so that it was to his advantage. "My brother is not so easily led as I was," she muttered to herself. "Rogan will not agree to what a Howard says."

"Yes, my Lady Howard," Margaret said softly, making Zared grimace.

Zared sat down on a window seat and looked out over the lovely rolling English countryside. "He will not agree to leave me here," she whispered. So I will have to return with my brother, and I will have to leave this beautiful place and my beautiful husband, she thought. I must return to a place of hatred and talk of war.

It was nearly sundown when Tearle returned to the room they shared. She jumped up at once and went to him, but she did not get close enough to touch him. "When do I leave?"

"Early tomorrow," he said, stretching. "Those men

of your brother's can eat. I do not wonder that your brother wants his title and lands back. It must cost much to feed men such as those."

"Do you jest about what is life and death to the Peregrines?"

He smiled at her. "I try to make a jest of everything. Have you not learned that yet? I am of the firm belief that laughter makes one live longer. Tell me, has that brother of yours ever so much as smiled?"

"Liana can make him smile," she said impatiently, then turned away. "So we have one last night together."

Tearle sat on the edge of the bed and began to unlace his tall boots. "Do you not plan to sleep with me when we are at your brother's house?"

It took Zared a moment to realize what he was saying, then she went to him. "You cannot go with us."

He smiled at her in a teasing way. "You can stand the place, but I cannot. Does this mean that you are more of a man than I am?"

She went on her knees in front of him. "Do not make a joke of this. My brother will kill you. If not directly, then there will be a falling stone, a blade that slips, an ax—"

"I did think of those things. I mentioned such to your brother." He paused in his undressing. "If he did not fear for the lives of those he loves, he would have killed me today. At least he would have taken great pleasure in the attempt. I have never seen such hatred in a man."

"He *will* kill you if given half a chance. You cannot think to go anywhere with him."

He put his hand under her chin. "I am not so fragile or so dumb and trusting as you seem to believe, nor is your brother as powerful as you think. Do you know

254

that when I was a child I thought my brother Oliver was the strongest, bravest—"

"Oliver Howard is fat and weak and—" She broke off, knowing where he was heading. "You cannot think that I do not see my brother as he is. Rogan is neither fat nor weak."

He leaned toward her. "Nor am I."

She sat back on her heels. Why did each man think he was invincible? "What have you and my brother arranged?" She looked up at him with narrowed eyes. "What have you talked my brother into?"

"Ah, at last you admit that there is something that I can best your brother in."

"Tell me," she repeated.

"He has agreed to what I have always planned to do. I am going with you to your home. Your brother will not believe that I want his sister for any purpose other than as some hostage of war. I told him that I wanted you only for your body, but even that did not make him laugh."

Zared grimaced. No, that would not make Rogan laugh. "Why would you want to do this? Why would you want to leave all this finery for my brother's poor place?"

He was silent so long that she looked up at him, and the tenderness in his eyes made her look away. She knew that he was going so that he could be near her. Rogan was so stubborn, so hardheaded that he would not believe any words that she spoke if she told him that she was with a Howard because she *wanted* to be. Rogan would always think that she had been forced. And he would do what he considered necessary to get her back. Zared *had* to go with her brother.

"You do not have to go with me," she whispered. "Perhaps I can return to you . . . later."

"Ha!" Tearle said. "I think your brother is worse

than you had described him. The man does not listen to reason. Do you know that I offered to give him this place if he would stop this war of his? I offered him half of the Howard estates upon my brother's death."

"He would refuse. All of what the Howards own belongs to the Peregrines."

He smiled at her. "He wanted you more than he wanted the estates." At Zared's look of astonishment Tearle nodded. "'Tis true. He said that he had lost too many of his family, and he could bear to lose no more. He would not trade you for all the riches in the world."

Zared looked away to hide her smile. It made her feel good that her brother loved her that much. She looked back at her husband. "You see that I must go with him."

"I understand that perfectly. I also know that I will not let you go either. Who will warm my bed at night if you are gone?"

She turned away. "You will find women. Men always do."

"Not women who chase me up trees and draw swords on me. Not a woman I find as entertaining as you."

She put her face in her hands. "You cannot go with me."

"I can and I will. Your brother, who has a head of rock, will have it no other way. I will go with you and stay with your family until he is satisfied that I have married you for some reason other than a personal feud." Tearle looked thoughtful. "Although I fear for my life if he hears the way I make you cry out in the night. He might think I am torturing you."

"I do not do that."

He gave her a smug smile. "Come and give me a kiss. Tomorrow we will ride with your brother, and we will see this place of yours. It cannot be as bad as you make it seem."

"It is worse," she said as she crawled onto his lap. "You will not be able to bear it."

He ran his hand down her hip and thigh. "I am made of sterner stuff than you imagine. In fact, I think that now I am made of steel. Do you know of a sheath where I could hide my sword?"

"Oh, Tearle, you fool," she said, laughing as she put her arms around his neck and began to kiss him.

Chapter Fourteen

Rogan's wife Liana lay back against the pillows of her bed and closed her eyes against the pain. Two days before she had given birth to a large, dark-haired little boy, and the birth had almost killed her. She still could not move without pain.

"How are they?" she whispered to her maid Joice, who was straightening the room.

"There is no change," Joice said solemnly, then she looked up at her mistress. "This cannot go on."

Liana nodded in agreement with her maid. It had been a month since Zared had arrived with her Howard husband, and since then the hatred in the Peregrine castle had grown darker and deeper. Liana had not been able to reason with her husband about his hatred for the man. "He is your sister's husband now," she had said to Rogan, but Rogan refused to bend, refused to see anything in the man except what he wanted to see. And what he wanted to see was a man who was an enemy.

For the last four weeks Rogan had done everything that he could to break the Howard man. He had trained him until Liana had seen the man's shoulders drooping from exhaustion. Rogan devised dreadful tests for the man, such as having six brawny knights attack him in the hallways, and this after a long day of "training" on the field. What Rogan called training would have killed most men.

But the Howard man took it all and never complained once. Liana had seen him look at Rogan with a glare of determination in his eyes, as though he were saying that he was going to survive whatever Rogan gave him or die trying.

In the last weeks Liana had been so heavily pregnant, so uncomfortable, that she had not been able to leave the solar and so could only see and hear what was happening secondhand. But as she had sat still, her sewing in her hand, and watched, she had seen more than she wanted to see.

When they had heard that Zared had been married to a Howard Liana had at first thought that her husband was going to die of apoplexy. The violence of his rage was something that she had never seen before. Years before, when Oliver Howard had taken her prisoner, she had later been told that her husband had gone into just such a fit, a fit of such severity that the people around him feared for his sanity.

No matter that Liana had protested day and night; Rogan raised a small army to go to the Howard house and get his sister. "Perhaps she married him because she loves him," Liana had said. "Perhaps she chose the man as I chose you."

Rogan would not listen to her. Nothing she said

made any difference to him. He was bent on gathering his army and going after his sister. "It will be the end of us all," Liana had said.

She spent long hours in the chapel praying for her husband's safety, knowing that she had just a few days to see him alive. The once grand Peregrine armies were too small to take on the many Howard men.

She sat by and watched as Rogan called his brother Severn to him, forcing him to leave his new bride at Bevan Castle. Severn was as enraged as his brother, and he told how he had been tricked and lied to by the Howard man. Severn kept saying that the Howard man had assured him that Liana had sent him to help them at the tournament.

It had taken her husband and brother-in-law some days to get ready to march to the Howard house. At the last moment Rogan had insisted that his brother remain behind, for he was sure that Oliver Howard would attack the moment Moray Castle was left with only a small force to guard it.

All the time Rogan had been gone Liana had stayed on her knees in the chapel asking God for the safe return of her husband.

She had not been prepared for the manner in which Rogan did return. He had come riding home beside a handsome dark-haired man dressed in finery such as Liana had not seen for years. And beside him rode Zared, but a Zared much changed from the boyish girl who had ridden off to a tournament weeks before.

Liana had watched the little group dismount, and at the sight of her husband's face her first hope that somehow the marriage of a Peregrine to a Howard would stop the feud fled. There was no happiness or forgiveness on her husband's face; only rage lived under his dark skin.

She stood at the window and looked down at the

group, and her heart began pounding, for it was a group full of many base emotions. "Send Zared to me," she had said to her maid. Liana knew that her husband could wait, but the misery she saw on her young sister-in-law's face was something that Liana wanted to understand.

Zared came stumbling up to Liana's solar and, without preamble, threw herself at her sister-in-law, going to her knees and putting her head in Liana's lap—what lap there was left. Liana had quickly dismissed the other people in the room and run her hands over Zared's thick red hair. "Tell me all," she said softly.

Words came flooding out of Zared as she told about the tournament and about making a bargain with the Howard man that she would marry him if he could arrange for Lady Anne to marry Severn. "I never thought he could do it," Zared cried. "I thought I was in no danger."

Liana stroked her hair and listened. She listened not only with her ears but with her heart, and she heard more than just words. Zared talked of being "tricked" into marriage and of having to marry the Howard man, but there was an underlying softness to her words that told Liana a great deal.

"Tell me about your time alone with him," Liana said softly.

Zared dried her eyes on Liana's silk skirt and started telling of the few weeks they had spent alone together. "His house was a worthless place, of course," Zared said. "A dozen men could have taken it." She paused. "Oh, but it was lovely." She told about the house and described in detail the clothes she had worn there, and she told about the fair and about some of the places she had gone and what she had done.

"And what of this Howard man you are married to? Is he *your* enemy as well as Rogan's?"

Zared clenched her teeth together to fight back tears. "I do not know what he is. I do not understand him. He is so soft and so gentle. He praises me and sings to me and gives me presents and reads to me, and sometimes I feel as though I would die without him, but . . ."

"But what?" Liana urged.

"But I do not know what is in his mind. I do not know if he can be trusted. He is not like any man I have ever met before. He says only that he does not want war, but what if I trust him and he is lying? What if I allow myself to believe him and he betrays me and my family?" She put her face in her hands. "How can I let go of a hatred that I have had all my life because of a few weeks of a man being kind to me? I must be made of sterner stuff than that. I *have* to be stronger than that. I cannot allow my passion for him to blind me to the fact that he is a Howard."

At that Zared began to cry again, and Liana could hear the anguish in her voice. Zared was more than confused about what the man she had married was and how she felt about him. "I was beginning to trust him, but I do not know why he married me. Sometimes I believe what he says to me, and sometimes I am afraid of my own belief. He says that he wishes to end this feud, but I fear that I am bringing the enemy into our house. If he gains our trust, he could open the gates at night and let his brother's army in here. He could kill us as we sleep."

"But what would he gain by that?"

Zared looked at Liana as though the older woman had gone mad. "He will have clear title to the dukedom and the lands. There will be no Peregrines to claim that he does not own the lands."

At Zared's answer Liana began to be afraid, too, and she wished she had never heard of the dreadful Howard man. She began to be afraid for the lives of all of her family: her son, her unborn child, her husband, and his sister and brother. Each night she quizzed Rogan on what he was doing with the Howard man, making sure that Rogan did not let up on his vigil over the man.

Once Liana took her son to the courtyard to see some new puppies and the Howard man walked by her, then stopped and smiled down at the lovely little boy with his bright red hair who held a puppy. He was still smiling as he looked back up at Liana, but the smile faded when she snatched her son to her in a protective way and glared at the man. He gave a sigh and walked away.

Liana did not have time to concern herself with how the brother of an enemy felt. She was much more concerned with the worry she saw on the faces of Rogan and Zared and Severn. Severn felt as though everything had happened because of him, and he worked hard to try to forgive himself, but he seemed to make no progress. He never left the training field, and Liana knew that he was pining for his new wife, whom he had left in the relative safety of Bevan Castle.

With each day Rogan's eyes sank farther into his head. As Liana well knew, he slept little, for fear kept him constantly on edge. He was afraid that at any moment his family was going to be attacked. One night she did no more than turn over in bed, and Rogan jumped out of the bed, his sword in his hand, before Liana could even get her eyes open.

But it was Zared who was the most troubled. With each day she seemed to grow thinner and grayer before Liana's very eyes.

It was at the beginning of the second week that Liana looked up at her little sister-in-law, saw the haggard look on her face, and understood a great deal. "You love him, don't you?" Liana said softly.

Zared tried to act as though the words meant nothing. "What does love matter? He is the enemy."

"But he's not your enemy, is he?"

"I am one person. I must think of my family."

Liana had no answer for her except to say that sometimes one must trust in one's own judgment and not the opinions of others. She spoke from experience, for years earlier she had trusted her instinct when she had agreed to marry Rogan. People had said that she was a fool and that he was a man incapable of love, but she had proved them wrong, for she had found the heart that he had managed to hide for years.

The birth of her child took three long, hard days, and afterward she could do little but lie in bed, but she watched what was going on within her family as closely as she could.

"Zared," Tearle said, "look at me."

They were in bed together, and she was as far to one side of the bed as she could get. She didn't want to touch him, didn't know if she should touch him. Yet she wanted to.

"I am tired," she said.

"You seem to always be tired," he said, his voice heavy. He was silent for a long while, then he spoke again. "I cannot do this alone."

She knew what he meant, but she had no answer for him. Every day was hell for her. Whenever her brothers caught her alone they pointed out the horses' skulls on the walls. Years before the Howards had laid siege to a Peregrine castle, and the inhabitants, who included Zared's mother, had starved to death. Before

264

they had died they had been reduced to eating the horses. The skulls of those horses hung on the wall as a constant reminder of the treachery of the Howards.

"It was you who wanted to come here," she said at last.

"No," he said softly. "I did not want to come to this house of hatred. What I wanted and have always wanted is for the woman I love to love me in return."

"I thought your desire was to stop the hatred," she said with some bitterness in her voice. Every day she watched what her brothers did to her husband, driving him hard enough to break a lesser man, but Tearle did not break. He did not so much as show anger.

She rolled over to face him. "What kind of man are you?" she half shouted. "Do you not know that all the men laugh at you? You take whatever Rogan gives you, and you do not fight back. The men are wagering on whether he will ask you to empty the slops next and whether you will do it."

He faced her, and his face showed some anger. "Were I to show what I felt to your brother he would strike me, and I would retaliate. Knowing your brother's anger, one of us would die. Is that what you want? A trial by combat? Shall we square off and fight each other for you like a couple of rutting bucks? Would you like to see one of us dead? Would that make you believe that I am as much a man as your brother is?"

He rose up on one elbow. "Tell me, Zared, is that what you want? Is that what I have to do to prove myself to you?"

He sat up. "It does not seem to be enough that I am willing to risk my inheritance by marrying you. My courtship of you seems to mean nothing. The fact that I, a Howard, walk into your brother's home, if one can call this den of hatred a home, alone and willing to face your two brothers, means naught to you. Whatever I do is not enough for you. You always want more from me. You said that I was not man enough to take what your brother could give to me, but I have taken it and more. I am tired and sore. And I am sick unto death of being hated. I am sick of the looks people give me."

He got out of bed and stood looking down at her. "But it would be worth it if I could change but one person's mind. If I could make you look at me with the trust I deserve, then all would be worth it."

He stopped and rubbed his eyes. "I will not fight your brothers. I will not see more bloodshed between these two families, and"—he looked up—"and you can tell your sister-in-law that I do not harm children."

He pulled on his clothes quickly and left the room.

Zared would have said something to him, but she did not know what to say. Could she tell him the truth? That every day she had to force herself to remember that he was a Howard? She saw him with Rogan or Severn, and she wanted to run to him and protect him, to keep their lances from coming at his back, to keep the men from laughing at him.

But she didn't interfere in what her brothers made him do. She was still a Peregrine, and he was still the enemy.

He did not return that night, and she did not sleep much.

It was three days later that Tearle and Rogan's three-year-old son disappeared together.

Chapter Fifteen

It was Liana who discovered that the boy was missing. For all that she had tried to raise the boy in a civilized manner, he was a Peregrine. His father had given him a wooden sword on his first birthday, and his uncle had given him a molded leather helmet. Rogan had set his son on a horse when the child was two. He was a child who had been raised amid horses' hooves and clashing swords. At two he was often out with his father on the training field, already imitating his father and uncle in the way they handled weapons.

By three years of age he was fearless. Liana had pleaded with Rogan to watch out for the boy and not allow him to run so freely about the courtyard where the men, who were usually half drunk or exhausted from Rogan's training, might easily step on the child. But Rogan had said that she was an old woman and that that was the way all the Peregrines had been raised, that he meant for his son to grow up to be a man and not a half-woman.

So when Joice had gone to see about the child and he was not in his room, she did not think anything of it. She had her weakened mistress and the new child to see to. She did not even mention to her mistress that the child was not where he usually was.

And Liana did not miss her older son because she had her husband's rage to deal with, for the Howard man had disappeared.

"Where is he?" Rogan had bellowed at his sister.

Zared had sat there in stony silence, for she had already answered her brother a hundred times. She did not know. He had spent the night with her, and he had risen very early and left the room. She had not followed him.

Zared did not tell her furious brother that they had had another fight, or actually a repeat of the same fight. Tearle had once again raged at her that she did not trust him and that he deserved her trust. But she had tried to tell him that even though she could not trust him, she was torn apart, that half of her sided with her brothers and half with him. Instead of appeasing him this had only seemed to make him more angry.

"Just as your brother will not accept only half of what belongs to the Howards, I will not accept half of what is my due." He had stormed out of the room, and she had not seen him since.

Severn said that the Howard man had not been able to take life with the Peregrines, but Rogan said that the man was probably going to his brother to tell him of the vulnerable defenses of the Peregrines.

"Stop it, all of you!" Zared had screamed. "He took whatever you gave him," she yelled at her oldest brother. "He did all that you asked of him, and he never so much as bent under the burden. He can take it all and more."

"Then where is he?"

Zared did not have an answer for them. Had he had enough of the Peregrine hatred and just ridden off? Would he have left her and not said a word? *Had* he gone back to his brother? Was war imminent? Would her family die because of what she had done?

She thought that she could bear no more agony, but it was nearly noon when Liana realized that her son was missing. Liana, already ill from the second birth, could not stand the misery of finding her son gone.

"The Howard man has taken my son," Rogan had whispered.

Zared wasn't sure that she was hearing correctly. "No," she said softly, then louder, "No! He would not do that."

Rogan gave her a look that said that he had no more use for her, that she was as much an enemy as the Howards.

Zared sat by and waited while her brothers and their men went out to search for the boy. Liana said that he might have walked into the village with one of the workers. But the village was scoured, and there was no sign of the boy or of the Howard man. Both had disappeared from the face of the earth.

By sundown Rogan was ready to wage war on the Howards, but both Liana and Zared pleaded for time. It was possible there was no connection between the disappearances of the boy and Zared's husband.

The moat was dragged with weighted nets, but there was no small body found, and Liana cried in relief.

Zared sat by a window in the solar, her eyes unblinking as she looked toward the north, hoping to see her husband come riding up. She hoped he had merely taken a day to get away from the Peregrines, a day to lie in the sun and look at the flowers. She could not tell her brothers that that was something that he might do, for they would not understand a man wanting to look at flowers.

At sundown the men took torches, went into the surrounding forest, and began to look for the child.

And it was in the forest that they found the poacher. At first the terrified man thought that Rogan and his men had come for him. His terror was so great that he could not speak coherently. When at last he realized that for once the Peregrine men were not concerned with who was stealing game from their lands he told them of having seen a large, dark man riding with a red-haired child in the saddle before him.

Rogan and Severn questioned the man for a long while until they were convinced that the child was Rogan's son and that the man who held him was Tearle Howard.

A grim Rogan and Severn went back to the castle and began to plan to go to war.

"Something is wrong," Zared said. "He did not take the child. He would not."

Rogan turned the full force of his fury on her, bellowing at her that all of this had been caused by her lust for a man, that because of her the Peregrine line was going to end. "If you carry his child now, I will kill it when it is born," he said to her.

Zared could not stand up against his rage or, she had to admit, against his logic. They had brought the poacher back to Moray Castle with them, and the man had repeated his story for the women. He had described Tearle to the color of the clothes he was wearing and the Howard emblem on his sword hilt.

270

And he had described Rogan's son with his bright red hair and his father's looks. There was no doubt that it was Tearle who had held the child. And with him rode three Howard men, all wearing the trappings of the Howards.

Zared wanted to believe in her husband, wanted to explain away what the poacher said he had seen, but she could find no explanation. Tearle had been seen with Rogan's son riding in the company of three Howard knights in the direction of the Howard estates.

The morning after his son disappeared Rogan rode out with Severn with nearly three hundred men behind them, all the men they could find. It wasn't enough men to wage a war on the Howards, but it was all the men the Peregrines could afford.

Zared had at one point suggested that she ride with her brothers, but Rogan had merely looked at her, his eyes blazing with rage. She knew that he considered her almost as much of an enemy as he considered her husband.

"Women wait while men go to die," Liana had said when the men rode off.

Zared was not very good at waiting, and she paced the parapets for days, paced until she wore the bottoms of her shoes out. She threw the shoes over the side of the castle into the moat, then walked barefoot, her eyes never leaving the horizon.

For two days she believed in her husband. For two days she told herself that he had not betrayed her and her family. She told herself that he could not have taken the child. She tried to remember all the sweet times they had shared and all the many times he had told her that he wanted to settle the feud between the two families.

In the middle of the third day Rogan sent a messenger back to his family. With the messenger came a man who told them that he had seen four Howard men who carried a red-haired boy with them, and they were heading toward the Howard estates. The man lived near enough to the Howard estates that he knew Tearle by sight.

It was then that Zared stopped believing in her husband. She was quiet, saying nothing after hearing the messenger, but she did not fool Liana.

Liana turned and saw that her sister-in-law had left the room, and she ran to find her. She found Zared putting on the armor that her brothers had had made for her.

"You are not going after him," Liana said.

"I brought him here, and I shall take him away. I shall find him and kill him. He will allow me to get close to him, and when he does I will kill him."

Liana knew better than to try to argue with a Peregrine. When it came to their hatred of the Howards, there was no reasoning with them. Liana left the room, called three men, all of them either crippled or too old to fight so they could not go with Rogan, and had the men hold Zared. She was not going to allow the young woman to leave the castle.

Zared was held under guard for two more days before the Peregrine army returned and Liana went to release her sister-in-law.

Zared's rage had not calmed under confinement, and she was so angry at Liana that she could not bear to look her in the eyes. When Liana started to touch her arm Zared moved away.

"They are returning," Liana said softly.

Zared pushed past Liana and ran up the stairs to the parapets. It was a long distance away, but she could see that her husband was with them. He rode beside

Rogan, his head down, and she could tell that his hands were tied behind his back.

She waited and watched as they rode closer, and as they neared she could see that Tearle had been beaten. For a moment, for just a tiny moment, she felt his pain, remembered his hands on her body, remembered his smile. But then she made herself remember his treachery and the way he had betrayed her family.

She went down the stairs and was waiting in the courtyard when they arrived. Liana stood behind her, and she gasped when she saw Tearle's face, his handsome face that was now black and blue and swollen.

Zared felt tears forming at the back of her eyes, but she would not shed them. She wondered why Rogan had not killed the man on sight, but then she knew that he had brought Tearle back for a public execution, an execution that Zared would have to watch.

She watched as they half pushed him from his horse and he fell, but he caught himself, having difficulty righting himself with his tied hands. When a man reached out a hand to help him up Tearle moved his shoulder away, accepting no help from the man.

Zared stood not three feet away and watched as her husband painfully struggled to stand up, and when he did, he saw her. His face was almost unrecognizable, and Zared winced, but she stood firm as she looked at him. She was not going to let her woman's softness betray her again. She straightened her shoulders and gave him a look that told him that he could expect nothing from her, that once she might have loved him but that she did not do so any longer.

He looked at her a long while, then he turned away and started up the stairs into the castle. Zared had almost gone after him then, for never had anyone looked at her as he did. Since she had met him he had looked at her in amusement, in exasperation and, lately, with love in his eyes. But never had he looked at her with hatred. She had not thought him capable of hatred. Perhaps she had thought that hatred was a prerogative of the Peregrines, an emotion that they had perfected and were especially good at.

But the look she had seen in Tearle's eyes put Rogan's hatred to shame. His hatred of her was not the impersonal hatred of one unknown family member for another, but of one person for another person. His look could only have been given by one who has loved but whose love has turned to the other side.

Zared looked away from him, could not watch him as he stumbled up the stone stairs into the lord's chamber.

"Go," Severn said from behind her. "You must hear his sentence."

Zared recovered her senses enough to look at her surroundings. Behind Tearle were several of Rogan's men, then came Liana, clasping her son to her. Behind her was Rogan, then more of his men.

"W-where was he?" Zared asked.

"We found him before he could reach the land the Howards stole from us. He was alone with the child." Severn turned from her and went up the stairs behind the others.

Glumly Zared followed him.

The sight that greeted her was worse than she had imagined. Tearle, barely able to stand, his clothes torn and bloodstained, was surrounded by Rogan's men. Liana, clutching her child, who was sleeping on her shoulder, was sitting near her husband, her eyes showing her relief at having her child back with her.

"What do you have to say for yourself, Howard?" Rogan said in a voice full of rage.

Tearle lifted his head and glared at his brother-in-law. "I have told you all," he managed to whisper through a swollen mouth. "You will hear nothing more."

"Take him and kill him," Rogan said.

It was Liana who protested, not out of any desire to protect Tearle, but out of fear of Howard retaliation. "You cannot do this. His brother is a duke." Her son woke at her outburst and immediately wanted to be put down. Liana, still too weak to hold a sturdy three-year-old against his will, set the boy on the floor. She stood up and went to her husband. "You will have to take him to London to the king."

Rogan gave Tearle a look of contempt. "The king will not see to justice. The man says that he did not take the boy. He says that he was saving him. The king will believe a Howard, for a Howard has enough money to buy even a king."

"Did not take the child? What do you mean?"

"I do not know," Rogan said. "The man is always full of words."

At the very idea that Tearle didn't take Rogan's son Zared's heart leaped, but she made it be still. She had believed in him once, but she was not going to believe in him again. She stood there rigidly, seeing that he was having difficulty in standing, but by some great force of will he was making himself remain upright. He had not looked in her direction since he had left the courtyard.

"Rogan," Liana said, "I want to hear what the man says."

"Nay," Rogan said. "I will hear no more of his lies." He turned to his men. "Take him below."

Zared would not have thought that Tearle had any fight left in him, but he struggled against Rogan's men when they put their hands on him.

It was at the struggle that Rogan's son let out a cry of protest and ran toward the men. The child, who was afraid of nothing, ran straight into their heavily shod feet.

Everyone else in the room was so intent on what was happening with the adults that no one but Liana saw the child. She gave a scream of fright, and when she did nearly everyone looked down and saw the boy just as one of Rogan's men's fists came toward the boy's head.

With his last bit of effort Tearle twisted and used his own body to protect the child from the blow. The fist hit Tearle's side, and everyone in the room heard the crack of Tearle's ribs.

For a moment all was still, everyone too stunned by what had happened to move. Tearle was on the floor, his body protectively over the child.

Liana went to her child, but the boy put his arms around Tearle's neck and held on.

Zared did not seem able to move as she stood to one side and watched. Tearle, with tears of pain in his eyes, rolled to a sitting position and took the child in his arms.

He looked over the boy's head to Liana, who was standing by, shaking with fear from having come, again, so close to losing her child, for had the man's fist struck the child, it would have no doubt killed him.

"We have become friends in the last days," Tearle said, his voice strained and shallow.

Rogan started toward the man and boy, but Liana put her hand out to stop him. "What happened?" she whispered.

They could all see that it was with utmost difficulty that Tearle spoke, and there was no imagining the pain

276

the sturdy child must be causing him as he moved about on Tearle's lap, but the boy would not leave Tearle even when his mother held out her arms to him.

"I could not sleep," Tearle said, and they could hardly hear him. "I went below, and . . ." He took a breath and closed his eyes for a moment against the pain. "The child was there. We . . . we played with a ball for a while." Tearle took another breath. "I must have fallen asleep. I opened my eyes, and the gate was open, and the child was gone." Tearle winced as the active little boy kicked him in the stomach, but Tearle merely put his hand on the child's foot and gently held it.

"I went to the gate and saw the boy walking toward the forest." Tearle took a breath. "My brother's men watch this place."

"We know that," Rogan snapped. "I will not listen to this."

Liana put herself between her husband and Tearle. She was protective of the child and anyone whom the child befriended. "What did you do?"

"I saddled my horse and went after the boy," Tearle said, and he looked at the boy fondly, his big hand on the back of the child's head. "My brother's men had taken him, just as I feared."

The boy sat down in Tearle's lap and began to play with the tattered remnants of his surcoat.

Tearle looked up at Liana. "I could not kill my brother's men, and I could not risk injury to the boy. I went with them in order to protect the boy."

"I will listen to no more of these lies. He is a Howard and is as dangerous as a snake," Rogan said.

Liana turned on her husband. "Do you think your son is so stupid that he does not know an enemy when he sees one? Was the boy so at ease with the other men?"

"He was frightened of the other men," Severn said. "Remember, Rogan? The boy screamed when one of the men came too near him."

"I remember nothing," Rogan said, but he didn't move toward Tearle.

Tearle looked down at the boy in his lap. "My brother's men are barbarians. They would have killed him for the sport of it. I could not allow that." He ran his hand down the boy's leg. "He is a fine lad."

Zared had not said a word, but it was at that moment that she knew he was telling the truth. He had done just what he said he had done: He had gone after the boy and stayed with him to protect him.

"He is telling the truth," she whispered to her brother, and she could feel Tearle's eyes on her.

"A Howard does not know how to tell the truth."

"He does, and he is," Zared said, her jaw clenched. "He did not take the child." She glared at her brother. "Where did you find my husband?"

When Rogan did not immediately answer her she knew without a doubt that her husband had been telling the truth, and suddenly she felt lighter than she ever had in her life. "Where was he when you found him?" she practically shouted at her brother.

"He was returning," Severn said.

"Returning?" Zared's heart became even lighter. "You mean he was coming back here? He was bringing the child with him and coming back here? I thought you said you killed the other Howard men."

Rogan had a look on his face that said he was not going to speak, so Zared looked to Severn.

"They were chasing him," Severn said quietly.

At that both women erupted, and they attacked the

two brothers. "He was running *away* from his brother's men? You killed the Howard men, and then you beat the man who was *saving* your son?" This last was from Liana.

Liana went to her husband and looked up at him. "Is your hatred so strong that it colors your judgment? For weeks I have seen you punish this man, and day after day he has taken your abuse, yet I have seen no evidence that he is the devil that you claim he is." She gestured toward her son. "Look you at them. Your three-year-old son has more sense than you do. He knows a friend when he sees one."

With that she turned to Tearle and bent to him. "You may be a Howard, but you have proven that you are a friend. Thank you for saving my child." She leaned forward and kissed Tearle's cheek, then took her heavy son from his lap and stood up. "Take our friend and care for him," she said to the men. "He is to be treated with the utmost care that we can offer him."

Tearle pushed the helping hands away, hands that a moment before had tried to kill him. Slowly, with much pain, he managed to rise without aid. "I will stay here no longer. I will go home."

Liana looked at him and nodded. She felt very bad for the way she had treated him in the past few weeks, but she understood that he did not want to see any of the Peregrines ever again.

Zared moved to stand beside her husband and looked at her brother in defiance. "I am going with him."

Before Rogan could protest Tearle turned to look down at her. "No," he said.

She looked up at him. "I want to go with you. Wherever you go, I want to go with you."

His swollen face was cold and hard. "No. I do not want you."

Cold fear washed over Zared. "But I trust you. I know you did not take the child. I know now that you are not my enemy."

His face did not soften. "You did not believe in me. I saw the hatred in your eyes. You thought I was guilty, just as your brothers did." He looked away from her as though the matter were settled and looked at Liana. "May I have the return of my horse? I would leave now."

Liana's eyes widened. "You cannot think to ride a horse. You are injured, and you have no men to go with you to protect you."

"I would leave this place now," he said, gasping against the effort.

After that no one stood in his way. No one tried to persuade him to remain in the Peregrine castle. Even Zared stood to one side as he walked out of the room and out of her life. She watched him go, and she wanted to go after him, but her pride wouldn't allow her to go. If he didn't want her, then she didn't want him.

"Go after him," Liana urged Zared.

But Zared shook her head and walked up the stairs to the hallway of bedrooms. She kept her shoulders back and her eyes straight ahead, trying to will herself not to think. If she allowed herself to think, she knew that she would remember how many kind things that Tearle had done for her. From the first he had been good to her. He had put his body between her and the trampling horse at the tournament, and she had no doubt that he had saved the life of Rogan's son.

Yet she had always doubted him. Liana had told her to go with her instincts, but Zared had not. She had allowed generations of hatred to influence her, and she had based her opinions of the man not on what she saw, but on what she thought to be true. Just as she wasn't as filled with hatred as her brothers were, just as she was different from them, she was sure that Tearle was different from his brother.

As she moved down the hall she became aware that something was different. She stopped walking and rubbed her arms as though from cold. Then, slowly, she turned and looked behind her. The door to the haunted room was open.

For a moment she stood where she was. She could see sunlight streaming out of the doorway and into the hall, yet she knew that it was gray and cloudy outside. The haunted room was always kept locked, and she had never been in it in her life. Before Rogan had married the second floor over the solar had not been used because everyone was afraid of the haunted room. It was said that when the lady inside was needed the door would be unlocked.

Zared looked about her and knew that she was the only one in the hall. If the door was open, then it must be open for her.

She took a step toward the open door, and her feet felt as though they were made of stone. She could barely lift them, but she shuffled along, inching toward the door.

As she rounded the corner she held her breath, not having any idea what she would see inside the room. Monsters, perhaps? Ghouls?

She was shaking as she entered the room, and the blood had drained from her face. For a moment her terror reached a peak, and she was ready to scream or run or both, but after a moment she let out her breath. There was nothing in the room but chairs with pretty cushions on them, a tapestry frame, and carpets on the wall. For all that the room had been kept locked for years, it was clean and fresh. And there was no one in it.

Zared began to breathe easily, and she walked to the frame and looked at the half-finished tapestry. She touched the design of the lady and the unicorn on the tapestry, and as she did so a piece of paper came floating down from the ceiling.

Zared's hand froze. She stood rooted where she was, her breath held, her body beginning to tremble as she looked at the paper on the floor. She was terrified to turn around, afraid of what she would see. Would a ghost be standing behind her?

It was some minutes before she could move. There was no sound in the room, nor did she hear anything from outside the room, even though the door stood wide open.

All at once, and with all the courage she could muster, she turned on her heel and looked behind her.

Nothing. No one. There was no one in the clean room that should have been dirty. There was only sunlight in a room that should have been as dull as the day outside was.

It took Zared a few moments before she could still her shaking body enough to look back at the piece of paper on the floor. Her legs felt a little weak from her fear, but she managed to make them work long enough to get to the paper and pick it up.

She hadn't had enough lessons from Tearle to be able to read the entire message, but she didn't need to know how to read to know what the paper said. It was the correct number of words, and it was shaped the same way as the writing above the fireplace in Rogan's brooding room. She knew the words by heart, as all the Peregrines did.

When the red and white make black
When the black and gold become one
When the one and the red unite
Then shall you know

It was a riddle that had been handed down in their family for centuries, long before the feud with the Howards and Peregrines began. No one had ever had any idea what it meant. When Zared was younger she had spent sleepless nights trying to figure out what the riddle meant. Sometimes she thought that if she could figure out the answer, then she could save her brothers from death. But she had grown up seeing her brothers and her father and her mother die. There had been times in her life when she had been frantic to solve the riddle, thinking that the responsibility of saving her family rested on her thin shoulders. She could not wield a sword with her brothers, but she could, perhaps, help in some other way.

She held the paper tightly in her hand and walked out of the room. Behind her she heard the door close itself and lock. She refused to think about such a happening. "It was the wind," she whispered, and she walked faster down the hall.

Perhaps if she could solve the riddle she could understand what was going on in her life, and perhaps she could get her husband back.

Chapter Sixteen

Tearle bit into the apple and watched his brother's men train. Or perhaps he should think of them as his men, he thought, since his brother was so ill. Tearle knew that he should feel some loss at his brother's approaching death, but he couldn't bring himself to do so. He was sure that hatred was killing his brother. Even on his deathbed Oliver Howard could speak of little else but his hatred of the Peregrines.

"They will try to take all that I have worked for," Oliver would whisper night and day. "You must be strong and keep them away from what we own. They will know that I am not here to keep them away."

Tearle didn't answer his brother. It seemed that all the world thought he was weak. His own brother thought he was not strong enough to hold the lands. The Peregrines had always thought he was made of softness. Even his own wife—

He did not pursue that line of thought. In fact, for

the three months that he had been back from the Peregrines' he had made a constant effort not to think of the woman he had stupidly made his wife. For weeks he had lain in bed, raging with fever, close to death as his body fought off the effects of the beating the Peregrines had given him when they had judged him without a trial.

On that day three months before, after that beating, on the long, painful ride back to the castle, he had kept the picture of his wife before him. He had thought that she would be enraged at what her brothers had done to him. He knew that at times she did not trust him and that sometimes she did not understand him, but he had been sure that she knew enough about him to know that he would never be so low as to take a child prisoner.

Yet when he had dismounted he had looked into her eyes and seen that she believed the worst of him. She thought that he had done what they accused him of. Even after having lived with him, after having spent a great deal of time with him, she thought he was capable of stealing a child. She thought that he had married her in order to perpetuate the feud between the two families. He looked into her eyes and saw that the hatred she felt was stronger than any love that she would ever feel for him.

For a while, between the pain of his body and the pain in his heart, he hadn't cared what the Peregrines did to him. It was instinct alone that had made him save the boy when he had seen the child was going to be struck by the man. That action had cost him much in pain, but in the end he guessed it had saved his life. At the time he hadn't cared much one way or the other, for his hatred of the Peregrines was equal to theirs of the Howards.

He had answered Liana's questions because for the

first time he'd seen a Peregrine with a face that was not twisted with hatred. He had watched as she had stepped between her husband and him.

It was only later, when Tearle had been proven innocent, that Zared stepped forward. She said that she was ready to go with him. She was ready to go once she had been shown that he was not the villain that she had thought him to be. But he hadn't wanted her then. She hadn't believed in him when all she knew was what she had seen of him. She hadn't believed him when he told her he loved her. She had believed only in her brothers and their hatred. Hate had meant much more to her than love.

Later he managed to get on his horse, and he'd managed to stay on it long enough to ride to where his brother's men were camped. They carried him home in a cart, Tearle only half conscious, and later Oliver's wife Jeanne had nursed him through his fever and his raging.

He was nearly fully recovered. He needed sunshine and air and some exercise and much food, for he had lost weight in his three months' recovery. Jeanne said that he would be as good as new in a few weeks, but Tearle knew that he would never recover from what had happened to him. He had been a naïve child when he had married the Peregrine brat. He had thought that love could conquer her hatred. But he had been wrong, for love had lost and hate had won.

It was while he was leaning against the wall, his body soaking up the weak sunshine, that he noticed something unusual about one of his brother's men. There was something familiar about the boy, something about the way he moved his sword. The boy didn't look very strong, but he was agile and quick on his feet and thus managed to miss most of the blows aimed at him.

Suddenly Tearle sat upright. That was no boy—that was his wife!

His first impulse was to grab her by her hair and pull her off the field, but his second impulse was to leave her where she was. But if one of his brother's men should recognize the brat as the youngest Peregrine, she would be ordered killed as fast as Oliver could speak the words.

He made himself lean back against the wall. How long had she been inside the Howard castle? How was she keeping her sex a secret from the boys? She must be living with the other men, sleeping in a bed with the boys.

Again he had an impulse to grab her, but he forced himself to stay where he was. Damn her and her whole family, he thought.

He watched her as she darted away from the boy's sword, and every time the boy came close to hitting her Tearle almost jumped up. It was when the boy knocked the sword from Zared's hand and sent it flying that he almost interfered, but he managed to make himself stay on the seat. He looked with disgust at the apple in his hand; he had crushed it.

He watched Zared dodge the boy, then run after her sword, and when she leaned over to pick it up she smiled at Tearle. She had known all along that he had been watching her, and she knew very well how it was affecting him.

He turned his head away. He wasn't going to allow her to see that he was concerned for her safety. In fact, he wasn't going to *be* concerned for her safety. He couldn't care less what happened to her or to any of her family.

At the sound of steel hitting steel he turned back quickly. The boy had Zared on the ground, his sword at her throat, and he was smiling as though he meant to skewer her.

Tearle was on his feet in seconds, and he pushed the boy away, sending him sprawling.

Zared lay still on the ground and smiled up at him. "You have recovered well, I see," she said softly.

"Not through the help of your family," he said, looking down at her, trying to remember the anger and loathing he'd felt for her on the day he'd left the Peregrine castle. What he noticed was that she was quite pretty. There was a smudge on her cheek.

"I came to be with you." She looked up at him with her heart in her eyes. "I have missed you. I . . . I do not like being without you."

He opened his mouth to tell her that he'd missed her, too. He had missed her laughter; he'd missed teaching her about the world. He'd missed her enthusiasm, her lack of artifice. He had wanted her with him even when he was ill. He had wanted her there telling him that he was weak and should have been up and about days earlier. Jeanne had been a good nurse, but Oliver had killed her spirit years before, and his convalescence had been a dreary affair.

"I have not given you a thought," he said haughtily.

She smiled up at him.

How did people not know that she was female? he wondered for the thousandth time. She was as feminine as the moon and the stars.

She started to get up, but he put his foot on her stomach. "I have but to tell anyone who you are and my brother will have you killed," he said softly.

She put her hand on his ankle. He did not put any weight on the foot that was on her. "Do you still laugh when your feet are tickled?"

"No," he said sternly, "I do not. You must leave here. I do not want you."

288

"But I want you. I have been miserable these months."

"You did not care on the day I left. That day you thought I had taken a child. You thought I would harm a child."

"People are staring at us," she said, and she started to get up, but he held her down. She gave a sigh, put her hand behind her head, and leaned on it. "Yes, I thought you were guilty. Can you blame me? You *had* gone with the boy. How was I to know that you would not harm him?"

"You had spent time with me. You should have known me."

"How can anyone know what is in another's heart?"

"You should have known then. You should have—"

"You should have taken me with you when you left. You should know what is in my heart *now,"* she yelled up at him.

At that Tearle turned and looked behind him. Every man on the field, every man, woman, and child in the courtyard had gathered behind them and was watching them with consternation on their faces. Tearle knew that it was only a matter of minutes before someone went to tell his brother that something very unusual was going on.

Tearle lifted his foot from Zared's stomach and glared down at her. "Come with me."

She stood up, dusted herself off, then gave him a hot look. "Gladly," she said in a provocative way.

He pretended to ignore her as he led the way into the main building and up two flights of stairs to his room. Since he was in front of Zared he did not see the way her eyes bugged and her mouth fell open at the sight of the riches in the Howard castle. She had seen something like it at the Marshall estate, but that was a stable compared to this rich place. Every surface gleamed with vessels of gold and silver. The walls were covered with tapestries, and there were thick rugs on the tables.

At last they arrived at his room, and he reached over her head to shut the door. "Now you will tell me what you do here. Have your brothers sent you to me to try to persuade me to give the estates to them? Have they heard that my brother is dying? Have they—"

He broke off because Zared had begun removing her clothes. She had wanted to talk to him, to tell him that it was her decision alone to come to him, that in fact she had had a raging fight with Rogan before he allowed her her freedom. But she knew that she could not out-talk Tearle. He had always been able to persuade her to do anything that he wanted, so perhaps she could keep him from talking.

Tearle stood where he was and watched her untie ties and slip cloth over her head. He hadn't had a woman since he had ridden away from the Peregrine castle. It wasn't that he hadn't wanted one. Twice he had chosen pretty kitchen maids and had wanted to take them to bed. The young women had been agreeable—so agreeable, in fact, that Tearle could practically hear the gold coins clinking in their pockets. In spite of himself he kept remembering that Zared had not come to love him for his money. She had come to love him for himself. She had come to love him when she finally realized that he wasn't her enemy.

"Do not," he whispered.

Zared removed the last of her clothes and looked at him. One minute she was standing in front of him and the next she had launched herself at him. He caught her as her legs went around his waist. He put his hands on her bare buttocks, and his lips fastened on hers, and the next minute his hose were around his ankles and he was in her.

They made love like two people dying for want of each other, as hard and as fast as their firm young bodies would allow.

When they finished Zared was half on the floor, half shoved against a wooden chest, while Tearle's back was bent in a backward curve that a spine could not manage under normal conditions.

He groaned. "You have killed me." When he could again move, he carried her to the bed, then pulled her on top of him, covering them both with the sheet.

She was still for a moment, eyes closed both in happiness and in fear. She had been in the Howard castle for four days. She had seen Tearle often during those days, but until that day he had not seen her. During those four days she had been terrified that he really did have no more feeling for her. But when she had seen him, seen the anger in his eyes when he had first recognized her, she had known then that he was still hers.

She lifted her head and kissed his chin. "Forgive me?"

"No." His lips said no, but his hand caressed her hair, and his eyes looked at her with love.

"Then I shall have to try harder to win you. When you are recovered from today I shall think of something new to do to your body."

"Oh?" Tearle said with some interest, then he pulled her hair back so that she looked up at him. "What are you doing here, brat? Is your brother waiting outside for you to open the gate for him tonight?"

"You can stay awake all night and watch me if you do not trust me," she said, wiggling her bottom against his hips.

He hugged her to him. "You are the curse of my life. I wish I had never seen you with my brother's men. Had I never laid eyes on you I would have been better off."

"You do not mean that." She raised herself up to look at him. "I have come not out of treachery or hatred, but out of love," she said softly. "I wanted to come to you long ago, but Liana begged me not to. Somehow she has managed to get messages about you. I . . ." She hesitated.

Tearle narrowed his eyes at her. "Do not think to hold back information from me."

"All right." She took a breath. "I think it was your brother's wife who sent word that you were well." Zared ran her hand down his cheek. "When you nearly died Liana and I spent long days in the chapel on our knees praying for your recovery. Anne Marshall came to Moray, and she prayed with us."

Tearle nodded. Perhaps he had felt the women's prayers. "I'll wager that your brothers did not pray for the recovery of a Howard."

"No, you are wrong." Zared paused. "Rogan has changed. I am not sure how yet, but he is different. I think it did something to him to almost lose his son and then come so close to killing the man who'd saved the child. I think that all the many words that Liana has spoken to him over the years are beginning to reach his ears. I do not think that he wants to raise sons to see them killed. I think he wants them to grow up and have children of their own."

"On whose estates?"

"I do not know. Liana says that with the money she brought and now with the dowry from Anne they could build a place or add on to Moray Castle. I think that Rogan is considering the idea."

Tearle knew that this was revolutionary thinking for

the hate-filled Peregrines. "What will your brother do without his hatred to fuel him?"

"You know only the worst of my brother. Underneath he is a kind and gentle man. He does not want to kill anyone. He was so . . . so hard on you because he thought you might harm his family. Had you thought what he did, you would have been difficult, too."

"Difficult? Is that what he was?" Tearle was trying to restrain his anger at the injustice that had been done to him, but it wasn't easy. He was cursed with being able to see both sides. "So what made you come here?"

She kissed his neck. "I have told you. I came because I did not like being without you. You make me laugh."

Tearle grunted. "Did I make you laugh on the day your brothers beat me?"

"No, I did not laugh that day. But that day I told you that I wanted to go with you, to stay with you."

"Until you believe that I have done something else to one of your precious brothers."

"No, I will believe you from now on. Now I will side with you against them."

He didn't move for a moment, then he lifted her head to look at her. He stared for a long while into her eyes, and he saw that she was telling the truth. There was more than just love in her eyes, there was commitment and loyalty and trust.

He put her head back down on his chest. "Now what do we do? You cannot stay here."

"I will stay wherever you are. Do you mean to go into battle? I will go with you."

He smiled at that. "I do not think that will be required. But if you stay here, it might be a battle. My brother will hear of what has happened this morning, and he will want an explanation."

"Tell him that you have taken a fancy to boys and—"

"Where have you heard of such?" He was genuinely horrified.

"Anne Marshall," she said simply, then she looked at him. "Oh, Tearle, she is the most interesting woman. She knows a great deal about many things. She is fascinating. Liana and I listen to her every word."

"The woman should keep her mouth shut."

"Her pretty mouth?" Zared said, looking at him. "She is beautiful, is she not?"

"Like a pretty, poisonous snake. Tell me, how does she get on with Severn?"

Zared laughed at that. "I rather think that she likes him. I do not think that he understands her any more than Liana and I do, but when he does not understand her he kisses her or takes her to their room. I sometimes think that she provokes him so that he will take her into privacy."

Tearle laughed at that. Perhaps his error had been in listening to women. Perhaps he should have behaved as Severn did; perhaps when a woman talked he should take her to bed.

"What else has Anne taught you?" he asked, hoping that her answer would be that she had been instructed in some exotic form of lovemaking.

"She has solved the riddle."

"I would think that Anne Marshall would be quite good at solving riddles." He said it in that tone that men use when they want to tell what they think of clever women. "What riddle did she solve?"

In spite of her intention of being the perfect wife

Zared gave him a look of disgust at his ignorance. "The Peregrine riddle."

"Forgive my stupidity, but I do not know as much about your family as you do."

"I will wager that your brother knows of the Peregrine riddle."

He didn't answer her but gave her a look that meant that she was to continue.

She repeated the riddle for him. "Anne said that she had little to do when she was at Moray Castle—I think that Severn was concerned that she might flee, and—"

"Wise of your brother to worry," Tearle said under his breath.

She ignored him, for she didn't like to think of what had gone on between her brother and his unwilling wife while they were away. When the subject was mentioned to some of the men who had been with them, they turned pale and shook their heads in disbelief. There were a few fresh wounds on Severn.

"Anne said it was hair color." When Tearle didn't seem to understand, she continued. "The red and the black. Hair color." She paused. "Rogan and Liana's first child has—"

"The boy whose life I saved?" he asked innocently.

"Their first child has red hair, like his father, but the second son has black hair, as Rogan's mother did."

"So this has to do with the riddle?"

"'When the red and the white make black.' See? Rogan's hair is red, Liana's hair is almost white, and they made a black-haired child."

Tearle smiled, understanding. "And the second line?"

"'When the black and the gold become one.'"

"Severn's gold hair and Anne's black."

Zared looked at him in admiration. He was indeed clever. "You and I are the last line. 'When the one and red unite.'"

He smiled at that, but then he looked at her in seriousness. "I take it that you are the red, so I must be the one. Yet I am not the one, assuming that 'one' means that I am the only Howard child. What is the last line of the riddle?"

"'Then shall you know.'"

"Know what?"

She took a while before answering. "Anne and Liana think that it means that we shall know who owns the estates." She could not look at him. If her brothers won, then it would mean that her husband lost. It wasn't that she so much wanted to own such a place, but she did not want to see her husband lose it. Nor did she want to see her brothers lose what perhaps should have been theirs.

Tearle looked at her and knew what she was thinking. "A dilemma, is it not?" He didn't tell her that he was glad that it had become a dilemma to her. A few months earlier she would not have had any doubts about who should have owned the estates. Then she had thought they should go to her brothers, and the man she married could go to hell for all she cared. But he was glad to see that she was confused about whom she should give her loyalty to.

He pulled her close to him and held her tightly. "Do not worry, my love. You will know what to do when the time comes."

"I know right from wrong," she said indignantly. "I know what must be done and who must—" She stopped when he kissed her to silence.

It was while he was kissing her that the door to his room burst open and four of his men charged inside. What they saw horrified them. It looked as though their master's brother was kissing a young boy, for all they could see was Zared's short hair above the sheet.

Tearle saw their looks and started to explain, but then he didn't know what to say. He couldn't introduce his Peregrine wife, and he couldn't very well pull the sheet down and show them that she was indeed a female.

For the first time in her life Zared saw her husband at a loss for words. She was not about to allow the opportunity to pass her by. She deepened her voice. "My lord," she said to Tearle, "you will buy me the armor you promised after I have done . . . this for you?" She motioned toward the bed.

Tearle gave her a quelling look as the men cleared their throats in embarrassment. He looked up at the men. "What do you want?" he snapped at them.

"Lady Jeanne begs you to come to her. Your brother is dying."

Zared didn't say anything as Tearle got out of the bed and began to dress. The riddle said that when the *one* and red unite then they would know. If Tearle's brother died, then Tearle would be the only Howard son left.

When Tearle was dressed he turned to her. "Remain here. Do not leave this room." He paused. "Can I trust you, or must I leave a guard on you?"

She was smart enough to know what could happen to her if word of her being in bed should get back to Oliver Howard. As long as the man was alive his hatred of the Peregrines was alive, too. "I will remain here," she said, ignoring the looks of the men at Tearle's back. There would be time in the future to show them the truth of who she was.

He started to kiss her but then straightened as he became aware of the men. "I expect you to keep your word," he said, then he was gone.

Alone in the room Zared leaned back against the pillows and looked about her. This room was what her family had fought and died for. It was what her family and Tearle's family had killed each other for.

She turned over onto her stomach and closed her eyes. Her husband no longer hated her, and that was all that mattered to her in the world. She fell asleep within seconds.

Chapter Seventeen

Zared didn't know what woke her. It wasn't a sound, for when she opened her eyes she heard nothing. It was night outside, so the room was dark, and she looked about, seeing nothing unusual or different in the room. Her eyes began to close again, but in the next moment she sat upright, clutching the sheet to her.

Standing at the foot of her bed was a woman. She was a pretty older woman dressed in a simple gown like the ones that Zared barely remembered seeing her mother wear. The woman looked at Zared with interest, then she smiled at her, a gentle smile.

Zared would have returned the smile to the woman except for one thing: She could see through the woman.

Through the woman's gown and body Zared could see the door behind her, could see the tapestry hanging to the left of the door.

Zared pulled the sheet closer about her and began to pray.

The woman's smile left her face, and she looked a bit sad that Zared should be so frightened of her. She turned away from the bed and walked to the door. At the door she paused and motioned to Zared to follow her, then she slid through the oak of the door and disappeared.

Zared sat paralyzed where she was. She had no intention of moving. In fact, she thought she might never leave the bed again in her life.

She was still shaking when the woman reappeared at the foot of the bed. Her face wore a look of urgency as she motioned to Zared to follow her.

Zared shook her head no. She was not going to go with a ghost. No doubt it was a Howard ghost who knew that she was a Peregrine.

The woman's mouth opened, and Zared put her hands up as though to protect her face. Would fire come out of the woman's mouth?

After some time Zared lowered her hands, and the woman was still there. She had a soft, patient look on her face.

"W-who are you?" Zared managed to ask. "What do you want of me?"

The woman held out both of her hands, palms up, in a pleading gesture.

Zared shook her head again. "No," she whispered. "I do not want to go with you."

The woman's face took on a look of urgency, pleading.

"No!" Zared half yelled. "I will not."

At that the woman looked about the room as though searching for something.

Zared didn't know if she was going crazy, but she was growing used to the woman. "What do you seek?"

The woman looked back at Zared, then pointed at her hair.

"Aye, it is short. I had to cut it again to be able to come to my husband. It will grow longer."

The woman pointed again and again, this time with some urgency. Zared tried to figure out what she meant, for she was beginning to realize that the ghost was not going to leave until she had something from Zared. She searched her mind to figure out what it was about her hair that intrigued the woman.

"This is as bad as the riddle," Zared muttered, and at that the woman began gesturing frantically.

"The riddle?" Zared asked, and the woman nodded her head vigorously. "You have something to do with the riddle?" Again the woman nodded.

Softly Zared repeated the riddle, and when she came to the last line she looked hard at the woman, seeing the small oak table through her. " 'Then shall you know,' " she said, and her face lit up. "My husband's brother is dead, and he is now the one."

The woman nodded, and her face showed her relief at Zared's understanding.

"You are here to tell me."

The woman again nodded.

Zared leaned back against the pillows and closed her eyes. The solution to the riddle was within her grasp. The solution to who owned the rich estates was near to her, yet all she could think of was, God, why have You chosen me? If the solution was given to Rogan or Severn, they would know just what to do, but Zared didn't know. If it was found that the estates belonged to her brother, should Zared take them from her husband and give them to her brother? Or did her love as well as her loyalty belong to her husband? *Could* she take away the estates from her husband? She had told Tearle that Rogan had changed, that some of his hatred was gone, but had she been telling the truth? If Rogan had proof that the estates belonged to him, would he take them from Tearle and leave him a beggar?

She opened her eyes and saw that the woman was still there, patiently waiting for her to come to a decision.

Zared sighed. It was no use agonizing over what was. For some reason she had been chosen to be the one to settle the feud.

Slowly she got out of bed and began to dress in her boy's clothes. It was, perhaps, better to know than not to know.

At last she turned and looked at the woman, who was still waiting for her. Zared took a deep breath. "I am ready."

The woman looked Zared up and down, and at first she thought maybe she disapproved of her clothes, but then Zared realized that the woman was probably a relative of hers, of hers as well as Tearle's, since she and Tearle were cousins, so perhaps the woman was studying her descendant. Zared was glad the woman had never seen her before, because that meant she hadn't been sneaking about spying on her.

The woman slipped through the oak of the door, but Zared quietly opened it and looked into the hall. There was no one about, but there were torches in iron holders on the walls, and the corridor was brightly lit.

Zared tiptoed out of the room and into the corridor, following the ghostly shape of the woman as she floated ahead of her.

After a while Zared's fear and her pounding heart made her feel that she'd followed the woman down corridors for hours. She had some trouble when four dogs came running from a dark alcove and, teeth bared, made straight for Zared.

Before she could run the woman appeared and put herself between the dogs and Zared, then the dogs, with fear on their faces, turned and ran the other way. For a moment Zared's knees were too weak to allow her to walk, but the woman gave an impatient look, and Zared managed to follow.

Zared followed her down corridors past brightly lit rooms and into the oldest part of the vast castle. There the rooms were not lit at all, and from the dirt and debris it seemed they were not used very often. A rat scurried under Zared's feet, but she hardly noticed it. What were rats when one was following a ghost?

At last the woman stopped and pointed at what Zared thought was a door. It was so dark in the corridor that she could barely see her hand in front of her face. Had it not been for the glow of the woman's body she could not have followed her.

Zared looked where the woman pointed but could see nothing. Then, as Zared watched, her mouth open in horror, the woman began to turn about in a circle, moving faster and faster. As she twirled about the glow of her body became brighter and brighter. When the woman stopped her body was as light as though sunlight were shining on it.

The woman smoothed back a strand of hair, then looked at Zared, who could feel her knees giving way under her. The woman reached out as though to touch Zared, but her hand slid right through Zared's arm.

That, added to what she had just seen, was almost the finish of Zared. She felt herself sinking to the floor and would have fallen had not the woman looked so annoyed with her. She started pointing in a vigorous way to the door that could now be seen quite plainly.

Zared did the best that she could to regain control of herself and put out her shaking hand to touch the latch of the door. The old door opened rather easily, and with a trembling body Zared entered.

It was a dirty old room, one that looked as though it hadn't had a human visitor in years. Great cobwebs hung from the shattered silk of the bed hangings. There were bats hanging in one corner of the room, and wind whistled in the broken glass of the large window.

Zared looked at the woman, who, now that they were in the room, was losing her eerie glow. She wasn't sure, but she thought there were tears in the woman's eyes. Could ghosts cry? she wondered.

The woman seemed to straighten herself, then she tightened her lips. She waved her arm and, to Zared's further horror, the room instantly changed. It was no longer dirty and dim and faded but was restored to its former glory. The bed hangings were once again a brilliant crimson, and the floor had fresh rushes on it. There were murals on the walls as well tapestries.

Zared's first instinct was to climb into the bed and hide under the covers, but something told her that it was just an illusion and that the bed was still covered in spiders and rat droppings that were quite real.

She took a deep breath and turned to the woman. "What do you want to show me?"

She watched the woman float toward the tapestry and point to it, and it took Zared some time to figure out that the woman wanted her to lift the tapestry. As soon as she touched it it fell off the wall. It *looked* clean and new and strong, but in reality it had decayed in the dampness.

Zared dropped the tapestry and kicked it aside. The woman floated toward the wall and put out her hand. To Zared's eyes there was only solid wall there. "Is something under here?"

The woman nodded.

"I don't see anything."

At that the woman began to turn about again, and Zared somehow knew that she was again going to turn until she became a human torch. "Please don't," Zared said. "I will look."

The woman seemed to understand and stopped turning about while Zared ran her hands over the wall looking for an opening. It was some time before she found a crack, but she could not get her fingers into the narrow opening.

"I will have to go back and get a tool. I can't budge the stone."

At that the woman seemed to panic. She went to the door and put herself before it, holding out her arms to bar the way. Zared knew that the woman was right. She couldn't leave the room. It had taken too long to find the place, and soon Tearle would return and search for her. He'd be quite angry that she had left his room after telling him that she wouldn't, and he would probably put her under guard if he had to, to keep her from leaving again.

"You are right," she said. "I cannot leave. Are there tools in here?"

The woman seemed to think for a moment, then she went to a large chest against the wall and pointed. Zared opened the chest. The only things inside were yarn and knitting needles. She held up a pair of the steel needles. "You want me to remove a stone block with knitting needles?" she asked.

The only answer she got was a weak smile from the woman, a smile so human that Zared smiled back at her. "Are you my grandmother?" she asked, and the woman nodded. Zared smiled again. "I think Rogan's oldest boy is going to look like you." Again Zared thought she saw tears in the woman's eyes, but she turned away too quickly for Zared to be sure.

Zared went to the wall and began to dig with the needles. She was so intent on digging the loose mortar away from the block that she did not hear the door open or the footsteps approach her. When Tearle spoke she jumped half a foot off the floor.

"What, may I ask, are you doing?"

She turned, her hand to her heart, and stared at him. "You frightened me half to death. What do you mean sneaking about like that?"

"Sneaking? In my own house? You swore to me that you would remain in my room."

She did some quick thinking about how he had found her. "And you said you would not put a guard on me. You must have had someone watching me if you could find me here. Is your brother . . . ?"

"Aye, he is dead."

"So now you own this pile of riches."

"I own this pile of blood," he said grimly.

Zared wasn't sure what to say to that, but she looked about the room. It was once again the filthy, untouched place that she had first seen, and there was no sign of the ghost, but there were two torches on the wall that had not been there before.

"What do you here?" he asked.

"Did not the person you had follow me tell you?"

He gave her a little smile. "He said you have the eyes of a cat and that he could see nothing. He did not know how you could see where you were going."

Zared realized that the man had not seen the ghost.

"How do you know this place so well to find this room? Do you not know that this room is said to be haunted? As a boy we used to dare each other to enter here."

"And did you see no one in here?"

He gave her a strange look. "Once I thought I saw a woman in here. She looked at me with great interest."

306

Probably wanted to see what her descendant looked like, Zared thought, but she said nothing.

"Again I ask you what you do here."

Zared took a deep breath. "I do not know for sure, but I think perhaps the ledgers that tell of the legitimacy of my grandmother's marriage are behind this stone."

He opened his mouth to ask her questions about how she knew this, but he closed it. After a while of looking at her he said, "Did you come back to me so that you might get near this room? So that you might find these registers and give the estate to your brothers?"

"No," she said softly. "I returned because I wanted you. I did not know of this place. Tonight I was . . . led here."

He searched her face. He didn't ask her who had "led" her or what she meant by that statement, but he could tell that she was telling the truth. He withdrew his knife from the sheath at his side and began pulling the mortar from the stone.

It took the two of them some minutes, but they managed to remove the stone. Tearle put the stone on the floor, then took a torch from the wall holder and held it to the wall. Inside they could see two fat old books. Tearle reached out to take the top book.

"No!" Zared fairly shouted, and she put her hand over his wrist to stop him. "Put the stone back. I do not want to know."

"Do not want to know what?" he asked softly.

"I do not want to know who is the rightful owner. *You* should have the place."

"No, your brother should have it. If the registers say that his grandparents were married legally, then the title and the lands are his, not mine." He lifted one eyebrow at her. "Do not tell me that you are in truth a

307

greedy woman. Do you want to keep it all for yourself?"

"I do not care for me," she said as she looked up at him. "What do my brothers know of running a place this size? All they know is war. You should have seen how filthy Moray Castle was before Liana came. Rogan will make this beautiful place as dirty as that."

"You would do your brother out of what is rightfully his because of a little dirt?"

She looked away from him. "No. Dirt does not matter. I am afraid of what Rogan will do to you. He might send you away. He might bar you from this place for all eternity."

Tearle put his hand under her chin and lifted her face so that she looked at him. "I have property from my mother. Will you go there to live with me?"

"Yes," she whispered. "I will go with you anywhere. But—"

"But what?"

"You will lose your title. You will not be the duke. It is a thing a man wants."

"Perhaps it is something that your brother wants. It was something that my brother wanted enough to kill for, and your other brothers were willing to die for the land and titles, but I am a different man. Do you not see that I am lazy?" He smiled down at her. "I want only to have a nice place to live in comfort and a wife to love me. It is all I have ever wanted. I should like some sons to ride and hunt with, and some daughters to play music to me when I am old and can no longer play myself. I should like to live long enough to have grandchildren. I want no more than this in life."

Zared looked at him and knew that he was telling the truth. He had never wanted any part of the feud, any part of the killing and the hatred, and, quite suddenly, neither did she. She wanted to walk away from the huge estate with all its riches, and, as Tearle said, with all its blood, and go back to his house and live there with him. The short time they had had in that house was the happiest time in her life. There the excitement was not over who had lost an arm or a foot but over which plants were blooming in the gardens and whether they could hear the baby owls at night.

She thought about him and his house and about the children they would raise, girls who did not have to dress as boys in order to stay alive and boys who would not die in battle before they reached manhood.

"That is what I want also," she said to him, then she stepped back as he pulled the first ledger from the hole in the wall.

She held her breath as he opened it and began to turn the brittle pages. She watched him as he scanned the writing on the pages, and when at last he stopped she waited until he looked at her.

"Your brother Rogan is the duke," he said softly.

Zared let out her pent-up breath and smiled at him. "Shall we go home?"

He returned her smile. Not many women loved a man enough to give up being a duchess. He put his arms around her and held her close.

Zared looked over his shoulder, saw the ghost of her grandmother behind them, and smiled at her.

The woman smiled back and nodded her head as though she was very pleased, and then she was gone.

Tearle pulled away, then took Zared's hand. "Yes, let us go home and begin those babies."

She smiled at him, and they left the room together, their fingers entwined.

Two great books— one great price!

Each book features two classics by your favorite authors together in one collectible volume!

Coast Road • Three Wishes
Barbara Delinsky

The Taming • The Conquest
Jude Deveraux

Twin of Ice • Twin of Fire
Jude Deveraux

Velvet Song • Velvet Angel
Jude Deveraux

Angel Creek • A Lady of the West
Linda Howard

Shades of Twilight • Son of the Morning
Linda Howard

Guardian Angel • The Gift
Julie Garwood

Castles • The Lion's Lady
Julie Garwood

Honey Moon • Hot Shot
Susan Elizabeth Phillips

Scandalous • Irresistible
Karen Robards

Homeplace • Far Harbor
JoAnn Ross

The Callahan Brothers Trilogy
JoAnn Ross

POCKET BOOKS
A Division of Simon & Schuster
A VIACOM COMPANY

Visit **www.simonsays.com**

13361